Baen Books
by Wen Spencer

TINKER

WEN SPENCER

Copyright © 2003 by Wen Spencer

A Baen Books Original

Baen Publishing Enterprises
P.O. Box 1403
Riverdale, NY 10471
www.baen.com

ISBN: 978-1-4814-8347-6

Cover art by Don Maitz

Baen mass market printing, November 2003
Baen trade paper back printing, September 2018

Distributed by Simon & Schuster
1230 Avenue of the Americas
New York, NY 10020

Printed in the United States of America

10 9 8 7 6 5 4 3 2 1

INTRODUCTION
ONCE UPON A TIME

A LONG TIME AGO: In a land, far, far away.

I was a rabid reader growing up. I read my way through categories in the local library. Obviously, fantasy was near and dear to my heart, but there's a handful of books that stand out as much beloved that weren't "fairy tales." At the time, they didn't seem connected in my mind. They were books like Laura Ingalls Wilder's Little House series, Jean George's *My Side of the Mountain*, Farley Mowat's books *The Dog Who Wouldn't Be* and *Owls in the Family*. Looking back, though, I can see the connecting thread. They were books which were set in the "here and now" of rural USA (as a child, I thought Saskatchewan was part of Minnesota.) The stories revolved around people using Swiss Family Robertson-like ingenuity in their day to day life. They had lives much like the one that I knew intimately.

I grew up in a small town north of Pittsburgh. I lived on the farm where my grandmother had been born in 1895. My great-great grandfather had given the land to her father; my family has lived on the same sixty-eight acres for over a hundred and twenty years. They were always "dirt poor" because the land was so hilly that it couldn't provide more than a basic living. My grandmother lost her father when she was around eleven. Her mother remarried and moved away, leaving my grandmother on the farm alone. She lost her husband when my father was eight. To make ends meet, she sold the outbuildings for their lumber and fieldstone foundations. The barn, a summer kitchen, and a springhouse vanished without trace.

Ancient farm equipment sat abandoned, slowly rusting away. Having never seen them in use, they always baffled me by their design. There was one that had a row of metal disks topped with narrow wooden boxes. Each box had a hinged lid and holes drilled into its bottom. Every summer I would stand and puzzle over it, cautiously opening the lids as the design made them perfect bee hives. I learned as an adult that the machine was a horse-drawn seeder, used to sow seeds in large fields.

At the turn of the last century, there had also been three oil wells on the farm. I'm not sure who got the proceeds of the wells as my grandmother only received free gas for lamps as "rent" from the drilling company. They'd taken down the derricks and removed all the pipelines but mysterious giant wood structures remained. I used to clamber over them, trying to figure out what they were used for since there were no clues in their location or surroundings. It often seemed like they'd been dropped by a passing giant. The largest was a set of wooden wheels which were twice as tall as a child, connected with a giant axle, sitting in the middle of nowhere. To this day, I have no idea what it was or why it was there. My best guess was it spooled rope on one of the derricks. After the oil wells were abandoned, it was likely that bored children (my grandmother? my father? my older sisters?) had pushed the wheels down the hill until they had gotten lodged on a tree.

When my father bought the farm from my grandmother shortly before I was born, the house had no running water, no indoor plumbing, no electricity, no central heat, no insulation, no basement, hadn't been painted for decades, and was in serious danger of collapsing. He worked days as an engineer at a manufacturer of safety equipment but in the evenings and weekends, he was a Jack of all trades, remodeling the house. He jury-rigged everything with whatever he could get his hands on, including using car radiator pipes to run cold water to the toilet. During my childhood, we had only one bathroom, so my grandmother used a chamber pot if she needed to go in the middle of the night. (She continued to live with us after my father officially 'bought' the farm.) The well was slowly giving out, so we needed to conserve water. These measures included the entire family sharing one bathtub's worth of hot water.

We had a massive garden every summer. August was spent slaving over a hot stove to can everything from green beans to tomatoes. We hunted in the fall for meat. We raised a weird range of animals to make extra money. Mink. Quail. Ring-necked pheasants. Chickens. Geese. Turkeys. Pigs. Beef cows. Ponies. And kids—lots of kids. There were four of us who were supposed to live there, a constant herd of little girls attracted by the ponies, and foster children that came and went.

Much as I loved *The Hobbit*, I identified closely with the life of Almanzo Wilder as told in *Farmer Boy*. When I daydreamed, it was escaping the horde of children normally at my home to live alone with a falcon like Sam Gribley of *My Side of the Mountain*. My first attempt at a novel when I was in first grade, it was about running away to live in the mountains. Fairy tales were too removed from my real world to see myself within them.

Urban Fantasy, when I first discovered it, excited me because it was no longer "once upon a time" or "far, far away." It was here and now. A dragon could live in our woods. Elves might move in next door. I could learn spells instead of spelling at school.

I particularly loved the borderland stories where the overlapping of worlds created a post-apocalypse feel to the characters' lives. It reminded me of growing up with so many mysterious relics of the past to puzzle over. It also meant that you could imagine yourself moving into any cool and interesting building that you liked. That beautiful Victorian in town. That nifty giant barn down the road. The imposing brick Catholic high school. The school bus turned into a tiny house/food truck. Money and logic need not apply.

Every time I read an Urban Fantasy, though, there was this niggling feeling of "But this isn't how I would have written this novel."

In 2001, I read yet another borderland Urban Fantasy that left me faintly dissatisfied. There wasn't anything strictly wrong with the story, it just went West when I would have gone East. It ignored the untraveled paths to go down familiar roads. The characters were solitary creatures, adrift in their unhappy lives without a solid course of action. I wanted characters with lives entangled with friends and family. I wanted the post-apocalypse feeling of our world reeling after it collided with a world of magic. I wanted the characters to have the can-do spirit of the Swiss Family Robertson or Pa Ingalls or Sam Gribley. I wanted to fight off monsters, claim abandon spaces, plant a garden, jury-rig a hot shower and most importantly, work magic.

In fairy tales, the dark woods were a mythical, unknowable place. The heroes ventured in, got lost, met odd and dangerous creatures but they never learned the ways of the forest. They needed magical animals or breadcrumbs scattered in their wake to find their way to safety. Even the dwarves were lost in Mirkwood. The Swiss Family Robertson would probably be eaten by giant spiders.

In Urban Fantasy novels, the city takes the place of the forest. Characters were supposed to be lost and bewildered by the unknowable, mysterious, dark metropolitan sprawl. That was at the heart of my dissatisfaction; what I wanted was incompatible for the genre.

At the time, I couldn't quantify my desire and how it conflicted with the tropes that defined Urban Fantasy. I finished reading a book and felt vague dissatisfaction. I liked all the bits and pieces of the world building. The modern American city. Swords mixed with guns. Elves. Magic. Normal humans attempting a normal life. I tried to put a finger on why I hadn't been completely happy with the end result. What would I do differently?

It boiled down to the basic bones of the genre. In the book I'd just finished, the land of the elves had been unknowable. The main character only brushed against the surface of the Elvish culture. He didn't speak the language, didn't know their motivations, and didn't understand the magic. Such total ignorance was common in fairy tales like Rumpelstiltskein. Who was Rumpelstiltskein? How did he spin the gold? What did he want with the king's son? While kings are greedy and stepmothers are selfish, non-humans in fairy tales operated on unknowable logic. Would they fill your mouth with gems or frogs? Why would they do either? A chance meeting, though, always resulted in incredible, life-changing repercussions.

I was unhappy with the Urban Fantasy because I wanted to know more. If I had written the novel, I would have had a main character that already knew how to speak Elvish. I would have an elf land in her lap that she needed to save. That would drag her into the heart of Elvish culture and have it all explained to her. I picked up a notebook and sketched a scene. It would take place in the here and now of Pittsburgh. I could pin down the gritty reality of being human with the city's steel and smoke and urban sprawl. I gave the heroine a junkyard filled with scrap metal and rusting cars.

At first, the villains of the scene were a human street gang armed with baseball bats and chains. I quickly rejected this because it didn't lead to my heroine being embroiled in Elvish politics and culture. She would be squarely in the human camp if the main conflict was between elves and humans. The moment that I decided that there would be a third race at war with the elves, which would force humans to choose sides, the story clicked. Girl Genius Tinker sprang out, fully formed, and ready to kick butt.

To get the post-apocalypse feel that I wanted, I decided to do a riff on Brigadoon. Pittsburgh would be a modern city that was only sometimes on Earth. It would be an island of normalcy deep within a forest full of magic creatures. The first Startup had been decades earlier. Most of Pittsburgh's population had fled back to Earth. It's the "can-do" individuals that remained, eking out a living in mostly a abandoned city. (I wish now that I had done less of an information dump in the first few pages. It makes the start a little cumbersome. Novels are like clay tablets; once the book is published, you can't change it.)

It's been nearly two decades since that day. I've written hundreds of thousands of words about the people living on Elfhome. Tinker. Oilcan. Jane. Law. Olivia. They all have a great deal of knowledge about their world but are still blindsided by things they don't know. They speak Elvish and know a little how elves think, but are often surprised by differences in their cultures. They have sprawling families and close friends. Some of them know how to cast spells. They've squatted in cool houses and jury-rigged daily needs. It's everything that I wanted in an Urban Fantasy. I hope you enjoy their stories as much as I enjoyed writing them.

Instant Message conversation dated
February 24, 2003, 7:00 p.m.

WS: To Don, who always helped me grow.

DK: Wow! Thanks. But that's kind of lame. How about:
To Don, cute, but prickly like a hedgehog.

WS: . . .*

DK: Um, don't use that. . . .

WS: To Don, who will someday get his hedgehog.
To Don, the hedgehog is just for you.

DK: To Don Kosak, King of hedgehogs.

WS: To Don, I will never look at hedgehogs the same way again?
To Don, Champion of the hedgehogs! To Don, "What, no, it's not a
hedgehog, it's his head!" To Don, it's hedgehogs the whole way
down. To Don, who is forever seeing hedgehogs.

DK: To Don, How do you know that Don doesn't know that the
hedgehogs are enjoying themselves in the spring.

WS: To zen Don, who may or may not be there.

DK: Hee hee. Okay.

* footnote: . . . is the Japanese way to indicate stunned or annoyed silence.

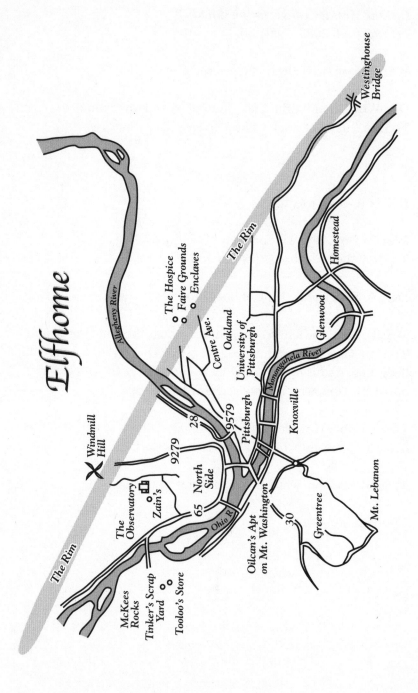

Elfhome

Westinghouse Bridge

The Rim

Allegheny River

Windmill Hill

The Hospice
Faire Grounds
Enclaves

Centre Ave.

Oakland

University of Pittsburgh

9279

28

9579

Pittsburgh

Knoxville

Homestead

Glenwood

Monongahela River

The Observatory

Zain's

North Side

65

Ohio R.

Oilcan's Apt on Mt. Washington

30

Greentree

Mt. Lebanon

McKees Rocks

Tinker's Scrap Yard

Tooloo's Store

1 : LIFE DEBT

THE WARGS chased the elf over Pittsburgh Scrap and Salvage's tall chain-link fence shortly after the hyperphase gate powered down.

Tinker had been high up in the crane tower, shuffling cars around the dark sprawling maze of her scrap yard, trying to make room for the influx of wrecks Shutdown Day always brought in. Her cousin, Oilcan, was out with the flatbed wrecker, clearing their third call of the night, and it wasn't Shutdown proper yet.

Normally, clearing space was an interesting puzzle game, played on a gigantic scale. Move this stripped car to the crusher. Consolidate two piles of engine blocks. Lightly place a new acquisition onto the tower of to-be-stripped vehicles. She had waited until too late, though, tinkering in her workshop with her newest invention. Shuffling the scrap around at night was proving nearly impossible. Starting with the crane's usual clumsy handling—its ancient fishing pole design and manual controls often translated the lightest tap into a several-foot movement of the large electromagnet strung off the boom—she also had to factor in the distorted shadows thrown by the crane's twin floodlights, the deep pools of darkness, and the urge to rush, since Shutdown was quickly approaching.

Worse yet, the powerful electromagnet was accumulating a dangerous level of magic. A strong ley line ran through the scrap yard, so using the crane always attracted some amount of magic. She had invented a siphon to drain off the power to a storage unit also of her own design. The prolonged periods of running the crane were overwhelming the siphon's capacity. Even with taking short breaks with the magnet turned off, the accumulated magic writhed a deep purple about the disc and boom.

At ten minutes to midnight, she gave up and shut down the electromagnet. The electric company changed over from the local Pittsburgh power grid to the national grid to protect Pittsburgh's limited resources from the spike in usage that Shutdown brought. She had no reason to risk dropping a car sixty feet onto something valuable because some yutz flipped a switch early.

So she sat and waited for Shutdown, idly kicking her steel-tipped boots against the side of the crane's control booth. Her scrap yard sat on a hill overlooking the Ohio River. From the crane, she could see the barges choking the waterway, the West End Bridge snarled with traffic, and ten or more miles of rolling hills in all directions. She also had an unobstructed view of the full Elfhome moon, rising up through the veil effect on the Eastern horizon. The distortion came from the hyperphase lightly holding its kidnapping victim, a fifty-mile-diameter chunk of Earth complete with parts of downtown Pittsburgh, prisoner in the foreign dimension of Elfhome. The veil shimmered like heat waves over the pale moon face, nearly identical to that of Earth's own moon. Ribbons of red and blue danced in the sky along the Rim's curve, the collision of realities mimicking the borealis effect. Where the Rim cut through the heart of Pittsburgh, just a few miles southeast, the colors gleamed brilliantly. They paled as the Rim arced off, defining the displaced land mass. Beyond the Rim, the dark forest of Elfhome joined the night sky, black meeting black, the blaze of stars the only indication where the first ended and the second began.

So much beauty! Part of her hated going back to Earth, even for a day. Pittsburgh, however, needed the influx of goods that Shutdown Day brought; the North American counterpart of Elfhome was lightly populated and couldn't support a city of sixty thousand humans.

Off in the west, somewhere near the idle airport, a firework streaked skyward and boomed into bright flowers of color—the advent of Shutdown providing the grounded airplane crews with an excuse to party. Another firework followed.

Between the whistle and thunder of the fireworks, the impatient hum of distant traffic, the echoing blare of tugboat horns, the shushing of the siphon still draining magic off the electromagnet, and the thumping of her boots, she nearly didn't hear the wargs approaching.

A howl rose, harsh and wild, from somewhere toward the airport. She stilled her foot, then reached out with an oil-stained finger to snap off the siphon. The shushing died away, and the large disc at the end of the crane boom started to gleam violet again.

In a moment of relative silence, she heard a full pack in voice, their prey in sight. While the elfin rangers killed the packs of wargs that strayed too close to Pittsburgh, one heard their howling echoing up the river valleys quite often. This sound was deeper, though, than any wargs she'd heard before, closer to the deep-chest roar of a saurus. As she tried to judge how close the wargs were—and more important, if they were heading in her direction—St. Paul started to ring midnight.

"Oh no, not now," she whispered as the church bells drowned out the hoarse baying. Impatiently, she counted out the peals. Ten. Eleven. Twelve.

In another dimension infinitesimally close and mind-bogglingly far, the Chinese powered down their hyperphase gate in geosynchronous orbit, and yanked Pittsburgh back off the world of Elfhome. Returning to Earth reminded Tinker of being on the edge of sleep and having a sensation of falling so real that she would jerk back awake, flat in bed so she couldn't actually have fallen anywhere. The gate turned off, the universe went black and fell away, and then, snap, she was sitting in the crane's operating chair, eyes wide open, and nothing had moved.

But everything had changed.

A hush came with Shutdown. The world went silent and held its breath. All the city lights were out; the Pittsburgh power grid shut down. The aurora dancing along the Rim dissipated, replaced by the horizon-hugging gleam of light pollution, as if a million bonfires had been lit. A storm wind whispered through the silent darkness, stirred up as the weather fronts coming across Ohio collided with the returning Pittsburgh air. On the wind came a haze that smudged what had been crystalline sky.

"Oh, goddamn it. You would think that after twenty years they would figure out a saner way of doing this. Let's get the power back on! Come on."

The wargs took voice again, only a block away and closing fast.

Was she safe in the crane? If the oncoming menace had been a saurus, she'd say she was safe on the high tower, for while the saurus was a nightmarish cousin of the dinosaur, it was a natural creature. Apparently designed as weapons of mass destruction in some ancient magical war, wargs were far more than pony-sized wolves; it was quite possible they could climb.

But could she make it to her workshop trailer, the walls and windows reinforced against such a possible attack?

Tinker dug into the big side pocket of her carpenter pants, took out her night goggles, and pulled them on. In the green wash of the goggles' vision, she then saw the elf. He was coming at her over the burned-out booster rockets, dead cars, and obsolete computers. Behind him, the wargs checked at the high chain-link fence of the scrap yard. She got the impression of five or six of the huge, wolflike creatures as they milled there, probably balking more at the metal content of the fence than at its twelve-foot height or the additional three-foot razor-wire crown. Magic and metal didn't mix. Even as she whispered, "Just leave! Give up!" the first warg backed up, took a running start at the fence, and leaped it, clearing it by an easy three or four feet.

"Oh, shit!" Tinker yanked on her gloves, swung out of the open control cage, and slid down the ladder.

"Sparks?" she whispered, hoping the backup power had kicked in on her computer network. "Is the phone online?"

"No, Boss," came the reply on her headset, the AI annoyingly chipper.

Her fuel cell batteries kept her computer system operational. Unfortunately, the phone company wasn't as reliable. That her security programs needed a dial tone to call the police was a weakness she'd have to fix, but until then, she was screwed. Shit, they could build a hyperphase gate in geostationary orbit and put a man in the seas of Europa, but they couldn't get the damn phones to work on Shutdown Day!

"Sparks, open a channel to the wrecker."

"Done, Boss."

"Oilcan? Can you hear me? Oilcan?" Damn, her cousin was out of the wrecker's cab. She paused, waiting to see if he would answer, then gave up. "Sparks, at two-minute intervals repeat following message: 'Oilcan, this is Tinker. I've got trouble. Big trouble. Get back here.

Bring cops. Send cops. I'll probably need an ambulance too. Get me help! Hurry.' End message."

"Okay, Boss."

She landed at the foot of the ladder. A noise to her left made her look up. The elf was on one of the tarp-covered shuttle booster rockets, pausing to draw his long thin sword, apparently deciding to stop and fight. Six to one—it would be more a slaughter than a fight. That fact alone would normally make her sick.

Worse, though, she recognized the elf: Windwolf. She didn't know him in any personal sense. Their interaction had been limited to an ironically similar situation five years ago. A saurus had broken out of its cage during the Mayday Faire, chewing its way through the frightened crowd. In a moment of childish stupidity, she'd attacked it, wielding a tire iron. She had nearly gotten herself killed. A furious Windwolf had saved her and cast a spell on her, placing a life debt on her essence, linking her fate with his. If her actions got him killed, she would die too.

Or at least, that's what Tooloo said the spell would do.

Sane logic made her question the old half-elf. Why would Windwolf save her only to doom her? But Windwolf was an elf noble—thus one of the arrogant *domana* caste—and one had to keep in mind that elves were alien creatures, despite their human appearance. Just look at loony old Tooloo.

And according to crazy Tooloo, the life debt had never been canceled.

Of all the elves in Pittsburgh, why did it have to be Windwolf?

"Oh, Tinker, you're screwed with all capital letters," she muttered to herself.

Her scrap yard ran six city blocks, a virtual maze of exotic junk. She had the advantage of knowing the yard intimately. The first warg charged across the top of a PAT bus sitting next to the booster rockets. The polymer roof dimpled under its weight; the beast left hubcap-sized footprints in its wake. Windwolf swung his sword, catching the huge creature in its midsection. Tinker flinched, expecting blood and viscera; despite their magical origin, wargs were living creatures.

Along the savage cut, however, there was a crackling brilliance like electrical discharge. For a second, the warg's body flashed from solid flesh to the violet, intricate, circuitlike pattern of a spell. That gleaming, rune-covered shell hung in mid-air, outlining the mass of the warg. She could recognize various subsections: expansion, increase vector, artificial inertia. Inside the artificial construct hung a small dark mass—an animal acting like the hand inside of a puppet. She couldn't identify the controlling beast, shrouded as it was by the shifting lines of spell, but it looked only slightly larger than a house cat.

What the hell?

Then the spell vanished back to illusionary flesh, reforming the appearance of a great dog. The monster rammed Windwolf in a collision of bodies, and they went tumbling down off the rocket.

These creatures weren't wargs, nor were they totally real. They weren't flesh-and-blood animals, at least not on the surface. Someone had done a weird illusionary enhancement, something along the lines of a solid hologram. If she disrupted the spell, the monsters should be reduced back to the much smaller, and hopefully less dangerous, animal providing the intelligence and movement to the construct.

And she had to try something quick, before the pseudo-warg killed Windwolf.

She ran twenty feet to a pile of sucker poles brought in last year from a well salvage job. They were fifteen feet long, but only two inches thick, making them light but awkward. More importantly, they were at hand. She snatched one up, worked her hands down it until she had a stiff spear of five feet fed out in front of her, and then ran toward the fight.

The monster had Windwolf pinned to the ground. Up close, there was no mistaking the weird-looking thing for a standard wolfish warg. While equally massive, the vaguely doglike creature was square-jawed and pug-nosed with a mane and stub tail of thick, short, curly hair. The monster dog had Windwolf by the shoulder and was shaking him hard. The elf had lost his sword and was trying to draw his dagger.

Tinker put all her speed and weight into punching the pole tip through the dog's chest. She hoped that even if the pole failed to penetrate, she might be able to knock the monster back off of Windwolf. As she closed, she wondered at the wisdom of her plan. The thing was huge. She never could remember that she was a small person; she had unconsciously used Windwolf as a scale, and had forgotten that he was nearly a foot taller than she.

This is going to hurt me more than it, she thought, and slammed the pole home.

Amazingly, there was only a moment of resistance, as if she had struck true flesh, and then the spell parted under the solid metal, and the pole sank up to her clenched hands. The beast shifted form, back to the gleaming spell. Both the spell form and the creature within reeled in pain; luckily someone had been careless in the sensory feedback limit. She reached down the pole, grabbed hold at the eight-foot mark, and shoved hard. The pole speared through the massive spell form, bursting out through the heavily muscled back, near the rear haunch.

The dog shrieked, breath blasting hot over her, smelling of smoke and sandalwood. It lifted a front foot to bat at her. She saw—too late to react—that the paw had five-inch claws. Before it could hit her, though, Windwolf's legs scissored around her waist, and she found herself airborne, sailing toward the side of the booster rocket.

I was right. This was going to hurt.

But then Windwolf plucked her out of the air on his way up to the top of the rocket. The crane's floodlights snapped on—the transfer of Pittsburgh to the national power grid apparently now complete—and spotlighted them where they landed. Beyond the fence, the rest of the city lights flickered on.

"Fool," Windwolf growled, dropping her to her feet. "It would have killed you."

They were nearly the exact words he had said during their battle with the saurus. Were they fated to replay this drama again and again? If so, his next words would be for her to leave.

Windwolf grunted, pushing her behind him. "Run."

There was her cue. Coming across the booster rocket were three of the monstrous dogs, the poly-coated tarp insulating their charge. Enter monsters, stage right. Exit brave heroine, stage left, in a dash and jump for the crane ladder.

What disrupted magic better than a length of steel was magnetism! With the power back on, the crane was operational. If she could get up to it and switch on the electromagnet, the dogs were toast. Through the bars of the ladder, she could see a fourth monster coming across the scrap yard, leaping from nonconductive pile to nonconductive pile like a cat transversing a creek via stepping stones.

She was twenty feet from the cage when it landed on the crane trusses and started up after her. And she had thought herself so clever in using ironwood instead of steel to build the crane tower.

"Oh damn, my stupid luck." She frantically scrambled up the rungs, fighting panic now. She was forty feet up; falling would be bad.

The dog was being equally cautious, taking the time to judge its jump before making it. She climbed fifteen feet before it took its first leap, landing nearly where she had been when it first reached the crane. It reared and stretched out its front legs, claws extended, trying to fish her down off the steel ladder without actually touching metal. She climbed frantically up and into the crane's mostly wood cage. She slapped on the power button and fumbled wildly through the dark interior for a weapon, tipping toward panic.

With the scrabble of claws on wood, the monster landed on the window ledge.

Her hand closed on the portable radio. *No. Well, maybe.* She flung it at the massive head. The tool kit followed. She snatched up the fire extinguisher as the monster growled and reached out for her like a cat with a cornered mouse. Cat? Dog? What the hell were these things? She'd have to figure it out later; it would bug her until she knew.

She started to throw the fire extinguisher and then caught herself. These things seemed to have full sensory feedback! Flipping the fire extinguisher, she yanked out the pin, pressed the lever, and unloaded the foam into the monster's face. The creature jerked back, teetering on the edge as it rubbed a paw at its foam-covered eyes. She changed her grip on the extinguisher, hauled back, and then nailed the dog with a full roundhouse swing to the head.

There was a nice satisfying *clang*, a wail of terror, a brief fast scramble of claws, and then it fell.

With luck, it wouldn't land on its feet.

She jumped to the crane controls. She had to lean way out to see Windwolf at the foot of the crane as she swung the boom around. Three of the monster dogs had him down, tearing at him like a rag doll. Was she too late? "Oh, gods, let this work!"

She activated the electromagnet, hit the siphon to drain off magic to the magic sink, and dropped the disc as fast and close as she dared onto the tight knot of bodies.

Luckily Windwolf and the dogs were on the booster rocket, which was far too big to be lifted by the electromagnet. The illusionary flesh of the dogs shifted to semitransparent shells. The spells unraveled, their power sucked away by the magnet, dropping the small animals controlling the monsters onto the rocket.

Dogs. Small, ugly, pug-nosed dogs, not much bigger than alley cats. Still, they launched themselves at Windwolf, barking and growling. She swore, swung out of the crane's cage, and slid down the ladder. As she landed, she saw a huge dark figure coming at her.

Shit, the monster dog she'd smacked out the window!

She raced for the booster rocket with the electromagnet still hovering over it, magic wreathing about the black disc. She could smell the dog's smoky breath, feel it blasting furnace hot against her back. With a strange clinical detachment, she remembered that cats killed their prey by biting down and breaking their necks. What did dogs do?

The dog hit her. She flung her hands back to protect her neck, and the massive jaws closed on her left hand. She screamed as they tumbled onto the ground. Gunshots cracked and echoed over the scrap yard as the dog shook its head, ravaging her hand.

"Help!" she screamed to the unknown shooter. "Help me!"

With a sharp crack, a bullet caught the dog in the center of its forehead, snapping its head backward. The flesh vanished to spell form, flaring deep violet, as the steel blasted through it. The dog released her hand, and she dropped to the ground. Immediately, she half crawled, half stumbled for the booster rocket. The shooter fired, again and again. She glanced back as she ran. The bullets struck the dog in a quick sharp hail, punching it backward. The runes flared with each shot, giving lightning flashes of the dog within, a vulnerable heart to the monstrous construct. The spell form, however, was robbing the bullets of their velocity and diverting them from a straight path. The monster came on, the dog within unharmed.

Sobbing in pain and fear, she hit the side of the booster rocket and clawed desperately for a handhold, leaving bloody smears with her savaged hand.

The monster launched itself at her—and hit the electromagnet's radius of influence. The spell flashed brilliantly, and then unraveled, the magic fraying upward in momentarily visible violet particles.

The small ugly dog within landed at Tinker's feet, growling.

"Oh, you're so dead!" she told it, and kicked it hard with her steel-toe boot. The dog landed a dozen feet away, struggled to its feet, and fled, yelping. "And it's good!" Tinker held her hands up like a referee judging a field goal. "And the fans go wild! Tink-ker! Tink-ker! Tink-ker!"

Elation lasted only a minute. The numbness in her hand gave way to pain. The wound bled at an alarming rate, though she suspected any rate would be frightening. Blood just had a way of being upsetting.

And there was still Windwolf to save.

"Sparks?"

"Yeah, Boss?"

"Is the phone working yet?"

"No dial tone, Boss."

Her luck, the phone company would only get the phones online an hour before Startup.

She struggled through cutting up her oversized shirt with her Swiss Army knife, reducing it down to a midriff. She had an individually wrapped feminine hygiene pad in her pants pocket. (They made good sterile bandages in such emergencies, and held twice their weight in motor oil.) She cut the pad in half and used her shirt to tie the two halves tight to either side of her bleeding hand. Not a great job, but it would have to do.

She walked around to the front of the booster rocket and clambered up the twelve feet to its top. Windwolf lay sprawled in a pool of blood. The ugly pug-faced dogs lay around him, dead. As she checked Windwolf's pulse, his almond eyes opened, recognized her, and closed.

The wounds that the dogs had inflicted on him were hideous. She needed to swallow hard to keep her stomach down. She noticed an empty shoulder holster tucked under his arm.

Oh, yeah, someone had shot the dog before it could kill her!

She glanced about for his gun, and finally thought to look up. An automatic pistol and a dozen shell cases were tacked to the bottom of the magnet. Windwolf was the shooter who'd saved her.

By the time she got Windwolf to the multiple trailers that served as the scrap yard's office and her workshop, she knew why vids always had men saving women and rarely the other way around. There just wasn't any way a woman—well, a five-foot-nothing woman—could carry around an unconscious, bleeding man in any *artistic* manner. In the end, she rigged a sling and used the crane to swing him across the scrap yard and down onto the front doorstep. She kept the electromagnet on until it was so close to the steel-shell trailers that they were shuddering. When she shut the magnet down, Windwolf's pistol dropped down into his lap.

She nearly fell climbing back down out of the crane and banged her head. She felt blood trickling down her face as she walked back to the trailers. She stuck Windwolf's pistol into her waistband. Getting the elf up into a firefighter's carry, she staggered through the office and into the trailer attached to it that she used as a workshop. Somehow, she got Windwolf laid out on her worktable without dropping or seriously banging him.

"Sparks." She sighed, head on Windwolf's chest, listening to his heart race.

Her computer churned slightly as the AI answered. "Yeah, Boss?"

"Are the phones online yet?"

"No, Boss."

"Oilcan check in yet?"

"No, Boss."

"What's the time?"

"Twelve fifteen a.m."

Fifteen minutes since Windwolf came over the fence. The longest fifteen minutes of her life.

Leaving Windwolf in her workshop, she staggered back into the office. It was a two-bedroom mobile home, complete with kitchen and full bathroom, forty years old and showing all of its age. She bolted shut the front door, got an Iron City beer out of the fridge, and then staggered back to the bathroom to wash her right hand well. Lava cleanser first, to scour off the day's layer of oil and grease, and then a rare soak in antibacterial soap for the upcoming messing with wounds. She cleaned around the bandage on her left hand, trying not to notice that it was blood-soaked.

The only clean place on her face was what the night goggles covered, giving her a weird inverse raccoon look. Her bottom lip was swollen, making her mouth seem even more full than normal. From somewhere within her haphazard hairline—a product of Oilcan's haircuts and her own occasional impromptu trims with whatever sharp object was at hand—blood trickled down. She hunted through her dark hair, looking for the source of the blood, and found a small cut. She wet down a washcloth and stood a few minutes holding it to her scalp, sipping her beer, and trying to figure out what to do next.

She had a weakness for strays. It was like someone early on had written "sucker" on her in magic ink. The weak and the helpless saw it, swarmed to her, and thrived under her care. Well, not all of them. Not plants. Her thumbs were black from motor grease and engine oil. She killed any plant she tried to doctor. Not the terribly fragile either. Baby birds and suicidal wrecks, she had found, all dropped dead in her care. They seemed to need more mothering than she could muster. Perhaps her lack came from never seeing the real thing in action.

The tough ones, though, survived. Perhaps more despite her care, she realized now, instead of because of it. When it came to healing, she knew enough to be dangerous. She could recognize that Windwolf was close to death. If he did die, she would find out if Tooloo was right about the life-debt spell. Except for throwing a few pressure bandages onto him, though, she didn't know how to deal with him. Usually elves healed at a phenomenal rate, but only in the presence of magic. The elves had mastered bio magic back when humans were doing flint weapons. Their dependence on magic to heal made Tinker theorize that their healing factor might mirror nanotechnology, that the elves had some type of spell interwoven into their genes that endlessly corrected their bodies, thus healing any damage and keeping them from aging.

She caught herself about to drift off into speculation on the type of spells they might be employing, and returned to the problem at hand.

Someone else would have to patch Windwolf up. Until she figured out who this mythical person might be and got Windwolf into his or her care, she had to keep the elf alive. It was Shutdown Day. They were on Earth. There was no ambient magic for his healing.

But she did have the power sink that collected the magic drained off the crane. She used a modified magnetic containment field to store magical energy—one of her more successful experiments. She couldn't use the stored magic directly on Windwolf's body—it would be like trying to link someone with an artificial heart up to a 110 outlet. She could, though, link the sink's energy to a healing spell.

"Sparks!"

"Yeah, Boss?"

"Search the codex for healing spells. Put the results up on the workshop screen."

"Okay, Boss!"

She got the first-aid kit out of the back storage room and went back to her workshop. She ran out of pressure bandages long before she covered all of Windwolf's wounds, so she raided the bathroom for feminine hygiene pads and affixed them with lots of Scotch tape.

Sparks had cued up twenty healing spells. Some were quite specific: broken bones, kidney failure, heart attack, and so on. She culled those out and looked at the more general ones. One was labeled "will not work on humans."

She had Sparks call up the spell schematics, wishing she understood bio magic better. It seemed to do what she wanted, which was focus energy into the body's existing healing abilities. She cut and pasted in a power distributor as a secondary ring. She made sure the printer was loaded with transferable circuit paper, sent the spell to the printer, and finished her beer as it printed.

Windwolf had worsened. Blood soaked the bandages. All color had drained out with his blood, and he breathed hard and shallow. She let the bandages be, but washed his chest. Peeling the protective sheet from the circuit paper, she pressed the spell to his clean flesh. She checked the spell's hertz cycle, hooked leads through a converter box, and taped the power cords into the power distributor.

"Here goes everything." She checked one last time to make sure all stray metal bits were clear of the magic's path, and flipped the switch. She checked her database, and winced at the activation word phonetically spelled out. Oh great, one of those ancient Elvish words where you try to swallow your tongue. A footnote gave the translation: Be healed.

The outer ring powered up first and cast a glowing sphere over the rest of the spell. Then the healing spell itself kicked in, the timing cycle ring clicking quickly clockwise as the magic flowed through the spell in a steady rhythm.

Windwolf took five shallow breaths. Then a long, deep breath.

Another. And another. He fell into a clean, easy breathing rhythm, color washing into his face.

"Yes! Be healed!" Tinker cried. "I am your magic god! Say Amen to me! Woohoo!" She danced around the room. "Oh yes, I am a god! The one! The only! Tinker!"

Still pleased to giggles, she went to look at Windwolf—really look at him—for the first time in years.

He was beautiful, but then again, he was an elf. They were all beautiful. (And unfortunately all snobs too.) A blue silk ribbon gathered his glossy black hair into a thick, loose ponytail that came nearly to his waist. She tangled her fingers in the curly tips of the ponytail and felt the smooth silkiness of his hair.

Deceptively delicate, his face held just enough strength in it to be masculine. All the fey features: full lips, sharp high cheekbones, perfect nose, pointed ears, almond-shaped eyes, and thick long eyelashes.

She couldn't remember the color of his eyes. They were the first elf eyes she had seen up close, within inches of her own, and they had been so stunningly vivid, she remembered that they left her breathless. But what color? Green? Purple?

She wrapped the lock of black around her finger and rubbed it against her cheek. So soft. It smelled wonderful—a musky spice. She held it to her nose, trying to identify the scent. Mid-sniff, she realized he'd opened his eyes and was looking at her with silent suspicion. His irises were the color of sapphires with the biggest price tags locked in jeweler's cases—the stunning deep blue that neared black.

She gasped with surprise, and then cried as he shifted, "*Naetanyau!* I've got a healing spell jury-rigged on you. If you move, it would be bad. Do you understand? *Kankau?*"

He studied the spell hovering over his chest, the power leads to the siphon, and then the bulky containment unit itself. "I understand," he said finally in English. He looked back at her.

She was still holding the lock of his hair. "Oh, sorry. You smell nice," she said, carefully dropping his hair.

"Who are you?"

He didn't remember her. Not that she was totally surprised—their minutes together, prior to today, could be counted on the fingers of both hands and had been shared with one nasty monster. She had been thirteen then, and still hadn't grown enough of a figure to distinguish her from the boys she played with. It seemed slightly unfair though; her imagination had decided that he stood as some kind of symbol and featured him often in her dreams.

"They call me Tinker." Tooloo had cautioned her against telling people her true name so often that using her nickname became habit. "You're in my scrap yard."

"Your eyes." He carefully lifted his right hand to make an odd gesture over his eyes. "They were different."

She frowned, and then realized what he meant. "Oh, yeah, I had my night goggles on." She fished them out of her pocket, demonstrated how they fit on. "They let me see in the dark."

"Ah." He studied her silently for several minutes. "I would have died."

"You still might. You're badly hurt. It's Shutdown Day, and we're on Earth. I'm afraid if I don't take some drastic actions, you're not going to make it."

"Then drastic actions it must be."

Tinker was trying to figure out what "drastic" might entail when a squad car screamed up the street and slewed in through the open gate.

The cop was Nathan Czernowski, shotgun in hand. "Tinker? Oilcan? Tink!"

"I'm in here!" she called to him, working the dead bolts. "A pack of warglike things attacked me. I think I got them all, but I wasn't taking a chance."

Nathan crossed the parking lot cautiously, scanning the yard, shotgun at his shoulder. "Someone stopped Cordwater out by the pike and said you were yelling for help over your radio line. There's an ambulance on its way. Are you okay? Where's your cousin?"

"One got my hand." She threw open the door, stepped back to let him in, and then bolted the door shut again. "It hurts like shit, but it's stopped bleeding. Otherwise, I'm fine. Oilcan is out with the wrecker. Sparks, edit the message to the wrecker: 'Oilcan, Nathan's here, the monsters are dead, and I'm fine. If I'm not here when you get home, I'll be at Mercy.'"

"Sure, Boss!"

"Can you wait for the ambulance?" Nathan pushed up his goggles and gazed down at her with dark concerned eyes. "I can take you to the hospital."

"I'm fine, but the—umm—the wargs were chasing down an elf." Normally she was a stickler for accuracy, but lacking a name for the monsters, it seemed easier just to say wargs. "He's in my workshop. They chewed him over good."

"He's still alive?"

"Barely. I jury-rigged up a healing spell, so he's stable."

"You've got a spell running now?" Nathan asked. "During Shutdown? Where's the magic coming from?"

"I'm running off of a power sink that I invented. I siphon magic into it while I'm running the crane."

Nathan grinned. "Only you, Tinker. Is he conscious?"

"He was. I'm not sure about right now."

"Did he tell you his name?" Nathan moved into "just the facts" mode, taking out a PDA and stylus.

"It's Windwolf. You know, the one with the saurus?" She traced a symbol in the air over her forehead. Nathan had been a rookie when he took her to the hospital that day, bleeding and crying.

"The one who marked you?" He noted it into his PDA. "The elves have a word for this."

"Shitty luck."

"It's like karma or something. Entanglement?"

"Entanglement is a quantum theory between photons. The polarization of one entangled photon is always the opposite of the other."

He worked his jaw as he thought. "Yeah. Once they're entangled, they stay that way, right?"

She looked at him, one eyebrow upraised.

"Well there's you, him, me, and a monster."

"Yeah, right." Strange, even after five years and with the monster dogs still fresh in her mind, it was the image of the saurus's mouth and the all-too-many ragged teeth that made her shudder. "Look, this has been pretty cranked. I talked to Tooloo about that symbol that Windwolf put on me. She said that's how elves mark life debts. Tooloo says that if Windwolf dies before I cancel the life debt, then some really nasty things will happen to me." Exactly what would happen changed every time she asked Tooloo about it. Once Tooloo had said that as

Windwolf's body decayed, Tinker's would too. Another time, Tooloo had insisted that Tinker would simply vanish. She tried not to believe the old halfie, but she still had nightmares after every conversation.

Nathan looked troubled. "Tooloo is a superstitious fool. I saw the mark. You told me how long Windwolf took making the mark. That wasn't a full spell, whatever it was. It was quick and dirty, and is not going to turn you into a walking zombie five years later. Why would he do that to you, anyhow? You were just a kid."

"He was angry with me. I got in his way while he was trying to kill the saurus and pissed him off. You know what they say about elves."

"What they say and what is true isn't necessarily the same thing. It was nothing."

"It will be nothing. I'm going to save his life. I'm going to cancel the debt. We'll be even."

"Good."

An ambulance came up the street, wailing, and pulled into the yard. Nathan went out to escort the EMT and Tinker swore when she saw who followed Nathan through the front door. "You? Damn, my luck is all bad today."

Jonnie Be Good was an elf wannabe; tall and slender, he wore his blond hair elf-long and had had his ears pointed back in the States. Why anyone would want to be an elf was beyond Tinker. True, the living forever came in handy, but their society sucked; the lower castes seemed practically enslaved by the castes above them, and they were all elegant nose-in-the-air snobs.

Odd, she usually thought of Jonnie Be Good as a good-looking slimewad—apparently after a few minutes' exposure to Windwolf's level of beauty, Jonnie seemed ugly as wood-grain, self-stick wallpaper.

Jonnie smirked and grabbed his crotch. "Oh, bite me."

Add stupid to ugly. Tinker sidestepped quickly to block Nathan; she didn't want Jonnie squashed before he had a chance to treat Windwolf. "I've got a chewed-up hand, and there's a guy really messed up in my workshop. Don't touch the spell I've got set up—it's keeping him stable."

"I like the shirt," Jonnie murmured, squeezing between her and Nathan instead of going around, and made it an excuse to slide his hand over her bare stomach.

"Watch the hands," Nathan rumbled, continuing his big-brother routine. Between him and Oilcan, it was no wonder she didn't date—not that there was anyone she wanted *to* date. Pittsburgh had a stunning lack of young male humans who weren't buttheads. And while elves were pretty, she had yet to meet one that didn't treat her like a subspecies.

Nathan glowered at Jonnie until the paramedic had disappeared into her workshop. "I'll take a look around. Make sure the wargs are all dead."

"That shotgun will only piss them off," she said, and pulled the dent-mender magnet off the wall. "Here, take this."

Because she spent most of her time at the scrap yard, either working or tinkering, she had her laundry machines hooked up in the small, second bedroom. She kept her clean clothes split roughly in half between her loft and a dresser in her workshop. She was annoyed, but not surprised, to find Jonnie pawing through her panties when she walked in.

He had the balls to act like nothing was wrong. He held up a pair of black silk panties. "Very nice."

She snatched it back and stuffed it into the open drawer, trying to pretend her face wasn't burning. "Do you mind?"

"Not at all." He grinned lazily, gazing at her groin. "Wouldn't mind seeing them on, either. Or off."

"Dream on."

"Let me see your hand." For a few minutes he managed to be professional, undoing her bandaging, washing out the wound with peroxide, applying an antibiotic, and rebandaging it. "It's too deep for artificial flesh. You're going to want to go to the hospital with this. You could take nerve damage if it heals wrong, and there's a good chance it can go septic."

"Okay." She mentally took back some of the things she had been thinking of him, until he got up and made motions of packing. Slowly, though, as if he wanted her to notice. "Aren't you going to do something about Windwolf?"

He stopped and shrugged. "Mercy won't take him. According to the peace treaty, elves are to be taken to the hospice beyond the Rim. The elves don't want us messing around with them. Nothing says I have to treat him."

At one time Pittsburgh was home to dozens of world-class hospitals. Amazing what being transported to an alien world can do to health care. Mercy was the only hospital left open, doing only emergency work. Apparently, only *human* emergency work. All elective surgery took place on Earth. There were other hospitals, beyond the Rim, but Tinker neither knew where they were, nor wanted to be stuck at one when Startup hit.

"It's Shutdown Day. The hospice is on Elfhome."

"So? He's stable; wait it out."

"I don't know if I have enough magic to last twenty-four hours. I want him patched up."

"Well, I could be persuaded to treat him."

She clenched her jaw on a few choice names. She'd let him know what she thought of him after Windwolf was patched up. "What do you want?"

"Your name appears on a very short list of women who have never put out."

She clenched her fists. "So, what of it?"

"Well, there's money riding on who gets the first dip in your pool."

"I can pay you anything that's riding on the bet." She sneered.

"Oh, the prestige is more important than the money, although the money has a good bit to do with it. And then there's the thrill of conquest, going where no man has gone before."

"Yeah, right, with Nathan Czernowski poking around outside, and Windwolf bleeding to death in here, you think I'm going to let you do me?"

"Your word is good for me. I do the elf, and later I come back, and do you."

Some sounds, she decided, are fated to be huge no matter how quiet they are. The sound of Windwolf's knife coming out of its sheath was only a whisper of silver on leather, and yet it rang out in the room like a shout. She supposed Jonnie's eyes bugging wide and his sudden frozen attention to the blade pressed to his groin helped to make the noise seem louder.

"You do her," Windwolf whispered, "and you will never do another woman."

"It was a joke." Jonnie swallowed hard.

"Get out," Windwolf commanded.

Tinker glared at Windwolf as Jonnie scuttled out. Why did Windwolf have to wake up now? "Great. That was the only man in the tristate area who could help you."

"I would rather die than stain my honor in that way."

"Your honor? What the hell does it have to do with your honor? It was my decision to make, not yours. I would have been the one to screw him."

"And you think this would not reflect on my honor?"

"Look, I didn't really even have to sleep with him. I could have *lied* to him, got him to treat you, and then backed out later. No one would blame me. He's a complete slimewad."

"Would you really break your word of honor?"

"We'll never know."

He caught her hand. "Would you?"

How could he be so close to death and still be so strong? She finally gave up trying to get free and answered him, anger making her truthful. She considered her honor much more valuable than her virginity, which was a temporary thing to start with. "No." But that didn't mean she couldn't think rings around Jonnie Be Good any day; tricking him without lying would have been easy, probably would even have been fun.

Nathan returned from checking the scrap yard, his head tilted as he listened intently to his headset. "I hate Shutdown Day. People just turn into raging idiots on the road. They've got like twenty cars piled up on the Veterans Bridge. There's possible deaths involved, and apparently a fight has broken out. I've got to go. I've checked around. There's no wargs skulking around." He frowned, noticing the lack of the third person. "What happened to Jonnie?"

"Oh, he opened his mouth, the normal sewage came out, and Windwolf pulled a knife on him. Says his honor would be damaged."

Nathan's eyes narrowed, and he muttered darkly, "I'm going to bust Jonnie's ass if he can't keep his mouth shut and his hands to himself."

"I can handle him myself." Men. All their posturing, yet she was going to have to pick up the pieces anyhow. She guessed it didn't hurt to ask. "What am I supposed to do with Windwolf?"

Nathan gazed at the battered elf bleakly. "I don't know, Tink. Just ride it out, if you can. I don't know anyone more qualified to take care of him than you."

"Damn it, Nathan." She followed him out to the front door. "I don't know anything about healing an elf."

"Nobody does. Take care of yourself, Tink!"

"Yeah!" She watched him get into his squad car and pull away. "Nobody else is going to do it."

She bolted the front door and glanced at the office clock: 1:20. Only a little more than an hour since Windwolf came over the fence, and another twenty-three before Pittsburgh returned to Elfhome and its magic.

Already there was a tiny slice off the top of the sink's power meter. She marked the one-hour's usage, feeling a growing sense of despair. The sink would last approximately another twenty hours. Alone she couldn't move the heavy sink, and if she disconnected Windwolf from it to get him to help, he would die. And according to Tooloo, if he died without the spell being canceled, so did she.

She remembered with a start that Tooloo had at one time given her a cancel spell. Tinker had transcribed it into her computer as an appendix to her family's spell codex. Windwolf seemed to be asleep; still, she did the search by hand, using the keywords of "cancel, life debt." Since the workshop screen was viewable from the table, she quickly sent the spell to the printer and closed the file. The printer hummed as it spit out a page of circuit paper.

Tinker picked up the paper and stared at it. Tooloo had scribed the single complex glyph out, and Tinker had copied it carefully; but the blunt truth was, she had no idea what the spell would do. The thought of using it smacked of putting an alien device to Windwolf's head, pulling the trigger, and *hoping* it didn't blow his brains out. Even if the spell didn't kill him outright, what if it disrupted his healing ability? At this moment, the result would be deadly.

And she only had Tooloo's often changing assertions that what Windwolf had done to her was harmful. Because Tooloo had taught her Elvish, and the fundamentals of magic, Tinker's scientific psyche allotted the half-elf with the same basic faith she had in her other teachers. (If her grandfather had ever lied to her, he had done it with a mathematician's consistency and had taken all of his secrets to his grave.) Oilcan warned Tinker often that she was too trusting in general, so she forced herself to consider that Tooloo could be lying.

She sat in her still workshop, Windwolf's ragged, uneven breathing the only sound, painfully aware of the empty streets for miles in all directions, trying to decide. Did she risk killing Windwolf to save herself?

Throughout Tinker's childhood, Tooloo took odd perversity at being impenetrable; there was no knowing if what she told Tinker was anything more than attempts to frighten her. Windwolf, though, had saved her twice this evening, and once five years ago. Simple, cold, rational logic dictated that she owed Windwolf the benefit of the doubt. She put down the spell, but she found no comfort in her decision. Why was the unknown so much more frightening than the known?

A half hour later, with a rumble of the big Caterpillar engine and the rattle of chains, Oilcan returned to the yard. He had his tow lights on and a small shrub stuck in the flatbed's ram-prow.

"Tinker?" he bellowed as he swung out of the cab, a crowbar in hand. "Coz?"

"Here am I." She came out into the yard, the dent mender in hand.

Tinker and Oilcan favored one another, which sometimes made Tinker wonder about her egg donor. She knew that her grandfather had selected her mother mostly on intelligence—he could be quite vocal about his scheme to raise a genius grandchild—but she wondered occasionally if he had also tried to make it so that she and Oilcan looked like brother and sister too. Oilcan was just shy of average height for a man, slender built as she was, with the same nut-brown coloring. When they were little, Tooloo had called them her wood sprites. Tinker always thought the overall effect worked better on Oilcan; he had a spry puckish kind of look—what people used to think of as fey before they met the real elves.

Oilcan stopped at the sight of the blood on her, his dark eyes going wide and solemn with concern. "Oh, shit, Tinker—are you okay?"

"Fine, fine. Most of it isn't mine. Windwolf is chewed to hell. Someone cooked up a pack of monster dogs that—" She stopped as implications finally seeped in. While created for a war waged millennia ago, the wargs now ranged wild, for all purposes a natural creature despite their magical enhancements. Simple bad luck could account for a warg attack. Windwolf's mauling, though, was clearly an attempt of premeditated murder. Someone had made the monster dogs, taking days to set up the original spell and then copy it onto the five pug dogs. "Someone sicced a pack of killer dogs on Windwolf."

"Windwolf? Not the elf that marked you? That's bad, isn't it? Is he still alive?"

"Barely. We have to make sure he stays that way. Jonnie was here. He wouldn't do anything for him, and he says that Mercy won't touch him."

"The hell they won't. Not everyone is a self-serving bastard like Jonnie. We can take him over and someone will take care of him. It's not like they're going to let him bleed to death in front of them. Is it?"

For a moment, she thought she could let him take charge. Then she realized that he was waiting for her to say yes or no. The problem was that Oilcan knew she was smarter than he was. He had a lot going on upstairs, but he always deferred to her. She was never sure if it was because she'd played too many head games with him while they were growing up, or if it was some crippling fear of failure. He had been ten before falling into her grandfather's care and can-do style of child raising, and it showed. He was four years her senior, but still he was more than willing for her to be the boss.

Of course, that had drawbacks.

"I don't know!" She retreated back to the workshop to check on Windwolf, finding him unchanged. Oilcan trailed behind her, waiting for her to think of something. "Certainly if we can't think of anyone else to help with Windwolf, we can take him to Mercy. Can't hurt. Might help."

"Who the hell else is there? Tooloo?"

"She stays on Elfhome on Shutdown. Let me think." Tinker bounced in place. Weird as it seemed, sometimes bouncing helped, like her brain just needed to be jostled around so a good idea could surface to the top. "Elf. Heal an elf. Elf healing. Elf biology. Xenobiologist! Lain!"

Oilcan studied the setup around Windwolf. "How are we going to move him? You need to take the power sink, and that's nearly five hundred pounds there alone. I don't know if the two of us can move it."

She considered the sink, the pale battered elf, and all the blood. "We'll just take the workshop trailer, load it onto the flatbed."

"You've got to be joking."

"That's how we got it here in the first place."

"Shit, but up to the Observatory? And we don't know if she's even home. The phones are still out."

"She's usually home on Shutdown Day," Tinker said. "She transmits data from her home computer. If she's not, well, we'll just drive on to Mercy Hospital. If they won't take him, I don't know, maybe we'll drive out to Monroeville and see if we can find a vet."

"Monroeville? You mean drive to Earth?"

"We are on Earth."

"We're in Pittsburgh," Oilcan said. "Pittsburgh hasn't really been part of Earth for a long time."

"Yeah, we'll go to Earth if we have to."

It took longer than she thought to fill up the flatbed's gas tanks, jury-rig a power supply for the trailer, disconnect the city's power connections, rig a sling under the trailer, and use the crane (magnet turned off) to lift the trailer carefully onto the flatbed and secure it. She made sure that they had Windwolf's sword and pistol; if he lived until Startup, they'd deliver him and his weapons to the nearest hospice. Tinker found the abandoned cancel spell, folded the paper carefully so the rune itself wasn't creased, and tucked it into her front shirt pocket. If things went wrong, perhaps the spell could still work after Windwolf died, severing any magical bond between them.

The trailer's now-empty air-conditioning slot conveniently fit up against the flatbed's back window, allowing her to crawl between the trailer and the truck's cabin. Oilcan would drive, being the more cautious of the two of them, and certainly also the more patient. Tinker made sure everything was green with Oilcan, then slithered through the hole to ride beside Windwolf.

"What is happening?" Windwolf peered through slit eyes, his voice paper-thin.

"We're moving the trailer to someone that can help you."

"The house is moving?"

"Yes."

He closed his eyes and exhaled a very slight laugh. "And you humans used to think of us as gods."

The Allegheny Observatory sat high on a hill, deep in an old city park. A steep and twisty road wound up to it. In the winter, the road made an excellent bobsled course. In the middle of the rainy night, in a teetering trailer, with a dying elf, it was nightmarish. The Rim, however, cut through on the other side of the park, taking out one vital bridge to a saner route.

At the turn of the millennium, the district of Observatory Hill had apparently been struggling; the gate effect, and the loss of the bridge, had killed it completely. Whereas in other parts of Pittsburgh, the Rim remained a sharply marked borderline between Elfhome and transported Earth, here a young forest of Elfhome trees, a mile in from the Rim, stood in testament to how much of the neighborhood had been lost. None of the houses had actually been torn down; a scattered number still stood, lurking like undead under the trees. Some of the buildings had caught fire, whole blocks burning to rubble before the fire department could check the blaze's progress. The rest had just been whittled away: the windows, the doors, the sinks, the toilets, the copper pipes, and finally the nails. Little by little, they'd been looted by those desperate for finished building materials. Soon only sodden white piles of plaster would be left.

Now Observatory Hill was just a commune of scientists huddled around the Allegheny Observatory bulkhead. A hundred years ago, the area had been moneyed, and stately Victorian homes remained, refurbished to act as dorms for the transient scientists. Mean age hovered at twenty-seven, postdoctorate but still under the authority of older, well-established scientists on Earth. Every thirty days the population changed. Because of the Observatory, lights were low, but always on. The astronomers studied the parallel star system during the night. Xenobiologists studied the alien life during the day. They shared resources of backup generators, kitchen facilities, cooking and cleaning staff, and computers.

Lain Skanske's home sat near but apart from the dorms. A pristine white fence guarded a lush garden of roses, hosta, *laleafrin*, and *tulilium*. Lain called the garden her consolation prize for giving up a life in space after being crippled in a near-fatal shuttle accident.

Oilcan pulled the flatbed to a stop, headlights aimed at the front door of Lain's grand Victorian home, and called back, "Tink, we're here!"

Tinker slid into the cab beside him. "He's still alive." She had spent the ride wishing she had asked Windwolf about the cancel spell in his few moments of awareness. There seemed no polite way to say, "What does this do? Do you mind if I cast this on you before you die?" to a man mauled while protecting you. She had kept her silence. Besides, there was still hope. "I'll go see if Lain's home."

"It's four in the morning, Tink."

"Well, if she's in town, she's here, then."

Lain's house had a massive front door with leaded glass sidelights extending the entrance out another two feet on either side. The doorbell was an ancient device—one turned a key located in the center of the door, and the key spun a metal spring coiled inside a domed bell bolted to the other side. Tinker had broken it as a child; last year, she had fixed it in an act of adult penitence. She spun and spun the key now, making the bell ring unendingly.

Lights came on, starting from the lab in the back of the house. Lain came up the hall, her figure distorted by the lead glass and the shuttle accident. The xenobiologist had trained to study the life in the seas of Europa. Crippled, she'd found a second chance studying the alien life of Elfhome.

"Who is it?" Lain called as she came.

Tinker stopped ringing the bell. "It's Tinker!"

Lain opened the door, blinking in the flatbed's headlights, leaning heavily on her crutch. "Tink, what in the world? This better not be another tengu you're bringing me."

"A what?"

"A Japanese elf. Related to the oni. Sometimes it looks like a crow."

"I've never brought you a crow."

"In the dream I had last week, you brought me a tengu, and wanted me to bandage it. I kept on telling you that it was dangerous, but you wouldn't listen to me. We bandaged it up, and it turned you into a diamond and flew away with you in its beak."

"I'm not going to be responsible for dreams you had."

This was the way conversations tended to go with Lain. Tinker was never sure if she liked talking with Lain. They were never direct, easy-to-understand conversations, and were thus an annoyance and a treasure at the same time.

Lain pulled an umbrella out of a stand by the door and stepped out into the wet to thumb it open. "Well, the phones haven't started working yet, so I might as well deal with this emergency now. You couldn't have picked a worse day to bring me something to treat."

"If this weren't Shutdown Day, I wouldn't be coming to you with this."

At the flatbed, Lain collapsed the umbrella, set it inside the chest-high door, unlatched her crutch, put it beside the umbrella, and then reached up and swung gracefully into the trailer. Lacking Lain's height and reach, and with one hand nearly useless, Tinker scrambled up in a less dignified manner.

Running off the flatbed's electric, Tinker had only managed to set up two lights. The dimness hid the worst of Windwolf's condition. Still, the sight of the bandaged elf seemed to shock Lain.

"Oh, my," Lain said. "It is a tengu."

"I am not a tengu," Windwolf whispered.

"Close enough." Lain shrugged, picking up her crutch. "What happened?"

"He was attacked by dogs," Tinker said. "A pack of them—really ugly and bigger than wargs. They were magical constructs."

"They were Foo dogs," Windwolf whispered.

Lain limped to Windwolf and eyed his many wounds. "Foo dogs. Can tengu be far behind?"

"A good question." Windwolf sighed. "Do you understand the strictures of the treaty between our people?"

"Yes," Lain said.

"Do I have your pledge that you'll abide by it?"

"You'll trust my word?"

"Tinker has vouched for you."

Lain threw Tinker a concerned look. "I see. Yes, you have my word."

"Word about what?" Tinker asked.

"The treaty allows for simple first aid." Lain scanned the equipment connected to Windwolf. "It theorized that since we can interbreed, humans and elves must be ninety-eight percent to ninety-nine percent genetically identical. But then, we're ninety percent identical to earthworms, so it's not that amazing, except that this is an alien world."

"We're that close to earthworms?"

"Yes. Frightening isn't it?"

"How close are Earth earthworms and Elfhome earthworms?"

"Do you know how many species of earthworms are on Earth?" Lain eyed the power sink. "Of course primates are also ninety-eight percent identical to us, and we can't interbreed."

"Has anyone tried?"

"Knowing humans," Windwolf murmured. "Yes."

Lain laughed, looking amused and yet insulted. "As a scientifically controlled experiment or a sexual perversion?"

"Both." Windwolf earned a dark look from Lain.

"What does that have to do with anything now?" Tinker asked to distract the two.

"The point is that the elves want to keep it all theory," Lain said. "It's against the treaty to cull any genetic samples from an accident victim. It's why Mercy won't treat elves." She shook her head. "This is going to be tricky. I'll need him in my operating room to properly treat him."

Tinker considered. "I have longer leads. We could leave the sink in the trailer and run the magic into your OR with the longer leads. There might be a drop in power, though."

Oilcan peered through the AC slot from the truck cab. "If I take down a section of the fence, we can back up almost to the OR's window."

"Oh, we can't," Tinker said. "We'll drive over the flowers and ruin them."

"A man's life is more important than flowers." Lain brushed the objection aside. "Will the spell let you disconnect and reconnect?"

"I am not a man," Windwolf whispered.

"Elf. Man. Close enough for horseshoes," Tinker said, shaking her head in answer to Lain's question. "I can print a second spell and activate it in the OR. We'll have to scrub his chest to get all traces of the old spell off."

"Horseshoes?" Windwolf asked.

"It's a game," Tinker told him. "Oilcan and I play it at the scrap yard. When you're better, I'll teach it to you."

"Okay." Lain limped to the door. "Let's make this happen."

Tinker printed off another copy of the spell and found longer leads. Oilcan found help at the Observatory in the form of astronomers. They took down much of the picket fence and eased the truck to the porch. Luckily Lain had a hospital gurney in her lab, and they wheeled it over a ramp into the trailer. After Oilcan and two of the postdocs slid Windwolf onto the gurney, they wheeled it as far as the present leads allowed, which took them inside the foyer of Lain's grand Victorian home.

There they let him sit, while Tink threaded the longer leads out the lab window. Then came the mad scramble of disconnecting leads, pushing Windwolf to the lab, moving the truck, cleaning Windwolf's chest, applying the spell, and reconnecting the leads. Windwolf lay still as death on the gurney even after Tink activated the spell.

"Is he dead?" Tinker had been entertaining herself with thoughts of Windwolf's aristocratic reaction to flinging large metal horseshoes at a metal peg. Would he even come see how the game would be played, she had wondered, or would he vanish out of her life like he had done last time? The thought of him dead and unable to do either sickened her. *Oh please, no.*

And then after that, an even more horrible thought. *Oh, no, the life debt!* She patted her shirt pocket, and the cancel spell crinkled reassuringly. There was even magic left in the sink to power the spell.

Lain pulled on latex gloves and then pressed a hand to his neck. "No. He's hanging in there. Barely."

Tinker sniffed as blinked-away tears made her nose start to run.

Lain looked at her strangely.

"If he dies," Tinker offered as an excuse for the sniffling, "I'm screwed."

Lain frowned at her, then swung the brilliant light over to shine on the elf's face. "Wolf Who Rules Wind." She used his full true name in Elvish, seemingly stunned to immobility.

"You know him? Lain?"

Lain looked at her. "When are you going to start taking notice of things beyond that scrap yard of yours? There are two very large worlds out there, and you are in an uncommon position of being part of both of them. Speaking of which, Oilcan, can you see if the phones are working? I have several hours of data to upload while we're on Earth. These Foo dogs—they have fangs, like a cat?"

"Yes."

"These puncture wounds must have been made by the fangs. There is crushing damage from the teeth between them. I'm going to treat all this with peroxide, or they'll go septic."

"They weren't genetic constructs—more like a solid hologram. When I hit them with the electromagnet, they unraveled back down to the original creature. Their breath smelled like—" Tinker searched her memory now that she didn't have one of the beasts breathing down her neck "—like incense."

"Foo dogs are actually Foo lions—protectors of sacred buildings," Lain said. "Temples and suchlike. They're supposed to scare demons—oni."

"I thought you said oni were elves, related to the tengu."

"Elves, demons, spirits. Two cultures rarely have one-to-one translations. So, you're saying that these bites were made by holograms? You're guessing there's no bacteria involved because they weren't eating, breathing, real creatures?"

"Solid illusions, possibly. Oh, who the hell knows?"

"I'd rather be safe than sorry. We have another"—Lain glanced at the lab clock, which read 6:10—"eighteen hours. The thing about animal bites is that they will go septic if you don't stay on top of them."

It took hours. News of Windwolf's condition spread through the commune. Despite the frantic shuffle of leaving and incoming postdocs, many of the scientists stopped by to lend a hand. Hot food was carried from the kitchens. Biologists came to help with the first-aid efforts. When the phones came back online at eight in the morning, the biologists fielded phone calls from Earth-bound scientists looking for specimens and data forgotten during the callers' last trip to Elfhome. They even ran Lain's data transfer.

At ten, a van arrived to pick up botanical specimens that Lain had collected and quarantined over the last thirty days. Lain had to supervise, making sure that only the most harmless of Elfhome's biological flora were loaded, even though the most deadly, like the strangle vines and black willows, probably wouldn't flourish without magic. The drivers complained about the ten hours to travel the ten miles in from the Rim, unloaded the truck of food and supplies, stared at the improving Windwolf in open curiosity, and then hurried off, hoping aloud that the twelve hours of Shutdown remaining would be enough time to reach the Rim again. They prompted an exodus among the scientists who were returning to Earth.

Finally the house emptied, and Tinker sprawled on a white wicker chaise stolen from Lain's sunporch. Lain found her nearly asleep and tapped her on the cheek with a printout. Tinker slit open her eyes, took the paper, and closed her eyes again. "What's this?"

"Carnegie Mellon University reviewed your application. Apparently they've been able to confirm your father's alumni-slash-faculty history prior to their hasty move out of Oakland. They were impressed by your placement tests and they've accepted you. They're offering you a scholarship, and your living costs would be handled by the displaced citizen fund. They're trying to decide if you qualify for the in-state tuition scale. If we get your reply out today, you can start in the fall."

"Lain!" Tinker kept her eyes shut, not wanting to see Lain's excitement. *They were impressed by my placement tests? How? I know I didn't get any of the questions right.* "I applied just to make you happy. I didn't think they would accept me." *I thought I made sure they wouldn't accept me.* "I don't want to go."

Frosty silence. Tinker could imagine the disapproving look. Even with her eyes closed, it had Medusa-like powers.

"Tinker," Lain said, apparently realizing the magic of her gaze alone wasn't working, "I didn't push this last year because you weren't legal yet, but now you can come and go without worry. You're wasting your life in that scrap yard. You are the most brilliant person I've ever met, and you're twiddling with junked cars."

Oh, the dreaded scrap yard attack! "The scrap yard pays the bills, gives me parts to work with and all the spare time I could want. It lets me do what makes me happy. If I want to spend three weeks inventing hovercycles, I make hovercycles."

"Any university or corporation would outfit you with a state-of-the-art lab."

Tinker made a noise of disgust. "No, they wouldn't." She cracked her eye, glanced over the paper, double-checking her facts before finishing. "See, I would be a freshman, whatever the hell that is, on probationary status *due to the unusual nature of my schooling and lack of exposure to normal human society.* They're not offering me a lab."

"They will. As soon as they see your full capabilities. Besides, a term or two of liberal arts classes could only help you. There's so much you don't know."

"Maybe about oni, but not about quantum mechanics."

"There's more to life than just physics. Shakespeare. Mozart. Picasso. You'll be exposed to the entire range of human culture, and meet intelligent people your own age."

"People my age are immature." She sat up, scrubbing at her hair and wincing as she hit a sore spot. "What's the bloody rush? Can't I think about this until next Shutdown?"

Lain pressed her mouth into a tight line, meaning she didn't want to answer the question, but her basic honesty forced her to. "You should go before you start to date." Lain held up a hand to check a protest. "I know you're not interested in any of the local guys yet, but it's only a matter of time before your curiosity overcomes repulsion, and once you get entangled with a man, it's so much harder to walk away."

With Jonnie Be Good fresh in her mind, Tinker said, "Oh, ick. I don't think that's really a danger, Lain."

"At CMU, there will be hundreds of intelligent boys your age who are more interested in graduating than getting married and having kids."

"Okay! Okay!" she cried to stop the flow. "Give me a little while to think about it. It was the last thing on my mind." Speaking of what was mostly on her mind, she asked, "How is Windwolf?"

"Stable. I'd like to think he's stronger than when I first saw him. I think he's out of immediate danger."

Rain still smeared the windows, graying the world beyond. The flatbed sat deep in Lain's prize flower beds. Rain-filled tire ruts ran across the yard and through the crushed flowers and the dismantled fence: six deep channels of torn-up earth zigzagging through the perfect lawn until it was more mud than grass.

Lain had spent hours, and days, and years working on her garden, crippled legs and all. It was going to take ages to right all the damage.

Tinker stared guiltily at the mess, and then looked at the paper in her hand. Lain had never asked, over the years, for any repayment for all the things she had done for Tinker. From comforting Tinker when her grandfather died, to advice on her menses, Lain had only given.

Classes would start in September and run until before Christmas. Three Shutdowns. Just ninety days, and she could always bail early if she hated it.

"Okay. I'll attend one set of classes and give it a try."

Lain went round-eyed in amazement. "Really?"

"Yes." Tinker cringed before her excitement. "One semester. Nothing more. I'll try it. I know I won't like it. And that will be that. We'll be square."

Lain gave her a sharp look, which probably meant she wasn't happy with the idea that Tinker viewed college as a prison sentence, but didn't debate it. She leaned forward and kissed Tinker on the forehead. "Good. I'll e-mail them your acceptance."

Tinker hunched in the chair, watching the rain sheet down the glass, feeling as if she herself were sliding down a slippery plane, gray and formless. There was no doubting she'd pleased Lain. The xenobiologist had always expected Tinker's best, and in doing so, usually got it. Tinker had learned all the levels of Lain's praise, from the scathing backhanded compliment for a job sloppily done, to the Mona Lisa smile and swat for a clever but naughty act. Lain had bestowed her ultimate seal of approval with the kiss.

Perhaps it was good that she was going to give Earth a try. Tinker had carefully avoided Earth her whole life, afraid that if she left Pittsburgh she wouldn't be able to return to Elfhome. Tinker grudgingly admitted to herself that it was childish to cling to the old and familiar, rebuking the new just because it was new. Didn't she pride herself at being extremely mature for her age?

And yet, with her whole heart and soul, she didn't want to leave home.

Tinker fell asleep sometime after that. Her sleeping mind twisted the day's worries and events and shaped them into her recurring "maze nightmare." As a new twist, Jonnie Be Good starred as a tengu, transforming into a crow's form to steal her diamond-shaped purity. Tooloo knew where Jonnie had hidden the gem inside the maze, but only spouted nonsense for directions. Windwolf did his typical "failing your potential" speeches—why him and not her grandfather or Lain, she never could fathom—and suddenly the dream went off in a new, erotic direction. Asserting that he knew what was best for her, Windwolf held her down and kissed his way down to her groin. His soft hair pooled over her bare legs as his insistent tongue caressed at a point of pleasure she barely knew existed. She woke with her abdomen rippling with the strength of her orgasm.

What the hell was that? She lay in the same position as in her dream, legs parted and hips cocked up. Her pose merged with the dream memory so strongly that for a moment she wasn't sure if she hadn't truly experienced the sex act. Common sense seeped in as she became more fully awake. No, it had just been a dream. Too bad. She squeezed her eyes shut, stealing a hand down the front of her pants, trying to recapture that roiling bliss.

Oilcan clunked into the room, rain darkening his shirt. "Hey."

Burning with embarrassment, Tinker yanked her hand out of her pants and tried to sound nonchalant. "Hey."

Oilcan shoved his damp hair back out of his eyes. "I went out to the trailer. The level indicators on the power sink are showing that we've only got a few more hours and then it's gone."

Tinker looked at the darkening sky, seeing that dusk was coming on. "What time is it?"

"Almost seven."

"Five more hours until Startup."

Oilcan shook his head. "The sink only has about two hours of power left."

"How's Windwolf?"

"At the moment, holding steady. Lain says that he's likely to worsen, though, once the power gives out."

Then they couldn't stay at Lain's. Magic wasn't like electricity; you didn't flip a switch and get current flooding the power lines. Instead, like a gentle rain after a drought, magic would need to saturate the area and soak in deep until the depleted earth couldn't hold any more and then form useable runoff. Even after Startup, it would take hours before the ambient level of magic in Pittsburgh would be where anyone could do a healing spell and expect it to work.

Tinker checked to see if she still had the cancel spell printout and then levered herself out of the chair. "We should be sitting at the Rim nearest to the hospice at Startup."

* * *

Windwolf woke as they prepared to move him back to the truck, blinking in confusion.

"Lie still." Tinker said to him, and repeated it in Low Elvish.

"Ah, my little savage," Windwolf murmured, lifting his good hand to her. "What now?"

"We're running out of time, which is unfortunately common for us humans." Tinker squeezed his hand in what she hoped was a reassuring manner.

"Does life go by so quickly, then?"

"Yes," Tinker said, thinking of leaving Pittsburgh in a few months and already regretting her promise to Lain. "It must be nice, having all the time to do all the things you want to do."

He turned his head and looked out the window. "There is a graveyard on that hill. I see them all the time here in your city. We do not have them. We do not die in such numbers. But it never truly struck me as to what these graveyards meant until now; all around you, the churches and the graveyards—death constantly stands beside you. I don't know how you tolerate the horror."

It scared her to hear him talking about death. "I'll get you to a hospice at Startup," she promised. "But you'll have to hang in there until then."

"Hang in?" He looked mystified by the English slang.

"Keep fighting."

"Life is a marvelous adventure," he whispered. "And I wish not to end it now. Especially now that things have gotten even more interesting."

They eased back down Riverview Road and through the maze of side streets to Ohio River Boulevard. There, the traffic snarled into knots as people fleeing the city collided with those trying to get back in. It took them an hour to travel the two or three miles to the first major split in the road. The night was sweltering, as only July in Pittsburgh could be. They rode with the windows down, and in the mostly stopped traffic, those without air-conditioning got out and stood waiting outside their cars for the chance to crawl ahead.

"There's Nathan's twenty-car accident." Oilcan indicated a score of wrecked cars and trucks sitting under the floodlights of the stadium parking lot. It wasn't difficult to guess which vehicle had been involved in the fatality. A red vehicle, make unrecognizable, sat to one side, smashed into an accordion two feet tall. "How do you suppose they managed that in this type of traffic?"

"One of the semis lost its load." Tinker pointed out the haphazardly loaded trailer. "It must have landed on the—minivan?— beside it." The parking lot's entrances, she noticed, had Earth Interdimensional Agency barricades up, and police tape strung at chest height about the cars created an imaginary fence. "Looks like someone got caught smuggling in the deal."

Judging by the amount of police tape and number of armed men, the EIA, the international agency in charge of almost everything in Pittsburgh even vaguely related to the elves, had stumbled onto a large illegal shipment. There were three tractor-trailer trucks, a dozen large Ryder and U-Haul box trucks, four pickup trucks, and the squashed car—any of which could have been the smuggler's vehicle. Unless they had been part of a convoy, it seemed strange that the EIA had impounded the whole lot.

"That Peterbilt is nearly new." The traffic opened up for a few hundred feet. Oilcan grunted slightly as he put in the clutch in order to shift out of first gear into second gear. The clutch in the flatbed, an ancient 2010 Ford F750, was stiff; Tinker nearly had to stand on it to shift when she drove. "It wouldn't take much to get it back to running."

Tinker drooled at it for a minute. "Yeah, but unless it's *the* smuggling vehicle and thus no one is willing to claim it, someone will have already made arrangements to get their truck back next Shutdown."

"One can dream." Oilcan grunted through another shift back down to first as they dropped to a crawl.

Speaking of next Shutdown . . . "I told Lain that I'd go to CMU for a term."

"You're kidding." He looked at her as if she had suddenly transformed into something slightly repulsive and totally unexpected, like one of those ugly pug dogs.

"It'll only be ninety days, and I'd get a chance to see what Earth is like."

"I've lived there," Oilcan pointed out. "Everything is too big. You can spend all day looking at thousands of people and not see a single person that you know."

They eased up onto the Fort Duquesne Bridge. Below them, barges choked the Ohio, the Allegheny, and the Monongahela rivers. It seemed possible to walk from one shore to the other without touching water. It happened every time Pittsburgh returned to Earth; trade goods coming and going by land, water, and air. She didn't want to think about living someplace this crowded all the time.

"You're not helping," she said.

"It's another world, Tinker. If you don't like it, you'll be stuck and miserable."

"Maybe I'll like it."

He shrugged. "Maybe. I don't think so. You hate having someone telling you what to do. *Think* about it. You're going for classes. You've never been to a regular school. Classes start exactly at eight a.m. Bang. A bell rings and you have to be sitting in your seat, quiet, facing forward. And you sit there, without talking, for hours, while you study what the teacher wants you to learn."

"Maybe college is different. Lain seems to think it's a good idea."

"And Lain likes to putter around in the garden, planting flowers. You tried that once. Remember how crazy it drove you."

"I already told Lain yes."

He scowled at her, and then focused on getting through the city.

Downtown, despite it being almost ten o'clock, was filled with activity. Stores were sorting hastily delivered goods, preparing for the Startup rush. Once the stores sold out, there would be no more until next Shutdown. Fall fashions were appearing in the windows; anyone who didn't buy early might be facing the Pittsburgh winter without gloves and sweaters.

The delivery drivers who were still trying to get home to Earth were few, and easily identified. They leaned on their horns, they cursed out their windows, and they disobeyed all laws of man, elf, and common sense in their rush.

"Watch, watch, watch!" Tinker shouted, bracing herself as one such idiot cut them off. It was a small rabid pickup truck, streaking through a recently changed red light with horn blasting. At the last moment, it recognized that the flatbed outweighed it by three times, and veered sharply to avoid them.

Only a motorcyclist was in the way.

A normal man would have died. The motorcyclist responded

with inhuman speed and strength, wrenching his bike out of the pickup's way.

"Is he an elf?" Oilcan asked as he responded to the blare of horns behind him and drove on through the intersection.

Tinker leaned out to look back. Strangely, instead of focusing on the pickup truck that nearly hit him, the motorcyclist was watching the flatbed drive away. He was far too homely to be one of the fey; under a wild thatch of black hair, he was long-nosed and sharp-featured.

"Nah. Just lucky," Tinker said, and scrambled through the back window to check on Windwolf.

The power sink read empty, and the spell had collapsed. Windwolf was cool to the touch, and for a moment she was afraid he had died. She stared at him for what seemed to be eternity before he took a long deep breath.

During the day, Lain had kept dryer-warm blankets on Windwolf. The current blanket was cool to the touch. Tinker called Lain. "The magic's out. Windwolf's cold. Is there anything I can do?"

"Lie down beside him, under the blankets with him."

"What?"

"Is he even conscious, Tinker?"

"I don't know." Lain was right, though. Tinker was letting the memory of her dream make her self-conscious. A moment ago she'd been afraid the elf was dead; how aware was he going to be of her? "Okay. I'll call you later, let you know how we're doing."

Tinker turned off the lights, took off her boots, and crawled onto the worktable with Windwolf. Sometime during the day, his hair had come unbound; it spread into a pool of blackness on the table. To keep from pinning his hair under her, she gathered it into her good hand and carefully moved it all to his right side. It felt as silky as in her dream. She stroked the long soft strands into order and then carefully cuddled up to Windwolf, trying not to press against any of his wounds. Lying in enforced idleness beside him, however, made her mind churn through possibilities at a feverish speed. Maybe, her brain suggested, she had dreamed so vividly of Windwolf because of the life debt, coupled with his proximity. Possibly he had shared the memory. Perhaps he had actually instigated the sex, since it was beyond her normal ken of experience.

She peered at his still face in the shifting beams of the passing headlights. Come on, Tinker, a male this beautiful—and in this much pain—doesn't dream about getting it on with scruffy little things like you.

Which left her solely responsible. Wow.

"Tinker. Tinker!"

"What is it?" She blinked awake and realized she was in Windwolf's arms, his head on her shoulder and his scent on her lips.

"It's the EIA," Oilcan whispered through the window. "They're checking citizen papers. Do you have yours?"

"Yeah. Hold on." She slid out of Windwolf's loose hold to the floor. Someone banged on the trailer door, hard, making the whole back wall rattle. "Who the hell is out there? The Jolly Green Giant?"

"All three are big guys." Oilcan's face was visible only from his eyes up, but it was a portrait of fear. Border guards spooking Oilcan?

"What time is it? Where are we?"

"Six blocks from the Rim. It's five minutes to Startup."

"And they're EIA border guards?" Something didn't ring true, and she glanced about for a weapon. "Give me a minute!" she shouted. "I'm—I'm getting dressed!"

Windwolf's shoulder holster and pistol sat by the worktable. She reloaded the pistol quickly, looped the holster into place, and pulled on a jacket over it.

She unbolted the door and swung it open. "Here." She held out her citizen papers.

Some estimated the elfin population to be a billion for the entire planet. Others thought there might be as few as a few hundred million. No human knew and the elves guarded the information closely. Regardless, the elves had allowed displaced humans to remain only on certain conditions specified in the peace treaty. All humans judged criminal or insane in nature were banished, and immigration was to be by elf approval only. While many people fled living on an alien planet under control of an alien race, the benefits outweighed the negatives for many people. Nonexistent unemployment, cheap housing, and a blissfully unspoiled planet proved too much of a lure for many. A brisk trade of smuggling immigrants existed. The responsibility of controlling it fell to the Earth Interdimensional Agency, EIA.

The border guards usually hugged the border, since anyone a foot within the Rim made the trip to Elfhome. This close to midnight, they should be at the fence, catching the last desperate few and then calling it a night as Startup made all things moot. Six blocks away from the Rim, with only five minutes left, was setting off alarms. They were big men, all three Nathan Czernowski's size, which was odd in humans.

The largest one seemed to be the leader. He took her ID but dismissed it and her in a glance. Nor did he hand it back. She noticed that he also had Oilcan's papers.

"Check the trailer," the leader told the smallest guard, although that was a relative "small." "See if the little bird was right. Get the car," he ordered the remaining guard, who moved off into the night. "I want to be gone when this is done."

The smallest guard grabbed the door frame and levered himself up into the trailer, barely squeezing through the door. His nose worked like a dog's. "It smells like a slaughterhouse in here."

"We're transporting a wounded elf." Tinker backed away from him, keeping out of range of an easy grab. "We're taking him to the hospice as soon as Startup happens. Wargs chewed him up. He got blood everywhere. That's what you smell." She sniffed to see if it was really that noticeable, and caught his scent.

Smoke and sandalwood.

The guard saw Windwolf. His eyes narrowed, and he grinned savagely. "He is here," he rumbled to the leader. "Laid out like the dead. Easy prey."

"Do them all," the leader ordered. "Quietly."

Tinker yanked out the pistol, sliding between the guard and Windwolf. "Don't touch him! Touch him and I'll shoot you! Get back! Get out!"

"Tinnnker?" Oilcan asked quietly in the startled silence that followed, and then started the flatbed's engine. "I don't know what you're doing, but you'd better do it quick! The one outside just waved down some kind of backup in an unmarked car."

The smallest guard started to move toward her and she fired a warning shot over his shoulder. He jerked backward like it had hit him.

"Get out!" She fought to keep her voice firm. "This is your last chance! Go!" Amazingly, the small guard tumbled out of the trailer, almost onto the leader, and they both scrambled away. She'd never felt so huge before. She slammed the door, bolted it, and raced back across the trailer, yelling, "Drive! Drive! Drive!"

The flatbed lurched forward, roaring up through first. "Tinker, I don't think I'm going to be able to make it! The car is cutting me off! Oh shit!"

A black sedan had raced past them on the left and was swinging right to cut them off. Oilcan was already slowing down when Tinker hit the window. She slid through the window, down into his lap, and jammed her foot down on top of his.

"Just go!" she shouted. "Shift!"

Swearing, Oilcan stomped down on the clutch, threw the truck into second, and let up on the clutch. "Watch the car!"

"I am watching it!" she shouted, nailing the gas pedal to the floor. The big truck leapt forward, caught the sedan at the front bumper, and smashed it aside. The flatbed shuddered at the impact and then shrugged it off, roaring forward.

They had been down a side street, and needed to turn onto Centre Avenue to reach the border. They were going too fast, though, for her to turn the truck alone. "Help me turn!"

Together they cranked the steering wheel through the sharp right turn onto Centre Avenue. There was a stop sign on the other side of the intersection. They mounted the curb, flattened the sign, and swung through the rest of the turn.

"That was a stop sign, Tink!" Oilcan complained.

"Yes! It was!" she growled. "Will you shut up? I'm thoroughly pissed off, and I don't need you complaining to me!"

They hadn't hit the sedan hard enough. It came sweeping up behind them, front panel gone and showing undercarriage.

The flatbed topped second gear.

"Shift!" Tinker called, easing minutely up on the gas. Oilcan clutched and shifted up to third.

The sedan took the moment to leap ahead, veering into their path again.

"Fuck them!" Tink growled and elbowed Oilcan in the stomach as he started to turn the wheel. She stomped on the gas, and the flatbed roared straight at the sedan. "Eat this!"

She hadn't grown up in the scrap yard without knowing the strength of the vehicle under her. Built heavy enough to carry over ten tons, backed with a 250-horsepower engine, it was a close cousin to a bulldozer. She aimed at the sedan's back panel, knowing that the car would pivot on its engine block. The sedan spun like a child's toy as they hit.

The narrow strip of no-man's-land of the Rim was now only a block before them. Beyond it was a tall chain-link fence and the Oakland of Earth rising up in full glory.

"Oh shit, it's not Startup yet!" Tinker cried.

"Two more minutes," Oilcan said.

"Damn!" Tinker slammed the brakes. The big truck fought her more than when she'd hit the car, the wheels locking up, slewing them sideways. She sent up a quick prayer that the bolts on the trailer held.

Oilcan yelped and caught the clutch before the engine stalled out. "What are we going to do?"

The guards were swarming forward to intercept her the moment they stopped. Behind them, the sedan was gamely straightening out.

"Shift!" Tinker said.

"Shift to what?"

"Reverse." She shoved his hand aside and worked the gear shift into reverse. "Hold on."

They started backward, gathering speed. She watched her side mirrors as the sedan this time scrambled out of the way. The flatbed shot past its bumper by inches. Would they chase? No, they seemed confused.

"A minute," Oilcan intoned.

A block. Two. Four blocks, and she said, "Okay, let's stop."

They shifted back to first and sat, their feet arrayed across all the pedals. Far off, so faint Tinker barely heard it over the rumble of the flatbed engine, came the ringing of St. Paul's bells.

"This is it," Oilcan breathed.

"One hopes," Tinker said.

Void. The odd sense of falling without moving. All the streetlights flickered out, and only their headlights cut the sudden darkness. The chain-link fence and Oakland vanished. The primal forests of Elfhome and the elfin enclaves lining the border took their place. The aurora effect gleamed directly overhead, dancing along the gate's curving veil.

"Let's go!" Tinker nailed the gas pedal.

The gate remained closed. The guards, gathered to watch her wild driving, scattered, except one fool waving like he thought she'd stop. Tinker reached up, caught the pull on the air horn, and blared her intention to barrel through. Said fool took the warning.

The gate was wood, and it sheared off with a sharp crack. The enclaves on either side of the road formed a chute of tall stone walls, three hundred feet in length, and then they plunged into the dark woods.

She had driven the road before, knew it to be a straight path. Roads on Elfhome were mostly fitted stone, following ley lines, acting as both road and power source. Unlike the wide-berm, multi-lane highways of Earth, they were more like paths. Branches scraped along the roof of the trailer and threatened to take out her mirrors.

Tinker leaned up. "See if you can check Windwolf. I don't have him strapped down back there."

Oilcan slid out from under her, squeezed through the window, and called, "He's fine. There are cars coming."

Reaally? Imagine that!

The side mirrors polarized to keep the car's headlights from blinding her completely. "I see them."

"We're in shit trouble, Tink."

"I know." She was determined not to be sidetracked into being upset. "We get through this, and then I'll worry about the mess."

The hospice was two miles in. Luckily the road remained too narrow for the EIA cars to try cutting them off. She geared down to make the turn into the hospice parking lot, swung the flatbed around, and backed up to the hospice's door as the EIA cars swarmed about her like gnats, hemming the truck in on the sides and front.

A moment later, and EIA men clung to every surface of the truck, pointing guns at her through the windows. Tinker raised her hands.

They hit her with a police override, and the door locks thunked up. They jerked the door open.

"I've got a wounded elf in—" she started to say, but finished with a yelp of surprise as they plucked her out of the seat.

"Tinker!" Oilcan shouted from the back.

"There's a wounded elf in back!" she said.

They pushed her up against the flatbed's hot hood, face down, and twisted her hands behind her back. Pain flared from her wounded hand. She couldn't bite back the cry of hurt.

"Tinker!" Oilcan threw open the back door and was yanked down himself. A moment later he was slammed up against the hood beside her. "She's hurt!" he growled. "Be careful with her!"

There were elves among the men. She could hear the rapid bark of Elvish. A man was leaning his weight into her back, while frisking her.

"She's got a shoulder holster on!" the man shouted in warning. "They've got a pistol someplace."

The gun! Where had she dropped it? It was lost in a blur of events.

He reached her pants pockets and started to upload them onto the high hood. "Damn, she's carrying a household."

"We haven't done anything except protect our patient," Tinker said, trying to turn to face him.

"Shut up, punk." He pulled her backwards and then slammed her against the hood again.

"Leave her alone!" Oilcan shouted.

The guard turned, nightstick upraised. Tinker shouted wordlessly in protest.

Then everything went silent and still. An elf had hold of the nightstick, and there were others, armed and hard-eyed, ringing them.

"They're not to be harmed," the elf said in Low Elvish. "Wolf Who Rules has placed them under his protection."

"*Naekanain*," Mr. Nightstick said, slurring the word as if he'd learned the phrase by rote. *I do not understand.*

"They have brought Wolf Who Rules here to be cared for," the elf clarified in Low Elvish. "He asked me to protect the young humans. I will not let them be harmed."

"What's he saying?" Mr. Nightstick asked the woman beside him.

"He's saying, 'Hands off the kids or we'll break your face.' Get the cuffs off them."

It quickly became apparent that there were two types of armed elves present. Hospice security appeared to be *laedin* caste, in camouflage green and browns done with elfin flare for fashion. They carried bows and spell-arrows and interceded between the humans of the EIA and Windwolf's personal security—which was all higher-born *sekasha* caste, armed to the teeth and thoroughly peeved. Even the hospice healers seemed intimidated by the *sekasha*, taking care to make no threatening moves as Windwolf was shifted off the worktable onto a stretcher and then handed out the trailer. The cousins were kept back, out of the way, as the healers and the *sekasha* carried the injured elf into the hospice.

By then, news of the cousins' arrival with Windwolf must have reached the enclaves that lined Elfhome's side of the Rim; elves drifted out of the darkness to gather in the parking lot. They were largely ignored by everyone, but seemed satisfied with swapping information among themselves. Only one rated attention from the guards; she drifted out of the woods like a will-o'-the-wisp, a gleaming beauty who made Tinker extremely aware of how short, dirty, and scruffy she herself really was in comparison. Obviously one of the high caste, the female crossed the parking lot and stopped one of the hospice guards with a touch of her luminous hand. The two made an effective roadblock, preventing the cousins and their joint elf/human guard from entering the hospice.

"Wolf Who Rules has been found?" the female asked in High Elvish. The guard bowed low and answered in a rapid flow of high tongue that Tinker couldn't follow. (Tinker had always found the more formal language to be too tedious and pretentious to become fluent in it.) She did catch, however, the female's name: Saetato-fohaili-ba-taeli. Roughly, it meant "Sparrow Lifted By Wind" though the "Saetato" could indicate soaring rather than lifted. While the female did not seem the type to take a human nickname, she would probably be called Sparrow.

As if collateral damage from Sparrow's beauty were not enough, the guard indicated the cousins, and Sparrow turned her stunning regard their way. From ankle-length hair, so pale blond it was nearly silver, with ribbons and flowers worked through it, to her tall lithe body encased in softly gleaming fairy silk of pale green, she was perfection taking humanoid form.

"These two wood sprites?" A soft musical laugh as eyes of deep emerald studied the cousins.

The guard clicked his tongue, the elfin way of shrugging, and added something about Windwolf putting them under his protection.

"Yes, of course." Sparrow clicked her tongue against straight pearly teeth and drifted away.

* * *

Minutes later the cousins were alone, under joint human/elf guard, in a waiting room, holding mugs of hot chai. Oilcan was quietly shaking off the adrenaline, which left Tinker plenty of time to think. They had done it—kept Windwolf alive all of Shutdown Day and delivered him to safety. With all of Pittsburgh, why though, had he ended up in her scrap yard? Just stupid luck, or had the life debt between them somehow guided him to her? And now what? Did he disappear out of her life again, until the next monster and the next life-or-death fight?

She touched her breast pocket to feel the spell within. If she got a moment alone with Windwolf, it might be the last time she could ever cast the spell. Even if she was sure the spell wouldn't harm him, did she want to sever the link? She scoffed at herself; what did she know of him except that he was arrogant? Strong. Brave. Altruistic. Honorable. Beautiful. That he was capable of wit and patience even while enduring great pain, facing probable death. And he was possibly a great lover.

The door swung open, and a man came in as if he ruled the place. He could nearly pass as an elf. He was tall, sleek, had blond hair drawn back into a braid, and was stylishly dressed from painted silk duster to tall, polished boots. He checked himself at the sight of the cousins huddled on the couch. Finally, the man let out his breath loudly and glanced at his PDA. "Which one of you is Oilcan, and which is Tinker?"

"I'm Tinker," she answered. "He's Oilcan."

He crossed the room to tower over them. "Brother and sister?"

"We're cousins," Tinker said.

"I'm Maynard." He didn't need to say more. Everyone knew Director Derek Maynard, head of EIA. In Pittsburgh, it was just short of saying "I'm God."

Oilcan moaned softly and sank deeper into the couch.

"You are in luck that elves believe that the ends justify the means, as long as it's done with honor. We've been told that the court would be most displeased with us if we press charges." He said it almost like the royal "we." "So the question is, what all do we need to pardon you of? Are you citizens, or do we have to draw you up papers? Is that truck yours, or did you steal it?"

"We're citizens," Oilcan said. "But we need our papers back. Your men never gave them back."

"We didn't do anything wrong until your men attacked us," Tinker said.

Maynard looked at her, eyes narrowing. "Was this before or after you destroyed the checkpoint?"

"We were waiting for Startup about a mile from the checkpoint when they forced their way into the trailer," Tinker said. "They were going to kill Windwolf. I had Windwolf's gun, so I pulled it on them. I made them get out. Then we rammed the gate."

Maynard studied her, all expression going from his face until he was unreadable. "What made you think they would kill Windwolf?"

"The one who got into the trailer called Windwolf 'sitting duck' or something like that."

"'Easy prey.'" Oilcan mimicked their thick rough voices. "He said 'He is here—easy prey.' Then the other said, 'Do them all. Quietly.' They were going to kill all of us."

"Yeah, no witnesses," Tinker said.

"What makes you think they were EIA men?"

"They had on the border guard uniforms and asked to see our papers," Tinker said.

"It is important for you to understand this." Maynard dropped to one knee so he was level with them. *The EIA did not try to kill Lord Windwolf.*"

"They were too big to be wearing stolen uniforms," Tinker said. "They were taller than you, with lots more muscle."

"Whether they were truly EIA or not is yet to be seen. I doubt very much that they were my men. If they were, *they were not acting under my orders.* It is *very* important that no rumors to the contrary start. Me sanctioning a murder of Lord Windwolf would mean war. Perhaps war isn't a strong enough word. It would be genocide. The elves would rid Elfhome of humans."

Had he ordered it? Tinker considered what she knew of the man. Everyone had something different to say about Maynard—some of it insulting. No one called him stupid, though, and sending men in uniform would be the height of stupidity.

"Okay," Tinker said. "You had nothing to do with it. So, I guess this means we won't get our papers back."

"I will see you are issued replacements," Maynard said. "We had reports that Windwolf and his guard had been attacked by wargs just before Shutdown. His guard had been killed, and he disappeared. We had no idea if he was in the city or still on Elfhome. We were hoping he made Elfhome. Apparently he didn't. How did he end up with you?"

"The wargs chased him into our scrap yard at midnight last night. I was there alone. They were temporary constructs, so I was able to disrupt them with our electromagnet. They reverted to dogs, and Windwolf shot them."

"And you've been sitting on him the last twenty-four hours?"

Tinker explained about Jonnie refusing to treat Windwolf and about taking the elf noble to the Observatory.

Maynard cursed softly. "None of them thought to call the EIA?"

"No," Tinker admitted. "What could you have done?"

"The hospitals don't treat the elves because the elves are worried we'll take blood samples in order to study their genetics and use it to tailor spells and germ warfare. You took a member of the royal family to a conclave of scientists while he was helpless. Do you have any idea what this might mean to our peace treaty?"

"We told him the choices. He agreed to it," Tinker said. "Besides, we gave him our word of honor. No one took samples."

"You know that for certain? You were with him every second?"

"When I wasn't with him, Oilcan or Lain was with him. We didn't leave him alone."

"Who is Lain?"

"Doctor Lain Skanske; she's a xenobiologist. She did the first aid on Windwolf. He asked her first if she understood the treaty and would swear to abide by it."

Oilcan nodded. "Tinker vouched that Lain could be trusted, and Windwolf said that was good enough for him."

Maynard looked at her in surprise. "He trusted you to vouch for someone?"

Tinker shrugged. "I suppose. I saved his life. He saved mine. He defended my honor. I helped stitch him together. I got into bed with him. It was one hell of a twenty-four hours, okay?"

"I see." Maynard continued looking at her, but she couldn't read his expression.

"Are we all free and clear with the EIA?" Tinker asked.

Maynard sighed. "We need you to describe the men who attacked you the best you can. We'll get someone in with a composite sketch program. I know you've been through a lot, but we need to nail these men."

He gave them no chance to say no. Standing, Maynard motioned to one of the human guards to go make his wishes reality.

"If Windwolf is out of danger, can I see him to say good-bye?" Tinker asked.

"I'll let his staff know," Maynard said. "They'll decide."

With that, he swept out of the room, apparently to start the search for the mysterious assassins. The cousins were left, once again, under the joint guard.

A police officer with a datapad showed up. They worked through sketches for the three big men. Oilcan proved to have a better memory for their faces, despite the fact that Tinker had interacted with them longer. The cousins were provided with forms to fill out and turn in later to replace their lost citizen papers.

As they finished up, an elf came and announced something in fast High Elvish.

"Windwolf is sleeping," Oilcan translated for Tinker. He had had the patience to learn high tongue where Tinker had not. "He left word that our desires be met."

"Can I see him?" Tinker struggled through the request in High Elvish, earning a surprised look from Oilcan over the top of his chai.

"*Batya?*" The elf asked. *Now?*

Tinker stood and did a formal bow. "*Shya. Aum gaeyato.*"

The elf returned her bow and led her to a door flanked by two stunningly beautiful elves elegantly carrying swords and automatic rifles. She ducked between them, feeling as scruffy as a junkyard dog.

They had worked serious healing magic on Windwolf. All his wounds were mere puckered scars. While he slept deeply, his breathing was regular and easy. All in all, he looked better than she did.

She took out the circuit paper, unfolded it, and looked at the glyph. *Now or never.*

Could she really lean over his battered body and place the glyph on his forehead? Cast the spell and hope for the best? Play magical Russian roulette with his life? She flashed suddenly to the weight and shape of his pistol in her hands, and shuddered at the thought of pressing that steel barrel to Windwolf's temple.

Never.

She dropped the paper into a wastebasket next to the bed. Bad as her luck was, she'd rather trust that Windwolf would outlive her by centuries than risk killing him by accident. Standing on tiptoe, she kissed Windwolf good-bye lightly on his bruised perfect lips. Perhaps in another five years, some monster would chase him into her life again. Strangely enough, she would miss him this time.

2: IN THE EYE OF GOD

TIME seemed to crawl by. The cousins went outside and found it was dawn. Someone had pulled the flatbed out of the way and locked it up. The keys needed to be found. Once they managed to get into the truck, they discovered that they'd made the break across the border on fumes. Oilcan dug out a fuel can and went off in search of gasoline.

Exhausted, Tinker bolted the trailer door, then stripped out of her day-old clothes and pulled on clean panties and her hoverbike team shirt. Curling up on her worktable where Windwolf had recently lain, she tried to sleep. Her torn left hand hurt, but she was too tired to check under the bandages that Jonnie had put on her. It wouldn't help to look anyhow; she'd killed all her first-aid supplies dealing with Windwolf. Jonnie had said that she would need to check into a hospital, she thought as she drifted off. When Oilcan came back, she'd have him drop her at Mercy.

A banging on the trailer door woke her. She felt cold and weak as she half fell off the worktable. She put out her left hand to catch herself, and the pain made her cry out; she curled tight around her hand, cursing. Whoever was at the door stopped beating on it.

The flatbed jostled oddly. Tinker squeaked in surprise as she suddenly found herself being hauled up and backward. Windwolf swung her up and sat her on the worktable.

"Windwolf!" She blinked at him, confused by his appearance, until she realized that he had opened the flatbed's cab door and crawled through the AC vent. "What are you doing here?"

"What is this for?" He held up the spell she had abandoned in the trash.

"Tooloo told me that's what I should cast when I paid the debt."

"Debt?"

"You put a life debt on me, during a fight with a saurus—five years ago."

He cocked his head and looked at her for a long minute. "You're the fearless little savage with the crooked metal bar? The one that put the saurus's eye out while I was dazed?"

When had he been dazed? "Um, yes. I had a tire iron."

"You were a boy."

She shook her head. "I've always been a girl. I was only thirteen. I was a child."

He gave a cold hard laugh. "And you're not a child now?" He crumpled up the circuit paper and flung it away. "And who told you about this debt?"

"Tooloo. I showed her the spell you put on me and asked her what it was. She said if you died, as your body rotted, so would mine."

He went still. "So that's the only reason you saved me?"

She waved his question away with her good hand. "It just made things scarier, that's all. As if the Foo dogs weren't enough to scare the shit out of me, I had this added little creepiness to deal with. I wouldn't have done anything different, but now we're even."

"We are not even."

"What? Look, I saved you! I risked my life, got my hand screwed up." She held up her hand to show the bound wound. "I tore my place into pieces so I could crate you around! We drove all over Lain's flower beds and yard, making big ruts and killing the plants, and I told her I would go to college to make it up to her! I pulled a gun on the border patrol—who weren't even border patrol, but that's another story. All to save your life! And you would have been dead! If I hadn't helped you fight those Foo dogs, and then hauled your skinny elf ass out here to the Rim, you would have died a couple times over."

He pulled his knife, making her yelp and flinch back. He caught hold of her wounded hand. A glint of light from the silver blade, and he cut off the bandage.

Don't argue with the elf! Yes, sir. No, sir. Then get the hell away from him!

He gazed at her hand, and then caught hold of her head, pulled her to him. His lips touched her forehead where he had once painted the symbol.

What the hell does that mean?

Windwolf reached over and unlocked the trailer door. He picked her up then, like she was a child.

Tinker squirmed in his hold. "What the hell do you think you're doing? Put me down!"

"No." He carried her out of the trailer and across the street. Various elves scurried toward them, bowing and speaking quickly in High Elvish. Windwolf gave curt commands that were instantly obeyed with a fluid bow and "*Shya, ze domou.*"

Windwolf carried her into the hospice, through a maze of hallways. A storm of High Elvish continued all around her, all too fast for her to understand.

"Please speak slower, please!" She hated High Elvish because it was so extremely polite. Yet no matter how many times she asked, no one seemed to take notice of her.

Windwolf stopped finally in a small room, typical of the hospice. The floor was a dark, warm blue color, the walls the color of honey, and the lighting came from the soft glow of the ceiling. Windwolf laid her on a high bed. Its pale birch headboard was more ornate than any human-style hospital bed, but otherwise it seemed to serve the same purpose.

Tinker sat up, swearing in a mix of Low Elvish and English. "Answer me, damn it! What do you think you are doing?"

A silver-haired female elf took a clear jar down from a birch cabinet. She handed it to Windwolf. He carried it back across the room, unscrewing the wide lid. Inside was a large golden flower.

"What's that for?" Tinker didn't bother with Elvish this time.

Putting the jar on the table beside the bed, Windwolf lifted the flower out and held it so close in front of Tinker's face that she nearly went cross-eyed looking at it.

"Smell it!" Windwolf commanded.

Tinker sniffed it cautiously. It reminded her of honeysuckle, a warm drowsy smell, with the soft drone of bees, the sway of green boughs, summer wind, blue skies, white clouds blistering white, softness piled and billowed upwards, wispy here, knife-edged sharp . . .

Tinker realized that she was going under, and jerked back. She tried to push the flower away with her wounded hand, too sleepy to remember it was hurt, and whimpered at the sudden flare of pain.

Windwolf caught the back of her head, holding her still, pressing the flower to her nose. "Just breathe it."

Tinker fought instead, not sure what was happening, only determined not to be helpless before him. She punched him as he bruised the sweet silken petals against her. She had aimed for his groin, but he turned and she caught him in the hip.

"Do not fight, little savage." He caught her chin between thumb and pinkie, holding her face as if in a vise, the flower cradled by his other fingers. He let go of her head and caught her wrists, forcing her back, pinning her down. "You are only going to hurt yourself."

She held her breath and squirmed under him, trying to kick him. He had his weight against her thighs and hips. Then she couldn't hold her breath any longer, and gasped. Sweetness, warm and sleepy as clean sheets on a feather-soft bed full in the early morning sun, white light through sheer curtains, open window to wind from a garden . . .

The female elf came across the room, laughing musically as only elves could, a silver knife in hand. The air went shimmering white, closing in around them, warm and liquid as honey, and sweet . . .

The Foo dogs chased her in her nightmares. Only they kept changing. One moment, they were great cats. Another moment—huge dogs. Other times—Chinese dragons, coiling through the scrap like giant poisonous snakes. She ran, her legs heavy as if she waded through mud. Suddenly the dream changed; Windwolf rocked her, warm and gentle as her grandfather's arms. His voice rumbled soft comfort into her ear.

"The Foo dogs!" she gasped, looking about wildly. The dream room held nothing more dangerous than shadows, a chair beside the bed, a low table with a pitcher of water and glasses.

"They are all dead," he murmured, stroking her back.

She clung to him as the dream wanted to slide back to the monsters in the scrap yard, the edges of the room blurring into heaps of metal. "Don't let go!"

"I will not."

She worked at forcing her dreaming to focus on him. She thought she heard the slither of scales over steel and whimpered, burrowing into his hair.

"Easy. You are safe," Windwolf stated calmly. "I will let nothing harm you."

Think of Windwolf. She ran fingers through his hair, found his ears and traced their outline. She investigated their shape and texture, the slight give of the cartilage, the softness of the lobe, and the intricate coil of inner part versus the firm, stiff points of the ear tip. After a few minutes, he gave a soft moan and caught her exploring hand. He moved it to his mouth, kissed her fingertips, the palm of her hand, and then ran his tongue feather light over the pulse point on her wrist.

Who would have guessed that would feel so good? She would have to try it awake some time. She gazed at him, stunned again by the beauty of his eyes.

"I don't think I've ever seen anything so blue. Cobalt maybe."

"My eyes?"

"Yes."

He studied her solemnly and then said, "Your eyes are the color of polished walnut."

"Is that good?"

This dream Windwolf looked at her with gentleness that she wasn't accustomed to from him. "Your eyes are warm and earthy and yet strong enough to face any adversity."

"Oh, wow, you like my eyes?"

"I like all of you. You are pleasing to look at."

Now she knew she was dreaming. "Yeah, right, with my hair and my nose." She twanged her nose a couple of times. It was numb, just like when she was drunk. Windwolf's nose, of course, was perfect; she traced her fingers over the bridge of his nose. Just right.

"I find your hair appealing," perfectly dreamy Windwolf said.

"You do?"

"It is very pure."

"I thought elves liked long hair." She tugged on a short lock to illustrate that hers was anything but long.

"There is beauty in functionality that makes fashionable seem jaded. In our case, fashionable has passed traditional and become something nearly geological."

She pondered this for several minutes before realizing that he meant that the length of hair in elves was set in stone. "Sounds boring."

"I am not sure if it is lack of courage or lack of creativity that dictates the length of elfin hair; unlike you, there is a notable shortage of both in our women."

"Me?"

"You are the bravest woman I have ever met, as well as the most intelligent."

"I'm brave?" *When?*

"Fearless."

Tinker blew a raspberry. "Hell, no, I was scared a lot in the past"—how long had it been since Windwolf came over the fence, disrupting her well-ordered life?—"days." At least it seemed like days. She could remember at least two nights, but the number of meals and periods of sleeping didn't add to anything reasonable. "I only did what had to be done."

"And that is true courage. As you pointed out, without you, I would have died many times over. Indeed, I hazard a guess that of all the people of Pittsburgh, humans and elves, you alone had the intelligence and fortitude to keep me safe."

It was such a weird dream. The edges of the room slipped in and out of focus, and she felt too light and bold. It was like she was drunk, only usually then her limbs felt huge and needed effort to move them about. Her hands now kept adventuring off on their own, exploring Windwolf.

His fingers proved to be long and slender, with the cleanest fingernails she'd ever seen. Of course, everyone she knew spent a good amount of time with their hands in dirt or engine grease. Under a loose silk shirt of moss green, only faint silvery scars remained where the Foo dogs mauled him.

"Why did the wargs attack you? Who wanted you dead?"

"I do not know. I have many enemies. Other clans are envious of the Wind Clan's monopoly on the Westernlands, and within my own clan, many consider me a dangerous radical. This, though, was not a simple political assassination. This was pure madness, to loose monsters that kill everything in their path. I can not imagine any of my enemies attacking me in such a cowardly method."

"Someone has."

"Yes. Who remains a mystery."

There seemed to be some barrier that she had breached. Normally she would not think of touching someone, nor did she need to rebuff most people. A quick hug. A handshake. A pat on the shoulder. It was like they all walked around with invisible shields, deflecting even thoughts of reaching out to another person. She had never noticed before, but now, snuggling against Windwolf, she noticed the lack of them. Like antimatter and matter meeting, their protection shields had collided and annihilated one another.

Windwolf allowed her to explore his scarred shoulder. She found herself nuzzling into his neck, once again tracing the outline of his ear. She drew back slightly in surprise of herself.

"I'm sorry," Tinker said.

"Why?"

She tried to form an answer and lapsed into confused silence until she forgot what she had been thinking about. He took her hand from his ear tip again.

"Does it hurt?" she asked as he lifted her hand away.

"It feels far too good to let you continue." He nibbled on her wrist, delighting her. "You are too pure to follow that course. You are not yourself right now."

"Who am I?"

"You are Tinker without her normal defenses. You are on the edge of sleep, still full of *saijin*."

"I'm drugged?"

"Very much so."

She considered her body. Yup. That would explain things. "Why?"

"I did not want you to lose your hand."

She peered at her right hand. Windwolf took hold of her left, opening it to expose a network of pink scars, and anti-infection spells inked onto both the palm and the back. She flexed the hand, discovering it hurt faintly, deep inside. Thinking back now, she vaguely remembered he had carried her into the hospice.

"Oh. Thank you." She kissed him. She meant it to be a chaste kiss, but it became something more. Suddenly it dawned on her that she was half drugged, half naked, and alone with a male in a bed. Her heart started to hammer in her chest like an engine about to throw a rod.

"Do you think you can sleep now?" he asked, stroking her cheek lightly.

What did he mean by that? "Sleep sleep" or "sleep?" Luckily, the Elvish was a much more concise language. "*Saijiata?*" The act of sleeping?

He nodded, looking inquiringly at her, as if the other possibilities had never occurred to him.

Interestingly, the moment of panic had burned out all thoughts of monsters. "Yes. I think I can."

Tinker woke with a start. Her head seemed big, and full of air. The pain in her left hand had deepened into a constant dull ache. Turning her head, she saw the empty chair beside the bed. Windwolf.

A vase of flowers sat on the nightstand next to the pitcher of water. The vase was elfin, a deceptively simple twist of glass, a thick base sweeping up to an impossibly thin rim, elegant beyond words. The flowers were black-eyed Susans. She guessed that the flowers were from her cousin and that the hospice staff had provided the vase. As usual, the bright wildflowers made her smile. A note card leaned against the vase, printed in Oilcan's neat, over-careful hand and smudged with engine grease.

When I got back with the gas, they told me that your hand was going septic and that you were in surgery. I'm sorry I didn't check it before I left. I looked in just now, but you were still sleeping. If we want food and fuel for the next thirty days, I've got to go make sure to get it now. I hate leaving you alone. I'll be back as soon as I can. Get well soon. Love, Orville.

Orville. He must truly be rattled if he was using his real name.

There was a light tap on the door, and Maynard, God himself, opened it up.

"You're awake."

"Yes." Tinker wondered what God wanted with little her.

"I didn't make the connection between you and *the* Tinker until Windwolf told me about some of what you did to keep him alive."

She shrugged. "Happens all the time. No one expects the legendary Tinker to be a little snot-nosed girl."

No smile. Maybe God didn't have a sense of humor. She often suspected that.

"How old are you?" Maynard asked. "Sixteen? Seventeen?"

"Eighteen, as of last month."

"Parents?"

Little alarms were going off. "Where's this going?"

"I like to know who I'm working with."

Make that big alarms. "Since when am I working with you?"

"Since today. I've got a bit of a mystery I need solved, and maybe you can help. They say you're fit to leave."

He left it nebulous as to whether this was a declinable personal request or an official demand. Maynard certainly wasn't someone she wanted to alienate; as god of Pittsburgh, he could make her life hell. Now that she was a legal adult, she had nothing to hide. At least, she didn't think she did.

"Okay. Let me figure out what they did with my clothes, and you can show me this mystery."

Clothes found, and Maynard carefully shooed off, she got up to change.

Under the cotton gown she was naked. She put on her panties and bra without taking off the gown, eyeing the door—which had no lock. Luckily no one burst in to catch her dressing. She pulled on her carpenter's pants, and then in one quick motion pulled off the gown and slipped into her team shirt. With her back to the door, she took her time buttoning it up.

The hospice had cleaned her clothes, managing to get all of Windwolf's blood off her carpenter's pants and to find a replacement for the bottom button of her team shirt. It had gone missing weeks ago, and she'd been at a loss as to how to replace it. Cleaning clothes she could do. Repairing was something she could only do to machines.

She stepped into her steel-toed boots, tied them, and clonked about the room, feeling more able to take on Maynard.

The contents of her pockets sat elegantly arranged in an elegant rosewood box. Elves stunned her sometimes. Most humans probably would have gone through her pockets and tossed most of her treasures. The hospice staff, however, had not only cleaned all the old grease-coated nuts and bolts, but had properly mated them together, and then arranged them by size on green velvet. They looked like bits of silver jewelry. Her spare handmade power lead (extremely crude looking but actually poly-coated gold) had been coiled and tied off with a strand of blue silk. They'd even kept the interesting-looking twig she'd pocketed the day before Shutdown, which now seemed weeks ago, instead of two days. It pleased her (she would have been unable to rebuild three separate projects without the various bolts), but still it weirded her out. When one was immortal, apparently, one had time to waste on other people's little details of life.

She pocketed her eclectic collection and went out into the hall to find Maynard waiting. He led the way out to the sun-blasted parking lot, towering over her. The flatbed was gone; Oilcan must have driven it back to the yard. Looking at the empty parking space where the tow truck had sat made her feel horribly alone and vulnerable. Stripped of her powerful toys and standing beside Maynard, she felt all of her five feet nothing. Nathan was as tall as Maynard, but he was a friend, so she never felt particularly small around him. Maynard was EIA. Her grandfather had viewed all forms of government with deep suspicion, which she of course had inherited in some part. After her grandfather had died, and she had been left an orphan in a town that exiled stray human children, the EIA had grown to bogeyman proportions.

I have nothing to fear from the EIA now. She and Oilcan had coasted a year, staying low, until Oilcan hit eighteen. At that time he could stand as head of household, and they were legal again, barely. There was the little matter that they were living in separate houses by that time. Last month, though, she had finally turned eighteen herself.

Maynard traveled in style; a big, black, armored limo rolled up to the curb, stopping so that the back passenger door could swing open without hitting them, and not an inch farther away. Maynard indicated that she was to slide into the air-conditioned comfort first.

"Parents?" Maynard asked after they pulled out of the hospice's parking lot.

"I'm eighteen—a legal adult." She tried dodging around the whole parent thing. Gods knew it was far too complex to go into. "I'm also a legal citizen: I was born and raised in Pittsburgh. I'm sole owner of Pittsburgh Scrap and Salvage. I did a quarter million dollars in business last year, and all my taxes are paid."

"Your cousin works for you?"

"Yeah."

"Any other family?"

She tried to bluff him off. "Should I save us both the effort and just dump a whole family history on you?"

"Like I said, I like to know who I'm working with."

She considered him and decided that meant "yes." She made a note not to bluff with Maynard again. "My grandfather had two kids: my father, Leonardo, and Oilcan's mom, Aunt Ada. That's all the family that I know of."

"Oilcan?" Maynard lifted one eyebrow. "Surely that's not his real name."

Apparently the loss of their ID cards had slowed down the EIA network. "No, it isn't. Aunt Ada was married to a man named John Wright. Oilcan's real name is Orville John Wright. I'm sure it was Grandpa's idea; he had a thing about inventors."

"Orville Wright." Maynard proved he had some sense of humor and smiled. "I can see why he goes by Oilcan. How did you and Orville end up here in Pittsburgh? You're too young to immigrate."

"Grandpa immigrated during the first year. I was born here. Oilcan came to live with us when I was six."

"What about your parents? Both yours and Orville's?"

"Both my dad and Aunt Ada were murdered."

"I'm sorry." Maynard thought for a moment, and then cocked his head. "Not here in Pittsburgh, or I would have known about it."

"My father was killed in Oakland before the first Startup. John Wright was a man with a temper; he killed Aunt Ada in Boston. I stayed with Lain when Grandpa went to Boston to get Oilcan; I've never been on Earth."

Maynard looked at her for several minutes through narrowed eyes. "Your father was killed—what—ten years before you were born?"

So, one couldn't slip things easily past this man. "Yes. My grandfather never got over my father's death. Grandpa used cryogenically stored sperm to have my ovum inseminated in vitro ten years after my father died."

"But your mother is still alive?"

"Technically, no." Tinker sighed—so much for trying to avoid complexity. "My birth mother wasn't the donor of the egg that my grandfather had inseminated. He also used a cryogenically stored egg. My real mother was also dead before I was born."

Maynard stared at her for several minutes before asking, "Did your parents, your real parents, even know one another?"

"I don't think so."

"Your parents, who had never met, were dead when you were conceived?"

"Yeah."

"Doesn't that bother you?"

"Mr. Maynard, if we're going to work together, can we just stick to scientific facts, and not go jaunting off through history and psychology?"

Maynard exhaled what might have been a laugh. "You hold your own."

Tinker wasn't sure what he meant by that. Sick of the whole inquisition, she forced the conversation off onto another track. "So what the hell do you want me to do?"

"Someone smuggled a large shipment of illegal goods in during Shutdown. Lucky for us, though, they were involved in a multiple-vehicle accident on the Veterans Bridge. Their vehicle was disabled, and they panicked in spectacular fashion, which makes us worried about what all they might have brought into Pittsburgh."

"You didn't catch them?"

"No," Maynard said. "They unloaded their truck, sorted through the shipment, and carried away what they deemed most important. The driver had been pinned by the accident; they shot him so we couldn't question him."

"Ouch." That earned her a dark look from Maynard. "So far it doesn't sound like a panic."

"Well, throw in a carjacking, assault on the other accident victims, picking up and throwing a Volkswagen Beetle over the side of the bridge in a fit of rage, engaging in a gunfight with police, and trying to blow up with C-4 what they couldn't carry away, and you start to get the idea."

Tinker gasped. *Nathan!* "Were any of the police hurt?"

Maynard looked surprised at the question. "Luckily, no. Not for the want of trying, though."

"And how do I fit in? I was in McKees Rocks fighting wargs when that accident happened."

"How do you know *when* it happened?"

"My friend Nathan Czernowski is a cop. He was with me at the scrap yard when the call came in. I'm assuming that there was only one multiple-vehicle pileup and fistfight on the Veterans Bridge."

"Yes." Maynard relaxed slightly, apparently accepting her alibi. "Well, you'll be interested to know that the description of the smugglers match that of your attackers at the Rim."

Tinker swore. "Smuggle in contraband one night, attack Windwolf the next?"

"Very busy people," Maynard said. "It denotes a large organization, of which these men are merely disposable muscle. So far, EIA has been able to keep such crime rings out of Pittsburgh. I want to pull this one up by its roots."

"Sounds like a plan. What does this have to do with me?"

"Some of the load wasn't contraband, just extremely expensive high-tech parts. The question is, what could they be used to make?"

"Oh, I see."

The impounded goods had been unloaded in a warehouse in the Strip District. Basically just one low room a block long, the place fairly crawled with armed EIA. While security for the building ran high, lighting and climate control left much to be desired. Natural light came in from windows lining an upper walkway. Work lamps tacked to support columns provided additional light, plugged into jury-rigged electrical boxes on newly strung Romex line.

Because of the virgin forests occupying most of the western continent, Elfhome usually ran several degrees cooler than Earth. Since Pittsburgh suffered from high humidity, the lower temperatures were a blessing. The rain storms of Shutdown and Startup over, a rare summer heat, however, had moved in. The warehouse's only nod toward climate control was ceiling fans, cloaked in the shadows high overhead, that barely moved the ovenlike heat of the building.

Tinker found herself wishing for shorts and a midriff shirt. In Maynard's company, she didn't even feel like unbuttoning her shirt.

Sweat trickled down her back as she followed Maynard through trestle tables set up and loaded with smuggled goods.

What she discovered made her forget the heat.

There were digital boards, stripping kits, and connector kits. For fiber-optics work, they had a full run of splice trays, hot-melt connector systems, and a curing oven. She found a spool of gold wire. Fault finders, microscanners, and status activity monitors. There were tech kits that set her mouth drooling. Punch boxes. Wire crimp tools. Small precision mirrors. There were even new digital markers that laid out a metal-based ink held in a buckyball matrix. Tinker poked through the stuff, wishing she could take the lot back to her place. Lain had told her tales about the world beyond the Rim where such stuff was plentiful. Much as Tinker loved Pittsburgh, she had to admit that there was a true shortage of goods.

Maynard interrupted her trolling to hand her a length of cable with a box at the end. "Do you know what this is?"

Tinker took it. She turned it in her hands, studying it. The box was molded plastic with two power ports. She tried the various screwdrivers she had tucked into her pockets, the third being the charm, and undid the screws. "Oh my, this is sexy."

"What is it?"

"It's a power transformer."

"You recognize it?"

"What's to recognize? This is a male 220 line, meaning you plug it into a 220 outlet. It would have a pull on par with an electric clothes dryer or an electric range. The female leads are typical magic connectors. It takes electrical power and transforms it to magic. The question is—what type of spell is it keyed to?"

"It would have to be keyed to only one spell?"

"There isn't any way to change the output frequency. It's preset. Although, if you knew the frequency it was outputting, then you could probably set up a secondary translation spell anytime you wanted to use it for a different spell. You'll see a loss in power efficiency on the order of eleven percent, but at this amperage, such a power loss would be negligent. Shit, I could have used something like this on Windwolf. I'll have to build one."

"You could build one of these?"

"Yeah. It wouldn't be too hard. Of course, there's the whole question of why bother. Here on Elfhome, there's enough magical power to fuel any spell without the cost of electrical energy. And on Earth, except for healing elves, there are already mechanical solutions for almost everything."

"Magic doesn't work on Earth."

"Does too." Tinker replaced the screws and tightened them down. "The laws of the universe don't change just because you hop dimensions. The difference is the amount of magical power in the dimension. Think of magic as a waveform passing through multiple realities. Elfhome exists at the top of the wave: Magic is plentiful. Earth exists at the bottom of the wave: Magic is rare. Magic follows the laws of physics just like light, gravity, and time. I could show you the math, but it's fairly complex. There are types of radiation more common in one reality than the other, but lucky for us, the generation waveform seems larger, so we fall close enough on the curve that it doesn't affect either species adversely."

"So you can do magic on Earth?"

"It's how I kept Windwolf alive," Tinker said. "I had magic stored in a power sink and used it to feed a healing spell."

"Can you tell what the smugglers might have been trying to build with all this?"

Tinker shrugged. "Not a clue. I'm afraid I don't have a criminal mind."

"Make a wild guess."

She sighed, glancing around. "Well, unless they scooted off with *all* the uncommon stuff, they're not going to make a wide range of items. I'm guessing all those power transformers are set to the same frequency, or else they would be labeled somehow. There's a lack of moveable parts, so it's not like a car or a bike or a printing press. It's magic-based, either many scattered copies of one spell, or one massive spell."

"Can you tell what spell?"

"You'd better check with the elves for that. The best I can do is to match the frequency to a known spell, but my knowledge of magic is fairly limited. For all I know, they're going to change the population of Pittsburgh into frogs."

Maynard sighed slightly, perhaps not looking forward to trying to pry information from the always-obtuse elves. "Anything else?"

"Well . . ." Tinker held out the power transformer. "You could let me take this home and play with it. I can figure out the cycle on the magic output and search through my spell database for a match. It would at least start eliminating possibilities."

"Take it then."

She lifted up the markers. "I don't suppose I could have these as part of my payment?"

Was that a smile that tugged his mouth slightly sideways for one second? "You can have them." Maynard produced a business card and presented it. "This is my direct number. If you figure anything out, give me a call. It is always answered."

Of course it was—he was god of Pittsburgh. There was no name on the card, only a phone number. Wow, God's private phone number.

Tinker pocketed it. "I'll let you know what I find out."

"I'll take you home."

She wasn't comfortable with the idea of God knowing where she lived, although, he certainly could find out easily enough. "I've got some shopping to do, before everything's gone. Could you just drop me at Market Square?"

3: ACCIDENTAL LOLITA

IT WASN'T UNTIL MAYNARD'S armored limo rolled away that Tinker realized she had just stranded herself downtown.

She had taken her headset off in the trailer, and thus Windwolf had carried her into the hospice without it. Pay telephones had started disappearing from Earth cities at the turn of the century as cell phones eliminated the need for them. Luckily, Pittsburgh had moved to Elfhome before the last wave of dismantling pay phones. Supposedly to maintain the lines of communication between Shutdown and Startup, the governments of Earth heavily subsidized Pittsburgh's phone system. Thus Tinker was able to find a phone, and with her lone rumpled dollar changed into dimes at the *okonomiyaki* cart, could afford ten calls.

The afternoon sun had heated the plastic of the pay phone to nearly blistering. Tinker winced at the pain it lanced through her newly healed hand, and juggled the hot receiver around while she called Oilcan. He didn't pick up, which was odd. She tried his home number, but he wasn't at his condo. She didn't bother leaving a message; most likely by the time he checked his home machine, she would be someplace other than Market Square.

Oilcan wasn't at the scrap yard either. Because she'd yanked her workshop to ferry Windwolf around, her office AI was offline at the scrap yard. After a dozen rings, she hung up, and called her loft.

Her home AI Skippy answered. "Hello, this is Tinker's residence. Tinker isn't in. Please leave an audio message, video clip, or data file."

"It's me. Let me have the audio messages." She used her voice code. "Tesla titillates treacle."

"There were sixty-seven calls," Skippy reported, and started into replaying the messages. "Message one."

Sixty-seven? Who the hell is all calling me? Tinker frowned as Nathan's voice came on.

"I was wondering what happened after I left," Nathan said. "Call me. I'm worried about you."

Skippy time-stamped the message from the morning of Shutdown and gave the number. She recognized it as the pay phone at the McKees Rocks gas station; Nathan might have stopped there after checking the scrap yard. She made a mental note to call him.

"Message two," Skippy queued into the next call, which was from Oilcan.

"Hey, I got gas for the shop, tracked down a load of fresh batteries, and even managed to snag you a new clutch system for your bike. I swung past again to pick you up, but you had gone already. I'm heading out to buy food now. I don't know about you, but all I have in my cupboard is instant oatmeal and brown sugar. I'll see you tonight at Lain's."

Lain's?

Skippy time-stamped the call at two hours earlier, meaning Oilcan must have been on Maynard's heels in his attempt to pick her up at the hospice. The phone number was a South Hills number, so Oilcan must have gone straight out to the food warehouses.

"There are no more audio messages," Skippy reported.

"Wait, what about the other sixty-five calls?"

"No other messages were left."

The phone company's automated system hijacked the connection and demanded more money. Tinker fed two of her dimes into the coin slot. Satisfied, the phone company's AI released the line.

"Give me a report on all calls."

Nathan's was indecently early, meaning he had probably left it as he came off shift. The second call hit at the ungodly time of 5:15 a.m. The third was at 5:30 a.m., and then the calls settled into an every-half-hour event. The first thirty-eight originated from an Earth phone number with an area code that she didn't recognize, and came with no ID flag. At midnight, when Pittsburgh returned to Elfhome, the Earth phone number dropped off the list.

At six the next morning, the calls started again, only this time the phone numbers were all local pay phones at systematic half-hour intervals. They moved in a widening circle around the scrap yard, starting at the gas station on the corner. She had just missed the most recent call.

Just out of curiosity, she had Skippy compare call times for all calls, Earth-based and local. All of them listened to the full outgoing message, as if checking to make sure nothing had been changed.

The phone company's automated system hijacked the line again, demanding more money if she was going to stay on. She hung up instead, not sure what to make of the mysterious phone calls. Obviously someone, apparently from Earth, was looking for her, but who?

Perhaps Lain knew, as all of Tinker's contacts with Earth came through the xenobiologist. Tinker used her fifth dime to call the xenobiologist, and got Lain's AI.

"It's Tinker," she told Lain's simple, unnamed AI.

"Tinker," Lain's recorded voice came on. "Oilcan called early this morning. He said there's nothing to eat out at your place. We're doing the traditional summer Startup cookout here at the Observatory. I'm probably outside, so just come on up. You can spend the night if you want."

Tinker's mouth drooled at the thought. Huge and crowded as Earth was, the scientific community of Earth remained small enough that the incoming scientists knew to bring food for a social gathering, each trying to outdo the rest. Since Pittsburgh pulled in people from all across Earth, the cookout was held the day after Startup, so those coming in at the last minute wouldn't miss out on the festivities.

Getting to the Observatory, however, might be tricky. Maybe she should have taken Maynard up on the offer of a ride. While South Hills still had a light-rail public transportation system, only taxis went to Observatory Hill. She now had only five dimes to her name.

She considered her dimes, then dropped one into the coin slot and called Nathan.

He picked up on the first ring.

"Czernowski."

"It's Tinker."

"Tink! What happened after I left? Where have you been? Are you okay? Where are you?"

"I—um . . ." She paused, not sure which question to answer first. The last two days' events seemed impossible to explain. "I'm fine. I'm downtown. Market Square. I'm kind of stuck. I need a ride out to the Observatory. I'm going to crash with Lain tonight."

"I'll be right there."

Which was what she had hoped he would say.

Nathan double-parked his Buick by the pay phone, twenty minutes later. "I've been worried sick about you," he called as he climbed out. "I'm sorry I had to leave you with that mess. The accident was unreal, and I was stuck there all night. By the time I got free, you had yanked your trailer and were gone."

"It's okay." She waved it away. "I had Oilcan and Lain to help me. You're here now."

"Lain! Of course." He surprised her by hugging her. What, was everyone suddenly touchy-feely? "How's your hand?"

She showed it to him, flexing it. "It got infected."

He dwarfed her left hand in his and eyed it with deep sorrow. "Oh, Tinker, I'm so sorry."

"It's fine now. They fixed it at the hospice." She wiggled her fingers in a show of health. She pulled her hand free. "I heard about your accident. You okay?"

"My accident?"

"Veterans Bridge," she prompted, heading for his car and its air-conditioned interior.

"Oh, yeah."

Nathan needed more coolant in his Buick. The air-conditioner struggled against the sticky summer heat. Tinker redirected the passenger vents to blow on her and unbuttoned her shirt above and below her bra line in an attempt to cool down.

"So, what happened?" she asked.

"Mass chaos is what happened." Nathan shook his head. "Shutdown traffic is usually so bumper to bumper you don't get much more than fender benders. This crew in a Ryder truck misses their turn, and they miss it big time, getting like halfway across the Veterans Bridge before realizing that they either wanted the Fort Duquesne Bridge to the Fort Pitt tunnels, or simply to get off at the North Shore. Who knows? Either one they could have gotten to by cutting through downtown. Instead, they try to back up. Of course they can't, everything bumper to bumper for ten miles. They block traffic for like half an hour trying to bully the drivers for a couple hundred feet behind them into backing up—but those people don't have anywhere to go. Meanwhile, all the traffic in front of them clears out."

"Let me guess. Once they stop blocking traffic, everyone races across the bridge trying to get in front of the jerks."

"Oh, yeah," Nathan said. "Only the Ryder truck is still lost. He's in the left-hand lane, and realizes either he's going to end up back at the Rim and a border-patrol check, or through the Liberty Tunnel and into the South Hills."

"And they're sitting on a truckful of illegal goods, so the Rim is out."

Nathan glanced at her sharply. "How do you know they were smuggling?"

"Maynard wanted me to look over their stuff; he told me a little about the accident. I was worried about you."

"Really?" The info seemed to please him greatly. "I'm fine. I was the first unit called, but by the time I worked my way around to the accident, the EIA and most of the cops in Pittsburgh were there."

"Good. So, go on. They tried to take the Sixth Avenue exit and cut through town."

"Yeah, only they did it at the last minute and cut off a Peterbilt fully loaded with steel girders and just getting up to full speed."

"Bad move."

"The Peterbilt tries, but he can't stop, not with the load he's carrying. He catches the Ryder in the back driver corner and rams them into the support beams for the overpass. His load comes off and crushes a minivan beside him, killing the two people inside instantly."

She recalled the flattened car. "Oh my."

"There's a pileup, cars everywhere, and of course police are called, and things start to escalate. The goons from the Ryder truck discovered that they couldn't free their driver and that their truck was totaled. They carjack a pickup truck, and unload the Ryder into it. While they're doing that, I start working my way across the Veterans Bridge, and that's when they get their guns out."

"Maynard says they shot their own driver, flung a Volkswagen off the bridge, and tried to blow things up with C-4."

Nathan nodded. "Even with the traffic snarled they managed to get away just by the sheer mess they left behind; it blocked everyone from chasing after them."

Tinker told Nathan of her run-in with the fake EIA agents.

He swore softly. "It certainly sounds like them. If I'd known there was any chance you'd get mixed up with them, I would have tracked you down yesterday."

"Ah, I dealt with them." Knowing that they had coldly killed one of their own made her encounter, in hindsight, more chilling.

Nathan shook his head. "That's my Tink."

The cookouts were held in the wooded grove next to the Observatory, handy to the dormitory kitchen. True to form, the picnic tables looked overcrowded with food, and the smoke from the charcoal grills, scented with the smell of cooking meat, drifted out into the parking lot. Oilcan's hoverbike sat on the grass beside the lot, almost as comforting a sight as Oilcan himself.

Nathan parked his Buick, and they got out.

"I'm going to have to go soon." Nathan scanned over the picnicking scientists, as if making sure none of them were the missing smugglers. "My shift starts in half an hour. Make sure Lain locks her doors tonight. If you need a ride home tomorrow, call me."

"Sure." Tinker was never sure how to take Nathan's protective streak. "Thanks for the ride."

"Any time." He turned to her with the start of a smile, which vanished with a look of surprise. "Tink!" He reached out to button the bottom of her shirt closed. "Please, try to stay decent."

"What?" She brushed away his hand and gave her middle button a slight tug. "You can't see anything important with this one done. Besides, I've got a bra on."

"I know," he said in an oddly husky voice. "It's a very sexy bra."

"You checked it out?" She would have been embarrassed except for the fact that he beat her to the blush. Weird seeing such a big guy turn red and knowing she had done it to him. Empowering. She tugged on the middle button again, flashing a bit of her bra's black lace. "Like what you saw?"

"Tink." He caught her hand with his. "Don't tease guys like that. The wrong guy will get the wrong idea."

"It's just you."

"I'll take that as a compliment." He surprised her by running his finger across her bare skin, just above the middle button—a glide of rough fingertip over the upper swell of her right breast. "And yes, I liked what I saw."

Her turn to burn. "You're just being nice." She frowned when he laughed. "What?"

"It's just you're so smart, and yet you're so naïve, innocent."

"What do you mean by that?"

He looked up at the sky for a minute, and then gave her a look like a boy caught stealing candy: guilty, but wanting so badly to get away with it. "You were just this skinny little kid until you turned about fifteen, and then, one day, I turned around and you were suddenly so drop-dead sexy."

She laughed out of total surprise. "Me?"

"You bloomed that year."

In plain English, she got breasts that year. "Well, yeah, but sexy?"

"Yes. I've been quietly obsessed with you since then."

"You've got a funny way of showing it. You've never laid a hand on me."

"You were fifteen, and I was twenty-five. I kept my hands to myself. I would bust any guy for doing what I was thinking."

"Big brother" Nathan thought she was sexy? She couldn't believe it. "Yeah, sure."

"That's always been the worst of it. You've never been aware of how sexy you are. Like the way you eat strawberries."

"What's wrong with the way I eat strawberries?"

He opened his mouth, and then thought better of explaining. "Nothing. Just forget it."

"Come on; tell me."

"You don't eat them; you make love to them. It's such a turn-on, I need a cold shower afterward."

"You get off watching me eat?"

"See!" He shook a finger at her. "You're innocent. You don't understand. And I do. I'm older, and—"

"If you say wiser, I'm going to smack you."

He held up his hands to ward off any blow. "Hey, when it comes to brains, you're clearly way ahead of me. I've never minded. This isn't about you; it's about me. I wouldn't be able to live with myself if I thought I was taking advantage of a kid."

"So? I'm a legal adult now."

"Hell, you just turned eighteen and never been kissed. And you still look young enough to be sixteen. I'm twenty-eight."

Tinker studied him, trying to reevaluate the last three years. How had she missed his obsession? Certainly he spent an inordinate amount of time with her and Oilcan—but he'd also had two or three girlfriends that she could remember. "Yeah, you're twenty-eight and definitely more experienced than me. That doesn't seem fair. You get to screw around while I stay a virgin."

He kicked at a weed growing up in a crack in the parking lot's cement. "I thought if I found someone else, I'd stop having a thing for you. It really hasn't been fun, wanting you and feeling like a filthy old man at the same time."

"You know, you are always going to be ten years older than me. There's nothing I can do about it."

"I figured that when you hit nineteen, if I was still hooked on you, that was old enough."

Was he serious about this? It was weird to think he had waited three years already for her to grow up, and planned to wait another year. Certainly at fifteen she couldn't have cared less about men, but in the last three years she had developed definite interest. Most guys she knew were like Jonnie, too slimy to consider. But Nathan Czernowski? She trusted him.

Everything inside her went suddenly, nervously aquiver. She looked at his mouth and wondered what it would be like to kiss him. "What am I supposed to do for the next eleven months? Sit and twiddle my thumbs until you feel righteous?"

He glanced at her, squinting in speculation. "You'll probably hit me if I say that would be nice."

"Yes," she growled. Eleven months of wondering would kill her. She was too used to satisfying her curiosity to wait that long. "Why don't we compromise? It would be stupid to spend the next eleven months, waiting, only to find out we can't stand each other in more than a good-friend way. We should try a date."

"A date?"

"You know. Go out to eat. See a movie. Go to the Faire. Date. That is, if your ego can stand being seen with me, and whatever people might think of you."

"Ouch."

"That's really it, isn't it? You're afraid that people will think you're as nasty as the guys you bust for molesting little kids."

"Okay, yes. You look younger than you are, and anyone who doesn't know how much you've got going on upstairs will see me as some kind of pervert. And that bugs me."

"I *can* look older. If I put some makeup on and some nice clothes, I can look twenty." Or at least Lain said so. "Especially in a dark restaurant."

A pleased grin spread across his face. "You really want to go out to eat with me?"

"I've watched you eat. What I actually want is to find out what it's like to kiss you, but I figured I'd scare you off if I told you that."

The smile vanished to a look of such intensity it seemed to solidify the air between them, making it impossible to breathe.

Oh my, he's totally serious about being gaga about me.

With infinite slowness, he leaned down and kissed her. His big hands caught her hips, pulled her to him, and then held her tightly. Her hands were momentarily pinned between them, and then they slid up, searching for someplace to go. She'd never realized how tall he was, or imagined how solid he would feel.

He nuzzled down her neck and kissed her where her shirt gaped open, exposing the top curve of her breasts. She clung to him, feeling suddenly small in his embrace, unsure if she wanted him to stop or go on.

He stopped, though, kissing her more chastely on the cheek, and then just held her. "I think anyplace we go," he whispered huskily, "should be brightly lit, with very little privacy."

"Possibly, that would be a good idea."

"Possibly." He sighed. "I need to work tomorrow night. Want to say Friday? We could do the Faire."

"Friday at the Faire would be good."

They kissed again, and she discovered that by knowing what to expect, the experience was even more enjoyable.

She waved as he drove away, feeling slightly silly doing so. Kids waved. What she really wanted was to pull him back and explore further—only more slowly. After he was out of sight, she pressed her hand to her mouth, capturing again the warmth and pressure.

Nathan Czernowski is in love with me!

Would wonders never end?

4: BEWARE ELVES BEARING GIFTS

⚭

WARGS, WINDWOLF, MAYNARD, interdimensional smugglers, and Nathan Czernowski were all pushed out of her mind at the sight of the loaded picnic tables. The competitive spirit of the scientists had produced amazing culinary feats. On the slim excuse of alerting people to possible food allergies each dish had the maker's name and the list of ingredients. The most elaborate dishes had the name first. The very simple donations had the makers listed last.

Even Lain was not immune to the competitive nature of the cookout. Her dish of fresh strawberries, spinach, walnuts, and homemade vinaigrette managed to be simple yet elegant.

Tinker loaded her plate with Lain's salad, dill potato salad, German coleslaw, three-bean salad, a linguine salad, a tortellini salad, baked beans, a sweet bean bun, a brownie, something made with pine nuts, and a cream cheese pineapple Jell-O salad.

She found Oilcan playing grill master, trying to smoke out his forming harem. Something about being stranded on a strange world combined with Oilcan's spry, puckish good looks seemed to make her cousin irresistible as a safe elf substitute to Earth women wanting to experience Elfhome to the fullest. Oilcan dodged the more aggressive attention, especially from the married women; he tended to be very moral in that regard. Still, Oilcan liked people, clever conversation, and playful flirting, so he went through something close to juggling fire sticks to attend any party at the Observatory. Already two women hung at the edge of the smoke, laughing at his witty remarks.

"Hey." Tinker braved the smoke to eye the meat on the grill.

"Hey!" Oilcan hugged her soundly. What had happened that suddenly everyone was hugging her? The harem eyed her with slight dismay. Oilcan chose not to introduce her, probably as a tactic to get rid of the women. He edged some of the food threatening to topple over the edge back onto her plate. "Think you got enough food?"

"I haven't had food since dinner yesterday." Tinker pointed out the largest hamburger on the grill. "Can I have that one cooked to medium?"

"Okeydokey." Oilcan patted it with a spatula. Red juices welled up in the slots. "It will be done in a couple of minutes. I came back to get you, and they said you'd left with Maynard. I tried calling you. Is everything okay?"

"I left my headset in the trailer." She balanced her plate in her left hand and ate with her fingers. "Where's the forks? Have you tried Lain's salad? Boy, is it good!"

"Here you are, little savage." Oilcan handed her a dormitory fork, unknowingly echoing Windwolf. "Try the stuff with the corn, if there's any left."

"I don't think I have room for more." Still, Tinker turned to scan the picnic table for the "stuff with the corn." "What about you? I couldn't get through to you."

Oilcan looked embarrassed. "I busted my headset on Shutdown. I had taken it off after it started to rain and put it on the seat next to me."

"We sat on it?" she guessed.

"No!" He laughed. "That would have been too simple. It fell out onto the ground at the yard sometime, and it got run over. I found it pressed into the mud, but in a thousand little pieces."

"Oh, crap, Oilcan, do you know how hard it is to get those things in Pittsburgh?"

"I know. I know. I knew you would be pissed, so I tracked down another one. You'll need to integrate it into my system for me."

"What? Where'd you find it?"

He glanced to the women still hovering on the edge of their conversation and dropped into Elvish. "It was probably stolen merchandise. Someone was selling headsets out of the trunk of their car down in the Strip District. The box was beat up, like it had been dropkicked. I do not even know if the thing will work, but I only paid ten dollars for it."

Tinker pondered the possibility that the headset was part of Maynard's mystery shipment, wondering whether she was obliged to tell the EIA or not.

One of the harem women took advantage of Tinker's silence and pointed out that Tinker's burger needed to be flipped. Having recaptured Oilcan's attention, the women laughed with him as he flipped the burger and pressed it down onto the blackened grill, the dripping grease making flame leap up. Tinker ate and thought.

The Veterans Bridge crossed over the top of the Strip District; a box dropped over the edge of the bridge would land on a rooftop or street. Depending on the packing, the box and contents could survive fairly intact. Oilcan had seen all of the men dressed as EIA guards, so he would have recognized any of them; thus the person who'd sold Oilcan the headset most likely found the box. Telling Maynard would probably result in having the headsets seized and the unlucky finder questioned and possibly jailed.

The important piece of information was that the smugglers had brought a box of headsets to Elfhome. Headsets themselves were useless without some kind of service plan, but once you had air connection they could tie together anything from a home/work/user tri-base to a multiuser network like the police ran to link together their officers.

Tinker heard her name spoken and looked up.

Oilcan had lost one of his harem girls and was finally introducing her to the remaining woman. "I told you about my cousin, the mad scientist."

"I am not a mad scientist."

"Yes, you are. You like to make big machines that make lots of noise, move real fast, or reduce other objects down to little pieces."

"You're only saying that because you know I can't hit you at the moment." Tinker considered throwing food instead, and then decided it was a waste of good food.

Oilcan grinned smugly at her as if he had guessed that she would decide against throwing food.

Recognition of Tinker's matching nut-brown coloring and slight frame dawned in the woman's eyes. She put a hand over her mouth to catch a laugh. "Oh, I'm sorry, I was expecting someone—"

"Older," Tinker guessed.

"Male." The woman winced. "I, of all people, should know better." She gave an honest smile. Not only was her left ring finger unadorned, there wasn't even a slight band of pale skin—honestly single then. "Hi, I'm Ryan MacDonald. Glad to meet you."

"Glad to meet you." Tinker bobbed a slight bow over her full plate. "Sorry for butting in earlier, but life has been a little insane for the last few days."

"Speaking of which," Oilcan said, "we really left the yard wide open. I bolted two metal plates over the workshop doorway, locked up, and padlocked the gate as we went out, but we *took* the whole security system with us. Someone broke in during Shutdown."

"Oh, shit." Tinker tried not to think of everything scattered haphazardly through the offices. At least her most expensive equipment was in her workshop trailer. "Were we robbed?"

"No. Whoever it was broke all the way in, and then walked back out without taking anything. They might have been looking for Windwolf." Was that supposed to make her feel better? "I went over to Roach's and picked up Bruno and Pete to keep an eye on the place until you get the security system back online."

Bruno and Pete were two elfhounds, on par in size with the Foo dog wargs, bred for intelligence, courage, and loyalty.

"Oh, that's horrible," Ryan said. "They said that Pittsburgh was safe."

The cousins looked at her and after a moment of silence said in unison, "If you don't count the man-eating animals, yes."

Ryan looked startled. "Are there a lot of those?"

"The elves patrol the woods around here." Oilcan waved his spatula at the Earth scrub trees slowly being overrun by elfin forest. "But you shouldn't go into the woods without a weapon."

Tinker ate a mouthful of the Jell-O salad before adding, "And if you hear an animal moving around outside, don't leave the building you're in, even during the day. Call nine-one-one, and they'll send someone to make sure it isn't a dangerous animal."

"Don't leave doors ajar," Oilcan said. "Always shut them firmly."

Tinker considered which of the other common safety practices

Ryan should know as she polished off the Jell-O salad. "Stay out of the swampy areas unless you have a xenobiologist with you who can spot the black willows and the other flesh-eating plants."

"Oh!" Oilcan waved his spatula at Ryan. "And the rivers aren't safe for swimming. The water is clean enough, but some big river sharks come up the Ohio."

"River sharks? Flesh-eating plants? You two are teasing me, right?"

"No," the cousins both said.

"There's a list of safety procedures that they usually hand out," Tinker said. "If you didn't get one, it's posted on the dorm's bulletin board. You really should read it; this isn't Earth."

Ryan glanced about the picnic grove with the red-checkered tablecloths on the picnic tables, the teams of scientists playing volleyball, and a portable stereo playing neon rock music. "Actually, things don't seem any different."

"Give it time." Oilcan cut Tinker's hamburger, peered at the center, and lifted it off the grill. "Here you go. Medium cooked."

"Are there buns?"

"Picky, picky, picky." Oilcan went off in search of a bun for her.

Ryan watched him go with a look that made Tinker view her cousin with a new eye. One had to admit he had mighty fine assets.

"Can I ask you," Ryan said hesitantly, her eyes still following Oilcan, "if your cousin has a girlfriend?"

"Look, you seem nice, but you're not staying. It might seem fun to you, to go to Elfhome and date a cute local, but it's not fair to Oilcan. Thirty days is just long enough to break his heart."

Ryan turned to consider her. "You've given this speech before."

"Every thirty days."

"Sorry," Ryan said. "They said that the elves don't socialize much with humans; I suppose it would seem like the same thing to them— here today and gone tomorrow."

Tinker winced. Did Windwolf view her the same way Oilcan saw the astronomers?

Oilcan came back with a bun lying open on a paper plate. "There. Tomato, lettuce, spicy brown mustard, chopped red onion, and real Heinz ketchup—the stuff made on Elfhome, not that new plant on the other side of the Rim on Earth."

"Oh, you know me so well it's scary." Tinker paused, considering the bun and her still overflowing plate. "Excuse me." She took the second plate. "I'm going to have to sit down to finish."

Lain slid onto the bench beside Tinker as she finished the hamburger. "How's your hand?"

"Good." Tinker licked her fingers clean and showed Lain her palm.

Lain examined it quietly, nodding at the pale scars. She closed up Tinker's hand, ending the examination, but continued to hold it. "I want to warn you about elves bearing gifts."

"Huh?"

"Windwolf gifted me with a new garden."

Tinker looked without thought in the direction of Lain's house, but the swell of Observatory Hill was in the way. "Is that a good thing or a bad thing?"

"Yes, that is the question, isn't it?"

Tinker winced at her carefully neutral tone. "What did they do?"

"They were very considerate in putting everything they dug up into pots. And I have to say that the specimens they planted are stunning. I dare guess that I have a garden to rival the queen's now."

They'd dug up Lain's flowers? Lain's work made it almost impossible for Lain to return to Earth. In Pittsburgh, she was as much an exile as she would be on Europa. And more importantly, the garden of Earth flowers she loved was a salve for not being in space.

"Oh, Lain, I'm sorry."

Lain hid away some of the pain in her eyes. "I can't say I'm completely displeased. Much of the garden would not have survived the root damage that the truck did. It would have taken me weeks just to fill the ruts. The new plants are all extremely valuable; it would have taken me years of wheedling to get any one."

"But it's not your garden of Earth flowers."

"No," Lain admitted. "It's not."

"I'm sorry. I'm really sorry."

Lain gave her a small, sad smile that vanished away before a look of true worry. "I'm nervous about what Windwolf might gift on you."

"Me?"

"There's no telling what he might decide to give you."

"I doubt he'll give me anything. There's still the matter of the life debt. Windwolf said that we weren't even." Tinker choked to a halt.

We drove all over Lain's flower beds . . . I told her I would go to college to make it up to her . . .

Oh, gods, he didn't replace the flowers because of what I said—or did he?

"Tinker?"

What else did I say? But she couldn't even remember exactly what she had said. The conversation was a feverish blur. Had she asked for anything for herself? Old fairy tales cautioning against badly worded wishes loomed suddenly large.

Lain watched her, worry growing.

"Can I turn it down?" Tinker asked. "Anything he might give me, if I don't like it?"

"Windwolf might not give you a chance to say no."

Tinker thought about it. What could he possibly give her that would be bad? "What do you think he might give me?"

"I'm not a superstitious woman, but our legends never have good to say about gifts from the fey."

"I'm not sure he's going to give me anything, Lain. He says we're not even."

Lain's eyes narrowed. "Did he say it in Elvish or English?"

Tinker paused to think. Windwolf had woken her up in the trailer, and they'd shouted at each other. But in what language? "English."

"Then it might not mean what you think it means, Tinker."

She thought it had been fairly straightforward, but Lain had much more experience dealing with elves. She recounted the conversation the best she could remember and ended with, "So, what do you think he means?"

"I'm not going to hazard a guess," Lain said. "But be careful around him. He meant well with my garden, but it was done in the arrogance of an adult catering to a child. He believes he knows what is better for us."

"Oh, great. I've got enough of that type of people in my life already."

"Tinker." Lain gripped her hand tightly. "I know I've pushed you into this college thing; I did it in the name of your own good. I've had a taste of my own bullying, and I'm sorry. Of all people, I should have realized that I was asking you to go alone to another world. If you don't want to go, you don't have to. I release you of all pledges."

The elves said that: I release you of all pledges. The irony of it kept Tinker from cheering. Knowing Lain, though, it might have been her reason for using the phrase. So Tinker said, "I'll think about it."

Dusk fell slowly. As the sky darkened and the stars started to peek out, the conversation turned from the world left behind, the experience of Startup, and the rustic amenities that the scientists found in the dormitories, and focused on the sky itself.

First Night was always fun; it was like watching children discover Christmas. Since it always rained during Startup—the warmer returning Earth air colliding with the chillier Elfhome climate—this was the scientists' first real sight of Elfhome's stars. Their faces were turned upward at the winking lights, and they murmured reverently, "Oh, wow!" Once Tinker's eyes adjusted, she could see the upraised hands, pointing out sights. As always, the cry of "Look at Arcturus!" went up. The elves called it the Wolf's Heart, on the shoulder of the constellation they called the First Wolf. One of the brightest stars in the sky, Arcturus was also the fastest moving; there was a fifteen-degree difference between the star of Elfhome and Earth.

"I can't believe this is the same sky we were looking at two days ago," someone close at hand said with awe. "A twenty-mile drive south, and all the constellations shift. Look at Corona Borealis! It doesn't look anything like a C anymore."

"Twenty miles south, and a side step into another dimension," another voice corrected the first speaker.

Because they would need to share the big telescopes, they all had personal telescopes set up. After minutes of fiddling, they excitedly swapped views.

"There are new stars in the star formation region of the Eagle Nebula—"

"Where?"

"M16—in Serpens."

"Look at the alignment of the planets. They'll be in full conjunction on Friday."

They ohhhed, and ahhhed, and talked about constellations that up to that point had only been textbook learning.

Tinker spent the night at Lain's. Oilcan picked her up in the morning and they headed over to the scrap yard. He went over the schedule he'd planned for the day. As usual, he was spending the days after Startup doing running, tracking down supplies and goods they needed. Tinker gave him a full report on her meeting with Maynard, Lain's garden, and finally the mystery calls on her home system.

Oilcan stopped at a red light at Route 65 and looked at her sharply. "I think I should leave Bruno and Pete with you."

"Please, no. I think it will be a while before I can deal with large dogs again."

"I don't like you being alone when everything is so weird."

"The weirdness is over," Tinker asserted.

"Someone is trying real hard to find you, Tinker. They're searching the neighborhood for you. Someone tried to kill Windwolf."

"Can't be the same people." She wished he wouldn't dwell on it— it was scary enough without him talking about it. "Windwolf was attacked on Elfhome before the Shutdown, and the calls started from Earth after Shutdown."

"So? Whoever's trying to find you is still *on* Elfhome."

"Whoever it is has nothing to do with Windwolf being attacked." Tinker could see where this was heading, and stopped it. "I'll arm the office security system first thing. My home security system is still running. I'll be okay."

Oilcan grumped a while longer but gave in, promising to check in with her often. No doubt he'd also find a way to let Nathan know.

Tinker tried to detour the conversation. "Can you do me a favor and see if you can track down some peroxide this morning? Lain says it's best for cleaning up large amounts of blood. We need to replace all the first-aid supplies, and I need pads."

"I restocked the first-aid kit," Oilcan said. "I also got you groceries. They're at my place. But you've got to get your own female stuff."

"It's not like they bite, Oilcan, and everybody knows they're not for you."

"It's embarrassing. Besides, I didn't know what type to buy."

"I used most of them to bandage wounds. Any kind will do."

"You get your own," he stated firmly. "Do you want me to bring the rest of the stuff over to your place tonight?"

A bid to make sure she was okay. Once there, he'd probably stay late.

"Nah. I'll eat out—get a pizza and some beer. Just bring it with you tomorrow."

He looked unhappy, but he let it go at that.

Windwolf came to the scrap yard late in the morning. One moment he wasn't there, and the next he stood watching her.

She stood looking back. She had been running in tight circles all morning—not wanting him to show, eager to see him, terrified of him appearing, cautioning herself that he might not come, and as the day wore on, nearly sick with the thought that she had read more into the situation and he wasn't coming. Now that he was here, she had no clue to her heart. That tight circle just spun faster, emotions whirling too quickly to latch on to.

Pick one, idiot, she growled at herself. *Happy. I'll be happy to see him.* Her happiness welled up so quickly and strongly that she suspected it was the truest of her emotions. She walked out to greet him then, a smile taking control of her face and refusing to give it up. "Hi!"

Elegantly dressed in elfin splendor, he looked out of place in the grimy scrap yard of rusting broken metal and shattered glass. He seemed a creature woven out of the glitter of sunlight on the river. Behind him, and well back, were armed elves—his bodyguard.

Windwolf nodded in greeting, an inclining of the head and shoulders that stopped just short of a bow. He presented a small silk bag to her. "For you. *Pavuanai wuan huliroulae.*"

It was High Elvish, something about talking together—at least that was what she thought *pavuanai* meant. She didn't recognize the word *huliroulae.*

Tinker eyed the bag suspiciously, thinking of Lain's garden and the xenobiologist's warning, but it didn't look dangerous. "What is it?"

"Keva."

"Oh." Tinker took the bag, opened it, and found indeed the golden cousin to soybeans. Genetically altered for millennia, keva beans were the elfin wonder food. Raw, roasted, fried, ground for flour, or even candied, keva beans were at the base of all celebrations. These were roasted with honey, one of her favorites. Still, this was her reward for saving his life? She noticed then that one of the guards held a fabric-wrapped bundle that looked for all the world like a present. Maybe this was a weird gift-giving appetizer. "Thanks."

Windwolf smiled as she popped one of the mild nutty beans into her mouth. "You said you would teach me horseshoes."

She laughed in surprise. "You really want to play?"

"Do you enjoy playing?"

She nodded slowly. "Yeah, it's fun."

"Then I wish to learn."

"Well, okay. Let me grab the shoes and the keys."

The keys were for the gate between the scrap yard and the small wood lot next to the scrap yard. Pittsburgh had many such pockets of wildness, places too steep to build on, full of scrub trees and wild grapevines. The lot was a series of level steps between steep drops, stairs cut into the hillside leading from level to level. There she and Oilcan had set up regulation-sized horseshoe pits.

"It's a simple game. You stand on one end, here, and throw the horseshoes at the stake. Like so." Tinker made sure she wasn't going to hit him with her swing, and tossed the horseshoe with a well-practiced underhand pitch. The horseshoe sailed the nearly forty feet and clanged against the stake in a single clear ringing note. "A ringer! That's what you're trying for." Her second shoe hit and rebounded. "But that's what normally happens."

He took the second set of horseshoes from her. He eyed the large U-shaped pieces of metal. "Are the horses on Earth really this big?"

"I don't know. I've never left Pittsburgh."

"So Elfhome is your home?"

"I suppose. I think of Pittsburgh as my home, but only when it's on Elfhome."

"That's good to know," Windwolf said.

And while she tried to decide what that meant, he copied her underhanded throw. He gracefully missed the stake by several feet. "This is harder than it appears."

"Simple doesn't necessarily mean easy," Tinker said.

They crossed the playing field to the pit to gather the shoes.

"Are you and your cousin orphans in this place?"

"Well, close. Oilcan's father is alive, but he's in prison. When he gets out, he won't be able to immigrate."

"Will Oilcan want to see his father?"

Tinker shook her head and concentrated on throwing the horseshoes. "His father killed his mother; not on purpose—he just hit her too hard in anger—but dead is dead." Not surprisingly, Tinker missed the stake. "Oilcan works hard at being the antithesis of his father. He never drinks to the point of being drunk. He doesn't yell or fight, and he'd cut off his hand before he'd hit someone he loved."

"He is a noble soul."

Tinker beamed at Windwolf, inordinately pleased that he approved of her cousin. "Yes, he is."

"My family is unusual among elves." Windwolf's horseshoe landed closer to the stake this round. "We elves do not life bond as readily as you humans, and I think sometimes it is because of the manner in which we are raised. Siblings are usually centuries apart, fully grown and moved on before the next becomes the focus of their parents' attention. We are basically a race of only children and tend to be selfish brats as a result."

"You're blowing my preconceived notion that you're a wise and patient race."

"We appear patient only because our conception of time is different. Amassing oceans of knowledge does not make you wise."

They collected horseshoes with oddly musical clangs of metal on metal.

"But your family is different?" Tinker prompted Windwolf.

"My mother loves children, so she had many, and she did not pace them centuries apart. She thought that when a child was old enough to seek out playmates on his or her own, it was time for another. Amazingly, my father put up with it, mostly. Perhaps their marriage would not have survived if we were not a noble house with wealth and Beholden." Tinker knew that Beholden were the lower castes that acted as servants to the noble caste, but she wasn't sure how it all worked. "The Beholden gave my father the distance he needed from so many children."

Given that his mother could have spent centuries raising children, Tinker blinked at the sudden image of the old woman who lived in a shoe, children bursting out at the seams. "How many kids are in your family?"

"Ten."

"Only ten?"

Windwolf laughed. "Only?"

"I thought maybe a hundred, or a thousand."

Windwolf laughed again. "No, no. Father would never submit to that. He finds ten an embarrassment he suffers only for Mother's sake. Most nobles do not have any children." Windwolf's voice went bitter. "There is no need for propagation when you live forever."

"Well, it keeps your population from growing quickly."

"The elfin population has only declined in the last two millennia. Between war, accidental death, and occasional suicide, we are half the number we once were."

That did put a different spin on things. "That's not good."

"Yes, so I try to tell people. I had great hope that with this new land would come a new way of seeing the world."

"Had?"

"The arrival of Pittsburgh was unexpected."

Tinker winced. "Sorry."

"It actually has been beneficial," Windwolf said. "Enticing people to an utter wilderness was difficult; few wanted to suffer the ocean crossing for so few comforts. Human culture, though, is attracting the young and the curious—the ones most likely to see things my way."

"Good." Tinker focused back on throwing the horseshoes. That's what she liked about the game. It encouraged a flow of conversation.

"What about you?"

"What do you mean?"

"Do you desire children?"

She missed the stake completely, only the chain-link fence keeping the horseshoe from vanishing into the weeds. "Me?"

"You. Or would you rather be childless?"

"No." She blurted out the gut reaction to the question. "It's just I've never thought about kids. Sure, someday I'd like to have one or two, maybe as many as three, but hell, I've never even—" She was going to say kissed a man, but she supposed that wasn't true anymore. "You know."

"Yes, I do know," he purred, looking far too pleased, and it put a flash of heat through her. Her and Windwolf? Like her dream? Suddenly she felt the need to sit down. As if he were reading her mind—gods, she hoped not—Windwolf indicated the battered picnic table beyond the horseshoe pit.

As she clambered up to sit on the tabletop of the picnic table, she wondered what it would be like to be with him, as they had been in her dream. "How old are you?"

"For an elf, barely adult. For a human, I am ancient. I'm two hundred and ten."

Or 11.6 times older than she was. Nathan suddenly seemed close to her age.

"Is that too old?" Windwolf asked.

"No, no, not at all." Tinker struggled for perspective. Elves were considered adults at a hundred, but until they reached a thousand, they were still young. Triples were what the elves called them, or those that could count their age in three digits. Windwolf could be compared to a man that just turned twenty; only he'd been born in the 1820s.

And she was like one of Oilcan's astronomers to him, staying only long enough to break his heart.

First Nathan and now Windwolf. Well, didn't her choice of men suck?

"Have you ever played ninepins?" Windwolf asked, breaking the silence.

"Bowling? Yeah. But only with humans."

"I am much better at ninepins."

"Tooloo says humans should never play ninepins with elves. It always ends badly for humans."

"This Tooloo is a font of misinformation. She was completely wrong about the life debt."

"How so?"

"The debt between us is not yours. It is mine," Windwolf said.

"Yours?"

"How could the count be any other way?"

"During the fight with the saurus . . ."

"You saved my life. I was dazed, and you distracted the saurus by putting out its eye at great risk to yourself."

She blinked at him, stunned as the events now rearranged themselves in her mind. "But the spell you placed on me?"

"If I did not survive the rest of the fight, I wanted others to know you had acted with courage. You were to be adopted into my household and cared for."

"Oh." She didn't know what else to say.

"We looked for you after the fight, but we thought you were a boy. We asked about 'the boy,' and no one knew who we were asking about."

How could Tooloo have gotten it so wrong? Or had Tooloo been lying all this time? But why? Tinker struggled to keep faith in the crazy old half-elf; Windwolf could be lying to her now. But why would he? His version of the events certainly matched what she remembered better, and made more sense.

"I must go. There are days when, even for elves, there is not enough time." Windwolf waved the guard with the present forward, took it, and banished both guards back to the scrapyard. "Last I saw you, you were a child, and now you are an adult. I want to grasp this moment before this too slips away."

He held out the present.

The keva beans had been harmless enough, and this gift looked no larger than the last. "Is this for me?"

"If you desire it."

Why did elves make everything seem so dangerous? It was just a small fabric-wrapped bundle. "What is it?"

"I thought it best to stay with the traditional gift for the occasion."

Trust elves to have a traditional gift for saving one's life. She unwrapped it tentatively. She was glad he had told her it was a traditional gift. Certainly it wasn't what she expected. She wasn't even sure *what* it was. It seemed to be a metal bowl, intricately worked as one expected of an elfin work, yet it stood on three legs anchored to a disc of marble. It had quite a heft to it, and what impressed her most was that Windwolf had made it seem so lightweight. She tried not to compare it with Lain's entire garden. The child in her, though, wanted to cry, *That's it?*

"Do you accept?"

"Yes."

He smiled. It was like the sun coming out. He spoke a word in High Elvish and kissed her on the forehead. The touch of his lips seemed to sizzle on her skin.

Tinker called Lain from her scrap yard. "He brought me a bowl."

"A bowl?"

"Well, I think it's a bowl." She described it at length to Lain, who identified the gift, after some thought, as a brazier, and explained that one burned incense or charcoal in the bowl, and the legs anchored into the marble made it stable and protected whatever it was sitting on from the heat.

A brazier? "Well, it's certainly not what I expected." Tinker eyed her gift. "I'm trying to figure out what the catch is."

A click of keys came from Lain's side of the connection. " 'Braziers are a symbolic gift.' " Lain read from something. " 'Great importance is made of the wrapping of the gift, which must be extravagant, and the presentation, which must be subtle.' Yes, but what does it stand for?"

"I don't know. He just said it was traditional for the occasion."

"Not you. Barron. He released his anthropology paper on the elves this spring, but don't ever repeat that. The elves don't study themselves and certainly don't want us studying them either."

"I was never sure why we compulsively study ourselves."

"How else are we going to learn and grow?"

"If the elves don't study themselves, does that mean they don't change?"

"Possibly. We certainly haven't been able to pry any information out to indicate that they have." There was a pause, and Lain murmured softly, skimming the info in front of her. "Tinker, what did you talk about with Windwolf?"

"I'm not sure. You know how it is to talk to them. It's worse than talking to you. Why?"

"The brazier is a customary gift for what Barron only terms as 'delicate arrangements.' I don't know what the hell that's supposed to mean. Apparently, accepting the gift implies agreement to the arrangements."

Tinker yelped, as the only delicate arrangement that sprang to mind was sex. "W-w-we didn't talk about any arrangements. At least not that I can remember. Doesn't this Barron list anything?"

"He says that this information was told to him in passing, and that when pressed, the elves stated that it wasn't a ritual that would occur between elf and human."

Tinker made a rude sound of negation. "Maybe Barron has it completely wrong."

"What did you talk about?"

"Horseshoes. Oilcan. His family." Tinker glanced in the mirror and yipped in surprise at her reflection.

"Tinker?"

"What the—" A triangle of blue marked where Windwolf had kissed her on her forehead. The spot wouldn't rub off, even with spit. "He marked me—somehow—after I accepted."

There was a long silence from Lain's side, and then, "I think you should come over."

Tinker and Oilcan had laid claim to an old parking garage between her loft and the scrap yard, thus convenient and inconvenient to them both. It easily held the flatbed, her hoverbike, and whatever miscellaneous vehicles they'd picked up and refurbished.

Tinker went round to the first bay and coded open the door. Her honey baby waited inside, gleaming red. She'd traded a custom-built Delta model hoverbike for a custom paint, detail, and chrome job at Czerneda's. Oilcan bitched that she was ripped off, because the detail job was so simple—gold pin striping—on a redshift paint job, but hell, it was perfection. She suspected that he bitched mostly because her own custom Deltas were the only serious competition she had on the racecourses, and every custom job she did chipped away at her odds of winning. Oilcan's loyalty wouldn't let him bet against her, but he liked to win.

Well, he'd have to get used to it. The Gamma models were being mass-produced by a machine shop on the South Side, kicking back a royalty to her for the design. At the moment, she was the only one who seemed able to grasp all the physics involved to make modifications. Sooner or later, someone would be able to bend his or her mind around the whole concept and beat Tinker at her own game. It was how humans worked.

She swung her leg over the saddle, thumbprinted the lock, and hit the ignition button. Ah, bliss—the rumble of a big engine between one's legs. She eased down on the throttle to activate the lift drive. Once the Delta actually lifted off of the parking studs, she retracted them and walked the Delta out of the garage. Once past the door sensors, she clicked the door shut.

She opened up the throttle. The Delta soared up and forward, the lift drive providing altitude while the spell chain provided the actual forward torque. Simple physics. Sooner or later, someone would twig to what she'd done.

Tinker set the dish of whipped cream beside her bowl of strawberries. Lain was the only person who seemed to understand the correct ratio of topping to fruit, which was three to one. "Have you found out anything more about the brazier or the mark?"

"Well, there's this." Lain put a slickie down in front of Tinker. "These are photos taken during the signing of the treaty. Look closely at the elves."

Tinker thumbed through the slickie's photos, dipping the strawberries into the whipped cream and idly licking it off. Despite the president's acting career, the humans looked positively dowdy next to the elfin delegation. It did not help that the humans kept to the stately solids of navy, black, and gray, while the royal party dressed in a brilliant riot of colors and sparkled with gems and gold. So vivid was the elvish beauty that it crossed the line of believability and became surreal, as if the images next to the drab humans were computer-generated art. It was a cheap slickie, so most of the photos were two-d, allowing no panning or rotation. The centerfold, however, was full three-d, and she rotated through the photo, zooming in on the faces of the elves.

Four of the thirty elves wore the same style of forehead marks. All four were female. Tinker frowned; the sample size was too small to use as a base for any good conclusion, but the marks certainly seemed to be a female thing only. Put there by males?

All four marks were of different colors—red, black, blue, and white—and shape. As she studied the one in blue, she recognized the female as the high-caste elf at the hospice, the one who had called her and Oilcan wood sprites. In the shadows of the parking lot, Tinker had missed the mark. What had her name been? Sparrow something or other.

Tinker dipped her current strawberry for the second time and studied the blue mark on Sparrow. Was it the same mark, or just the same color? "Do you have a mirror?"

Lain went off to her downstairs bathroom and returned with a small hand mirror. They carefully compared marks.

"No, they're not quite the same," Lain announced after several minutes.

Tinker grunted. "What do you suppose it means?"

"I don't know," Lain said. "But you seem to be in good company. This is the royal majesty herself and her court. They're the world leaders of Elfhome."

Good company or not, she didn't want to be part of it. In her book, elves made colorful neighbors but she was glad not to be one of the family. She'd seen enough of their stiff formality and causal cruelty between castes to know it would drive her nuts.

Tinker was startled at another familiar face. "This is Windwolf."

Lain leaned over to check the photo. "Yes, it is."

Tinker realized that despite a growing awareness that Windwolf was important in the local politics, she didn't know exactly what his title was. "This might be a silly question, but who exactly is Windwolf?"

"Lord Windwolf is the viceroy of the Westernlands."

Viceroy? Before Tinker could ask what that meant, the doorbell rang.

"Looks like I have company," Lain said, reaching for her crutch.

"What am I? Sauerkraut and kielbasa?" Tinker muttered.

"Hush, my little pierogie," Lain called back as she limped up the hallway to the front door.

Tinker considered the photo of Windwolf as Lain answered her front door. Tinker had thought him stunning the few times she had seen him, but now she knew she hadn't yet seen him at his best. The creature in the photo seemed as untouchable as a god.

Lain's visitor, in a deep raspy male voice, introduced himself as the son of her fellow crew member who had died in the training exercise that crippled Lain. "I don't know if you remember me at the memorial. I was about five at the time."

That drew Tinker out of the kitchen. Lain stood, apparently rendered speechless by the sudden appearance.

The man was in his early twenties, tall with a shock of black hair and a long sharp nose. He was in biking leathers, wore a pair of sunglasses, and had a helmet tucked under his arm.

Tinker recognized him with a start. He was the motorcyclist she and Oilcan had seen nearly hit on Shutdown Day. "I thought you might be a half-elf."

He looked at her, frowning, and the frown deepened. "No. I'm not, lady. You're mistaken."

"Tinker!" Lain admonished with a single word, then turned her attention back to the man. "I remember you. My, how you've grown, but children do that, I suppose. You were such a grieving little boy; I don't think I heard you say a single word that day."

"It was long ago. I've moved past that," he said.

"Riki was your name, wasn't it?"

He nodded. "Yes, you do remember me. I was afraid that you wouldn't."

"Your mother spoke a lot about you before the accident." Lain indicated Tinker. "This is Tinker, who is very worth knowing."

Riki turned to look at Tinker. She reflected in his sunglasses. He nodded and turned back to Lain. "I was hoping you could tell me about my mother."

"You stranded yourself on Elfhome just for that?"

"No. I'm going to be attending the University of Pittsburgh once fall classes start. I've got a grant from Caltech as part of my graduate studies. I showed up a little early so I'd have a chance to experience Elfhome fully. It would be exploring an alien world, just like my mother hoped to."

Lain clicked her tongue over what she certainly considered the folly of youth. Tinker had heard the sound often enough to recognize the thought behind it. "Pitt is a shadow of what it was; it's barely more than a community college right now. Well, there's not much to be done about that now. You're here. The question is, what is to be done with you now? Do you have a place to stay? Money enough to last?"

"I have the grant money." Riki tapped a breast pocket, making paper inside wrinkle loudly. "It's supposed to last me six months, but I've got to make it stretch to nine. I'm hoping to find a job, and a cheap place to stay."

"Housing shouldn't be too hard; it's summer—just find someplace that looks empty and squat," Lain said, and limped back to the kitchen. "Come have something to eat and drink, and we'll consider work."

Riki followed Lain, glancing around with vivid interest, pausing at the doorway of the living room to scan it fully. "It's a nice place you have here. I expected something more rustic. They talk about how backward Pittsburgh has become, cut off as it is. I half expected log cabins or something."

Lain laughed from the kitchen.

Tinker had stayed in the foyer. She picked up her helmet and called, "Lain, I'm going to go."

Lain came to the kitchen doorway. "You! Stay! Into the kitchen."

Tinker put down the helmet and obediently went into the kitchen. One didn't argue with Lain when she used that voice. "Why?"

"All the positions up here on the hill are government funded; all hiring has to be written out in triplicate and approved in advance. You have more contacts than I do down in the city."

Tinker winced. "Lain, I'm not an employment agency."

Riki regarded Tinker with what seemed slight unease. It was hard to tell with the sunglasses. "You seem too young to be anything but a high school student."

Tinker stuck her tongue out at him and got smacked in the back of the head by Lain.

"Behave." Lain filled the teakettle and set it onto the gas range. "Tinker is much more than she seems. She's probably the most intelligent person in Pittsburgh. Now if she could learn a bit of common sense and get a more rounded education . . ."

"Lain," Tinker growled. "I don't want to beat that horse right now."

"Then be nice to my guest. Offer him a job."

"I doubt if he wants to do demo work at the yard," Tinker said. "He certainly doesn't know anything about magic, and it's nearly as unlikely that he knows anything about quantum physics."

"I've got a master's degree in quantum physics," Riki said.

"Eat crow, little girl!" Lain cried, laughing at the look on Tinker's face.

Riki startled at Lain's reaction.

"You're kidding," Tinker said.

"I'm going to do my doctorate on the quantum nature of magic. No one has done research on magic in its natural state. That's why I'm studying at Pitt."

"If you want to learn about magic, you need to work with Tinker. She's the expert."

"No, I'm not; elves are."

"True, true, their whole society seems to be based on the ability to cast spells." Lain laughed, putting out cups. "But that does him no good, not as closed mouthed as they are."

"What do you mean? Anyone can cast spells."

Lain looked at her with surprise. "Tooloo has never explained why the nobles rule over the other castes?"

"I'm never sure when Tooloo is telling me the truth," Tinker said. "She's told me that nobles can feel ley lines and can cast certain spells with gestures and words instead of written patterns . . . which might be true. Certainly the spoken component of spells is merely setting up certain subtle resonance frequencies. I'm not sure about the hand gestures. Written spells follow a logic system similar to the and/or gates of computer circuitry, creating paths for energy to follow toward a desired effect. The only way I could see it working was if somehow the noble's body replaces the circuitry. . . ." She fell silent, thinking of energy following fingertips while the hands moved through the pattern of a spell. The ability to feel ley lines could result by simply bioengineering an organ like the inner ear that was sensitive to magic. How would you manipulate magic with your hands? She looked at her own oil-stained hands, the left one with its new patchwork of pink scars. With what she knew of biology, it was unlikely that they fitted new organs into their fingertips, unless it was on the tip of the bone, or perhaps their fingernails. She flexed her fingers as if typing. She supposed fingernails would work, although if one could engineer it so each finger bone had a separate function, then each finger could perform three functions instead of just the one. . . .

"Tinker. Tinker." Lain interrupted her thought process.

"It might work that way," Tinker conceded. She added, "Tooloo also tells me stories about elves making gems or frogs falling out of people's mouths when they talk, and unless you have an N-dimensional space filled with frogs, it couldn't work. Besides, what would the frogs eat? How would you deal with the heat they generated packed together like that? I suppose you could use that energy to move a frog into our dimension."

A smile spread across Riki's face. "I like how your mind works."

That startled Tinker into silence. No one had ever said that to her.

"If you hire him," Lain said, pouring tea out, "every minute he frees up, you will have for fiddling around with your inventions."

Tinker opened her mouth and shut it on a protest. She

remembered the condition of the offices—her workshop still on the back of the flatbed and thoroughly splattered with blood. Suddenly the idea of having help, and thus more time, was seductive—and Lain knew it. "That's not playing fair."

"I don't like wasting time."

Tinker frowned. The words "sucker for strays" on her forehead were coming into play. "Well, I could offer part-time at minimum wage, but nothing more than that. Tooloo might have some work."

He looked at her for a minute, and finally said, "I don't know if this is rude—I don't know elf customs—but what's the mark for?"

Speaking of casting spells with just a gesture. Tinker rubbed at her forehead, wondering how exactly Windwolf had marked her. "I don't know. We were just trying to figure that out."

Lain looked troubled. "That worries me. Why don't you see Maynard about that? You should find out why Lord Windwolf marked you."

"The viceroy?" Riki asked.

Tinker got up, annoyed that this newcomer knew more about Windwolf than she did. "Look, if you want the job, show up at my scrap yard tomorrow morning. Lain can tell you how to get there. And I'll need to see your papers. I'm not getting into trouble with the EIA for hiring an illegal immigrant."

Lain gave her a look of disapproval, but Tinker clumped out. She'd had enough motherly scolding for the day.

5: VARIABLE SUBSITUTIONS

TINKER'S GRANDFATHER had often told her that moving Pittsburgh to Elfhome raised the intelligence of human bureaucrats. He commonly cited the Housing Act as proof. People fleeing Elfhome registered their property with the EIA in return for displacement vouchers. The United Nations redeemed the vouchers for a house of equal value (prior to the gate of course) anywhere on Earth, doling out the Chinese Compensation money to those most affected by the gate. The EIA resold the Pittsburgh real estate for a dollar to anyone who pledged to make the home his or her permanent primary residence. The system encouraged squatters to maintain property that would otherwise stand empty. Housing, which had always been affordable and easy to find in Pittsburgh, became basically free.

Her grandfather, Oilcan, and she had lived in an old hotel looking out over the river on Neville Island. It was a four-story palace bought for a dollar.

The locks and dams that controlled the Allegheny, Monongahela, and the Ohio rivers, however, stayed mostly on Earth. Every spring, the muddy river water would creep up the steep bank and swirl into the hotel's downstairs. The basement had slowly filled with river silt, as they only pumped out the water. The first floor they shoveled out and sprayed down with fire hoses. All the wallpaper had long peeled off, leaving stained plaster behind. They left the windows open all summer to dry out the wood. When Tinker and Oilcan rode their bikes through the large empty first-floor rooms, or played street hockey using the old fireplaces as goals, they would kick up clouds of fine dust. Come fall, they would loot empty buildings for window glass, and patch the plaster anywhere the winter winds would be able to blow through.

Her grandfather had converted the second floor to the kitchen, workshop, and classroom. The third floor contained the library, away from the lower-level floods and the fourth story's dripping roof. They slept on the fourth floor, drips and all, as it was the safest place in case of flash flood.

Oilcan moved out the winter of his sixteenth birthday to Mount Washington, claiming he wasn't going to spend another spring worrying if the river would wash into their bedrooms. When their grandfather died the next year, Oilcan offered to take Tinker in with him. Nothing could make him move back to the river's edge. Nor would he let her stay at the hotel alone when she refused his offer. Showing surprising strength of character, he insisted she find someplace above the floodplain.

Tinker had scoured the hill around the scrap yard. After the high ceilings, long halls, and sprawling first floor of the hotel, everywhere else had seemed small and cramped. Finally she'd found a large loft. The living room was thirty by sixty, and the one bedroom was a roomy fourteen by twenty.

Now she went up the steps to her loft wearily, unlocked the door, mumbled her security code to her security system, and slammed the door behind her. She was at the fridge, opening the door to get a cold beer, before she realized her security system hadn't acknowledged her. She jerked around, hand still on the refrigerator door handle, and found she wasn't alone.

A woman—tall, leggy, with dark spiky hair and armed with a stocky handgun leveled at her—drifted out of the shadows to block the front door. "Durrack?"

A man appeared at the bedroom door. He quirked up one eyebrow. "Well, what do we have here?"

"She let herself in, and gave a security code," the woman said. Her taste in clothing ran to black, and very tight fitting. If she had any weapons other than the handgun, they were small, or strapped to her back. Tinker couldn't tell how lethal the handgun was. It seemed too large to be loaded with something as mundane as bullets.

"Who are you?" Tinker asked, and was somewhat pleased she

didn't sound as scared and angry as she was. When was her life going to go back to normal? "What are you doing here?"

"We're going to ask the questions," the man said. "We're looking for Alexander Graham Bell. He goes by the name of Tinker. This is his residence."

He? Hell, they were confused. They had her name right, but certainly not her sex. Not that she was about to point out the error in their thinking. "And I take it that he's not here."

"No," Durrack said, closing the distance between them. "What's your name? Let me see some ID."

Tinker backed away. "Look, I don't want any trouble. My name is Lain. My ID was stolen two days ago by some big goons. I've had a really shitty week, and I haven't seen Tinker for days. Skippy, activate emergency system!"

"We turned the AI off." He checked his forward motion. "Cooperate with us, and you're not going to get hurt."

"You break into my house, wave guns at me, and expect me to turn over my boyfriend?" It was weird talking like this, keeping pronouns straight. It was like a math problem, substituting in values.

"You live here with him?" Durrack asked.

"Yeah."

The woman made a disgusted noise. "How long have you two been together?"

What would the right answer be? A few weeks or months? It didn't seem long enough. "Three years."

Durrack and the woman exchanged dark looks. Perhaps three years was too much.

"I hate this assignment more and more," the woman muttered.

"Patience, Briggs. It's a whole new world."

"Doesn't mean I have to like it."

And while they murmured together, Tinker said lowly, "Tripwire."

Briggs jerked her head up, and then swore. "She's activated a backup defense system!"

Durrack caught Tinker under the arm and hustled her out of the house. Out on the street, he pushed her up against the wall. Not as hard as he could, but still she found herself dangling a foot from the ground.

"Look, you little twit. We've been down to your boyfriend's scrap yard, and there's blood everywhere. We've been to Mercy. We checked with all the Earth-based hospitals. He wasn't checked in at any of them. If your boyfriend is still alive, he's running on borrowed time. If someone finds him before we do, he'll end up roadkill just like his father did. Do you understand?" She didn't understand any of that, but she wanted him to let go of her, so she nodded. "Now, where is Tinker?"

Oilcan's? No, he probably wasn't home. Lain's? No, keep her out of this, whatever it was. Nathan's? He was most likely on duty. She thought of a dozen more places and rejected them. Tinker needed someplace with lots of people where, if these folks really turned out to be American agents, the U.S. government carried little weight. "He's at a hospice just beyond the Rim."

"What's he doing there?"

"Wargs attacked the scrap yard at Shutdown. They downed a high-ranking elf. Tinker took him out to the hospice after Startup."

"That was two days ago."

"Tinker was hurt. One of the wargs messed him up, and the wound got infected."

Durrack swore and took hold of her. "Come on. I'm not letting you out of my sight until I have your boyfriend under my thumb."

Tinker hunted for signs of squad cars responding to the tripwire distress call, but the police weren't showing. Pittsburgh police were spread too thin.

Their car was tucked out of sight, half a block down. A sleek late-model sedan, it looked out of place in Pittsburgh and especially in Tinker's neighborhood. It didn't need the D.C. plates to identify it as out of town. Briggs unlocked the car with a remote.

Durrack opened the back passenger door but held Tinker in check. "Search her."

Briggs moved Tinker so her hands were on the car roof and her legs were slightly spread. The woman combed fingers through Tinker's short, dark hair. The search went down the back of Tinker's neck, up under her shirt and into her bra. Durrack averted his gaze. Briggs' hands stayed impassive, but Tinker clenched her hands into fists on the car roof, until her knuckles showed white, as the search moved to her groin.

"You have no right to do this." Tinker blinked to keep tears out of her eyes. "I haven't done anything."

"Sorry, kid, them's the breaks." Durrack actually sounded like he was sorry.

Finally Briggs moved down to the less personal territory of Tinker's pants pockets. There the search slowed to a crawl. Tinker's pants had a half dozen pockets, and all of them held something. After the first handful, Briggs dumped the items onto the floor of the backseat.

"Please don't lose the nuts and bolts," Tinker said. "They're irreplaceable."

The pockets empty, and double-checked, Briggs stepped back away from Tinker. "If she kicks you with those boots, you're going to know it."

"Take them off," Durrack ordered Tinker.

Briggs sorted through the pile on the car floor, confiscating "dangerous" items: three different-sized screwdrivers, a pocket acetylene torch, and her Swiss Army knife. They went with her boots into the trunk.

"Can I have the rest of my stuff back?" Tinker asked, nearly whispering in an effort to keep from showing how much she wanted her possessions.

"Just get in. You can pick it up while we drive."

Tinker scrambled into the backseat. There was no lock switch, door handle, or com device.

Durrack slid into the passenger seat, letting Briggs drive. "Where's the hospice?"

"You cut through downtown and go up past where the Hill District used to be." Tinker stuffed away her things.

"Where?"

"Centre Avenue out of town. Corner of Old Center and Old Penn."

"New roads named after old roads that don't exist anymore." He programmed it into the nav system. It must have been tied to one of the few government satellites, because it actually seemed to be working.

Distantly a police siren rose, but they were already turning off her street. Tinker slumped back in the seat. If the police arrived at her place now, she wouldn't be there to be rescued.

"Who are you two, anyhow?" She contented herself with kicking the back of the front seat.

"I'm Corg Durrack. My associate is Hannah Briggs. We're with NSA."

"What's that?"

"National Security Agency."

It just didn't make sense. What had she done to bring these guys down on her? "What do you want with Tinker? He's never been in the United States."

Durrack made a negation sound. "He was born in the United States—someplace. He would have been five when the gate first moved Pittsburgh to Elfhome."

Oh, this made sense why they didn't suspect her of being Alexander Bell. They were looking for someone nearly ten years older than her. They hadn't considered that Tinker was anything but a naturally inseminated child. Add in her male name, and they were obviously completely lost. Still, that didn't explain why they were *looking*.

"We want to protect Tinker," Hannah Briggs said. "He's in a lot of danger."

"So you keep on saying." It was a good line to have someone betray a loved one. "Why would anyone want to hurt Tinker? He runs a scrap yard. He keeps his nose clean. He's a good guy."

Briggs gave a flat laugh and murmured, "Yeah, right."

Durrack gave Briggs a hard look. "He's an extremely intelligent young man who apparently understands the working of the phase gate and in all possibility could build one."

Understood it, yes. Build one? She'd never considered doing that, mostly because the parts were too exotic to find as scrap in Pittsburgh. "So?"

Durrack threw her a surprised look. "Do you have any idea how rare that is?"

"Apparently not."

"People like that can be counted on one finger. No one has been able to develop a hyperphase device since Leonardo Dufae's death. The Chinese figured out how to build it off the designs they stole, but they can't change it or improve it. If they could, we wouldn't have this little weirdness called Pittsburgh. Then up pops Tinker, son of the gate's inventor, trained by the same man, and one assumes privy to any family secrets."

"Yeah. Energy equals mass times constant squared."

Durrack turned in his seat now to consider her in a silent study. They crossed the heavy McKees Rocks Bridge, all stone and steel, hopping parts of the riverbank before crossing the Ohio River proper, still choked with barges. It would be a week before river traffic returned to normal. The roads, though, were clear, and minutes later they were crossing the Allegheny River on the Fort Duquesne Bridge.

"Tinker applied to Carnegie Mellon University last Shutdown. It took them a while to put all the pieces together and notify NSA. We've blacked it out, except letting them issue an acceptance letter. Hopefully, no one else put the pieces together either."

"What pieces?"

"That Alexander Bell listed Leonardo Dufae as his father, and that according to the testing AI, he understood all the questions, even though he answered them wrong. That includes the filter questions on hyperphase that no one is supposed to be able to answer."

Shit. She hadn't considered that they would have an AI filtering the placement testing. Lain had explained that the test was just to see what courses she would need to attend: *You can test out of the basics and only take advanced courses.* By tracking eye movement, keystrokes, length of time per question—and correct answers changed to wrong ones—a good AI would easily have determined that she had comprehended all the questions and just chose to get them wrong. "What an idiot."

"If he meant to confuse people, he's succeeded. Why did Tinker bother to apply to Carnegie Mellon University?"

"He only applied to humor a friend. He doesn't want to leave Pittsburgh, so he tried to keep them from accepting him."

Durrack made a slight noise of discovery. "Why doesn't he want to leave?"

Tinker snorted. Durrack had said it with faint disbelief that anyone would want to stay. "Earth has nothing that interests Tinker."

Durrack's eyes narrowed, and he exchanged glances with Briggs. "What about you?"

"Me?" Tinker squeaked. Oh, please, don't pay any attention to little old me.

"Would you like to go to Earth?"

Tinker laughed. "No!"

"We can set you up at a nice house. All new furniture. Cleaning robots. Two new cars. Basically replace everything you might lose in a move. You could go to school if you wanted. Earth has malls, the net, cable television, first-class restaurants, and Disney World."

"Disney World? I'm supposed to give up my family and friends and everything I know for Disney World?"

"Offer her candy and ice cream," Hannah murmured. "At her age, that might still work."

They were coming up to the Rim. There were long-standing jokes about the slowness it took to move across the border. One joke was that the border was an event horizon of a black hole, something that you could spend a lifetime trying to reach. Another sarcastic prod was that elfin magic made any event last longer than a human lifetime, which was why they'd bioengineered themselves to be immortal.

Hannah, apparently feeling the need for privacy, slid up the sound barrier behind the front seat.

Tinker took out the digital marker that Maynard had given her from the smuggler's loot and traced a quick eavesdropping spell on the back of the seat.

". . . so chances are, Tinker isn't going to want to come with us."

"That's a possibility," Durrack said. "I say that if we don't find the boyfriend at this hospice, we tuck the girl away for safekeeping."

"Durrack, sometimes you scare me. The Pittsburghers are still American citizens—"

"Whose willingness to live on a foreign planet makes their loyalty to the United States suspect."

"Don't feed me that line. You don't give a shit about that."

"Yes, but it looks good on a report when you bend the hell out of the rules."

"Making the girl disappear would do more than bend rules."

"Protective custody. If we've thought to use her to get to Tinker, then she's fair game to anyone looking for him. Do you want the kid in the middle of this? You want to deal with that again? I sure as hell don't."

"It isn't all black and white. There's a lot of gray out there, Durrack."

"It's not the black, white, or gray that I'm worrying about. It's the blood red. I say if Tinker is out here, we stick them both away until next Shutdown and then smuggle them out to the States."

"We should make sure they actually like one another first. She might be lying about their relationship."

More than you can guess. Tinker watched as the second car in front of them got waved through. Tinker or Tinker's lover, she was slated to disappear after the hospice search, which meant she had to get away from them at the hospice. She mostly needed to get out of the car. She considered the tactics she could try, from asking to go pee to stating that she wanted to stay in the car. Just because they'd made the one mistake on her identity didn't mean they were truly stupid. Her real name was misleading, and she didn't remember the application asking for gender or age.

She considered the hazards of being locked in the car, in case her ploy failed. Could she get out? Unlikely. Trying the reverse-psychology ploy of refusing to leave the car was too risky.

Might as well start working on the bathroom ploy. She tapped on the divider.

It was their turn through the security checkpoint.

Hannah slid down the window and handed out her NSA ID. Durrack handed his across via Hannah.

"We're looking for a human male," Hannah said in rough, slow Low Elvish. "The girl has no ID. She is our prisoner. We are responsible for her."

While they talked, Tinker pieced together a plea for help in High Elvish.

The elfin border guard glanced in the window at her. She mouthed the plea, just in case she didn't get the chance to talk to an elf at the hospice.

"Where do you seek this human male?" the elf asked Hannah, gazing intently at Tinker.

"The hospice."

The guard went off with their papers into the guardhouse. Tinker whispered, "Come on, come on," crossing the fingers on both hands. That simple magic didn't work, if it ever really worked. The guard returned and waved them through.

Hannah drove to the hospice and parked. Tinker's stomach

churned nervously as they walked in. She needed to do this quickly, because the NSA were about to find out that she had been the only human ever treated here.

She picked the brawniest-looking of the elves in the foyer as the NSA agents checked stride, apparently scanning about for an equivalent of a reception desk. She locked eyes with the elf and said quickly, "Please, help me. I am in grave danger. Wolf Who Rules . . ."

Durrack jerked her back and slapped a hand over her mouth. "What the hell did you say?"

Hannah produced her ID and was saying carefully, "This one is in our care and might be charged with crimes. She is young and foolish."

Tinker hadn't thought of what the elves might *do* in response to her plea. She expected demands for identification and long legal proceedings. She was stunned as the elf unsheathed his sword in a ring of metal.

Durrack reacted instantly, shoving her aside to pull his own weapon. Hannah shouted, "Drop it! Drop it!"

Tinker scrambled to one side, swearing. This wasn't what she'd planned! Still, she'd be an idiot not to take advantage of the opportunity. She darted through the door and into the maze of hallways.

What had happened to her life?

One minute it was all so sane and orderly, and now look at her! They say that the elves really couldn't curse anyone. Elves could use their magic to turn a person into a toad, cause someone to become incredibly uncoordinated, or drop one's inhibitions like a six-pack of Iron City Beer, but really rotten, everything-turns-against-you-bad luck they couldn't do.

So why did it seem that someone had cursed her?

Tinker skittered on the slick stone to round the corner; then yelped as she came face-to-face with armed men in EIA uniforms. EIA? How did they get here so fast? Were they real EIA? She tried to turn, her stocking feet went out from under her, and she went sliding directly into them. *In a frictionless universe, objects in motion stay in motion.*

Durrack and Briggs came around the corner, and there was sudden excited shouting. She looked up to find the EIA and the NSA pointing guns at one another.

"NSA!" Durrack shouted. "Put down your weapons!"

"EIA!" the others yelled back. "Drop it!"

Tinker edged toward the closest doorway. No one really seemed to be paying attention to her, but then, she didn't have a gun.

"This girl is in our protective custody," Briggs growled.

"Drop the guns!" the EIA or EIA look-a-likes shouted. "You're not doing anything until we see proper identification and clearance papers."

Tinker bolted through the door.

Behind her, Durrack didn't seem to notice she had fled. "This is code black!"

Nor had the EIA. "I don't give diddly what color it is. This is Elfhome!"

After thoroughly losing herself, she slid through a door and discovered she was at a dead end in an empty patient room. She could hear booted feet echoing through the halls, rapidly approaching her, cutting off other possible exits.

Hiding looked like her only course. Other than the bed, nightstand, and guest chair, the only piece of furniture was a large wardrobe. She opened the door and found that the bottom was taken up with drawers. What kind of wardrobe was this? The upper part was one tall shelf, about the size of a dress shirt. Oh well! She scrambled up onto the shelf and closed the door with her fingernails.

The pounding of her heart covered all sound until someone entered the room in long booted strides. The footsteps continued straight to the wardrobe. The door opened, and Derek Maynard studied her. Hovering over his shoulder was a locate spell.

"There are times I hate magic," Tinker sulked, remaining tucked on the top shelf.

"You are a hard girl to keep pinned down." Maynard motioned her out.

"Unfortunately, not hard enough." She reluctantly unfolded and swung down off the shelf.

Maynard reached into his pocket and produced a bright yellow rectangle. "Gum?"

"I've been told not to take candy from strangers."

He raised one eyebrow, as if saying "Get real" or "How wise" or something truly witty. Tinker supposed that was one of the benefits of keeping one's mouth shut—people made up better dialogue for you than you yourself could imagine. Then again, the trick would never work for her; she couldn't stay quiet. She scowled at him and took the offered piece.

The gum filled her mouth with sweetness, and ran counter to her banging heart.

"Juicy Fruit," She identified the brand. "They say that elves love this stuff."

"Juicy Fruit and peanut butter." Maynard unwrapped a piece for himself. "I have always wondered if it's a cultural thing or something more genetically based. Gods know there are human cultures that have weirder tastes."

She shrugged, not knowing or caring. Why were they standing there trading inane remarks? If Maynard had tracked her down, did it mean that he was going to turn her over to the NSA and correct all their misconceptions? Maynard had been studying her while making what seemed to be a deliberate show of chewing the gum. He reached out now to rub the triangular mark between her eyebrows.

"Where did this come from?"

"Windwolf." She jerked her head away. It occurred to her that if any human knew what it was, Maynard would. "What does it mean?"

"The elves run a rigid caste system, but sometimes a high-ranked elf can elevate a lower-rank elf. He marks them with a *dau*." Maynard tapped her forehead again. "And they become part of his caste, with all rights and privileges."

"Why'd Windwolf do it to me?"

"Why didn't you ask him at the time?"

"I didn't notice the mark until after he left. I haven't seen him since."

"Ah," Maynard murmured, and nothing more.

He had been dealing with elves too long. Maynard was nearly as obscure as they were. It seemed as if they would spend all day simply chewing gum.

"So, are you going to turn me over to the NSA?"

"Can't," Maynard said.

"Can't? Won't? Shan't?"

"By the rules of the treaty, no elf of any caste can be moved to Earth by any human agency for any reason."

"Rights and privileges?"

Maynard nodded.

Well, the day was suddenly looking up, but it seemed too good to be true. Tinker tested her luck. "I don't think the NSA will see it that way."

"I don't give a fuck," Maynard said. "Lord Windwolf will not allow it, and that's all I care about. I'm walking a delicate line with the elves. I'm not going to piss the viceroy off to make two gun-happy American agents' jobs easy."

"What the hell is a viceroy?"

"You, girl, need a lesson in politics."

6: A DATE WHICH WILL LIVE IN INFAMY

A VICEROY turned out to be a very high position in the elfin government. The word *viceroy* was a weird smash-together of the words *vice* and *royal*, kind of like vice president, but with the idea that the president was somewhere else. In Windwolf's case, it was the queen of the elves, who lived in an area that corresponded with Europe. Windwolf apparently was the youngest elf ever appointed to be a viceroy, but Tinker got the impression it was by default. Windwolf had researched human explorations of the Americas and then led the first elfin landing in the Westernlands once he reached majority. As a colony, it hadn't rated a viceroy, but with Pittsburgh's arrival and the sudden boom in trade, Windwolf had been elevated solely because he was the principal landowner.

This made him a target both inside and outside his clan. Elders in his clan thought someone older with less radical ideas should replace him. The other clans were split—half wanted control of the trade with the humans and the rest wanted to break off contact totally. The queen, though, favored Windwolf, so he remained viceroy.

All things considered, girl genius or not, Windwolf was depressingly out of reach for a human teenager that ran a scrap yard.

Maynard tried to explain the elfin politics to Tinker while escorting her out to his limo. He was hampered by the fact that her grandfather had taught her nothing about human government and very little world geography. (*No use cluttering up one's mind with things that change*, as he'd put it. What she did know came from Lain, who believed in a rounded education: *insects specialize, not humans.*)

"It's in humans' best interest that Windwolf stay viceroy," Maynard finished. "He's an intelligent, honorable being with an open mind. It's also in our best interest to stay on his good side. Letting two minor human agents kidnap his newest family member would surely infuriate him."

"Family member?" Tinker squeaked.

"I'm keeping things simple," Maynard said cryptically. "The elfin guard at the border saw a member of Windwolf's family with two humans, and the humans claimed that person—you—as their prisoner. That's a basic violation of the treaty—I'll have to finesse things to calm the waters. If Windwolf doesn't know about this already, he will shortly. Luckily the border guard called the EIA to help extract you safely."

"You mean I did all that running around for no reason?"

Maynard slanted a look in her direction. "It did keep the NSA from learning the truth about your identity and the whereabouts of Alexander Graham Bell. And it delayed their attempts to remove you from the hospice until I had a chance to arrive. It wasn't a waste of time."

"Where are they now?" Tinker glanced out of the limo's back window at the hospice.

"They've been arrested for violating the treaty. If they're lucky, they won't be summarily executed."

"You're joking."

"I'm not," Maynard said. "The NSA has committed a serious breach of protocol out of ignorance. They're making it worse by refusing to discuss why. Did they explain anything to you?"

She considered him. He currently was the only thing standing between her and the NSA, but that was for Windwolf's sake, not hers. She was only important because of Windwolf. She hedged. "I told you my father was murdered. The NSA think I could be in danger from the same people."

"The NSA don't usually commit two agents for thirty days to protect a little girl."

She glared at him. "I'm not a little girl; I'm a woman."

"Or a woman."

She supposed that keeping the truth from him when he was bound to discover it from the NSA agents sooner or later would only serve to annoy him. "My father was Leonardo Da Vinci Dufae."

She hadn't expected him to recognize her father's name, and was thus surprised when he did.

"Leonardo Dufae? The man who invented the hyperphase gate? Where did the name 'Bell' come from? Is that your egg mother's name?"

Tinker winced. "It's complicated. On the night Leonardo was killed, his office was ransacked and all his notes and computer equipment stolen. About a month later, someone tried to kidnap my grandfather. Grandpa always claimed it was Leonardo's murderers, who realized that what they stole off Leo wasn't complete and thought Grandpa could fill in the missing information. The government stepped in and gave Grandpa a new identity and relocated him out of Pittsburgh. When the Chinese started to build the gate, Grandpa left protective custody and disappeared totally. I'm not sure what he did during the next five years, and what names he went by, but when Pittsburgh was first transported to Elfhome, he was living here under the name of Timothy Bell."

"And to stay in Pittsburgh, he couldn't change it," Maynard guessed. The hasty peace treaty had allowed only residents listed on the census to remain after the first Shutdown, a ruling carried out by armed forces.

"Even when I was born, he was still too afraid to give me the name Dufae. He kept his inventions hidden. Lain always said he was a little loony in that regard."

"Then how did the NSA suddenly find you?"

"I applied to CMU. Since I'm basically homeschooled, and didn't want to be stuck on Earth for a month in order to take the standardized tests, Lain thought I should use my father's legacy to get in. After all these years, with Grandpa dead and all, I didn't think anyone would care who my father was."

Maynard gazed out of the window of his limo, considering what she'd told him. After a moment of silence, he said, "You said the stolen information wasn't complete."

"No. It wasn't." She'd never thought it important, but now maybe it was, and so she tried to piece it all together in her own mind. "If I had just lived with my grandfather, I probably wouldn't know the whole of this, but Oilcan lived with his mother until he was ten, so there are family things he knows that Grandpa never told me. The founder of the Dufae line, hundreds of years ago in France, was an elf. Dufae was a physician to the nobility, and was beheaded in the French Revolution; his wife and son fled to America. When my father and aunt were children, my great-great-"—she paused to count it out—"- great-aunt lived with them. She was over a century old, and she recounted stories that her great-grandmother had told her about the first Dufae.

"What made my father's work so groundbreaking was that much of it wasn't an extension of someone else's work, but was extrapolated from anecdotal information handed down through my family for generations. Apparently Dufae had traveled from Elfhome to Earth, but couldn't get back. If you believe the stories, then Dufae was proof of parallel dimensions."

"The elves had gates?"

"No, not really. It seemed to be a natural phenomenon in certain cave systems, most likely an iron ore embedded in quartz with a great deal of ambient magic present. In human legends, elves were a race that lived 'under a hill.' By all accounts, including Dufae's, elves and humans crossed back and forth between the two dimensions quite freely. Then something happened, and Dufae became stranded on Earth."

"Something happened?" Maynard echoed, puzzled. "Like the 'gates' stopped working?"

"From the stories, yes. Dufae traveled Europe, trying all the gates he knew about, and none of them worked, but he didn't know why."

Maynard frowned over this news for a minute, then turned his mind back to Tinker's father. "I'm not sure I follow. What does this Dufae have to do with Leonardo's plans being incomplete?"

She considered telling Maynard about Dufae's Codex, but decided not to. Let that remain a long-kept family secret. "Because of the great-aunt's stories about Dufae, my father started work on his theories as early as ten, writing down the tales and trying to conduct scientific analyses of them. This was the 1980s and 1990s, just as computers were becoming exponential in ability. When he upgraded to a new computer, he would only move his most recent files across and continue work from there. After Leo's death, my grandfather consolidated everything into one system, but on the night of Leo's murder, his work was spread across half a dozen machines. The thieves only took the one at his offices without realizing there were five more at home. They got information on how to build the gate, but not why it was designed the way it was in the first place."

Maynard groaned at the stupidity of the thieves. "I've seen the intelligence reports showing that the gate was definitely your father's work, but there have always been things that puzzled me about the whole thing. Most inventions have been a footrace to see who could make the breakthrough first. With the gate, your father's work came out of the blue, and it's been a scramble to work backward to see how he designed it. This explains why there were no small-scale experiments, but it leaves the biggest question."

"Which is?"

"Why in the world did the Chinese steal the design and sink so much money into building the gate when there was no proof that it would work? It's stunning that it does work."

"Mostly works. The little problem of Pittsburgh swapped to Elfhome is because the plans were flawed, but the Chinese haven't been able to fix the problem."

Maynard turned his focus on Tinker. "NSA thinks that you can build a gate from scratch, without the design flaws of your father's."

"It's a possibility that they're seriously entertaining."

"Can you?"

It would be safer to say no. Straight-out lie. There was the matter of the placement-test questions, but there were levels to understanding. One has to know enough to answer rote questions. The higher level was understanding to the point of creation. It was an invisible barrier that divided the likes of Newton and Einstein from the rest of the scientific world. Could a test question expose that level of understanding? Did she even have it? She thought she understood her father's theories, but she could be wrong. Certainly she'd never played with them, attempting to create or correct.

"You can," Maynard said while she wavered.

"I might." She tempered it. "There's a profound lack of parts for such items in Pittsburgh."

"And there's the matter of getting into space," Maynard quipped.

"It doesn't have to be in space. My family's stories are filled with foreboding as to what might have caused the gates to fail. My father thought that space was just the safest place to put a doorway between worlds."

"So he wasn't predicting the veil effect?"

Tinker looked out the side window, past the river to the elfin forest. "No. To be quite frank, I think he would be horrified."

She had Maynard take her to the yard, and as she hoped, Oilcan was there. Her cousin hugged her and held on—he had heard about her kidnapping. His obvious source of information, Nathan, was there, glaring at Maynard as if he were responsible for dragging her away instead of returning her.

Tinker kicked him. "Act nice. He's one of the good guys. This is Nathan Czernowski. He's a close friend of the family. Nathan, this is Derek Maynard."

"I recognize him," Nathan stated, barely civil, but extended his hand.

"Officer Czernowski." Maynard shook hands.

It struck Tinker that they were the same height and coloring. Nathan, though, was nearly twice the width, all muscle, and had a steady plainness to him, like a piece of stone.

"What the hell happened?" Nathan asked. "Your front door was wide open, your tripwire was activated, but your home system was shut down."

Tinker sighed and tried to explain, keeping the facts bare. She didn't bother to mention the NSA misgivings that her life was in danger. Maynard, however, added them in.

"I need to get back and deal with the NSA agents," Maynard finished. "There's a slim chance they'll be freed by morning, but I'll let you know before they are."

"Thanks."

After Maynard left, Nathan hugged her, lifting her off the ground.

"Hey!" she complained, tired of being manhandled for the day.

"I was worried about you." He put her down.

"I can take care of myself," she said, more for Oilcan's sake than Nathan's.

"What's this?" Nathan rubbed the mark between her eyes.

"Oh, that." She sighed. "Windwolf has elevated me to elf status or something like that. Maynard says it's kind of like he adopted me into his family."

Nathan frowned and rubbed the mark harder. "You let him tattoo you?"

"No!" She jerked her head back. "He had the spell initialized and coded to a word and a kiss. Apparently the mark is a big deal, so it could have some authorization coding in it so someone with a temporary tattoo kit can't duplicate it."

"He kissed you?"

She had never seen jealousy on Nathan before, but still she recognized it on his face. "Oh, cut it out. It was a little peck on the forehead." She turned away from him as she recalled cuddling with Windwolf at the hospice. Had that actually happened, or was it some drug dream? "Look, it's a good thing. The NSA tried to kidnap me, and Windwolf's mark kept them from doing it."

It was hard to tell what annoyed Nathan more—that the NSA had grabbed her or that Windwolf had permanently marked her. She hadn't suspected that Nathan would react with such primal male chest beating. "He's the viceroy, Nathan, get over it!"

And even Nathan could see the unlikelihood that an elf noble would be interested in a little junkyard dog. "I'm sorry, Tink."

He turned her toward him and leaned down to kiss her, cautiously at first, and then hungrily. She was too tired and annoyed with life to enjoy it completely.

When he broke the kiss, he leaned his forehead against hers and asked huskily, "Do you want me to take you home?"

That put a thrill through her. Nathan. Her place. Her big bed. No. That was too scary a thought, despite the sudden wanting throb inside of her. The couch? Yes, she could deal with the couch, but still, the bed was frighteningly close by.

"No," she said once she swallowed down her heart. "I've got some things I want to do here," she lied. Then, because she knew Nathan wouldn't allow her to go home alone, not after today, she said, "Oilcan can take me home."

Oilcan looked struck dumb. When he realized that they were talking about him, he nodded. "Yeah! Sure!"

"Okay." Nathan stepped away reluctantly. "If you need anything, just call me."

"I will," she promised.

"See you tomorrow night." Nathan went to his squad car and drove away.

It wasn't until after he left that she realized he meant for their date.

"What the hell was that all about?" Oilcan broke the silence. "What's tomorrow night?"

"We're going to the Faire tomorrow night."

"You're dating Nathan? Since when?"

"Friday! You've got a problem with that?"

"I don't know. It just seems weird. You two kissing?" He squirmed. "It's like you're dating me."

"What the hell does that mean?"

"Well, you know Nathan's like family."

"So?" She kicked a dead headlight sitting on the ground. It sailed off to smash with crystal clarity. "You want me to date a complete stranger like . . . like"—she couldn't say Windwolf because that would hurt—"Maynard?"

"No! Well, maybe." Oilcan rubbed at the back of his neck. "I don't know. Nathan knows you're smart, but I don't think he knows how smart."

"What does that have to do with anything?" She didn't want to point out that she and Oilcan got along fine, even though they both knew she was smarter than he was.

"You're only going to get smarter. You're not happy unless you're learning something. Nathan, he's at the top of his game right now. He sees you and thinks he can handle it, but he doesn't realize things aren't going to stay the same."

"Could you at least let us get one date in before you doom the whole relationship?"

"As long as you keep in mind that it's probably not going to work out."

"Why not? You said yourself that Nathan already knows what I am."

"I don't know if Nathan has ever really *listened* to you. I mean, when you're talking about racing, or bowling, or horseshoes, he's listening to you. But when you talk about what's really in your soul, the real you, he's tuning you out. His eyes glaze over, and he does all sorts of fiddly things, and if you go on too long, he tries to shut you up."

He does? Embarrassingly enough, she had never noticed. She shrugged it away. If she didn't notice, it couldn't be something hugely important. "I'm going to have to date someone, sometime."

"Have you told Nathan about CMU?"

"Actually, Lain released me from that. She said I only had to go to college if I really wanted to."

"And?" Oilcan asked, as if it was still a possibility.

She opened her mouth to say no, but for some reason it came out, "I don't know!"

Nor did she know later as Oilcan dropped her off at her loft. She cleaned up the mess that the NSA agents had made of her place, trying to wrap her mind around the sudden changes in her life. Too much had hit at once. If it had just been Windwolf, or the EIA, or CMU, or the NSA, or Nathan, maybe she could have dealt with any one. She finally drew decision trees to map out her possible actions.

Windwolf yielded no branches; there was nothing for her to actually do, so she tried to delete him from her mind. Unfortunately, sometimes a mind wasn't as obedient as a piece of hardware.

Nor did the NSA tree provide actions; they were dealt with for the time being. EIA worked out to be a simple "help Maynard or annoy Maynard." While Windwolf's adoption obviously provided her with protection from the EIA, it seemed wiser to help the EIA.

Nathan broke down to the simple "go on the date or cancel." Because of her age and Nathan's reticence, neither would lead to massive changes in her life.

The tree for going to college, however, disturbed her greatly. The branch for attending splintered into multitudes of possibilities. Staying in Pittsburgh yielded unending sameness. For the first time she wondered if Lain was right; was she in danger of stagnating if she stayed in Pittsburgh?

She glanced at Nathan's tree. If she dated him, at least that was some change. She circled the "go on the date." She had promised him to try to look older. That required better clothes and makeup, of which she had neither. She made a note to get both in the morning.

* * *

Maynard called and told her that the NSA agents would be released in the morning. "Unfortunately the elves don't deal with gray very well. We either had to execute Durrack and Briggs or let them go. While killing them would keep them safely out of our hair, it was a little excessive."

Tinker made sure the door was triple bolted, and she armed her security system before going to bed. The events of the last few days combined oddly in her mind until she was dreaming of Foo dogs, crows, Riki, the NSA agents, and Windwolf all jumping through magic hula hoops. Despite the teleporting abilities of the hula hoops, the dream played out entirely at the EIA warehouse. At some point, the Foo dogs ran off with the magical toys, reducing her to tears.

"Do not cry." Windwolf produced a ring. "This works just as well. The gates can be quite small, if you understand the quantum effect of magic."

"What about the veil effect?" Tinker breathed as he slid the ring onto her oil-stained finger.

"Here it is." He placed a bridal veil on her head. The shimmering fabric was at once invisible and a glistening black caught full of stars.

Proving that she had paid attention to the handful of weddings she'd attended, Maynard married them in what seemed a fairly accurate though amazingly short ceremony.

"Do you take this woman to be your lawfully wedded wife?"

"She is already mine." Windwolf parted the veil to touch the spell mark on Tinker's forehead.

"Do you take this man to be your husband?" Maynard asked.

"I really just want to mess around," Tinker said.

"Oh, okay." Maynard stepped back out of the room, saying, "You can kiss the bride."

Windwolf did more than kiss her. She was riding a wave of orgasm when her doorbell woke her. She opened her eyes, the morning sun spilling across her bed, an echo of the pleasure still washing through her. The doorbell rang again, and she stirred in her nest of rumpled white linens to find her bedside clock.

It was seven in the morning.

Who the hell was ringing her doorbell at seven in the freaking morning?

She fumbled with her spyhole display and discovered the NSA agents actually standing on her doorstep and ringing the doorbell like real people instead of breaking in.

She thumbed the display to two-way sound. "What do you want?"

Briggs located the camera and microphone first and pointed it out to Durrack while saying, "We want to talk to you, Ms. Bell."

Corg ducked slightly to look earnestly into the camera, as if trying to make eye-to-eye contact with her. In an apologetic mood, he actually had a boyish face with dark eyes and thick eyelashes. "We're sorry about yesterday; we let our concern for your safety carry us away. We really crossed the line, and we're very, very sorry. We promise it won't happen again."

"You sound like you get a lot of practice at groveling, Durrack."

Hannah laughed at her partner while he rubbed an embarrassed look off his face.

"Well, actually, being a federal agent is hard on relationships," Durrack confessed. "Chicks really dig the spy thing, but they really get pissed off when you miss their birthday because you were off saving the world."

Tinker laughed despite being annoyed at the NSA agents. "So you save the world a lot?"

"Small American slices of it, yes."

Briggs pushed Durrack impatiently aside and leaned close to the camera. "Ms. Bell, we believe you're in a great deal of danger."

Tinker sighed, resting her forehead on her nightstand. Let them in or chase them away? Neither seemed like a good idea.

"We promise to behave," Durrack added.

Yeah, right. She didn't believe them totally, but she suspected they weren't going away—at least not without talking to her face-to-face. She crawled out of bed, pulled on some clean clothes, and padded out to her front door, rubbing sleep out of her eyes. She supposed it was a good sign that they didn't rush her when she unbolted the door and swung it open.

Why was everyone suddenly coming in jumbo sizes? Both NSA agents towered over Tinker. Corg Durrack was broad-shouldered with deep chest and lean waist, giving him the proportions of a comic book hero. He fairly bristled with weapons and carried a white wax paper bag that he held out as a peace offering. "We brought donuts."

Briggs scoffed quietly at this. The female agent wore a long-sleeve shirt and pants that looked like black wet paint. Apparently the shirt doubled as a sports bra, and if she wore panties, they were thong. Still, Briggs was a stunning example of what strength training could do to the female body. As she stalked through the loft like a caged cat, the outfit showed off muscles on her long legs that Tinker didn't know women could develop.

"Do you want to start over from the top?" Tinker accepted the bag and swung up onto her countertop in an effort to keep a level playing field. "My life is in danger, oh ah, and you want to drag me back to Earth in order to lock me up in protective custody."

"Well, I'm glad you're taking this seriously." Briggs matched Tinker's sarcastic tone.

"I know all about protective custody." Tinker peered cautiously into the wax paper bag. Inside were four large coffee rolls of pure decadence. "My grandfather did some time in it, and he had choice stories to tell of the victim, rather than the criminal, being the prisoner."

Durrack sighed. "The sad truth is that we can't arrest all the bad guys."

"'Sorry, madam, I couldn't get your rapist, but I did lock up the baby girl next door just in case.'" Oops, judging by the look Durrack gave Briggs, there was only so far Tinker could push the NSA agents—or at least Briggs—and she had just hit it. "Come on; let's do a history update. Twenty-five years ago, a quarter of a century, someone killed my father. They've got their gate. They don't know that I exist, unless someone leaked the CMU information, but even then, there's no proof I can *build* a gate. Hell, even I don't know if I can build one. There's a big jump between knowing something well enough to answer elementary questions and being able to create a working prototype. Oilcan does as well as I do on just about any test, and can understand what I create, but he can't develop things on his own. The spark isn't there."

"But you have the spark, and anyone who puts Alexander Bell together with Tinker is going to know it too."

Tinker picked up a dog-eared copy of *Scientific American* off the counter. "In the last quarter century, scientists have been working feverishly to understand what Leo did. This magazine is two years old, but there's an article in here from some Norwegian who's doing field manipulation using quantum particles."

"Torbjörn Pettersen," Durrack said.

"Pardon?" Tinker said.

Durrack tapped the magazine. "The Norwegian was Torbjörn Pettersen, and he's been missing since that article hit the streets."

"Oh." She dug out the most recent issue—although the mailing lag made it the December issue and not the May one. She noted with a sudden relief that even though she paid the exorbitant subscription, it was still addressed to *Timothy Bell, Neville Island, Pittsburgh on Elfhome.* "What about"—she checked the table of contents—"Lisa Satterlund?"

"Dead," Briggs said simply.

Durrack expanded the single word: "Satterlund was killed during a kidnapping attempt in December."

"Marcus Shipman? Harry Russell?" Tinker named the two scientists she could remember who had published important advances in gate theory.

"Missing," Briggs said.

Durrack sighed. "Harry Russell had a GPS chip on him after a DWI arrest. We found the chip in the stomach of a catfish in St. Louis. The forensic scientists are trying to determine when he died. The thing is that, for at least four months, the chip wasn't in North America."

"You think he was here in Pittsburgh?"

"Yes."

"It's a possibility," Durrack allowed. "It's possible that the kidnappers just managed to block the signal while holding him in the United States. It seems more likely that they brought him to Elfhome."

"To kill him and dump his body into the river?"

"These people use excessive force," Briggs snapped. "His death was probably accidental."

"How he died isn't as important as the fact that you're still in peril," Durrack said. "At the moment, we have an advantage. You're a complete blank: no fingerprints, no retina scans. The other side is going to be looking for a guy about to hit middle age. With just a name change, you could vanish into the general populace. Hell, you could go to MIT or Caltech and live in the dorms. That's assuming you want to attend college. If you don't, we could set you up with a lab."

"Like I want to turn my life over to you." Tinker shook her head as her stomach growled. "I have a life here. There's my cousin, and all my friends. Besides, I thought you couldn't take me off Elfhome since technically I'm an elf now."

"We can't *take* you off, but you can request permission to leave," Briggs said. "Elves have traveled to Earth in the past, but they usually only stay thirty days, until the next transfer. They don't like living without magic."

"Neither do I," Tinker said, and gave in to the temptation of the donuts, taking out one of the still-warm pastries. "There's lots of cool possibilities with magic I haven't explored yet. If I go back to Earth, I'd lose that ability."

"The U.S. government would be willing to make it worth your while," Durrack said. "Everything we offered before and then some. A house. Someone to cook and clean so all you have to do is invent. A fully equipped lab. A law firm to file your patents."

"What does the government get out of this?" Tinker unrolled the spiral coffee roll, tearing off bite-sized pieces. "I know there's a price hidden in there somewhere."

"The U.S. gets insurance that the Chinese don't get a land-based gate first."

"Why does the U.S. want a gate?"

"Part of it is that they're used to being the ones with the new toy, and it annoys them to no end that the Chinese have something that they don't. But there's also a fear of what a land-based gate can and can't do. What if it lets you travel through time, or to several dimensions? If the Chinese get it first, they're not going to share information any more than they've shared details on the gate."

"I'm not going to leave my cousin," Tinker said.

"He could come with you," Durrack said. "We set him up a new identity. He could pick out a name nicer than Orville or Oilcan. He could go to college too. I hear he's an intelligent young man—it seems a waste for him to spend his life as a tow truck driver when he's got the smarts to be anything he wants. It could be a great opportunity for him."

Durrack would say anything to manipulate her, but it didn't make it any less true. While Oilcan occasionally stated that Earth had been too big and crowded, he complained about the lack of people their own age and temperament. He hovered around the Observatory, drawn to the women postdocs, but was never able to do more than watch them come and go.

The NSA agents waited for her response.

"Let me talk to my cousin. See what he says."

"We can take you over to his place."

"Oh, stop pushing," Tinker said. "I'm going to take a shower, and then go shopping for clothes. I've got a date tonight." And Nathan wasn't going to be happy about any possibility of her leaving town; his whole family clung to Pittsburgh, refusing to leave. "And I've got lots of hard decisions to make. So just go away; leave me alone to figure out what I want in life."

Tinker took the well-worn path down through the steep hillside orchard, carefully avoiding the beehives, to Tooloo's store at the bottom of the hill. The store itself was a rambling set of rooms filled with unlikely items, many ancient beyond belief. One section was secondhand clothes, where Tinker often found shirts, pants, and winter coats. Some of the clothes were elfin formal wear that Tinker drooled over from time to time but never found any reason to buy. Even secondhand they were pricey.

There was an odd collection of general goods, but the main focus of the store was food—often the rarest items to find in Pittsburgh. In an area behind the store, Tooloo had an extensive garden and various outbuildings: a barn, a henhouse, and a dove coop. She had fresh milk, butter, eggs, freshwater fish, and doves all year. During the summer, she also sold honey, fruit, and vegetables.

Tooloo herself seemed to be an eclectic collection. Locals referred to her as a half-breed, left over from the last time elves visited Earth. Tooloo certainly had the elfin ears, spoke fluent Low and High Elvish, and could be counted on as having in-depth knowledge on matters arcane. Unlike any full elf, she looked old, a face filled with wrinkles and silver hair that reached her ankles. Her elfin silks were faded and nearly threadbare, and she wore battered high-top tennis shoes.

Whereas Lain was a known quantity, comforting in her familiarity, Tooloo refused to be known. Asked her favorite color, it would be different each time. Her birthday ranged the year, if she would admit to having one. Even her name was unknown, Tooloo being only a nickname. In eighteen years, Tinker had never heard Tooloo mention anything about her own parentage.

If Tinker's grandfather was the source of Tinker's scientific thinking, and Lain the source of all common sense, then Tooloo was her font of superstition. Despite everything, Tinker found herself believing a found penny meant good luck, spilt salt required a pinch thrown over the shoulder to ward off bad luck, and that she should never give an elf her true name.

Thinking about what she'd say to Oilcan about the NSA proposal and her date with Nathan, Tinker wasn't prepared for Tooloo's reaction to recent events.

"You little monkey!" Tooloo swept out of the back room that served as her home, shaking a finger at Tinker. "You've seen Windwolf again, haven't you? I told you to stay away from him."

Tinker turned her back so she didn't have to look at the scolding finger. "You've told me lies."

"No, I haven't. Only bad will come of this. He'll swallow you up, and nothing will be left."

"You said he marked me with a life debt." And as Tinker said it, she realized that Tooloo had told the truth, only the half-elf had twisted it somehow. "You didn't tell me that he was in debt to me."

"It's a curse, either way." Tooloo came to rub the mark between Tinker's eyebrows. "Oh, he's got his hands on you now. The end begins."

"What do you mean?"

"What I've said all along—but then you've never listened. You come asking again and again for the same story and go away not listening despite how many different ways I tell you."

"It can't be the same and different at the same time."

"Windwolf is dangerous to you." Tooloo used the scolding finger again. "Is that simple enough for you? I've tried to keep you hidden all these years from him, but he's found you now, and marked you as his."

Tinker realized suddenly that as one of the few people in Pittsburgh who spoke High Elvish, Tooloo would have certainly been the one asked about Tinker's identity after the saurus attack. "I don't understand."

"Obviously." Tooloo snorted and moved off to rearrange stock.

From years of dealing with Tooloo, Tinker recognized that the conversation had come to an impasse. She changed the subject to the reason she was at the store. "I have a date with Nathan Czernowski. We're going to the Faire."

"Ah, what is with you and fire?"

"What does that mean?"

"It's dangerous to offer a man something he wants but that can't be his."

"Why can't it be his?"

Tooloo caught her chin. "When you look at Czernowski, do you see your heart's desire?"

"Maybe."

"You know your heart so little? I don't think so. You do this to satisfy that little monkey brain of yours. Curiosity is a beast best starved."

"Nathan wouldn't hurt me."

"If only the same could be said of you."

Tinker stomped to the clothes, trying to puzzle that warning out. Was it something in the water that made older women impossible to understand?

At Tooloo's she found an elfin jacket. Or at least, on an elf it was a jacket. On her it was a duster, coming down nearly to her ankles. The sleeves were slightly long, but she could fold them back. A mottled gold silk, it had a purple iris hand painted on the back. She fell in love with it but could find nothing to complement it, so she took her hoverbike into Pittsburgh in search of an older self.

Kaufmann's was a Pittsburgh tradition, the oldest department store located downtown. It had withstood flood, suburbia, the invasion of foreign department stores, and being transported into the fey realms.

"I need some clothes to make me look more mature," she told the saleswoman in an area marked "Women's," who pointed her firmly toward "Petites." She found a push-up bra that made the most of her chest, a clingy black slip dress, and high-heeled shoes.

"I need a cut that makes me look older," she told the hairstylist, who eyed her hacked hair with slight dismay.

"Did you tattoo yourself, sweetheart?" the stylist asked, gingerly touching Windwolf's mark on Tinker's forehead.

"Umm, ah, it's a long story." Remembering Nathan's reaction to the mark, Tinker raked her hair forward with her fingers. "Is there any way I can cover this with my bangs?"

"What bangs?" The stylist found the longest lock and pulled it forward to show that it fell short of the mark. "Sweetheart, at this point all you can do is wear it proudly."

In the end, the stylist could do little more than even out the length of her hair and then rub a gel into it so it stood up in little spikes. "It's retro chic," the stylist chanted. "Very elegant."

The makeover woman eyed Windwolf's mark and pronounced it extremely cool.

"Is there anything that will cover it up?"

The woman laughed again. "Not without an inch or two of concealer. Why would you want to? It becomes you; it makes you very exotic looking."

"The guy I'm dating tonight doesn't like it."

The woman swabbed the mark with cleanser and shook her head. "He better learn to like it; it's there to stay."

"Can you make me look older then, like I was in my twenties?"

"Why does every woman under twenty want to look over it, and every other woman in the world wants to look under it?" She resoaked the cotton ball, took Tinker's face in one hand, and started to clean her face gently. "Men, that's why. Honey, don't be in a rush to change for a man. You might make him happy, but most likely only at the cost of making yourself miserable. . . . You've got wonderful skin," she cooed.

"I've got freckles."

The makeup woman tsked. "Here's the secret, honey; you've got what men want. You're young, and pretty, and nicely padded in all the right places. You might be saying, 'Oh, my hair isn't down to my ankles, I have freckles, and my ears aren't pointed,' but men see the chest, the hips, the butt, and the pretty face—in that order—and little else. You can have any man in this city, so take your time and be picky. Make *him* work to get you."

Perched on a bar stool, Tinker spent nearly two hours and nearly a hundred dollars learning the arcane skill of applying makeup and dealing with men.

To some degree, she managed to achieve looking older than her real self. How much older, she wasn't sure, but she felt a little wiser in the ways of the world. She detoured on her way back to her bike for condoms and a can of mace for "protection, just in case of any emergencies."

It wasn't until then that she remembered Riki.

Someone had been busy while she was gone. Her workshop trailer was back into place, square and level as if it had never been moved. All the various power links were reconnected, and the air conditioner was even back in its slot. Someone had also gathered up all the blood-soaked bandages into a plastic garbage bag and then scrubbed the floor and worktable clean of blood until the air smelled sweetly of peroxide.

She would have suspected Oilcan of the progress, except that the flatbed was missing and Riki's motorcycle sat next to the office door. When she found the offices empty, she wandered through the scrap yard, wondering where the grad student was. Had he gone with Oilcan on some errand, or just taken a walk?

Finally something drew her eye toward the crane, and she found him at last, perched on the boom, sixty feet straight up. Still dressed in the black leather pants and jacket of yesterday, he sat on the end of the boom, a black dot on the blue sky.

"What the hell?" Tink scrambled up the ladder to the crane's cage. What was he doing out there? Was he planning on jumping? How had he even gotten out there? She leaned out the window and saw that with the boom level, it was basically a straight walk out from the cage.

"Riki? Riki?" she called in a low pitch, trying to get his attention without startling him.

He glanced over his shoulder at her, the wind ruffling his black hair. "Oh, there you are."

"Sorry that I was late. I got busy and forgot about you." She winced. Maybe that wasn't the right thing to say at a time like now.

"Your cousin was here." Riki stood up and casually picked his way back along the narrow boom. He had her datapad with him, and it caught the sun and reflected it in blazes of sheer white. Blackness and brilliance, he moved through seemingly open sky. "Oilcan called Lain, and she let him know I was legit."

She drew back from the window, gripping the operator's chair. Just watching him made her suddenly afraid of falling. "What the hell are you doing out there?"

"I have a thing about heights." He leaned in the window. Unlike yesterday, he seemed relaxed and pleased, a lazy smile on his face. "They clear my head. I think better when I'm high up."

"Get in here; you're making me nervous."

He laughed and swung his long thin legs in and sat framed in the window. "Sorry. I forget how much it bugs people. The sky was too perfect, though."

She looked out the other window. The sky was a stunning deep blue, with massive stray clouds dotting it, huge and fluffy as lost sheep; only when you gazed at them, you saw how complex they were, with lines so crisp they were surreal. A cool wind scented with the endless elfin forest just beyond the Rim moved through the blueness, herding the sheep. It was the kind of sky she had sat and stared at as a child. "Yeah, it's perfect." When she turned back to him, he was watching her, head cocked to one side. "What?"

"Just that you gave that thought before you passed judgment."

"Thanks. I think."

He held out her datapad. "I was reading over your notes. They're brilliant."

She blushed as she snatched it back. "I really didn't mean for other people to see them." She glanced down at the pad. He had her theory for magic's waveform pulled up. In the scratch space, he'd worked through her equations, double-checking her work. "You followed this?"

"Mostly." He held out his hand for the pad.

She reluctantly surrendered it back.

He closed her documents and enlarged the scratch space, clearing out his work. "If I'm understanding this right, the multiple universes can be represented by a stack of paper." He drew several parallel lines. "Earth is at the bottom of the stack, and Elfhome is somewhere higher up." He labeled two of the lines appropriately. "Now magic is coming through the entire stack as a waveform." He drew a series of waves through the stack. "Since both the stack and the waveform are uniform, the point where the wave intersects the individual universe is constant; it always hits Earth at N and Elfhome at N+1."

"In a nutshell, yes." Tinker looked at him in surprise. She had tried to explain her theory several times, but never using this model. It seemed so clear and simple. Of course, one of the reasons it was easy to understand was that Riki had ignored the fact that the universes weren't stacked like paper, but were overlapping in a manner that boggled the mind. To reach out and touch a point meant that your finger would almost be touching a zillion identical points across countless dimensions, separated only by that weird sideways step that made it another reality. Of course, only in the nearby realities were you touching that same spot. Farther away you were touching another position, and farther away, like on Elfhome, you never existed because at some extremely distant time, life took a different path and elves came about instead of humans.

"This is what I don't follow." Riki pulled up her notes again, scrolled through them, and found what he was looking for. "I came here to see if I could wrap my brain around it."

"It's not fully formed." She sighed unhappily at it. "I hate it when there are things in the universe that I don't understand."

"It looks like you're trying to figure out how to reach other dimensions."

"Well, the real question is: Why do we always return to the same Elfhome? At least, we seem to. All indications are that we return to the exact dimension."

"Well, the gate generates the same field."

"Consider all the universal changes. We start on Earth, which is spinning with the gate in orbit over China, so the veil effect has to travel through the Earth's core. Then the planet is slowly wobbling through the precession of equinoxes. We've got the Moon's effect on Earth, and then the Earth moving around the Sun, which is moving around the center of the Milky Way galaxy.

"We're talking about numerous vectors that we're traveling in at any one time. That Pittsburgh returns to the same Elfhome, again and again, indicates something other than just dumb luck."

Riki grasped what she was talking about. "Like we're dealing with a universal constant. If you can travel from one dimension to a second dimension once, you'll always be able to?"

"Yeah, some commonality between the two dimensions."

"So how do you make a gate to a third dimension?"

"A third dimension?"

"Well, with countless dimensions available, why only travel to just one?"

"Two seems to be plenty for us to handle right now."

"Well, surely there are more than just two dimensions with the same commonality. You'd expect something more like a string of pearls, linked together on a silk thread."

"Oh, that's elegant." Tinker gazed out at the perfect sky, but she was looking at a strand of planets strung together in a black universe. Earth. Elfhome. Worlds unknown. "But what's the thread?"

"The gate traverses the thread."

"Yes."

"Do you understand how the gate works?"

"Oh, not you too!"

"What?"

"All of a sudden, that's all anyone seems to care about," Tinker snapped. "Gates and babies."

"Babies?" Riki cocked his head at her. "What did you do to your hair? I like it that way."

She frowned at him. Her hair? She put a hand to her hair, touched the gelled tips and suddenly recalled Nathan's date. "Oh, no, what time is it?"

Riki tugged up his leather jacket's sleeve to show his watch. It read 4:38.

"Oh shit, I'm going to be late!"

"Where are you going?"

"On a date! To the Faire! Hey, you should go. It's Midsummer Eve's Faire tonight, so it's extra special. The Faire grounds are out just beyond the Rim." She leaned out the window but the Hill blocked any sign of the Faire. She pointed out the Hill, explaining that the Faire grounds lay behind it. "Just ask anyone for directions. On any old map, it's off of where Centre Avenue used to be."

"Will there be a lot of humans there?"

"Yeah, sure, don't worry; you won't stand out."

"Okay then, I'll be there."

There was a note tacked on her front door. By the style of paper—thick, creamy, handmade linen—and the elegant script, she guessed that it was from Windwolf. A single piece of paper trifolded, the note was sealed shut with a wafer of wax and a spell that would notify the writer that the note had been opened, and perhaps by whom. The outside had her name written so fancy that she didn't recognize it at first:

Tinker

The inside gleamed softly as she unfolded, a second spell being triggered, but it faded before she could tell what it did. Unfortunately the writing was in a language that she could only guess to be High Elvish.

She considered driving to Tooloo's to get it translated, but the old half-elf would probably only lie to her. Maynard? She glanced at the clock—after five. Nathan would be here within an hour, which didn't give her time to go downtown and back. If she took it with her to the Faire, though, surely someone would be able to read it to her.

Nathan knocked at exactly six o'clock, and looked slightly dazed when she opened the door. "Wow, you look wonderful."

"Thanks!" She stepped out onto the sloop, armed her security system, and locked the door. Her outfit had no pockets, and it had taken an hour to pare things-to-be-carried down to a single key and Windwolf's note; she stood a moment, unsure what to do with the key. The note was fairly simple to carry, but she couldn't hold the key all night. Her bra presented a natural pocket, so she tucked the key under her breast. Would it stay there? She jiggled a moment. Yes. "Are we going to eat first? I forgot to eat all day."

Embarrassingly enough, Nathan had watched the whole key thing and now stammered, "Y-y-yeah, I've made reservations at one of the Rim's enclaves, Poppymeadow."

She tried to ignore the burn on her face. "I didn't think you liked elfin food."

"Well, it's like eating at my mom's; you get what's being served, and if you don't like it, they still make you eat it."

"They do not."

"Okay, they make you pay for it, and they don't give out doggie bags."

He wasn't being logical. "So why are we going?"

"Because I know you like it."

She thought of the makeover woman's advice and nodded slowly. "Okay."

In the car, Nathan became oddly silent as he headed for the Rim.

"What do people normally talk about on dates?" Tinker asked to break the silence.

Nathan shifted uncomfortably, as if this stressed that he was older and more experienced than she was. "Well, normally you get to know each other. Where you're from, who your parents are, if you have brothers and sisters. You know. Background info."

"We know all that."

"Yeah," Nathan said unhappily. "Common interests and if nothing else, the weather."

Common interests? Bowling? That made her think of Windwolf. No, no, not a good idea.

"It sure was hot this Shutdown." She started the inane conversation about the weather.

As the steelworkers had at one time divided themselves into richly ethnic neighborhoods, so did the current inhabitants. The UN workers, which made up the bulk of the EIA, lived within downtown's triangle of land, using the rivers to shield them on two sides against packs of wargs, the occasional saurus, and other Elfhome creatures with big mouths and sharp teeth. On the South Side, sheltered less so by the Monongahela River and the bulk of Mount Washington, was a set of Americans whose expertise was the freight trains that did the East Coast run. Mixed in with them were the oil workers who kept a steady supply of natural gas flowing throughout the region, supplied by gas wells long since tapped on Earth. On the sliver of the North Side remaining, a Chinatown had grown up, part of the treaty with China when their gate triggered the whole mess. Native Pittsburghers were sprinkled everywhere, refusing to move despite everything.

Lastly, in Oakland, were the elves.

The elfin businesses sat just beyond the part of old Oakland that had been razed by the Rim. The southern side of the street was graveled parking lots with large warning signs that the lot fell into the Rim's influence during Shutdown and Startup. The northern side of the street was elfin enclaves, half a block wide, high-walled and gated, built firmly on Elfhome. Once through the gates, one was in lush private gardens filled with exotic flowers, songbirds, and glowing cousins to fireflies.

Since it was Midsummer Eve, the traffic was heavy for Pittsburgh, and Nathan had to cruise the parking lot for several minutes to find a space. Most of the crowd, however, were heading several blocks to the west where the Earth street ended abruptly in the Faire grounds.

There was a group of mostly elves waiting to be seated as Tinker and Nathan came down the garden path of the Poppymeadow enclave. A female elf with long silvery hair that nearly reached her ankles glanced toward Tinker. Her eyes went wide in surprised recognition. "Tinker *ze domi!*"

Tinker startled; of the handful of elves she knew, this wasn't one. She glanced behind her to see if maybe an elf noble named Tinker was standing behind her. The garden path was empty.

The other waiting diners turned, saw Tinker, and bowed low, murmuring, "Tinker *ze domi!*"

She didn't recognize any of them. To cover her confusion, Tinker bobbed a shallow bow to the crowd and gave a semi-informal greeting. "*Nasadae!*"

The *domo* of Poppymeadow pushed through the diners, bowed low, and gushed out High Elvish faster than Tinker could hope to follow.

"Please, please, *Taunte*," she begged him to use the low tongue.

"You honor me!" the *domo* cried, taking hold of her hands. "Come. Come. You must have the finest seat in the house."

He guided the bewildered Tinker through the waiting diners, into the public eating areas, and to an elegant table set into a small alcove. Nathan followed, looking as mystified as Tinker felt. "Here! Let me be the first to wish you merry!"

"Thank you, but . . ." Tinker started to ask why they were fussing over her, but the *domo* was already gone.

"What was that all about?" Nathan asked.

"I'm not sure," Tinker said slowly.

"What were they saying?"

"You don't speak Elvish?"

"Not really. Just enough to do a traffic stop. What did they say?"

Tinker flashed to the patrol guard who had roughed her up at the hospice on Startup. She pushed the ugly comparison away; no, Nathan wasn't like that. Wait. The hospice.

"Tinker?"

"Um, they recognized me somehow, but I don't know them." Or did she? Was the silver-haired female the one who had helped with the surgery on her hand? Startup had been a blur, but that would be a whole crop of elves who would know her.

"Maybe they know you from the hoverbike racing," Nathan suggested.

Elves called her Tinker-*tiki* at the races, which was a friendly informal condescending address, on the order of "baby Tinker." This had been Tinker *ze domi*, an address of extreme politeness. More likely these *were* elves who knew her from the hospice. Certainly between her arrival with the flatbed at Startup, and Windwolf carrying her through the hospice yelling the next morning, and this morning's fight with the NSA, she had made herself memorable enough. All the elves at the hospice most likely knew that she had saved . . .

Realization hit her. She barely kept her hand from reaching up and touching her forehead. The elves had to be reacting to Windwolf's mark! She glanced worriedly at Nathan. If he thought this weirdness meant that Windwolf did have some claim on her . . . She winced; she didn't want to deal with a jealous Nathan again. What a mess.

The *domo* returned with a bottle labeled in Elvish, two drinking bowls, and a small silver dish of something white. While she was trying to decide if it was sugar or salt or something more exotic, the *domo* flicked it onto her, exclaiming, "*Linsa tanlita lintou!*" He continued in Low Elvish, saying. "May you be merry!"

What the hell? Tinker blinked in surprise, too confused even to form a reaction.

The *domo* pushed one of the small drinking bowls into her hands, saying, "Praise be to the gods."

She at least knew how to react to that. "Praise be," she said, and drank the wine. What was in the glass was clear, sweet as candy, and burned the whole way down. While she gasped for breath, the *domo* vanished again.

"You okay?" Nathan asked, and she nodded. "What did he throw on you?"

"I think it was salt."

"Why?"

"I don't know." Nor could she guess. What had the *domo* said? *Linsa* and *lintou* were both forms of the same word—purity. *Tanlita* was the word *tanta* meaning "will make" in its female form. Pure into purity? Purity into cleanliness?

The food began to arrive on tiny delicate hand-painted dishes. At an enclave, you ate what you were served. Tinker usually liked it because there were no choices to be made, and you weren't stuck with a large portion of something that was only so-so, or in envy of what another person ordered. Sure, you never knew what you were about to be served, or sometimes had already eaten, but it made the entire meal an adventure.

She could really do without adventure and mystery in her life right about now.

Like most businesses in Pittsburgh, the enclaves relied heavily on local produce to supplement the supplies brought in during Shutdown. Thus the dishes appearing before Tinker and Nathan featured woodland mushrooms, walnuts, trout, venison, hare, keva beans, and raspberries. Luckily the dishes came with built-in conversation: *What do you suppose this is? Oh, this is good. Is there more? Are you going to eat that?*

It made it easy for Tinker to ponder what the *domo* meant by "wish you merry." Had she translated that right? Merry what? Merry dinner? Merry Midsummer's Eve? Merry Christmas? Why did languages have to be so vague? This was why she loved math!

During the third round of dishes, the other diners started to appear at the table. They would slip up, eye Nathan doubtfully as he grew more and more surly, then smile warmly at Tinker and press something into her hand, saying, "I wish you merry!" The first was the silver-haired female, with a flower plucked from the enclave garden, which seemed innocent enough. It wasn't until the second diner pressed a silver dime into Tinker's hands that she realized she should have refused the flower. Now she couldn't refuse following gifts without grave insult, something you didn't do with elves. So she smiled and accepted the dime and prayed that Nathan wouldn't blow a gasket. Flowers, coins, note paper folded into packets containing salt, and a small cage of slender vines woven into a cage holding a firefly followed.

"What's with the bug?" Nathan asked.

"I don't know." She winced as she realized that she was whining. "It is kind of cute, in a weird kind of way."

"Why are they doing this?"

"If I told you, you'd get all bent out of shape, and I don't want to deal with that."

He frowned at her and pushed his latest dish away. "Look, why don't we just go to the Faire? I don't feel like eating any more."

The *domo* saved her from having to abandon all the gifts behind. He came forward with a basket while Nathan went off to settle up the bill.

Under all the gifts, she found Windwolf's note. "Please, can you read this—and translate it to low tongue for me?"

"Yes, certainly." He glanced over the note. "It is from Wolf Who Rules. He—" a pause as the *domo* worked through translation from formal to informal "—will see you at the Faire."

Oh wonderful.

"What is it you say: I wish you merry?" she asked awkwardly. "Merry what?"

"Life. I wish you a merry life. May all good things come to you."

That seemed harmless enough. Nathan appeared, waiting, so she didn't ask about the salt or the gifts.

They stopped at the Buick and dropped off the basket. Night had fallen, and the Faire had awakened a gleam of multicolored lights and the beat of exotic music. There by the car, they seemed to be in their own envelope of space-time. Nathan pulled her close, kissing her while slipping his hands under her silk duster and running his hands down the back of her dress. For a little while, it was very nice; his strong warm body holding her, the smell of his musky cologne, and the excitement of kissing in the open darkness. It felt similar to when she raced her bike fast down Observatory Hill, exhilarated by the speed, heart leaping to her throat every time she slid out of control toward the edge of the tree-lined road.

At some point, though, Nathan realized that the duster shielded his hands from any chance passersby, and he slipped them down and then back up, this time under her dress. He straightened slightly, pulling her off her feet, at the same time kissing down her neck to nuzzle into her breasts.

"Nathan." It was getting too scary, and she was a little angry that he was taking it so fast, out in the open, as if he wanted to be seen, so that everyone would think that she belonged to him. It was as if this was his way of marking her.

"No one's here." He was strong enough that he could support her easily with one hand. Their joint focus became his free hand, rough fingertips on her inner thigh, exploring higher.

"Nathan!" she hissed, wriggling in his hold. "Someone might come. Put me down."

"We could get into the car," he groaned into her hair.

Into the car and what? Did he think the car afforded shadows deep enough to disguise what he wanted to do? Or in the car, they could go to someplace more appropriate? His place? Her place?

"No." She squirmed more, tempted now to use elbows, knees, and the practically sharpened tip of her shoes. "I want to go to the Faire."

He gave a long-suffering sigh. "Are you sure?"

"Yes!"

"All right." He set her back onto her feet. "Let's go to the Faire."

The first booth beyond the gate was a portable shrine to Redoeya; she paused to clap and bow to the statue and drop a dime into his silver-strewn hands. She considered, eyes closed, hands clasped. What was it that she wanted? In earlier years she had prayed for things as simple as winning something from one of the booths. Searching her heart, she found only conflicting desires. Finally she prayed simply: *May I figure out what it is I want in life.*

"Why do you do that?" Nathan had hung back, looking a mix of annoyed and bewildered.

"I always do that." She headed for the sweet bun stands as Faire custom number two; one needed to get them fresh and hot. "Tooloo said that if Grandpa wasn't going to put me in the protection of human gods, then she'd see me protected by the elfin ones."

He made a face.

"What?"

"Oh, I was fairly sure you weren't Catholic, but I expected you to be at least Christian."

"And?"

"Nothing."

Nathan bought sweet buns for both of them, and they drifted on, pulled by the tidal force of moving bodies.

There was more of everything at the Faire than she'd ever seen before. Another row had been added to the basic grid to accommodate the additional booths. Despite the extra space, more people strolled through the aisles: elves dressed in human fashions, humans dressed in elfin fashion, parents with infants, couples of mixed races, and most surprisingly of all, armed guards of both races. Tinker had never seen on-duty guards at the Faire before. She wasn't sure if the tension she felt came from the armed presence, or her own sudden unease with Nathan.

"I can't believe there are armed guards here," she said to Nathan as they passed the third guard, her dark EIA uniform and flat black gun a black hole for attention.

"The viceroy was nearly murdered twice," Nathan said. "And then there's the whole thing with the smuggling ring. With this many people in one place, it's the smart thing to do."

"I don't like it."

"You wouldn't have ended up tangling with that saurus if there'd been more than Windwolf and his bodyguard at the Faire."

Tinker flashed to that day, the saurus standing with a foot pinning the lower half of Windwolf's bodyguard to the ground and his upper half in its mouth. In an image that haunted her nightmares, the saurus pulled upward, stretching the guard's body obscenely long before shaking its head, tearing the male in half. She shuddered. "Let's not talk about that."

But once called up, she couldn't stop thinking about the day. Strange how she couldn't recall Windwolf's location until he was yelling in her face to run, and how, even now, she didn't remember him as wounded, only angry.

In a sudden rewrite of history that was almost dizzying, she realized that Windwolf had lost a friend that day, not only torn to shreds but also eaten. How long had they known each other? A hundred years? Poor Windwolf! No wonder he had been so angry.

"Guess." Nathan interrupted her thoughts.

"What?"

"So guess what they named the baby."

Baby? She glanced around and spotted a human woman showing off her baby to curious elves. She had always thought it odd that elves seemed fascinated by babies, but considering what Windwolf had said, a young adult elf may have never seen an infant in his or her life. She had to admit there was something intriguing about the miniaturization of a being that babies represented, but they were, on a whole, too fragile for her to deal with. She supposed that if someday she had "kids" she would have to deal with "babies"—an utterly frightening thought.

Nathan was still waiting for her to guess the baby's name and was growing impatient.

"I don't know the mother. Who is she?"

"What?" A frown quirked at the corner of Nathan's mouth as he scanned the brightly dressed crowd. "No. Not her," he said, spotting the baby being passed around the knot of adults. "My sister's baby. Guess what they called my niece."

Oh, yes, his sister Ginny lived in Bethel Park. She had been waiting for Shutdown to go to Earth in order to have her second child, but the baby came a week early, and she delivered at Mercy Hospital. When Tinker had talked to Nathan before Shutdown his sister hadn't named the baby yet.

"Oh. Um. After you?" Was there a female version of "Nathan"?

"No. Mercy. Mercy Anne."

Yuk! Tinker tried to keep her face neutral and made polite noises. Luckily they'd collided with the mass of people listening to the musicians onstage at the edge of the Faire ground. She didn't recognize the group's name, but they were a common mixed-race band, blending the raw American rock beat and guitars with traditional elfin instruments and melodies. They featured an *olianuni*, and an obvious master playing it, his mallets a blur as he hammered. The guitars snarled around the rich deep bell-like melody beat out by the *olianuni* player. The lead singer was human, growling out a song about the shortness of human life and the reckless abandonment in which the race embraced its fate. In a high pure counter, the elfin backup singer chanted out the thousand blessings of patience.

"Want to dance?" Tinker shouted to Nathan, bobbing in place to the beat of the music.

"Actually, I was working my way to something. Can we find someplace quieter to talk?"

"Okay." Still moving with the beat of the song, she threaded her way through the crowd, trusting him to find a way to follow.

"You know"—he caught up with her beside a fishing booth, where people were trying to fish brightly gleaming *pesantiki* out of a pool with small paper nets—"if you let me go first, I'd open up a path for you to follow."

"Then all I could see would be your back. You can see over me. Here, let's sit."

The next booth down was the *okonomiyaki* cart that usually sat in Market Square. Side benches folded down from it, and there were banners hanging down from the bamboo awning to give the deception of privacy.

"You're still hungry?" Nathan asked.

"I didn't get to eat a lot at the enclave." She felt a little guilty. Enclaves charged a set price that was rather steep. She held up the bag of silver dimes. "Let me pay."

"No, I'll pay." Nathan thumbed out some coins to the Asian man on the other side of the griddle.

They ordered their toppings, and the chef started to mix up the eggs, water, flour, and cabbage for the pancake.

"So?"

"The family across the street from my sister decided to emigrate back to the States, and they signed over their house to the EIA. They had a nice place: a four-bedroom Cape Cod with a two-car garage, and a natural-gas furnace with a wood burner backup system."

"Your point being?"

"Well, it got me thinking," Nathan said. "The house would be a nice starter place for you and me."

"What?" Her cry startled the chef.

"It's a nice place, well maintained. We could nab it now and move in later."

She could only stare at him in surprise.

"We put up curtains," Nathan said. "Buy a few pieces of furniture, and no one would know the difference. It needs sprucing up, so we take our time painting and such."

"You want to live together?"

Nathan took her hand. "I want to marry you."

"Whoa, whoa, whoa. What happened to waiting until I'm nineteen? I thought this was just a date."

"I don't mean right away. I don't want to rush you."

"I don't know—talking about marriage on a first date sounds like rushing."

Nathan winced. "Sorry, I suppose it is. It's just that this house is so perfect. My brother-in-law took me through the place. The rooms are large and sunny, the woodwork is all natural, there's this marvelous stone fireplace in the living room, and there's a level backyard for kids."

Kids?

Her face must have reflected her shock. He laughed.

"It's only eleven months until you're nineteen. In less than two years you'll be twenty." Nathan sounded like he was trying to convince himself. "We've got to look ahead. Sure there are lots of houses out there. Most of them have been standing empty for years; the pipes and windows are broken and roofs need to be replaced. This place is cherry."

"Nathan, I really meant it when I said we should date to see if we liked one another as more than friends. I don't know if I want to marry you."

There was a moment of hurt hidden quickly away. "I'm sorry, Tink; I shouldn't be pushing. I'm the one, after all, who wanted to wait until you're nineteen."

"Yeah." Tinker shook her head vigorously and then looked down, embarrassed to be suddenly so eager to wait. "Is this about the mark? You're rushing because Windwolf made me part of his family?"

"That has nothing to do with it," Nathan said, so surlily that she figured it had everything to do with it.

"Oh, come on, Nathan, he's the viceroy. He's rich and powerful and could have any woman, elf or human, that he wants."

"Exactly."

"Look at me!"

"You're beautiful."

"Not when you compare me to high-caste elf females. You've seen them; everyone on the street stops and stares until they're out of sight."

"Maybe he has a thing for human women," Nathan said.

The possibility that Windwolf might like human women made her insides go weird, like someone had dropped them through hyperspace to some point billions of miles from where she stood. She tried to root herself back to reality and ignore the possible "delicate arrangements" that the brazier might indicate. "I saved his life, twice now. He feels indebted to me. I'm an orphan. He's an elf; he's nearly twelve times my age. He's probably just acting like a father figure to me."

"This has nothing to do with Windwolf." Nathan reached out and took her hand. "It's just made me think, that's all. You're a legal adult. There's no *real* reason to wait."

Having just compared herself to elfin females, Tinker felt a stab of sympathy and guilt for Nathan. How could he compete for her attention when just the idea of Windwolf kept making her feel all goofy? Nathan's interest in her had been intriguing until he started to talk about marriage. All of Windwolf, from his thoughts to his interest, did weird things to her emotions.

Nathan was waiting for an answer, and she didn't know what to say. She scrambled for something, and came up with, "I've got to go pee."

Nathan let go of her hand, and she fled. Why did he have to go all serious on her? Why couldn't he just take it slow and let her get used to the idea? And what was that scene at the parking lot? Was he going to try that again the moment they were alone in his car? Did he think they were going to have sex tonight?

Suddenly she just wanted to be home in her own bed, alone.

She headed for the Faire entrance, but her tight skirt and high heels were making it difficult to run away. And how was she going to get home? Like a fool, she hadn't brought money enough for a taxi. She could call Oilcan, but how would he react? He might think something worse had happened between her and Nathan—and that would be bad.

She hit a patch of soft dirt, and her heels sunk deep, making her trip. Hands caught her before she fell, righting her.

"Thank y—oh." Her words dried in her mouth as she realized it was Windwolf holding her lightly.

What was it about him that inspired so many emotions all at once? She peered up at the viceroy for all of the Westernlands. Gosh, what did she even call him? Your Majesty? All she managed was a faint, "Hey."

"I am glad to see with my own eyes," Windwolf said as quietly, "that you are well."

"I'm okay." She balanced against him while she took off her shoes. High heels in dirt being mistake number ten or eleven for her tonight. "Maynard took care of me."

"Ah, good." Windwolf relieved her of her shoes, handing them off to one of his guards. "Come with me. My car is waiting."

"Great!" She took a step forward and then stopped. "Oh, wait. I told Nathan I was just going to—um—going to the rest room. He'd worry if I just disappeared." He'd also probably call out a manhunt for her, and that might get the NSA involved.

"Describe this Nathan. I will send someone with a message."

Oh, that was tempting. Whatever had caused her to bolt suddenly—it wasn't quite fear, she told herself, just huge anxiety— receded in Windwolf's presence. "No." She held his hand tightly, drawing strength. "I should go back and tell him myself." Tell Nathan what, she wasn't sure. Oh, gods, what a mess. "It would be proper."

Windwolf bowed his head, and they started to retrace her route. Now, what was she going to say? *Nathan, I'm going home with Windwolf.* No. *Windwolf is taking me home.* No. *Windwolf is dropping me at my loft.* That sounded innocent enough. Nathan was going to ask why. *Because—because—because you're scaring the shit out of me.* "Oh, be real, this is Nathan after all."

"Pardon?" Windwolf leaned closer to hear her mumbled comment.

"Nothing. I'm just trying out apologies."

The crowd had been parting like waves when Nathan appeared before them, a rock to smash up against.

"What's going on here?" Nathan stared at Tinker's right hand holding Windwolf's.

Tinker hadn't even been aware that she still held tight to Windwolf. She fought the urge to snatch her hand free. She wasn't doing anything wrong. "I—I—I need to go home. Windwolf is dropping me at my loft."

"I'll take you home." Nathan took her left hand.

"Nathan!" she whined. Why did he have to be so dense? "Things went too fast tonight. I just want to go home."

"So I'll take you home." Nathan gave her hand a gentle tug.

Windwolf stepped in front of Tinker and caught Nathan's wrist. "No. She is coming with me."

"Look, you stay out of this." Nathan dropped into cop mode, and his voice went hard. "This is between me and her. Elves have no say in this."

"You did not listen to her. She is saying no. Now let her go."

The two males locked angry gazes at one another, ignoring her completely, while each holding on to one of her hands. She felt like a bone between two dogs.

"Nathan!" She tried pulling free of him. "Look, I just need some time to think about things. Give me time."

Nathan finally looked at her, and there was a world of pain in his eyes. "I'm sorry if things went too fast. Just don't go away with him."

Things went too fast? No, you went too fast! But she didn't say it aloud because she'd used the phrase first: It bothered her that he didn't own up to his actions, though. "Please, Nathan, let me go."

Nathan glanced hard at Windwolf, but then sighed and dropped her hand.

"I'll see you later," she promised. "We'll talk. Okay?"

"Yeah. We'll talk."

Having done the proper thing, she fled with Windwolf.

7: CARBON-BASED TRANSFORMATION

WINDWOLF'S CAR was a silver Rolls-Royce. Buttery-soft leather covered the seats. The privacy shield between the front and back sections turned opaque. The door shut, enclosing them in a womb of darkness, and Tinker discovered that the barriers between her and Windwolf remained down. Despite the couch-sized backseat, Windwolf sat close beside her, their bodies touching in the dark.

"You look lovely," Windwolf murmured into her ear.

She breathed in his warm scent, of sandalwood and leather. "How did you find me?"

"I had notes delivered to every place you might be today. You opened one and triggered the tracking spell on it. I would have found you anywhere tonight."

"Oh."

He cradled her left hand in his. "I would have come for you sooner, but there was much to prepare." He bowed his head over her hand, and kissed her palm, soft as butterflies alighting. "I wish there was more time, but that is something that you, as a human, do not have. Just yesterday, it seems, you were a child. I lost that chance to protect you. Now that I have found you, and come to know you, I do not wish to lose you again."

He ran his tongue feather light over the pulse point on her wrist, just as he had done at the hospice. Gods, it felt even better when she was fully awake.

Her fingers curved and touched the supple pearl of his ear lobe. She found herself exploring the alien beauty of his ear, so different from her own. "You don't mind me touching you?"

"Tonight it is you, not the *saijin*," he said huskily.

She took that as permission to explore. No stubble marred the line of his jaw, as elves did not have facial hair. He kissed her fingers as she glided them over his full mouth. In the strong column of his neck, she found his pulse just over his high shirt collar. Hard muscles played under the warm silk. By touch she found the structure of his shoulders, the solidity of bone. She came to the line of his buttons, and he undid them before her curious fingers. His skin under the shirt was soft and smooth as the silk, sculptured into taut muscles.

"Do you lift weights?" she whispered as he shifted them, lifting up her knee as he settled back against the seat, pulling her after him. In one graceful motion, she found herself straddling his lap, facing him.

"It is the sword play, it is hard work."

Her exploration peeled back his shirt, laying bare his upper torso. The cloth lay draped across his back and over his forearms. His nipples were dark coins and his abdomen a stack of well-defined muscles. His shirttails were still tucked into his pants; white silk cut off by black suede. Her dress had ridden up where she straddled Windwolf, and they pressed together with anatomical correctness, only leather and silk separating them.

What was she doing? She just bolted from Nathan, afraid of going too fast, and here she was, stripping the clothes off of Windwolf.

But being with Nathan had been like losing the brakes on a big truck—careening out of control. He had scared her. He picked her up, and overwhelmed her with his strength. What's more, there had been none of this gentle exploration; Nathan had zeroed in on her private zones, ignoring the tiny erotic places that Windwolf exploited. Windwolf had yet to touch her beyond her arms and back.

If she had gone home with Nathan, what they would have had was sex.

What she was doing with Windwolf—it felt like making love. She rested her hand on his chest, and felt the beat of his heart, and knew that she trusted him. She leaned forward and kissed him tentatively. He opened his mouth to her, and he tasted of plums.

"Can the driver see us?" she whispered, her heart hammering in her chest at her own boldness.

"No. Nor can he hear. We are in our own private space here."

"Make love to me. I want you to be my first."

"Gladly." He touched her cheek. "But not here. We're nearly at the lodge."

Lodge? The landscape beyond the windows was dark, and she suddenly realized that they hadn't gone through downtown, that they weren't heading for her loft. Pittsburgh was far behind them, and they traveled now through the primal forests of Elfhome.

"Where are we going?"

"When I'm in Pittsburgh, I use this hunting lodge." Windwolf looked out into the passing darkness. "It was the only structure here before Pittsburgh arrived. I've had it enlarged, but it is not very convenient. We're just arriving."

She got the impression of the forest growing only slightly less dense before the Rolls came to a stop. For a moment she was annoyed that they hadn't gone to her place, and then she thought of all the dirty dishes piled in her kitchen sink, and her dirty clothes strewn on her bedroom floor. Okay, so Windwolf's place would be classier than hers.

"Come." Windwolf slid out from under her. "There is not much time. We must hurry."

The driver opened their door. Windwolf got out without bothering to button his shirt.

She scrambled after him, puzzled and frustrated. She thought things were working up to them making love. "Why are we hurrying?"

"There are times when a spell is more likely to succeed than others." Windwolf took her hand and led her through a row of tall trees, branches interwoven, their pale bark gleaming in the candlelight. Moss-covered boulders lurked like giants in the shadows beyond the trees. "It has to do with the alignment of stars and planets, the sun and moon, the nature of the magic. A blessing should be done at noon, when the Moon is full and in the day's sky. A curse should be done at night, after the set of the new Moon, when none of the planets are on the horizon."

Windwolf chose a path down into a steep ravine, across a stream on an arched wooden bridge, and up steps cut into living rock. "Sometimes there is leeway. An optimal effect comes when the conditions are right, but still, the spell can be cast even if the time is wrong. A blessing can be placed at night, but it will not be as strong."

"Perhaps it has to do with gravity." *Where were they going?*

On the summit sat a lone structure; an open shelter with fairy silk hung from the eaves. It glowed softly like a Chinese lantern, surrounded by dark, silent forest. Tinker paused, glancing back the way they'd come, and found they'd climbed up above the treetops. Pittsburgh was nowhere to be seen on the night horizon. The moon was rising, bright as a spotlight, already washing out the brilliance of Jupiter, Saturn, Mars, and Venus' conjunction.

"This spell should be done now." Windwolf kissed her brow, his breath warm on her face. "The conditions will never be this perfect again, not in a human's lifetime."

"What spell?"

"Come." he urged her to the shelter.

One of the silk panels had been tied back, and looking inside, she recognized the building for what it was.

One heard of such places, where elves did powerful spells. Secluded away from anything that could affect a spell, the sites rested on the intersection of strong ley lines, tapping directly into an incredible amount of power. Those ley lines were permanently carved into a floor of white marble. White to show the tracings of a spell. Stone to act as a natural insulator. The marble sat on limestone bedrock, and the wooden shelter was constructed with no nails, containing not a single scrap of metal.

"Wow!" Tinker whispered.

A massively complex spell was inked out onto the shelter's stone floor. Even without knowing the spell, Tinker recognized it as a major enchantment. She studied the design, trying to find any components she knew. She could pick out that they built in an error-testing loop, and a slight blur on the tracings indicated that they had done a debugging run already.

"Take this off." Windwolf slid her jacket off her shoulders. "There is metal woven into it."

Tinker shuddered at the thought of wearing metal near an active spell. She stepped out of her high heels, balancing with one hand on Windwolf's arm; her shoes might have a steel shank worked into them. Jacket and high heels went onto a wooden table beside them, well outside the shelter. Tinker fished through her bra until she found the key to her loft. The key joined the others on the table.

"So, what is this?" Tinker asked. "I thought we were going to make love."

"We will." He kissed a line up her bare shoulder to the nape of her neck.

"Oh, good." She reached for him and found his shirt still unbuttoned, all that wonderful, warm skin to explore.

He unzipped her dress and eased it off her, murmuring, "This too must go."

She pressed against him, using him as a shield against prying eyes. "What if someone comes?"

"No one will come." He held her close as he dropped her dress onto the table. "They know we wish privacy. You have more metal on. Once we remove it, the curtains will shield us."

She glanced downward at her bra and panties. "More metal? Where?"

"This." He indicated the bra's wire under her breasts and then the tiny hooks clasping the fabric tight.

"Remove my bra?" *Yes, Einstein, you have to take off your clothes to make love.* She swallowed down the jolt of fear, and, turning her back to him, she fumbled with the hooks.

"Let me." Windwolf undid the clasps—his knuckles brushing her back—and her bra went loose. She trapped the fabric to her chest, as the straps slid down over her shoulders, making her feel suddenly naked.

"Do not be afraid." He kissed her on her spine. "Nothing will happen that you do not allow."

You want this. You want him. Stop being a coward. She tossed her bra toward the table and turned to face Windwolf.

Amazingly, a moment later, in his loose hold, skin touching skin, she no longer knew why she'd been so scared. It seemed that the more nerve endings were involved, the better kissing became.

"Much as I wish there was more time, we must start." Windwolf stepped away from her, voice husky, and unbuttoned his pants.

Tinker turned away from him, blushing furiously. She had just gotten used to the concept of being half-naked in front of him. Despite being raised by men, she had never seen a male nude outside of Lain's anatomy books. "What's the rush?"

"The spell must start while the moon is high."

The spell? She'd forgotten all about the mysterious design inked out onto the white marble. "Wha-wha-what exactly—"

He eased her back to settle against him, only the thin silk of her panties separating them. Naked and aroused, he felt like a shaft of polished wood. Awareness of him forced the air out of her lungs.

"We are at a branching." He held her, letting her grow accustomed to his presence. "To the left, every path leads to death. No matter which way you go, you will die."

"Me?"

"Yes, you." He nibbled lightly on her ear lobe. "And I do not wish to lose you. You have become very dear to me."

"I'm going to die?"

"If we do this spell, no. It is the path on the right, which leads to life. I wish there was more time for you to decide, but the full moon rises, and the planets align tonight. This is the perfect time, which will quickly pass."

She huddled in his arms, stunned by her mortality. She was going to die? Her stay at the hospice must have revealed something. She shuddered, remembering how quickly her grandfather died once he fell ill.

"Trust me, my little, savage Tink." He kissed her neck, finding some pleasure zone that she didn't know existed.

Trust him? Wasn't that the line that men always used? But she did trust him, perhaps more than she knew, perhaps more than she should.

"Shall we do the spell?" Windwolf asked.

She nodded her head, mute with shock.

He hooked his thumbs into the band of her panties and slid them down. With gentle pressure, he pushed her out across the spell to its center. She could feel the power shimmering through the spell tracing through her bare feet, the marble warm with resistance-generated heat.

"This isn't exactly what I expected when I asked you to make love to me."

"I will make it good for you." He stopped her at the center of the stone, the spell radiating out around them. "And because of tonight, there will be other times, at our leisure."

Other times.

He pulled her close, his right hand following the curve of her body, slipping down to caress her with shocking intimacy. He was at once hard as stone, and soft as petals. She could do nothing more than squirm in his grasp as he gently touched her. Electric shocks of pleasure shot through her with every caress.

She felt like a rag doll in his arms. He handled her with his incredible elfin strength. She seemed to weigh nothing. She had no form, bent supplely to give him access to her pleasure points. He lit a golden ember of sexual pleasure in her, and then stoked it to a molten heat. He would not let her touch him, returning her hands to her own body until she realized that all of her focus must remain on herself.

As she started to moan, he spoke a word of power, activating the spell. The outer shell of the spell took form and rose up to rotate clockwise. When her first tremors of impending release hit her, changing her moans to cries of joy, he spoke a second word. A second and third shell shimmered into being, canting up to spin counterclockwise at 45- and 135-degree angles. The magic grew dense, a visible shimmer.

Windwolf muffled her then with his mouth, and shifted himself so that he moved now between her parted legs, a hardness sliding through her wetness. She wanted him with a sudden wanton desperation. She wanted him inside of her, wanted to be taken. The force of it frightened her, and if she had been less a captive, she would have wriggled away, fled her own desires. He held her in his iron grasp, muffling anything she might have said, so she could neither plead with him to stop nor urge him on.

When she trembled on the peak, he slid into her to her maidenhead.

She bucked and cried out at the intrusion, the sense of being filled spilling her over the edge into release.

He lifted his mouth, spoke a word, and muffled her again.

The fourth shell rose, and it reflected that moment back at her, intensifying it, and then reflecting the next level back. She barely noticed the pain as he broke through and thrust into complete union. She was aware only of the golden tide of pleasure. He spent himself, uncoupled, and then turned her in his arms. Cautiously, he released her, touching her briefly on the mouth to remind her of silence. She clasped her hand over her mouth, unable to keep silent in any other way.

The pleasure continued, rolling like the tide, over and over her, each wave stronger than the last. Her skin gleamed with its essence, and she drifted in mid-air, suspended by magic.

He dipped his fingers into her, and then traced symbols on her skin, dropping words of power like stones.

"*Nesfa.*" Seed. "*Nota.*" Blood. "*Kira.*" Mirror. "*Kirat.*" Reflect. "*Dashavat.*" Transform.

He stepped away from her, made a motion, and leaped out of the shell. Turning her head, she saw him land at the part in the curtain. He gazed into her eyes, raised his hand, and spoke the final word.

Her universe became brilliant, blissful oblivion.

The elfin ceiling was quite amazing. Arched somewhere high above her, it had been dark when she awoke, but phased slowly to a pale rose color like the morning sky would as the sun crept to the horizon. After that, it blushed slowly to a pale white, then deepened into a delicate blue.

She felt hollow, and fragile, an eggshell, broken and empty, the life released and flown away. Her mind seemed to come online as gradually as the ceiling. In a calm, detached way she reasoned out that the ceiling looked odd because it was unknown, and then guessed it was the one at Windwolf's hunting lodge, and finally figured out what she was doing under it. *Oh yeah, we made love. So that's sex? Oh, hoo-chee mama! I definitely want to do that again.*

Windwolf said there would be other times. That thought made her squirm with delighted anticipation. She lolled in a nest of soft, white linens recalling all the sensations of being with him, the feel of his hard muscles, strong hands, and warm mouth. She tried not to think how pissed Nathan would be at what she'd done—and failed. She'd bullied him into a date, dropped him in public, and went off to make love to another male. And the worst thing about it, everyone else seemed to see it coming but her, so she was going to get the "young and inexperienced" speech from everyone.

Groping about, she found a pillow and screamed into it. Oh, why did Nathan have to be such a jealous butthead? If he hadn't started talking about marriage and kids, she wouldn't have gone off with Windwolf—or would she? Certainly it had been Windwolf she had been having kinky dreams about and the one that made her heart do silly things.

But Nathan would be the one waiting for her back at the scrap yard. She groaned but forced herself to sit up. While Oilcan could run the business short-term, and now had Riki to help, she still had to get back to work. Between saving Windwolf, her stay at the hospice, the NSA's kidnapping, and a day wasted getting ready for Nathan's aborted date she'd lost four days out of the week already.

Tinker crawled from the bed. Her clothes, cleaned, pressed, and folded, sat at the foot of the bed. Something was odd about her body, but she couldn't figure out what. Everything looked the same. Her underwear, at least, fit comfortably. For some reason her dress seemed stiff and uncomfortable. No matter, she'd need to change before heading to the yard. Her house key had been strung on a silk cord; she slipped it over her head, and it lay ice cold on her chest.

The stone floor was warm underfoot, so she carried her high heels to the door and slid it open. The hallway beyond opened directly to woods idealized; surely no random lot of trees could be so beautiful without careful, invisible work.

There was an elf in the hall too, of the heavily armed guard variety. His hair and eyes were black as engine grease, and he had a build that imparted a sense of sturdiness, which was rare in elves.

"Tinker *ze domi,*" he said in careful Low Elvish, and bowed deeply to her, which creeped her out. "*Domou* is not here. He and Lifted Sparrow By Wind were summoned away. He left word that you were to be given anything you wanted."

"Who? Windwolf?" And getting no reaction, Tinker struggled the full mouthful of Elvish that was Windwolf's real name. "Windwolf?"

"Yes. Windwolf." Obviously the elf had never used Windwolf's English name. He pronounced it as if he didn't speak English, or didn't recognize the two words that made up Windwolf's name. "Windwolf is not here."

"I want to go home."

"*Do-do-domi,*" the elf stammered out, "Aum Renau is very far away."

Huh? "I want to go to Pittsburgh." She tried again, slower. "*Pitsubaug.*"

He looked to his right and left, seemingly seeking someone to translate. Surely her Low Elvish wasn't that bad. "Pittsburgh? Now?"

"Yes, now."

He considered her for a silent minute, a foot taller and a foot wider than she, and then bowed again. "As you wish, *domi.*"

She'd missed quite a bit during the trip north while making out with Windwolf in the Rolls' backseat. They traveled half an hour just on elfin roads cut through dense forest until they reached the Rim, coming out near what was left of Sewickley. They went directly to the scrap yard gate, and from there she gave directions to her loft.

"Stop here," Tinker said as they pulled up to her building. She got out, and then put out a hand to block the elf, who showed every sign of following her into her loft. She knew her nerves wouldn't take someone underfoot. "Um, thanks for the ride. Let Windwolf know I got home safe."

"I'm not sure if—"

"I want to be left alone."

The elf nodded, and closed the door.

There were messages from Nathan on her home system, the scrap yard's line, and at her workshop. She let them play while she showered, piloting on automatic. The hollow feeling persisted, and it was hard to concentrate, as if her thoughts wanted to float around the empty space.

What had Windwolf done to her? What had been wrong with her? She hadn't felt sick.

There was a banging at her door, and Nathan's voice. She wrapped a towel around her and went to answer the door.

The Rolls was still at the curb when she opened the door. Nathan took in that she was naked except for the towel, and pushed into her loft. By the smell of him, he'd been at a bar; there was beer on his breath, and smoke clinging to his clothes.

"Where in the world have you been? You've been gone for three days." He roved the loft like a SWAT team looking for snipers.

"Three days?" No wonder she felt empty and dull-witted. When was the last time she'd eaten?

"I tagged my later messages so I'd be notified when you picked them—" He had turned to her and froze. "Oh, God, what did he do to you?"

"A major enchantment of some sort," she said, toweling her hair. "I'm starved. Want to go out for something to eat?"

He closed on her, staring. "Why did you let him do this to you?"

"I don't want to argue about this right now. I'm hungry. Let's just go get something to eat."

He caught her wrist as she started to turn. "You don't want to talk about it? Jesus Christ, Tink. I thought we had a future together and you pull this."

She was missing something here. Something visible, that he was staring at with dismay. She yanked her hand free and rushed to the bathroom. The mirror she had ignored earlier was partially fogged, but there was enough to show her what Nathan saw. For several minutes, she could only stare in silent shock. Nathan came to the bathroom door, filling up the frame.

It was *her* in the mirror—but it wasn't. It was an elf that looked like her. Her damp brown hair. Elf-shaped eyes—that slightly almond-shaped, almost Asian look. Had her eyes always been that color? They *were* brown, but hers couldn't have been that vivid. Right? Those brown eyes widened on a fearful thought, and she pushed her hair back.

Elf ears.

"All the gods in heaven!" she swore. "I'm going to kill him!"

"He didn't tell you that he was going to change you? He just took you out to the woods and changed you?"

"Yes!" Tinker answered without thinking, and then caught the dangerously hard look on his face. "No. No. He didn't. He asked me, but I didn't understand. You know how he is. How they all are. I didn't understand."

"What did he say?" Nathan asked.

"He said I was going to die, and that he cared too much about me to let that happen, so if I let him do the spell, then I wouldn't . . ." She wouldn't die, because elves were immortal. "Damn him. Why couldn't he say it in plain English?"

"So you're," he stumbled on the words, sounding physically sick, "you're immortal?"

"I don't know. I think that was what he was trying to do. He wasn't there when I woke up, so I just came home."

"It's taken three days for the spell to run?"

Three days. Three days to work through her entire body and transform every cell into elf. Tinker stared intently at herself. Her skin had the creamy perfection of elves. Her nose—not even being an elf fixed that. Her lips seemed fuller, a red of subtle lipstick. "I can't believe he did this! I'm not human anymore! Of course I was going to die. All humans die!" She noticed that her teeth had that unreal look of elves and Hollywood actors. She grimaced, pulling back her lips to bare teeth and gums to examine them closer. "I think even my one filling is gone. It was one of those white poly-cement ones. It was this tooth, I think."

She stared now at her fingers. All her fingernails were long and hard like she'd had them done at a salon. They seemed longer and more graceful. Were they? Would she be able to do the fine work that she was used to with a stranger's hands? Her hands started to tremble, and she found she was shaking all over.

Nathan's officer training took over. He guided her out of the bathroom, saying, "Why don't you sit down? I'll get you something to drink. You've had a shock."

A bark of laughter slipped out and threatened to explode into something longer, completely uncontrolled. She clasped her hand over her mouth, those delicate elfin hands over those full, cherry red lips. Oh gods, she wasn't human anymore. The bastard had turned her into an elf without even asking.

Nathan got two beers from the fridge, opened them, and came back. He handed her one. "I didn't think it was possible to turn a human into an elf."

"They can change a little Shih-Tzu into something the size of a pony, why not a human into an elf?" She took a large drink and nearly choked on the taste. "What the hell? This beer is bad."

He took it and handed her the one he had been drinking. She took a drink and choked it down. "This one is bad too."

"It tasted okay." He took it back and sipped it cautiously. "Tink, it's not the beer. It's fine. It must be you. The change did something to your taste."

He gave her back her original beer and finished his own. She tried to drink the vile-tasting stuff, but after the second swallow, handed it to him, saying, "I can't drink it."

So he drank it also. "What was the spell like? Did it hurt? What do you remember? Can he undo it?"

She flopped back, pressing hands to eyes. What a mess! There was no way she could tell *him* everything Windwolf had done. What she had *let* Windwolf do. What she had *enjoyed* having Windwolf do to her. "He had a big enchantment room set up with the spell inscribed and everything. I remember him activating it, but nothing afterward until I woke up about two hours ago."

"So he could have raped you while you were unconscious and you won't know."

She turned and kicked him, partly because he focused on sex, partly because Windwolf had gotten into her without having to rape her. "I would know."

Nathan put down the empty beer bottle next to his first, leaned over, and pulled open her towel.

"Nathan!" She tried to keep the towel closed. "What do you think you're doing?"

"I want to see what you look like now."

"No!" Surprisingly, a blush can start at the tips of one's toes and go all the way up. At least, it can when you're an elf.

"Let me see!" He pulled away the towel.

"Nathan!" she cried, trying to tug the towel out of his hands, but it was like trying to move a mountain. Then the mountain moved of its own will, lowering itself to kiss her bared skin. When Windwolf had kissed her in the same way, it had been like plugging straight into a 220 line. This hurt in a way that had only a little to do with bruising flesh. "Nathan! Don't! Stop!"

He did, only to kiss his way up her body. "Don't you see, Tink?" He supported himself with one hand, his other undoing his pants. "There's no reason to wait now. There's no getting older for you."

He was up against her, hard as steel, large as the rest of him. His weight was on her thighs and hips and chest, pinning her down so she couldn't even kick at him.

"No!"

"You're going to look this way for the rest of my life." He moved, seeking her entrance. "But the beauty of it is that with you being an elf, no one will think anything of you being young."

"Get the hell off me!" She got her hands to his face, thumbs pressing in warning at the edges of his eyes. "I said no! You of all people should understand that no is no."

"I love you, Tink."

"Then get off me. We're not doing this, not now, not this way. Be nice, and there's still a chance for us. Force me, and I'll press charges."

He stilled, hurt and guilt warring for control of his face. "Tink."

Was it a plea for forgiveness, or permission to continue? She couldn't tell, and it was rendered moot by a sword blade suddenly appearing at Nathan's neck.

"*Naetanyau!*" The elf from the Rolls growled, pressing the sword tip until it cut Nathan's skin and Nathan's blood dripped onto Tinker's breasts. "*Batya!*"

Nathan jerked back, shoving Tinker up and over the back of the couch like a rag doll as he moved. While she found herself deposited behind the sofa, Nathan tumbled back, coming up with his pistol. "Put down the weapon!"

"What the hell are you doing?" she shouted at the elf in Low Elvish. "I told you to leave me alone!"

Both males moved toward her, and checked as it brought them closer together.

"Put down the weapon!" Nathan commanded again.

"*Ze domou ani* said that I was to watch over you," the elf said to Tinker in Low Elvish. "This man was forcing himself on you. I couldn't allow that."

"Put down the weapon!" Nathan cocked his pistol. "Drop it or I'll shoot!"

And he would. Tinker edged between the men, facing Nathan, holding out her hand in warning. "Nathan! Nathan! Don't. He's just protecting me. He thought you were going to rape me."

Nathan flinched at that. "Tell him to put the sword away."

God, what was the word for policeman? "He's—he's a law enforcer," she said to the elf. "Put the sword away, or he'll kill you." That just got a look of stubbornness from him. "I command you to put your sword away."

That got a startled look. The elf obeyed grudgingly.

"Put your gun away, Nathan."

"Who the hell is he?"

"He works for Windwolf. Put the gun away."

Nathan holstered his pistol and zipped his pants. Tinker picked up her towel and wrapped it around her again; it seemed to have shrunk in size over the last few minutes and was woefully inadequate at covering her.

"What's his name?" Nathan asked.

Tinker looked to the elf, expecting him to answer, since the question had been fairly basic English. He gave no indication of understanding. "Do you know any *Pitsupavute*?" The human language spoken in Pittsburgh, or in other words, English.

The elf nodded stiffly and said in English, "No. Stop. Don't. Water. Rest room. Please. Thank you. Yes. Go." Had he listed them purposely in order, to indicate he understood her refusing Nathan? His English used up, he switched back to Elvish. "Windwolf did not expect you to leave home, so my lack of *Pitsupavute* seemed unimportant."

"What's your name?" Tinker asked the elf.

"Galloping Storm Horse On Wind." He gave it in Elvish, which was *Waetata-watarou-tukaenrou-bo-taeli,* which made her grimace. "My family calls me Little Horse, so *domi zae* says I would be *Po-nie.*" Po-nie? Pony! "If you find that easier, I would be pleased for you to call me that."

"Yes. Thank you," she said. She switched to English. "His name is Stormhorse, but he says I'm to call him Pony."

Nathan snorted at the name, then sighed deeply. "I'm sorry, Tinker. I had no right to do that."

"Damn right you didn't." She had trusted him more than almost anyone else on the planet. She wished Stormhorse had waited, given Nathan a chance to back off and apologize. She wanted desperately to believe he would have, that her trust in him could remain intact. That things could go back to the way they were.

He raked a hand through his hair, and then stood tugging at it, as if he wanted to yank the whole handful out. "It's just I spent all those years, wanting you so badly, and I finally had you. You were going to be mine. There was nothing stopping the whole marriage and kids and growing old together thing. Then Windwolf walked up, waltzed you away, and I let him. I fucking let him take you to do anything he damn well pleased to you. I've been going nuts the last three days, trying to find you, and now . . ." He held out his hand to her, tears coming to his eyes. "It's like he killed you, and all I have left is an elfin shadow. I just wanted to claim you, before he took that too."

"Your timing sucks. If—if—if . . ." If what? She didn't know what to say to make things right. Could anything make things right after he'd almost raped her? After Windwolf had made her into an elf? After she'd gone molten in Windwolf's arms? Would she have said no to Nathan if Windwolf's smell and touch weren't still lingering in her mind?

"If things were different?" Nathan asked. "The shitty thing is, they were different until Windwolf did this to you without even asking."

"I know," she whispered. "Look, things are too screwed up right now. I'm hungry, and confused, and hurt, and scared. Don't ask me to make decisions like this. You're just hurting me."

"I know. I'm sorry."

"Go home."

"Tinker—Tink—please . . ."

The front door opened, and Oilcan walked in.

8: REDEFINING SELF

OILCAN called out, "Tinker? Are you here?" as he came through the door and then checked at the sight of angry Stormhorse, flustered Nathan, and Tinker in a towel.

The sight of Oilcan destroyed all control Tinker had, and she went to him, suddenly crying. Her cousin held her without asking questions, and the males regarded each other in tense silence.

"I think it's time for you to go," Oilcan said quietly, and Nathan left without another word.

Stormhorse's hand rode his hilt, and he eyed Oilcan with open suspicion.

"*Nagarou.*" Oilcan identified himself as a sister's son of Tinker's father. His Elvish had always been better than hers. He and Stormhorse launched into a High Elvish discussion, faster than she could follow, which ended with Stormhorse bowing and letting himself out of the loft. And then Oilcan held her until she wept herself out. Then, in fits and starts, mostly from editing out what she didn't want him to know, she told him about Windwolf and Nathan.

"Look at me; I'm shaking so bad."

"If you haven't eaten anything for three days, then you're probably weaker than you think. Stormhorse went to get you something to eat."

"He did?" She got up. "Where would he get anything this time of night?"

"I don't know. Why don't you get dressed before he comes back?"

So she went back to her bedroom to dress. She found herself pawing through her underwear drawer, looking for the plainest pair of panties she owned. She stopped herself, picked a pair randomly off the top, and pulled them on. Clean jeans, a T-shirt, socks, and then her boots. She stomped around, feeling more like herself.

Oilcan had cleared her kitchen table, wiped it clean, and was washing her few pots and dishes. She got a clean towel and started to dry.

"How long do you think it will take him to get back?"

The sweep of headlights through her loft announced Pony's return.

"Not long," Oilcan said dryly.

She smacked him with the towel and went to open the door.

Pony came in carrying stacked wicker baskets, wreathed in the perfume of heavenly smelling food. Setting the baskets lightly on her table, he undid the lid and lifted it off to reveal noodle soup in the hand-painted bowl of an enclave restaurant.

"I didn't think enclaves did takeout." Tinker sat down on the footstool, leaving her two battered and mismatched chairs for the males.

"I persuaded them to do so this one time." Pony sat the noodle soup in front of her. "It would be best if you eat this first."

"Why this?" The noodles were long as spaghetti but nearly as thick as her pinkie and had a slightly waxy appearance. After her experience with the beer, she eyed the soup with suspicion.

"Rich foods on an empty system might upset your stomach, and you need to eat as much as possible. This has very little fat."

Oilcan found her a spoon, and she tried the stock. It was keva bean paste mixed with hot water, simple but delicious. She had to fight to get the noodles into her mouth. Despite their looks, they were mild but good.

"I told them of your *nagarou,* and they sent enough to share." Pony unlocked the top basket and lifted it off, exposing the next level of food: steamed meat dumplings.

"*Mauzouan!* You can count me in." Oilcan fetched plates and silverware, got himself a beer from the refrigerator, and settled at one of the chairs. Pony unloaded the rest of the baskets, but remained standing.

"Why don't you sit?" Oilcan paused in sharing out the *mauzouan* to three plates.

"I am Tinker *domi*'s guard. I should stand."

"Sit," Tinker snapped.

Pony wavered a moment, then pulled out a chair and sat unhappily. "This isn't proper."

"Currently I'm too peeved to care," Tinker snapped.

Wise man that he was, Oilcan set a dish of *mauzouan* in front of Pony without comment.

With Pony on the other side of the table, and food in her hands, Tinker could study him now at leisure. While pretty as all elves tended to be, he was by far the most solid of elves she'd ever seen. He wore wyvern armor, harvested from a beast that ran to the dark blues, with an underlining of black leather to keep the sharp edges of the overlapping scales from cutting him since they themselves couldn't be dulled. The armor left his arms bare from the shoulders. Permanent protection spells were tattooed down his arms like Celtic knots. For reasons she thought were no more than artistic, the spells were done in graded shades of cobalt; they shifted with the play of his muscles. Unlike most elves she knew, who wore dazzling jewelry, from complex dangling earrings to rings, Pony's only decoration was dark blue beads woven into his black hair.

While previously it had seemed to Tinker impossible to judge an elf's age, Pony struck her as young, but she couldn't tell if that was from some hint in his face or just his manner. He fairly bristled with weapons: a long sword strapped to his back, a pistol riding his hip, and knife hilts peeking out of various locations. Still, he met her gaze with a look that shifted from open honesty, to slight embarrassment, to bewildered confusion, and back around again.

"Where is Windwolf?" Oilcan asked as Tinker ate her soup and studied Pony.

"A message came from Aum Renau." Pony glanced at them to see if they understood. *Aum Renau* was the name of the palace on Elfhome in roughly the same place as the Palisades were on Earth—overlooking the Hudson River, near New York City. "His presence was requested by Queen Soulful Ember. He couldn't refuse the summons. He had to go. He wished to leave Sparrow to care for you. She's quite fluent in *Tanianante*"—the Elvish for "those many human languages"—"and *Pitsupavute*. The queen, however, requested her appearance specifically along with Windwolf's."

"The queen is in the Westernlands?" Oilcan asked.

"It is very unexpected. She has not been here since the treaty signing," Pony said. "He wished to bring Tinker *domi* with him, but he didn't want to take her so far away without consulting her first."

That would have pissed her off proper, but at least it would have saved her from Nathan being a jerk.

"How did Windwolf change me?"

"I-I do not really know, honestly." Pony screwed up his face, and Tinker suddenly liked the sturdy dark elf. "I am only of the *sekasha* caste, and still considered young. The *domana* understand the great transformation spells. Windwolf took blood samples while you slept; by the old reckoning, you're genetically *domana* caste now."

She shivered. "What do you mean 'by the old reckoning'?"

"There was a time when clan leaders often transformed their most trusted followers to *domana* caste. They were then considered full equals by the rest of the caste."

"And now?"

Pony touched his own forehead where Tinker bore Windwolf's mark. "There is the *dau*."

Which Maynard said elevated her to Windwolf's caste.

"When is Windwolf coming back?" Oilcan asked.

"He couldn't say," Pony said. "But if he can't return soon, he might choose to send for Tinker *domi*." Seeing the look on her face, Pony added, "If she wishes to join him."

Unfortunately, all the wonderful food meant lots of delicate dishes to be cleaned. Still, with all three of them washing and drying, the work went quickly. Pony, however, made no sign of leaving.

"Shouldn't you go back to the lodge?"

"Windwolf told me to guard over you. I can't do that at the lodge."

"So, you plan to stay with me until Windwolf comes back to say otherwise?"

"Yes."

Oh, great.

Tinker saw the look on Oilcan's face. "What?"

"You're sleeping at my place tonight," Oilcan said in English. "I wasn't crazy about you being alone, but him here too—I'd feel better being close."

"Then stay the night."

"You only have your bed and the couch."

"Oh, yes. Okay." She sighed and yawned. "Your place."

Oilcan had lucked into a place on Mount Washington, a sprawling three-bedroom condo in a high-rise apartment building, on the sole condition that he keep the elevator, air-conditioning, and heat working. His balcony looked out over downtown Pittsburgh and the endless canopy of elfin forest.

Pony worked to make himself invisible to them, keeping still and quiet. As Oilcan went to check on his rarely used guest beds, Tinker strolled out onto the balcony and looked down at the city.

Why had Windwolf changed her? Was it a gift for saving his life—a life for a life? Or was it more, as the sex implied? Did he love her? And what exactly did she feel about his gift? It was too frighteningly huge to handle. She was an elf.

"You okay?" Oilcan padded out onto the balcony with her.

"I'm fine—just a little rattled. What about you?"

"You mean, how am I with this?" Oilcan flicked his hand up and down to indicate her new body. "I'm cool. So you've got dorky ears." He leaned out and fingered one tip, and it felt embarrassingly good.

"Hey, don't mess with the ears."

Oilcan jerked his hand back and looked hurt. "Sorry."

"It's just—they're erogenous zones."

"Oh. *Oh!*"

"Exactly."

"Are we still cousins? At least in the genetic sense?"

"Would it matter if I'm not?"

"No, but it would be comforting if you were." Oilcan took her hand. "After my mother died, Grandpa said something to me. He said that as long as I and my children after me lived, my mother would be alive, living on through her bloodline. It's how humans reach immortality. It's why he made sure you were born, even after your father had died so long ago."

They lapsed into silence.

"Lain could check and see," Tinker whispered. "We could go see her tomorrow."

"But what if she says we're not?" She wondered how much it meant to him. If it meant a lot, she wouldn't give up Oilcan for Windwolf; she'd find some way of getting back to her real self.

"Whatever Lain finds, you'll always be my best friend and little sister."

"Little sister?"

"Based on love, not blood," Oilcan said. "Nobody can touch that if we don't let them."

She hugged him hard and wondered if he wasn't the smarter of the two of them.

They made an odd threesome on Lain's porch. Oilcan with his blatant humanity, Pony unmistakably elfin, and Tinker caught somewhere between the two. Lain answered the door, went pale at the sight of Tinker, and murmured, "Oh dear. Oh dear."

"It's really not that bad." Tinker tried for a brave front, and then failed. "Is it?"

Lain gazed at her for another minute before saying, "No, love, no. It's fine. Come in. I'd ask what in the world happened, but it's obvious that Windwolf happened."

"Pony, this is Lain." Tinker introduced the warrior. "Lain, this is Galloping Storm Horse On Wind, but he goes by Pony. He's one of Windwolf's bodyguards, but he's been told to guard over me. He doesn't speak English."

The two bowed to each other.

Lain led the trio back to her sprawling kitchen. Pony ranged through it and the connecting rooms, looking for danger.

"Where's his master?" Lain asked quietly in English, avoiding Windwolf's name.

Tinker followed suit as she explained about the queen's summons as Lain put the teakettle on. "Oilcan and I want you to test us to see how much *he* changed me—are we still cousins?"

"Of course you are!" Lain cried, then saw the looks on their faces. "There's a good chance you'll only be disappointed. He's obviously done something quite radical."

"But I'm still me. I feel the same. I think the same way. I have all my memories." Tinker had woken in a blind panic the night before, searched through old memories, factored out several large numbers, and considered a fix to one of her newer inventions before satisfying herself at that level. "The only thing different seems to be my sense of taste. Beer tastes awful, and I couldn't stand the instant hot chocolate this morning. Pony wouldn't drink it either."

"Well, beer is bitter because of the hops." Lain shooed Pony out of her path to the fridge with her crutch. "Elves seem to have evolved an intolerance to alkaloids. That's why they avoid coffee, tea, and nicotine in addition to the many toxic alkaloid-containing plants we stay away from as well."

"Well, that kills most of my favorite drinks," Tinker said.

"I have some herbal tea you can drink, but I think you'll have to be careful. A strong allergic reaction can be quite deadly." Lain took out a bowl of strawberries. "I've also found that elves are sensitive to certain types of fats we put in commercial food products. They love natural peanut butter, but the brands with trans-fat cause them trouble."

Tinker named her favorite brand of peanut butter.

"Sorry, love." Lain sat the strawberries in front of Tinker. "Luckily I make my own whipped cream, or that would be out too. Depending on the brand of instant you're using, it might be why you couldn't stand the hot chocolate."

Tinker considered her well-stocked kitchen at her loft. "I don't have any food I can eat, then."

"You'll have to rely on Tooloo more for fresh foods, then." Lain fetched the whipped cream. "Vegetables, meat, eggs, butter, and even the bread she bakes is most likely safer. Can I get you anything, Oilcan? Coffee? Tea?"

"I'll take coffee." Oilcan settled near to Tinker, fidgeting. "How long will the tests take?"

Lain shot a glance toward Pony standing guard by the door. "It's against the treaty to do gene scans of elves."

"I'm not an elf," Tinker growled, and dunked one of the strawberries.

"I know," Lain murmured. "But we can't let your guard know what we're doing."

Tinker controlled the urge to glance toward Pony. "Ah. Yes." She nibbled at the strawberry, considering. "Well, he seems to do what I tell him to do."

Oilcan also studiously avoided looking at Pony. "If we station him at the front door, then we can be in the lab unwatched."

So Tinker finished her strawberries, moved Pony to the foyer, and went back to the lab to have her blood drawn.

"When we're done, I'm going to destroy the samples and the results." Lain tied a tourniquet around Tinker's arm and swabbed down a patch of skin inside her elbow with alcohol. "It's a whole little Pandora's box we're peeking into. You will not tell anyone—not humans or elves—about this."

"We won't," Tinker promised.

Oilcan echoed it, and then added, "It's just for us to know."

Lain not only took a blood sample from Tinker, but also swabbed the inside of Tinker's mouth, plunked out a hair, and then asked for a stool sample.

"What?" Tinker cried. "Why?"

"Please, Tinker, don't be squeamish." Lain motioned Oilcan to sit in the chair Tinker just vacated. "The cells of the intestinal lining are excreted with the stool and are a source of DNA. I want to see how invasive this change is."

Lain was just untying the tourniquet on Oilcan's arm when the doorbell rang.

"Oh, who can that be?" Lain grumbled. She put the vials containing the blood out of sight, and stuck a bandage on Oilcan's arm. "Pull your sleeve down, Tink."

The woman on the front porch looked familiar. She brightened at the sight of Tinker and said to Oilcan, "Oh, wow, you found your cousin!"

"Yeah." Oilcan actually looked sheepish under Tinker's puzzled stare. "You remember Ryan. She's one of the astronomers?"

Oh yes, the one she'd tried to warn off the night of the cookout.

"I came over to see if there was any news." Ryan waved toward the Observatory. "I'm just getting done for the night, and I thought I'd check in before hitting . . ." She stopped and cocked her head. "You weren't always an elf, were you?"

"I've got work to do," Lain announced into the sudden silence.

"No, no! She—she—" Oilcan looked to Tinker for help.

"Don't look at me," Tinker snapped, then picked up on Lain's cue. "I want to go to Tooloo's to stock up on some food I can actually eat. Do you want anything, Lain?"

"Actually, yes. See what she has in the way of fish. A dozen eggs."

Lain listed her needs as she crutched to the kitchen and returned with her shopping basket and a glass milk bottle that she held out to Tinker. "A pint of whipping cream. And some fresh bread would be nice."

Tinker took the empty return and wicker basket. "I'll be back in . . . two hours?"

Lain nodded. "That would be good."

That left Ryan to be kept out from under Lain's feet. Oilcan blushed slightly at his assignment, but indicated the dorms with a jerk of his head. "Let me walk you back to the dorms, Ryan, and I'll explain."

So they split up, each to their own task.

Pony insisted that Tinker sit in the back of the Rolls, so she hung over the front seat to give him directions to Tooloo's store. She noticed that he handled the car smoothly as he took it down the sharply curving hill of the Observatory.

"How long have you been *driving*?" Driving was an English word, since the nearest Elvish words implied horses and reins.

"*Nae hae*." No years. The full saying was *Kaetat nae hae,* literally "Count no years" but actually meant "too many years to count"—a common expression among elves; it could mean as few as ten years or as many as a thousand. After a thousand, it changed to *Nae hou,* or roughly, "too many millennia to count." In this case, however, *Nae hae* had to be less than twenty years, since that was when the elves were introduced to modern technology with Pittsburgh's arrival.

"The Rolls were part of the treaty," Pony explained. "It required that the EIA provide quality cars for *ze domou ani*'s use. All of his guard learned, as did *husepavua* and *ze domou ani*, though not all enjoy doing it."

"Do you?"

"Very much. *Domou* lets me race, although *husepavua* says it is reckless."

She directed him onto the McKees Rocks Bridge. The morning sun was dazzling on the river below. "Who is *husepavua*?"

"Lifted Sparrow By Wind."

The name sounded familiar, but it took her a moment to place it; Sparrow had been the stunningly beautiful high-caste elf at the hospice. Pony had mentioned her once or twice the night before, calling her just Sparrow.

"Is Sparrow . . . Windwolf's wife?"

He looked at her with utter surprise on his face, reinforcing her impression that he was fairly young. "No, *domi*! They are not even lovers."

Oh, good. Pony was giving her amazingly direct answers, something she hadn't thought possible for elves. Perhaps it had to do with his willingness to obey her—had Windwolf told him to do so? Or was it an offshoot of being young? "How old are you, Pony?"

"I turned a hundred this year."

While that seemed really old to her, she knew that elves didn't start into puberty until their late twenties and weren't considered adults until their hundredth birthday. In a weird, twisted way, she and Pony were age-equals, although she suspected that he was much more experienced than she could hope to be.

"Is this the place?" Pony asked, pulling to a stop beside Tooloo's seedy storefront. To conserve heat in the winter, the old half-elf had replaced the plate glass with salvaged glass blocks. Somehow, though, she'd tinted the blocks, so the wall of glass became a stained-glass mosaic on a six-inch-square scale. Typical of elfin artwork, the picture was too large for a human to easily grasp. If one stood in the kitchenette and looked through the entire length of the shop, one could see that the squares formed a tree branch, sun shafting through the leaves, with the swell of a ripe apple dangling underneath. From the outside, though, one only saw the salvaged block and the muted colors in a seemingly random pattern—keeping the store's secrets just as the storekeeper kept hers.

The only nod toward advertising the store's function was painted under the length of the windows: Bread, Butter, Eggs, Fish, Fowl, Honey, Pittsburgh Internet Access, Milk, Spellcasting, Telephone, Translations, Video Rentals. Of the words that could be translated into Elvish, the rune followed the English word. It mattered much to Tinker that she could remember standing in hot summer sun as the cicadas droned loudly, carefully painting in the English traced onto the wall by Tooloo's graceful hand.

"Yes, this is it." Tinker slid out.

She hadn't considered Tooloo's reaction to her transformation.

When the old half-elf saw her, Tooloo let out a banshee cry and caught Tinker by both ears. "Look at what that monster did to my dear little wee one! He's killed you."

"Ow! Ow! Stop that!" Tinker smacked Tooloo's hands away. "That hurt! And I'm not dead."

"My wee one was human, growing up in a flash of quicksilver. Dirty Skin Clan scum." Tooloo spat.

"Windwolf is Wind Clan." Tinker rubbed the soreness from her ears.

"All *domana* are Skin Clan bastards," Tooloo snapped.

Tinker winced and glanced to Pony. Thankfully, the exchange had been in English, but Pony obviously had picked up Windwolf's name and was listening intently. "Don't insult him, Tooloo. Besides, if you'd just warned me, I might have been able to avoid this."

"I told you the fire was hot! I told you that it burns! I told you to be careful. So don't cry that I never told you it could burn down the house. I warned you that Windwolf would be the end of you, and see, I told you and there it is."

"You have told me nothing." She went and got a basket, angry now but determined to keep her calm. "Knowledge is not cryptic warnings, indistinguishable from utter nonsense. 'All *domana* are Skin Clan bastards.' What the hell does that mean? I've never heard of the Skin Clan."

"There wasn't a need for you to know if you'd just stayed away from Windwolf. I know humans; if it's ancient history, it doesn't pertain, so I would have been wasting breath to explain a war that happened before the fall of Babylon."

Tinker picked up a crock of honey, intending to put it into her basket. "Well, tell me now."

"Too late now." Tooloo stalked away, flapping her hands over her head as if to swat away questions. "Done is done!"

Tinker barely refrained from flinging the crock at Tooloo's retreating backside. "Tooloo, for once just tell me, damn it! Who knows what mess I might get into because you've kept me ignorant?"

Tooloo scowled at her. "I have things to do. Cows to milk. Chickens to feed. Eggs to gather."

"Well, you don't feed chickens with your mouth. I'll help you, and you can tell me what I need to know." Besides, Tinker had to keep Pony out from under Lain's feet for a full two hours.

Tooloo sulked but went to the store's front door, flipped the "Open" sign to "Closed" and threw the dead bolt, muttering all the while.

Tooloo lived in the one big back room of the store, a house done at miniature scale with changes in the flooring to indicate where walls should be. Mosaic tile delineated the kitchenette. The two wing chairs of the living room sat on gleaming cherry-wood planks. The floor around Tooloo's fantastically odd bed was strewn with warg skins. Tinker had spent countless hours on the floor, from studying the dragon shown coiled on the kitchenette's tile to building forts under the bed. She thought she knew it well.

Entering the room, Tinker discovered she didn't know it completely.

It felt like stepping into a pool of invisible warmth. No. There was movement, a slow current to it, heading east to west. She stopped, surprised, looking down at the wood. It did more than gleam. It shimmered as if heat roiled the air between her toes and her eyes. As she studied the floor, an odd, pleasant sensation crept up her legs until her whole body felt strangely light.

Even odder was the change in Tooloo's bed. The pale yellow wood seemed at once sharper and brighter, almost surreal, like someone had overlain computer graphics onto reality.

Pony followed Tinker's gaze, and grunted in surprise. "Dragon bones."

"Yes, dragon bones," Tooloo snapped, wrapping her braid loosely around her neck like a scarf of thick, silver cording. "That's how I survived on Earth all these centuries. Silly beast died without the magic, but its very bones stored massive amounts that slowly leaked off. Every night I slept in that bed, *nae hou*, aging only when I strayed away from it. I was tempted to burn it after the Pathway reopened, but waste not, want not, as the humans say. There were times I grew so depressed that I wouldn't stir out of it for months on end."

"Why is the floor so weird?" Tinker asked Tooloo, but the half-elf had stepped out the back, so she turned instead to Pony. "Can you feel that?"

"It must be a ley line."

"I can *see* it—I think."

"Yes, you should be able to." But he explained no further.

Deciding to focus on one mystery at a time, Tinker went out into the backyard after Tooloo. What used to be a small public park lay behind the store, but Tooloo had claimed every patch of green in the area plus several nearby buildings to use as barns, regardless of what their previous functions might have been. Fenced and warded, her small yard gave way to a sprawling barnyard.

Tooloo had already filled a pan with cracked corn from the feed room and now stood throwing out handfuls, calling, "Chick, chick, chick." All the barnyard fowl ran toward the falling kernels. She kept a mix of Rhode Island Reds (which were good egg layers), little bantams (which fared better on the edge of Elfhome's wilderness), and a mated pair of gray geese called Yin and Yang (that acted more like watchdogs than birds).

"Tell me about the Skin Clan." Tinker picked her way through the pecking and scratching birds. Pony hung back, staring in fascination at the chickens. She wondered if elves had chickens, or if they were one of the species that hadn't developed on Elfhome.

"Tens of thousands of years ago, in a time past reckoning, the first of our race discovered magic." Tooloo tossed out handfuls of corn. "It is said that we were tribes then, nomadic hunters. Our myths and legends claim that the gods gave magic first to the tribe that became the Fire Clan, and perhaps that is true. It is fairly simple to twist magic into flame.

"But one tribe rose up and enslaved all the rest—they were the ones who practiced skin magic. They learned how to use magic to warp flesh, and to remake creatures stronger and faster. They were the ones who discovered immortality, and they used the beginning of their long lives to make themselves godlike in beauty, grace, and form."

Tinker scooped out handfuls of corn and flung it at the chickens to speed up the feeding process. "I don't understand how they enslaved the others; surely not because they were pretty."

"Can you imagine the advances that your famous thinkers might have made if they had lived a thousand years? What would Einstein be creating if he were still alive today? Or what Aristotle, da Vinci, Newton, Einstein, and Hawking could create if they all worked together."

"Wow."

"As a race, we went from being bands of nomadic hunters to an empire with cities in a fraction of the time it took humans. As their realm expanded, the Skin Clan crafted fierce beasts to wage war and enforce their laws: the dragons, the wyverns, the wargs, and many other monstrous creatures. In time, they spanned the known world, which was roughly Europe, Asia, and Africa on Earth.

"All of this happened before humans dreamed of building their first mud hut." Tooloo dumped the last of the corn, tapping the fine dust and small bits of broken kernels out to be fought over by the chickens. "See, old news."

Exchanging the feed pail for wicker baskets, Tooloo headed for the one-car garage converted into a chicken coop. Long used to helping Tooloo with chores, Tinker took one of the baskets and worked the east wall of cubbyholes, lifting the day's eggs out of the still-warm nests. It was easy to tell which nest belonged to the bantams, as the eggs were much smaller. Pony stepped cautiously into the coop, peered into one of the cubbyholes near the door, and lifted out an egg, which he examined closely.

"Okay." Tinker carefully deposited her discoveries into her basket. "But there's some reason you're telling me about the Skin Clan."

"They are the seed of everything elfin." Tooloo systematically worked through the western cubbyholes. "Human are like snowflakes; nothing about humans is the same. They've chopped their planet up into thousands of governments, cultures, traditions, religions, so forth and so on. At their dawn, though, the elves were all gathered together and forced into the same mold and then made immortal. As we were when the humans started to build the pyramids, we are still."

Windwolf had talked about the stagnation of his race, but Tinker hadn't realized that it was so profound.

"Why haven't I heard of the Skin Clan before?"

"Because they're all dead, except for their bastard children, the *domana*."

"What happened? How did they die?"

"They didn't die, silly thing; they were killed. Hunted down. Killed to the last one—in theory."

With that Tooloo ducked out of the coop and swung around to her back door to set her basket in the store before heading for the small milk barn.

"Wait!" Tinker snatched up the last of the eggs, including the one Pony still held, and scurried after Tooloo. She caught up to her at the pasture where Tooloo's four milk cows waited to be let out. "Tooloo!"

"What?" Tooloo opened the pasture gate and the cows ambled to their stalls without guidance. "I'm trying to compress twenty thousand years of history into a teaspoon, and you complain? History isn't easy stuff. It's a tangled web full of lies and deceit. There's no easy way of pouring it out."

"Okay, fine, the *domana* are the Skin Clan's children?"

Tooloo scoffed loudly as she poured grain out to the cows. "The Skin Clan was the first of the castes, for they raised themselves up to perfection. Then they created the other castes. The *filintau* born for a clean breeding stock. The *sekasha*." Tooloo thumped Pony in the chest. "Sound and strong, able to withstand massive damage, but not necessarily smart. It's the same that humans did with dogs, chickens, and cows." She gave one of the cows a similar pat. "Breed a bloodline for certain properties until they're nearly a different species—and when they no longer suit, let them die off. When I lived in Ireland, I had this lovely herd of small, hardy Kerry cows that nearly went the way of the quagga."

"The what?"

"It was like a zebra. It went extinct in the days of Queen Victoria. Ah, there was a woman!"

"So, the Skin Clan set up the castes and fathered the *domana*?" Tinker tried to steer the conversation back to elfin history.

"As you will no doubt learn, you don't wake up and fully realize you're immortal. It takes a few hundred years." Tooloo washed her hands, took down a clean milk bucket, and moved the milk stool beside the first cow. "Once the genetic tinkering started, the Skin Clan grew increasingly infertile, so they originally accepted all their offspring into the caste. About a thousand years into their immortality, they realized that they were diluting their power by sharing it with their 'half-breed' children, so they ruled that only those born to a Skin Clan female could be accepted into the caste. It did not keep the males, however, from fathering children among the lower castes, and that's where the *domana* came from."

Tinker leaned against the stall side, watching Tooloo wipe the udder clean and position the milk bucket. Tinker drew a line at milking the cows, as she'd been swatted in the face with a tail once too often. Pony watched in complete mystification. Head tucked against the cow's flank, Tooloo settled into a fast milking rhythm, shooting alternating streams of milk into the bucket. "This happened a long time ago; Windwolf wasn't even born. And even if his father is a Skin Clan bastard, so what? Oilcan's father killed his mother, and that doesn't make Oilcan a bad person."

"Nah, nah, Longwind—Windwolf's father—is just a young buck too. Politics does what time can't; Windwolf's grandfather, Howling, was murdered and Longwind took his place as clan head. Howling, though, he was ten thousand years old when the blade found him, and he had been part of the Skin Clan downfall. But to be precise, he wasn't the bastard—it was his father, Quick Blade, before him, who was the bastard, but Quick Blade died in battle during the war."

"How do you know all this?"

"How do you know about George Washington and Thomas Jefferson? These were the 'heroes' of the war and the leaders of our people afterward." Tooloo said it with such bitterness that both Tinker and the cow flinched. "It was, though, a simple trading of masters. Perhaps more benign than the Skin Clan, but iron-fisted all the same."

That Windwolf was one of "them" made Tinker uncomfortable with the conversation. Tooloo said whatever suited her with little regard to truth, and she hated the concept of being poisoned against Windwolf with lies. Still, it was fairly obvious from the caste system that the *domana* ruled and the others served.

"I don't understand," Tinker said. "If Quick Blade was Skin Clan, how did Howling get to be Wind clan?"

Tooloo sighed into the cow's flank. "The Skin Clan tried to wipe out the use of other magic, but they only drove it underground. And exactly what they were afraid of happened—the seeds of power became great trees. The ignorant but physically strong—like your strapping young *sekasha* there—pledged their services to those with arcane knowledge. Over time the castes linked together into the current clans, but they were slowly losing during the Years of Resistance."

"Until the *domana* joined the clans against their fathers."

"There's still hope for you, my bright wee one. Yes. The Skin Clan had added the ability to wield magic to their blood, and then fathered bastards among their rebel slaves." Tooloo stilled for a moment, considering the past. "There is, I suppose, an inevitability to it all."

Tooloo finished with the first cow and carried the milk to the scales to be weighed. "Thirty pounds. Nothing to piffle at, though Holsteins have been bred to output twice that amount. Here, take this back to the cooler."

Tinker reached for the bucket, but Pony stepped forward and took it.

"What are you doing?"

"It will be heavy for you, but nothing for me to carry."

Tinker snorted but let it go because, unfortunately, he was right. She found it disgusting that, while Oilcan wasn't much taller or more muscled, he was proportionally stronger than she was.

Pony eyed the bucket of milk as they walked to Tooloo's large walk-in cooler. "Ah, they are cows."

Tinker considered that the elves had a word for cows and chickens. "Yes. You seem . . . surprised."

"They don't look like our cows," he said. "And I have never seen any of ours milked before. *Kuetaun* caste handles livestock, not *sekasha*."

"Oh, I see." That would explain his reactions to the chickens too. "Not in a hundred years?"

"I devoted a great amount of time to training. Only the best are chosen to be bodyguards, and that is what I wanted."

"Why?"

"It is what I'm good at. I enjoy it."

"But, doesn't it mean you're setting yourself up as a sacrifice to someone else's life?"

"If I do my job right, no. But if I must, yes."

"I don't understand how you can make yourself anyone's disposable servant."

"I choose who I guard, that is the only way it can be. Windwolf values my life as much as I value his; he protects me as I protect him."

They had stopped in front of Tooloo's ten-foot-square walk-in cooler. Tinker unlatched the heavy door, frowning at what Pony had said; it seemed to defeat the whole concept of bodyguard.

"Windwolf protects you?"

Pony cocked his head. "Why do you find that so hard to believe?

You put yourself between me and harm, do you think that Windwolf would do anything less than that?"

She what? When did she protect Pony? Oh, when Nathan was being a butthead. "That was nothing."

She yanked open the door and cool moist air misted out into the sunshine.

"You put yourself in harm's way to save Windwolf." Pony let her take back the bucket and watched with interest as she poured the warm milk into wide-mouth crocks. "Not only against the EIA imposters at the Rim, but against the wargs at the salvage yard."

"I don't plan to make a living out of it." From another crock that had already separated, she skimmed off the cream with a clean ladle, filling a pint bottle for Lain. "Grab me one of those quart jars."

"In all things, there must be those who are willing to guard and protect." Pony picked up the bottle of milk. "It is the way of nature. You humans have *police* and *firefighters* and *EIA*. It is not that I do not value my life, but if I risk it, it is for a worthy cause."

Tinker supposed that Pony's job was not much different from Nathan's. Stepping back out of the cooler, she latched the door and headed back into the store. Drat Tooloo, the half-elf had her seeing everything in a bad light already. And the comparison to Nathan dragged that whole mess up. Damn him, why had Nathan betrayed her that way? Beyond Lain and Oilcan, there wasn't another person in the city she would have opened the door for dressed only in a towel. The more she thought on it, the more she realized how much she misjudged Nathan. She had been looking at the cop, not the man. She expected him to stay the nice big brother type, only with kissing thrown in. In one giant step, they'd moved into new roles, and Nathan, the boyfriend, was a different person. That Nathan was possessive and overpowering. Perhaps her instinct to flee him at the Faire was for the best; perhaps no matter when or how they'd ended up on her couch, it would have led to Nathan trying to force her into something she didn't want.

And if that was the case, what did she do now? She'd opened the door and let the warg in; how did she get it back out?

Tinker tried, but she couldn't stretch the shopping out to the full two hours without alerting Tooloo or Pony that she was stalling. She and Pony returned to Observatory Hill a full forty minutes early, but Lain had already finished up and sat in the kitchen with a cup of tea and a stunned look on her face. The expression set off alarms in Tinker. She quickly stashed away the perishables from Tooloo's store and banished Pony to the foyer so she could safely discuss the results of the DNA tests with Lain.

"It's bad, isn't it?"

Lain raised an eyebrow. "What? Oh, no, I'm still stunned at the amount of change Windwolf accomplished in an adult seemingly without fear that it would kill you. You look so much like yourself that it didn't really click until I started working with your DNA. I-I-I'm in awe."

"Lain, please, you're freaking me out."

"You have no idea of the enormity of this. It changes everything we know about the elves' ability. We've considered the concept of elves being able to turn people into frogs with magic just folklore and urban legend."

"So you're saying I'm lucky not to be a frog?"

The stunned look vanished before annoyance. "Oh, Tinker!"

"Where did scientists think the gossamers and wyverns came from?"

"Humans have made amazing changes in animals over thousands of years of breeding. One only has to look at the extreme phenotypic variation of the canine genotype."

"What?"

"Dogs. From Chihuahuas to Irish Wolfhounds, they're thought to be all descendants from a species of small Northern European wolf."

"Lain, can we focus on me. What did you find out?"

"Don't you want to wait for Oilcan?"

"No. I think—if it's bad—he'll take it a lot worse than me. I want to deal with it so I can be strong for him."

"I wish I had thought to analyze your original DNA." Lain limped to her lab with Tinker following her. "This was a stunning chance to learn so much about the difference between our two races."

"Lain!"

"I'm sorry, but it's like watching someone destroy the Rosetta stone."

"The what?"

Lain sighed, picking up a thermometer. "You need a more rounded education."

"I am not in a mood to have my inadequacies discussed."

"Fine." Lain poked the thermometer into Tinker's ear, made it beep, and then took it out to look at the readout. "Ah, that's what I was afraid of." Lain limped to her medicine drawer and picked out several bottles. "Here, I want you to take these."

"Why?"

"Your white blood cell count is extremely high. Elves seem more resistant to disease, which suggests an aggressive immune system, so it's possible that an elevated count is normal. But you're running a low-grade fever, which isn't surprising considering all the cells of your body have been radically altered."

"They have?"

"All four of your samples were identical, which indicates the change was global."

"Oh. What are these?" Tinker eyed the pills that Lain shook out into her hand from several different bottles.

"Tylenol to control the fever." Lain recapped the bottles. "Calcium, folic acid, iron, zinc, and a multivitamin. I have no idea what Windwolf has done to you, but it might be viral in nature, so trying to stop the process might be disastrous. Those will help keep you strong through this; you probably should take a nap after this afternoon. Pushing yourself now could be very bad."

"So, all of my DNA samples were the same. What about mine compared to Oilcan's?"

"I separated the DNA out of all the samples, and used a restriction enzyme to cut the DNA into a defined set of fragments." Lain opened up a window on her workstation. "Those I stained with a fluorescent dye and passed it through the flow cytometer. As the laser strikes the fluorescent dye molecules that are bound to the DNA fragment, a photon 'burst' occurs. Because the number of photons in each burst is directly proportional to the fragment's size, the cytometer counts the photons in a burst to obtain an accurate fragment-size measurement."

Lain clicked open an image file showing a line of smudgy dots in a vertical row. "The resulting distribution of fragment sizes in the sample shows the raw DNA fingerprints. It's rough, but it's enough for our purposes. Basically, the more closely related two people are, the more gene sequences they will share."

"The smudgy dots?"

"Yes, those are gene sequences. This is the fingerprint of your blood."

"Okay." Tinker braced herself. "And Oilcan's?"

Lain reduced Tinker's sample and clicked open a second scan. "This is his."

At first glance, they didn't match. As Lain made them the same size, and placed them side-by-side, the differences only seemed greater.

"Oh." Tinker sat down, amazed at how much it hurt. She didn't think it would matter so much to her.

"It isn't as bad as it looks." Lain pointed to a cluster of dots in the center of Tinker's fingerprint. "These spots are from DNA on the telomere."

"The what?"

"Telomeres are segments of DNA at the ends of chromosomes. Each time a cell divides to make a copy of itself, the telomere gets shorter. Once it gets too short, the cell can't copy itself and dies. That's how we age. We've theorized that the elves would have longer telomeres than humans and thus age much slower; this is evidence that we're right."

"And the extra DNA is muddying the fingerprint, so to speak."

"Yes." Lain pointed to a second cluster. "This is from telomeres, and here too." Lain tapped a third section. "If you try to ignore these three regions, you'll see that the rest of the fingerprint is very similar."

Tinker squinted, trying to see "around" the smudges, wanting desperately to see the similarities. "I don't see it."

"Here." Lain opened up a third image. "This is my DNA."

"This is supposed to help?"

"Wait. I'm now isolating telomere DNA on your sample."

Red shot through Tinker's sample as the sections that Lain had pointed out as telomeres shifted color.

"Okay, let's find matching probe locus points in lane one and two." Lain flicked through another menu. Green flooded through Tinker and Oilcan's samples as ranks of black smudges turned to jade.

"That's what we share?"

"Yes." Lain pulled up a fresh copy of Tinker's DNA, isolated out the telomere, and placed it next to Lain's sample at the bottom of the screen. "As a control, let's compare your sample and mine."

Only a trace of green appeared.

Tinker looked back to the top of the screen, and all the lovely jade in the first two samples blurred slightly until she blinked away the tears. "So we're still cousins?"

"In my professional opinion, yes."

Tinker clapped, making the gods aware of her, and said, "Thank you."

"That settled, I have questions. How did Windwolf do this? Did he inject you with anything? Did he give you something to ingest?"

They spent the next ten minutes with Lain asking detailed questions and taking notes.

"You don't have to put down that we made love, do you?"

"Obviously it was vital to the spell. Sperm is made by nature to be a perfect carrier of DNA."

"Lain!"

"No one will know. This is just for me to know." Lain saved the notes, making them disappear into her computer system under heavy encryption. "So, Windwolf was the tengu of my dream after all."

Tinker paused, trying to remember exactly what Lain was talking about. "Oh, the raven elf."

Lain looked out her window at the garden Windwolf gifted on her. "You brought the tengu to me to bandage up. It turned you into a diamond and flew away with you in its beak."

"Lain, I'd rather not talk about prophetic nightmares and Chinese legends."

"Japanese," Lain corrected absently. "Just as the Europeans had brownies, and pixies, and elves, the Japanese have tengu, oni, and kitsune, and so forth."

"And Foo dogs."

"Well, the Foo dogs are Chinese, but they were imported along with Buddhism. The original religion of the Japanese is Shinto, a worship of nature spirits."

"If the tengu are the elves that can become crows, what are oni and kitsune?"

"Kitsune are the fox spirits. They usually appear to be beautiful women, but they really are just foxes that can throw illusions into their victim's mind."

Tinker made a face; silly nonsense was what she hated about fairy tales.

Lain tapped her on the head to stop Tinker from making faces. "Oni are fearsome ogres usually depicted as seven feet tall with red hair and horns. I've heard a theory that the oni are actually lost Vikings with horned helmets."

Now that sounded familiar. It all clicked together in her mind. "The three men who attacked us were very tall, with red hair. Windwolf called the pseudo-wargs Foo dogs. He also recognized your references to tengu. If we have legends of elves, and they are real, by simple logic then, the oni are real too."

Lain admitted Tinker's theory might be true with a thoughtful nod of her head, and then poked holes into it. "The world doesn't always follow simple logic. The cultures of the ancient worlds were highly contaminated by each other. The Chinese interacted with the Japanese, and then traded on the Silk Road to the Middle East, which spread into Europe. You can find the same children's story of Cinderella with the evil stepmother and the magical fairy godmother in almost every culture now. The oni could be just the Japanese version of our elves."

"But someone used Foo dogs and onilike people to try to kill Windwolf."

"There's so little we know about the elves, even after twenty years. For all we know, these attacks are part of political infighting."

Tinker considered it, and shook her head. "No. Tooloo just gave me a history lesson and—provided it's all true—the elves are quite homogeneous."

"Ah." Lain murmured and thought for several minutes. "Then maybe there's something about oni that the elves aren't telling us."

Tinker glanced toward the foyer where Pony stood guard. "Weren't telling us. Windwolf has changed the game by swapping one of the players to the other team."

"Well." Lain locked up her workstation. "You crack that nut, and I'll make lunch."

Tinker felt guilty when she walked into the foyer and realized that

Pony had been standing there since they returned from Tooloo's. "Why don't you sit down?"

"It's not proper—"

"Oh, sit down!" She pointed at the chair beside the door.

Pony sat, unhappy but obedient.

Tinker settled on the fourth step of the staircase, which put her level with Pony. "What do you know about oni?"

"Oni?" Pony lifted his hands to his head and made his index fingers into horns.

"Yes, oni."

"They are cruel and ruthless people with no sense of honor. Their weapons are crude, for they are a younger race than either elves or humans, but they spawn like mice and would crush us with sheer numbers."

So much for oni being mythical. "They live on Elfhome?"

Pony looked puzzled at this. "No, then they would have been elves. They live on Onihida."

"So, where is Onihida?"

Pony screwed up his face in the way that Tinker recognized as him reaching the limit of his ability to explain something. Finally he held out his left hand, palm down. "Elfhome." He waved his right hand under it. "Earth." Then, holding his right hand still, he moved his left hand under his right and waved it. "Onihida."

She pointed at his left hand. "How did you get to Onihida? Or did the oni come to Elfhome?"

"We found them." Pony looked daunted. He sat silent for several minutes, thinking. "There were at one time certain caves and rock formations that formed Pathways to walk from one world to the next. They were perilous, for the movement of the Moon and the planets made them inconstant."

It confirmed her family legend of caves being gates. Tinker suspected that a mineral deposit running through quartz next to a strong ley line could mimic the hyperphase field of a man-made gate. Like the gate in space, the power needed to be supplied to only one side to create two-way travel. Based on what Windwolf told her about gravity affecting magic, then perhaps ley lines had "tides" which would cause the gates to occasionally fail.

Pony plunged on. "While we bent our minds to shaping magic,

humans learned to forge bronze and then steel. For goods we could not make ourselves, we walked the Pathways to Earth. We kept close to the Pathways and traveled heavily cloaked and mostly at night, for without magic we lived a breath away from death. But the risks were always well rewarded with rich trade goods."

Obviously Pony was using the historic "we" since the Pathways had mysteriously failed prior to the 1700s, and he had just hit his majority.

"But some of these Pathways led to Onihida," Tinker guessed.

"In a manner, yes." Pony scratched at the back of his head, pondering how to—as Tooloo put it—compress history into a teaspoon. "Where a Pathway opened on Earth, magic would flow out. While humans would only find a Pathway through blind luck, a *domana* could sense it from a distance. Still maps were made to keep careful track of the Pathways. One day on Earth, a *domana* found a Pathway that was not on our maps. Nor, when the matching location was investigated on Elfhome, could it be found where it opened. A group adventurous in spirit decided to investigate where the Pathway led. Twenty journeyed out, only two returned."

"The oni killed them?"

Pony nodded. "At first, the explorers had thought they'd somehow traveled to Elfhome, for Onihida—unlike Earth—flows rich with magic. Then they realized that the plants and the animals were unknown to them, and showed signs of being spell-worked." The elfin way of saying the object had been bioengineered. "Whereas on Earth, they would have easily traveled undetected, wards revealed their presence, and they were surrounded before they could flee back to Earth. The oni lords 'invited' them to a nearby fortress. The explorers were treated well, served rich foods, and offered beautiful whores. The oni called them their brothers and tried to deceive them, but a dragon always shows his teeth when he smiles."

"The oni wanted to know where the gate to Earth was?"

"Natural gates apparently were usually quite small." Pony measured out four feet with his hand. "Many only wide enough to take a pack horse through, and sometimes much smaller." He reduced the width to only two feet. "They were within dark caves, and like the veil effect," he waved his hand about to take in the house around him, shoved from Earth into Elfhome, "invisible. Anyone without the ability to detect a ley line could search closely, even to the point of stepping in and out of worlds, and never find it. Like the elves prior to the birth of *domana*, no oni passing through a gate to Earth had ever returned."

So that the oni didn't realize a gate wasn't just a deathtrap to be avoided until the elves showed up. "Obviously the explorers didn't reveal its location."

"At first, they easily evaded the questions, for they did not know the oni language, and deliberately misunderstood their gestures and the demands for maps to be drawn. But they were forcibly detained, taught the tongue, and asked more directly. Then they were tortured, then healed, and tortured again until their minds broke."

"That's horrible!" Tinker shuddered. "But the gate only led to Earth. The elves could have given it up to the oni without risking Elfhome."

Pony stood to pace. "The oni had spell-worked their warriors to be far stronger than the average man. What's more, they had discovered the secrets of self-healing and immortality, yet continued to breed like mice. With their numbers and abilities, they would have flooded Earth unchecked."

"I'm surprised that the elves cared that much about Earth."

"The explorers had traveled Earth for centuries; some had taken human lovers and sired half-breed children." He leaned against the banister to give her a soulful look. She found herself suddenly aware of his eyes, dark and full of sincere concern. "We have always seen humans as our reflection, good and bad. Man was how gods made the elves before the Skin Clan remade them."

Pony spoke with the same bitterness as Tooloo used while explaining the origin of the *domana* as the ruling caste.

"If elves hate the Skin Clan so much, why hasn't spell-working been banned?"

"It was for a while. Blight struck our main grain crop, though, and a great famine followed, so one of our most holy ones, Tempered Steel, petitioned for reform. *Evil lies in the heart of elves, not in magic.*"

This was one bit of elfin history she knew—learned from puppet shows during the Harvest Faire—only she had never understood the full context. Much was made that Tempered Steel was a *sekasha* monk, which made sense now, since a *domana*'s motives for bringing back spell-working would have been questionable. The creation of keva beans was linked to Tempered Steel's reform, saving the elves from starvation.

"Two of the explorers survived?" She steered the conversation back to the oni.

"Two escaped, reached the gate and returned to Elfhome. Once their tale was told, *sekasha* were sent to destroy the gate from Onihida to Earth, and then systematically all gates from Earth to Elfhome were destroyed."

"That seems rather drastic."

Pony clicked his tongue. "They say an elfin carpenter is more thorough than a human one, for he has forever to hammer down nails."

"Did they warn travelers first?"

"We had no way of contacting all the far-flung traders."

Thus her elfin ancestor and Tooloo were trapped on Earth. While long lived, without a source of magic, even elves age and die.

Pony half-turned, head cocked. "Someone is coming."

There were footsteps on the porch, and the front door opened. Oilcan paused in the doorway, surprised to find Tinker and Pony in the foyer, focused on his arrival. He tried for nonchalant but Tinker could read the tension in him. "Hey."

"Hey." Tinker held out her hand to him. "I got back early too."

He lifted his arm to take her hand and allowed her to pull him warily into the room. "Is it good?"

He meant the news about the tests.

"It's good." Tinker gave his hand a squeeze before letting go. "Everything's cool."

The tension flooded out of him with a huge sigh, and he grinned hugely at her. "Ah, that's great."

"Lain's making lunch."

"And she's finished," Lain called from the kitchen. "Come eat while it's hot."

The EIA was located in the Pittsburgh Plate Glass corporate headquarters, the Rim having cut it off from all of PPG's factories and most of its customers. The building was a fairy castle done as a modern glass skyscraper. Pony parked the Rolls in the open courtyard, ignoring all the "No Parking" signs. Tinker wasn't sure if he couldn't read English, or if such things didn't apply to the viceroy's car.

There seemed to be some protocol to walking together. Outside she hadn't noticed it, but as she wandered about the crowded lobby, looking for an office directory and gathering odd looks, Pony tried matching her step in awkward starts and stops.

"Do you know where Maynard's office is?" she snapped finally.

"This way, *ze domi*." Pony led her to the elevators, where she gathered a few more double takes before the elevator's doors closed them off from curious stares.

What tipped people off that she was now an elf? Her ears weren't really visible, and certainly her hair was in the same "pure" hairstyle as always. It had to be the eyes—the shape and vivid color. She made a mental note to get a pair of sunglasses.

They hit the top floor, the doors opened and Pony pushed back an EIA employee by mere presence. It was still startling to see Pony go from invisible to in-your-face in a blink of an eye. After assuring himself that the floor was clear of menace, he allowed Tinker off.

On second thought, it probably wasn't anything about her tipping people off, it was the six-foot-something elfin guard.

The space beyond the elevator was small, elegant, and tastefully decorated to elfin sensibilities. The only furniture was two chairs for waiting visitors, and a receptionist desk staffed with a woman pretty enough to be mistaken for a high-caste elfin female.

"I'd like to see Director Maynard, if I can."

The woman was definitely staring at Pony as she asked, "And you are?"

Tinker gave the receptionist her name—making the woman's eyes go wide as if this were some startling news—and added, "Tell him it's very important that I see him."

Maynard came out of his office, saying, "Where have you been—" He took in first Pony's presence and then her new eyes. "Tinker?"

"Tinker *ze domi*," Pony corrected Maynard.

Maynard flashed a look back to Pony and then bowed to Tinker. "Tinker *ze domi*. It is good to see you're safe."

Oh, this couldn't be good if Maynard was doing it too.

A few moments later Tinker was in Maynard's office and, with careful maneuvering, Pony was not.

"I need language lessons," Tinker complained, ranging his office nervously. The reason for the tiny foyer was Maynard's office seemed to take up a large portion of the top floor. Must be a bitch to heat in the winter, although the AC seemed to work fine. The wall of windows looked out over the North Shore to the elfin forest beyond.

"I thought you spoke Elvish." Maynard anchored the conversation to his desk by sitting down behind it.

"Tooloo taught me like any elf would, cryptically. I would like a more direct routine, like a dictionary! I want to know for sure I understand what the hell is going on, instead of walking around thinking I know but probably getting it all wrong."

"Such as?"

"What the hell is this whole *ze domi, ze domou, ze domou ani*? I thought it was like Mr. and Ms., only politer. And what exactly does *husepavua* mean?"

"*Husepavua* literally means 'loaned voice'; figuratively it means an assistant. Lifted Sparrow By Wind is Windwolf's *husepavua*. *Sedoma* is the word for 'one who leads.' *Domou* is 'lord.' *Domi* is 'lady.' *Ze* denotes a level of formality. *Ani/Ana* indicates the tie between the speaker and the noble. When it's *Ana* it means the speaker doesn't share a tie with that lord or lady. *Ani* means the speaker and the person he or she is addressing shares a tie with the noble. Basically 'my lord' or 'our lord.'"

My Lady Tinker. That's what Pony had been calling her. And the elves at the enclave. All the little presents. She'd nearly forgotten that. *May I wish you merry, my lady.*

Her knees went, and luckily there was a chair close enough to collapse into. "Am I—am I—*married* to Windwolf?"

"It seems a very strong possibility." Maynard spoke with what seemed like exaggerated care. "What exactly has happened since you left the Faire with Windwolf?"

She was surprised for a moment that he knew her movements and then remembered that he was the head of the EIA. "We went north to his hunting lodge and . . . and"—she swept a hand down over herself to indicate the transformation—"he cast this spell on me and I woke up yesterday like this. Pony says that Windwolf was called back to Aum Renau, and that he ordered Pony to guard me, so Pony hasn't left my side since yesterday. He slept on the floor of my bedroom last night. I think he slept."

Maynard winced slightly. "Yes, a very strong possibility that you're married to Windwolf."

She sat there stunned for a few minutes. Maynard got up, opened a cabinet to expose a small bar, and poured out a drink for her. She eyed the clear liquid, dubious after the beer, but it was strong and sweet and burned its way down. After she drank it, she realized it was the same stuff that the elves at the enclaves had used to toast her during Nathan's date—only it tasted much better now. "What was that?"

"Ouzo. Anisette liqueur. The elves love it."

She groaned as she realized that the elves had toasted her marriage in front of Nathan. Oh, thank goodness he hadn't understood what was going on—a pity she hadn't known either. "I just want to know when I supposedly agreed to all this. I didn't ask him to do this." She meant making her an elf. "At least I don't think I did. And I *know* there wasn't any wedding."

"You probably accepted a gift from him?" Maynard made it a question, clueing her.

"Well, there was this weird brazier that he gave me. That's when he marked me."

Maynard pinched the bridge of his nose as if to ward off a headache. "I'm guessing that the brazier was a betrothal gift. Windwolf offered marriage—and everything it entails—and you accepted. When he put the *dau* mark on you, you were, in essence, married."

"You're kidding."

"In elfin culture, it is offering and acceptance that are important. Everything else, as we humans are wont to say, is icing on the cake."

"That's it? No priest? No church? No vows? No blood test?" Well, strike that. Pony had said that Windwolf gave her a blood test.

"That your word of honor is binding is the keystone of elfin society."

"I don't know if I want to be married to him! What if I want to get out of it? Do elves have divorce?"

"Frankly, I don't know." He sighed. "I'm sorry, but the last thing I want to do is to disturb the marital bliss of the viceroy. That would be bad for relations between the two races."

"Are you saying that you can't help me?"

"No." Then he clarified himself. "I'm not saying that." He spoke slowly, obviously studying what he'd say before speaking, looking for traps. "This is a very delicate situation. On one hand I'm going to have humans, on Elfhome and Earth, see this in the worst possible light. And on the other side, any complaints might seem to be questioning Windwolf's honor."

"Big whoop-de-do!"

"Windwolf is acting head of the Wind Clan in the Westernlands."

It irritated Tinker that she had such an incomplete understanding of elfin society. She knew that there were clans and castes and households and families but, like most humans, could never get a clear picture of how they all worked. While she knew that major clans were named after the four elements, and that there were lesser clans, she'd only met elves from the Wind Clan. They had names like Lifted Sparrow By Wind, Galloping Storm Horse On Wind—and Wolf Who Rules Wind. As a child, she'd assumed that "Wind" meant they were part of the same family, until Tooloo explained that it denoted clan alliance, that most clan members were not related, and that a family usually shared the same clan, but not necessarily always. Clear as mud, as her grandfather would say.

What Tooloo had taught her thoroughly was the elfin code of honor. You kept your word, and you never implied that an elf's word wasn't as solid as cash. A single slur could pit you not only against the elf you insulted, but all the elves "beholden" to them. Implying that the head of a clan wasn't honorable would be slurring the entire clan, in this case, all the elves in the Westernlands.

"Let's start with the simple things first," Maynard said. "Are you in love with Windwolf? Do you want to be married to him?"

If those were the simple questions, then they were in trouble. Life as an elf was easier to imagine than being married. What did married people even do when not having sex?

Maynard sat, waiting for her to decide, saying nothing to sway her.

"I don't know," she finally admitted. "I've never been in love before; I don't know if I'd recognize it when I felt it."

"But it's a possibility?"

"It would be easier for you if I said yes."

"Yes, it would, but I'm not going to close my eyes to a rape, if that was what it was."

"No!" Tinker squirmed in her chair. "I can take care of myself. I wanted him. I just didn't expect this!"

"I've heard you speak low tongue; you're extremely fluent. Windwolf might have assumed that you knew his culture better than you do based on your fluency of his language."

"Well, I don't. I can't believe that there's nothing in the treaty to cover this." Tinker pushed back hair to expose her ear. "You made laws against this, didn't you?"

"We didn't know the elves could do this," Maynard said quietly, "in order to prevent it. Is that why you're here? Do you want charges pressed?"

"No. At least I don't think so. Depends. I haven't had a chance to talk to Windwolf yet."

"Why are you here?"

Tinker shifted in her chair. "It's weird. Before this, if I found something out, I'd consider things in a 'me versus the EIA' way. What do I get out of it? Will I get into trouble knowing this? Will this bring the EIA down on me? And now—maybe I'm afraid people will think I've changed loyalties as well as my ears."

"What did you learn?"

"There were, might still be, natural gates on Elfhome. It's a matter of getting magic to resonate on the right frequency, and you open up a wormhole to another dimension. Most of Westernlands is unexplored, so there might be gates here that the elves don't know about."

"Between Elfhome and Earth."

"Or someplace else," she said. "We have legends of more than just the elves. In Japan, the people from other worlds are known as the oni. Pony told me this morning that the oni are from Onihida, and they're the main reason that elves stopped trading with humans a millennium ago. The oni are very tall, and red haired, with a grudge against the elves."

"Windwolf's attackers."

"Somewhere, there's a gate to a third world open, and the oni are coming through. They're here, in Pittsburgh."

"Does Windwolf know?"

Tinker considered and nodded. "I think he might. Certainly, it might be the reason that the queen of the elves is in the Westernlands."

9: A GATHERING OF WYVERNS

THERE, she had done her duty to the human race, and reported her suspicions to Maynard. Only it didn't make her feel better. She'd repeated Pony's story and Tooloo's history lesson and gone away feeling like an alarmist circulating dangerous rumors. Maynard had nothing he was willing to add to her news, so she left still in the dark and feeling grumpy.

On top of that, it felt ridiculous to ride into the scrap yard in the back of the Rolls-Royce: the elegance of the car rolling into the lot of wrecked machines, and her handed out like a fairy princess. She was tempted to kick Pony just to protect her junkyard-dog image. Checking the impulse, she unlocked the offices, disarmed the security system, and got gently put aside so Pony could check out the offices.

"My system was up and running, so no one is in here," she complained, following him in. She should have kicked him. The air was stale, smelling still of blood and peroxide. The offices suddenly struck her with their worn, cluttered ugliness. All the office equipment was second-hand, jarring in its mismatched, battered appearance. Despite her best efforts to stay paperless and organized, the paperwork sprouted out of every nook and cranny.

"Forgiveness," Pony murmured, but continued looking. In the small, crowded rooms, he seemed larger and more imposing.

She ignored the impulse to get out a beer. One, it was way too early to start drinking; secondly and more importantly, the beer would just taste like piss. She was going to have to find some ouzo somewhere.

Sparks had nearly a hundred messages cued up. She told her bot to skip past all messages from Nathan, and the number of waiting messages dropped by half. There were messages from Oilcan, Lain, Maynard, and the NSA from the time she had been with Windwolf, covering all bases as they tried to locate her. Those she had Sparks delete. The last two dozen messages were from actual customers, looking for parts and wanting to sell scrap.

"Sparks, make a list of wanted parts."

"Okay."

The door burst open, and Riki rushed in. "Where the hell have you—"

Pony had his sword out and to the grad student's neck, cutting off the words while almost cutting open his neck.

"Pony!" Tinker cried.

Riki had rebounded, hitting the door frame in an attempt to get back out the door, his hands up in a hopefully universal signal of unarmed surrender. "Hey! Watch it!"

"Put your sword away, Pony," Tinker commanded. "He works for me. This is Riki."

Pony eyed the tall gangly human suspiciously, even as he sheathed his sword. "Riki?"

"Yeah, dude, Riki."

"He doesn't speak English," Tinker told Riki. "Windwolf told him to guard me."

"I see." Riki continued to eye Pony, but Tinker could only stare at Riki. A cut split the skin of his cheek, his nose was clearly broken, and his sunglasses couldn't completely cover the fact that both eyes were blackened. Everything was purpling gloriously, which meant the damage had been done soon after she last saw him, three days ago.

"What the hell happened to you?"

"I got in a fight." He glanced at her for the first time and stared. "Oh, shit. What the hell did you do?"

"I didn't do anything."

"Oh, you did something! You're a fucking prissy elf!"

She was stunned at the venom that he put into the word and projected at her. "What's your problem?"

"You sold yourself to them like a whore, only you did it body and soul. I didn't think you were such a slut. How many of them did you fuck until you found one that could remake you?"

"*What?*" It took a moment to actually get something else out. "You're one word away from being fired. You don't know anything about me, about what's happened to me. You have no right to talk to me that way."

He snapped his mouth shut and spent a moment or two choking on whatever he wanted to say. "I'm sorry," he finally managed to growl. "It's not you I'm mad at, and you're here and they're not."

"If you're pissed at someone else, go scream at them."

"Okay." He ducked his head down again. "I'm sorry."

She glanced to Pony, slightly surprised that he had let the shouting take place, even if he didn't understand the language. Pony stood tense, one hand gripped around his hilt. Okay, he was ready to shish kebab Riki. The danger of Pony actually doing just that helped cool Tinker's anger.

"Look, there was a misunderstanding between me and Windwolf. I didn't know he was going to do this to me, and I'm not sure how I feel about it. So can we just ignore it for a while and get some work done?"

"Fine," Riki snapped, much too fast to have really thought about it, but she'd deal with that if and when he brought it back up.

"Who did you get in a fight with?"

He blinked a moment at the sudden change of subject before saying, "Some elves at the Faire. I said the wrong thing. The jerks took it as an insult."

She'd never heard of elves ganging up on anyone before. Usually honor dictated that fights were one against one. "What did you say?"

Riki sucked his teeth a second before saying, "I'm not sure. I was really drunk, and I thought I was being friendly."

Well, if Riki was drunk, then anything could have happened, including him just tripping and falling flat on his face. It at least explained why he suddenly hated elves.

She searched the top of her desk, found her headset, and pulled it on. It fit oddly on her new ears and refused to stay in place. "Sparks, upload the list to my headset."

"Yes, Boss."

Now if she could get Riki to be as cheerful and helpful.

She fought with her headset long enough to scan the parts list, and then stuck it in her pocket to be modified later. The quickest order to fill was an alternator for a turn-of-the-century Dodge truck. She dragged Riki through the yard to where she knew a Dodge sat already partially stripped of door panels, back axle, and windshield. Pony made sure no one was hiding in among the salvaged cars, and then settled into a guard position a couple dozen feet back.

Tinker leaned into the cab to pop the hood latch. "Do you know anything about engines, Riki?"

"I know the basic parts. Why?"

"It would be nice to know what I can trust you to do. Lots of different jobs go into keeping this place profitable. If you can't buy your own food, keep clothes on your back, and heat your place in the wintertime, the EIA ships you back to Earth."

She found the latch, slipped it aside, and hoisted up the hood. As usual, she couldn't reach it up high enough to fit the brace into place. God, she hated being short. Why couldn't Windwolf have fixed that while he was turning her into an elf? Maybe she would start growing again. It would be nice to be taller.

Riki pushed the hood up and slipped the brace into its slot.

"Thanks." She spread out her catchall. "So, what's the alternator?"

"Here." He tapped on it.

"Good." She stepped up onto the bumper so she could lean over the engine to reach the fist-sized part. "Okay. Carburetor."

They played name-that-part while she used WD-40 and patience to loosen up nuts and bolts untouched for years.

"Nuts and bolts are important here." She coaxed one set after another off and tucked them into the catchall's pocket, where they couldn't fall to the ground and possibly be lost. "Don't strip them if you can help it, and don't lose them. If you find one on the ground, pick it up. I've got boxes of spares back in the offices. Lose a vital bolt, and you could wait two months for a simple repair to be done."

"Two months?"

"One Shutdown to order the lost piece, a second Shutdown for it to be delivered."

Riki grunted. He was looking at her oddly. With slow carefulness— as if he expected her to hit him if he moved too fast—he took out his handkerchief and wiped grease off her nose. "I can't figure you out. If you just went to Earth, you wouldn't have to be mucking around with junk like this."

"I like this," she growled. "What's so great about pure science? So what if the universe is expanding or contracting? What difference will it make?"

"What difference will a used alternator make?"

"It makes a hell of a difference to the poor schmo with his Dodge up on jacks, waiting for this part."

He grinned briefly, and then sobered. "I don't know what Windwolf offered you, but remember that everything has costs. Sometimes the price is out in the open, and sometimes it's hidden."

"One fight makes you an expert in elves?"

"I don't need to know about elves to know how the universe works. There are always strings attached, and it's the hidden ones that are the real bitches."

Yeah, like suddenly being married. "I said I didn't want to talk about it. I'm pretty freaked out about it."

"I'd be more pissed than freaked, especially with a watchdog thrown into the deal." Riki jerked his head in the direction of Pony. "I would hate having to hide everything from a spy on top of dealing with the change. Or are you so naïve that you don't realize everything you say and do is going to be reported back to Windwolf?"

"Can we just drop this?" Tinker cried. "And I'm not naïve! I've been careful all morning about what I said and did around him." But all the juggling had been for Pony's sake alone. Having a total stranger invade her life had been intrusive enough without making him privy to all her personal conversations. It hadn't occurred to her that Pony might report her activities back to Windwolf, or that Windwolf might have arranged a guard just for that purpose. Had he? Her gut instincts said no, but what did she really know about Windwolf?

"I'm just trying to warn you. You do know it works two ways."

"What do you mean?"

"He can also keep you from doing anything Windwolf doesn't like."

"Like what?"

"I don't know." Riki raised his hands to show he was innocent of the knowledge. "I can only guess. I'm fairly sure that I can't take you out for a drink, just the two of us, on my bike. Which is a shame, because you seem like you could use a drink."

She shifted uneasily. "I've got a ton of work to do."

"You really amaze me. If I were you, the last thing I would want is to go through the motions with some watchdog keeping an eye on me. I'd take off, take a little *me* time to deal with being jerked out of the human race."

"That would be immature."

"News flash: You're still a kid. And here's another important announcement: You're now stuck that way."

"I'm an adult."

"As a human," Riki said. "As an elf, you're about sixty years shy. You're not going to be an adult for a long, long time."

She could only stare at him in horror. "Oh, no, no, no."

"Like I said, if I were you, I'd ditch the watchdog and fly."

She barely kept from looking toward Pony. "Yeah, with him watching every minute?"

"Duck around the car where he can't see you, and I'll stand here and keep talking. He'll probably assume you're working there."

"And what about you? When he figures out I'm gone?"

"Don't worry about me. I'm very good at pretending to be harmless."

It was blind panic that took her out of the scrap yard and halfway back to her loft. True to his word, Riki stood at the Dodge and talked to thin air as she crept to the back of the truck, around an old PT Cruiser and into the Fords. Then, before she knew it, she was walking faster and faster until she was running.

She started for her loft out of pure instinct, which became more rational as she grew nearer to home. Without thinking, she'd taken Pony to the three places she'd most likely lie low: Oilcan's condo, Lain's house, and Tooloo's store. That left the hotel on Neville Island. She'd need the keys to the front door, her shotgun and fishing pole, and some money. A change of clothes would be nice too, but if she delayed at her loft too long, Pony might catch up with her. Rounding the last corner, she glanced over her shoulder. No sign of her watchdog yet.

Thus Tinker nearly collided with the stranger.

That the person was tall and redheaded impressed Tinker first. She jerked back away from the stranger, gaining an arm's distance to realize that the stranger was a female elf, not one of the tall male humans who had attacked her on Shutdown. The elf was slender and beautiful, with hair the color of fire, pulled back and braided into a thick cord. Like Pony, she wore a vest of wyvern-scale armor, and permanent spell tattoos scrolled down her arms; both were done in shades of red that matched her hair.

"Sorry, I didn't see you," Tinker said in English.

The elf's eyes went to the *dau* mark on Tinker's forehead. "Tinker *domi?*"

Oh, hell, the elf knew her name. At least the elf didn't have horns. Unfortunately, the female wasn't alone. She had two brothers or cousins: tall, elegant redheads loaded with weapons. The one farthest back actually stood on her doorstep—they had been coming from or going to her loft. Either way, they blocked her from the safety of her place and the gas station down the street. Everything behind her was abandoned until one hit the scrap yard.

"Who are you?" Tinker edged away from the elf. "What do you want?"

"Kiviyau fom ani. Batya!"

Or at least that's what she thought the female said. The elf had an odd accent that made her hard to understand. The first and last words were fairly clear. *Kiviyau.* Come. *Batya.* Immediately. Tinker could also read the body language fairly easily. The female definitely wanted her to come with them.

"*Chata?*" Tinker tried for a stall by asking why while taking a step backward. Every muscle in her body had gone taut as a stretched elastic band, thrumming with the chorus of "run, run, run" so loud she was sure the elves could hear it.

"Kiviyau. Batya!"

"I don't understand. *Naekanat.*" She took another step backwards. "*Chata?*"

There was some weird universal law that stated, when faced with someone that didn't understand, humans spoke loud and slow, and elves talked polite and fast. The female went into a rapid tirade of High Elvish.

"I don't understand," Tinker said. "Please, explain in Low El—"

"*Kiviyau!*" The female stepped forward, lifting a hand to catch hold of her. She might as well have pulled a trigger; Tinker bolted.

Later Tinker would realize that her brain had mapped out an escape route, but at the moment, she went blindly. She didn't expect to get anywhere; no one won footraces with elves. She ducked into the narrow space between two buildings and had reached the next street over before she knew that she was running. As she darted across the empty street, then through the obstacle course of the old school yard playground, she realized that she was running as fast as a startled rabbit. It dawned on her that she was an elf too, shorter of leg, but that she otherwise had all their advantages. Well, except the guns. And the fact that there were three of them. She would have to do something about that, but gently, just in case these were rude cousins of Windwolf's.

As she plunged down Tooloo's steep hill, she detoured off the path through the apple trees to cut through the beehives. As she flashed past the wooden boxes, she thumped the sides hard and was gone, leaving behind a growing angry buzz, and a moment later, shouts of surprise and pain. At the bottom of the hill, she dropped to the ground and rolled under the lowest strand of barbed wire, then scrambled on hands and knees through the barnyard muck. Yin and Yang came at her, hissing, wings half spread.

"Not me, you stupid things. Them! Them!" Tinker cried, risking a look back.

The female had discovered that the top wire was electrified and was backing up to vault the fencing.

Shit! Tinker picked up gravel and tossed it toward the fence, calling, "Chick, chick, chick!" Instantly, all the barnyard fowl ran toward the falling pebbles, pecking and scratching for corn.

She ducked into the barn while behind her Yin and Yang started to honk out warnings at the stranger landing in their midst. The warehouse Tooloo used as a haybarn had little in common with a real barn except the deep shadows, the scent of hay, and the drift of dust on the air. The female elf barked commands, and there were answering calls, spiraling in around the barn. Tinker had planned to just cut through the barn, but now she tucked herself into one of the smaller nooks, panting, scared. What now?

She shouldn't have ditched Pony, that's what. What the hell had she been thinking? Obviously she hadn't been thinking. Someone had tried to kill Windwolf, and someone had killed her father, and how did she know that these weren't the same someones?

She spied a pile of things and scrambled toward it, muttering, "Stupid, idiotic, moron, brain-dead ass"—which might have made her feel better if she hadn't been talking about herself. Tooloo must have traded someone for several yards of fishnet, a set of ninepins complete with two balls, a spring hinge, a length of cord, and a collection of hickory walking sticks. She grabbed the hinge, two of the sticks, and the fishnet.

Minutes later, the far door creaked open and one of the male elves slipped into the barn with her. She flung the first ninepin ball at him. The ball was weighted differently than a horseshoe, but she managed to nail him in the temple. As he went down, the female came through the near door and rushed her. Tinker tripped the spring hinge; it flung the netting—weighed down with the ninepins threaded through the holes of the net—over the female. Snatching up the hickory stick, Tinker swung as hard as she dared.

The elf shouted, throwing up her arm. Magic spilled out of the ruby on her earring, traced down the crimson tattoos on her arm, and flared into a shimmering red force.

It was like hitting a brick wall, inches from the elf's body.

A shield spell! Oh shit, I'm in trouble now!

The female flung off the net, the pale red aura of the shield pulsing around her arms. She balled up her fist, hauled back, and swung at Tinker.

Oh, this is going to hurt! Tinker flung up the stick, trying to block the blow.

But then, appearing like magic, Pony was there. "*Domi!*" He caught Tinker from behind, and jerked her backward out of range of the female.

The male she'd nailed with the ball was staggering to his feet, and the much stung and vastly annoyed second male was closing fast.

"Pony!" Tinker tried to run, but couldn't pull free of his grasp. "They're coming!"

Pony tucked her behind him, maintaining his grip on her. He held out his empty hand to the strangers. "Hold! Hold!"

"What are you doing?" Tinker cried, still trying to get free. Surely he wasn't going to fight all three unarmed.

"You must not fight them!" Pony said quietly. "They're Wyverns."

"Wyverns?" Tinker twisted in his hold to peek around him. What the hell did that mean? They looked like regular elves to her. The three halted, so perhaps there was the time for an explanation.

"Promise me, please, that you will not fight them," Pony pleaded.

"Okay." Tinker, who had been considering running, had no problem with not fighting.

Pony turned, keeping her tucked behind him, and spoke carefully in High Elvish. He went on at length. The looks cooled from anger to slight disgust and total annoyance.

The strangers finally replied, which generated another long elegance from Pony.

"I have explained that you are only recently transformed and that you do not know the high tongue nor recognize their uniforms. They understand the situation now, and while they are the Wyverns, they are also merely *sekasha* and do not wish to face the full anger of Windwolf."

Tinker grunted to keep in snide remarks. Annoyed as she was, even if it was one-on-one and without swords, they would probably still beat the snot out of her. It was so lowering and frightening to discover exactly how small you were in the world.

"Are you hurt?" Pony asked.

"I'm fine," Tinker said.

"I am sorry. I should have been here to forestall such a misunderstanding."

"Who the hell are these guys?"

Pony raised an eyebrow. "I told you. They are Wyverns."

"What the hell are Wyverns?"

"Oh," Pony said. "I see. They are the queen's guard. They bring a summons from the queen."

"Summons? Is that like being arrested?"

"No. Not completely. The Wyverns have come on the queen's personal airship to take you to Aum Renau. It is not a summons that we can refuse."

"You mean, we have to leave now?"

"Yes. The order indicates all speed must be taken."

"Why?"

Pony turned to the waiting elves and spoke with them. When he turned back, he was wincing slightly. "They did not ask; it is not in their manner to do so."

On the way back to the Rolls, she remembered she had her headset stuffed into her pocket. She guessed it was just as well; getting the police involved would have only complicated things. She called Oilcan and let him know that she was safe but being taken to Aum Renau.

"I want to come with you," Oilcan said.

"No, no, no. I'm fine." She didn't want to get him caught in the mess she was in. "Someone has to keep the yard going."

"There's Riki."

Yeah, Riki, who talked me into ditching Pony, she thought and then sighed, knowing that wasn't fair. Riki couldn't have known that the Wyverns were standing on her doorstep. "I went and saw Maynard. He says—well—that Windwolf probably thinks we're married. If that's the case, then the queen probably just wants to meet the viceroy's new wife."

"You're *what*?"

"Married. Please don't tell anyone yet, at least until I know for sure. Windwolf is at Aum Renau. He won't let anything happen to me."

There was long silence from Oilcan's side, and finally, "Okay, okay, okay. Don't get hurt."

"I won't." She folded away the headset.

"I've been thinking," Pony said quietly. "If we are going to court, it would be best that you did not have a guard, but have a guard."

She considered the sentence. He was using two different forms of have; she had thought the words were equal, but obviously they weren't. "What do you mean?"

"It would raise your esteem in court. Unless you do not wish me to be your guard."

The idea of being completely alone raised sudden panic in her. "No. I want you to be my guard. I don't want a stranger."

"I would be honored to be your guard." He paused to bow low. "I will not disappoint you."

10: BLIND SIGHT

A GOSSAMER AIRSHIP was moored over the Faire Ground's now-empty meadow. Tinker had seen many gossamers at a distance, but never one close enough to appreciate their true size. Something so huge, living, floating in mid-air challenged the mind to accept it as truth. The gondola alone was a hundred feet long and sixty feet wide; the gossamer rippled in the wind above it, dwarfing the teak structure. And that was the portion of the animal easily seen—the cell structure of the creature fractured the sunlight into a million prisms, giving substance to the nearly transparent form. The creature's countless frilled fins, extending far beyond the glittering mass, showed only as a distortion high overhead, like water running over a glass roof.

"How much tinkering did you have to do to get the gossamers that big?"

"I believe getting them large was not the problem," Pony said. "They occur in nature nearly that size. Probably making them float in air was the difficult part. Originally they were sea creatures."

"Why wouldn't they start with something that already floated in air?"

"You can grow wings on turtles, but they still crawl on the ground."

"What the hell does that mean?"

Pony struggled a moment to put it into words. "Those that float in air naturally go where the air takes them. They needed something that could choose its own course—a swimmer."

It took her a moment to realize he was talking of instinct. "You can give turtles wings—somehow—but not the understanding of flight."

216

"Yes!" Pony beamed a smile. "There are some side considerations. Redesigning a body structure to take the stresses of such a massive size in strong currents would have been difficult, so they selected an animal already quite large."

"Who are 'they'?"

"The domana."

On a signal from the Wyverns, there was a loud clank above their heads as safety locks disengaged. An ornately carved, wooden elevatorlike cage smoothly lowered from the gondola. The doors were handmade works of art, and they folded aside to reveal the stunningly beautiful Sparrow Lifted By Wind. Her shimmering white gown of Faire silk was cut so far off her shoulders—displaying her pearly skin, delicate bone structure, and full breasts to perfection—that Tinker wasn't sure what was keeping the dress on, except for the fact that it was too tight to otherwise slip down. What kept her from being the antithesis of Hannah Briggs' tight black was an overdress of cerulean that drifted around her like smoke and matched the blue of Sparrow's *dau* mark. Sapphires, cerulean ribbons, and pale blue forget-me-not flowers weaved through her intricate pale blond braids, not a hair out of place.

Instantly Tinker realized that she was covered with motor grease, engine oil, dirt, and chicken shit. That she wore Oilcan's hand-me-down T-shirt, her worn carpenter pants, and boots large enough for Minnie Mouse didn't help either. "Oh, hell," she breathed.

"*Husepavua.*" Pony bowed in greeting.

Tinker started to bow too, but Pony checked her with a hand to her shoulder and a slight shake of his head.

Sparrow's eyes narrowed slightly at the gesture, and she flicked her hand dismissively at Pony. "You are released from this duty. Take the car and return to the enclave."

"I am *ze domi ani*'s"—Pony stressed the plural—"guard. I will be going with her."

Pony startled Sparrow into showing cold deep anger that smoothed away a moment later.

"Come, then." Sparrow motioned toward the elevator cage. "I am needed at Aum Renau and can ill spare my attention for this baby-sitting run."

More than three would have crowded the elevator, so the Wyverns waited on the ground while Sparrow, Pony, and Tinker boarded. The doors had to be closed manually, and a bell rung to signal that all was ready for the cage to be raised. Still, the elevator rose as smoothly as it had descended.

Sparrow studied Tinker as they rode upward, and gave a slight sniff. "She smells so much of mud, one would think Wolf Who Rules fashioned her out of dirt."

Pony did not bother to hide his anger. "You fumbled badly, Sparrow. The Wyverns dealt with her in their normal heavy-handed manner and nearly hurt *ze domi ani*. You should have accompanied them."

"And you should remember I'm *domana* now, not *kuetaun*," Sparrow chided him. "As for the Wyverns . . ." She clicked her tongue in an elfin shrug. "The fault does not lie with me. No one would expect the Wyverns to be stupid enough to attack the viceroy's wife."

The cage slid up into the gondola and the safety locks reengaged with a thud under their feet, muffled now by wood and carpet.

Sparrow folded back the door to reveal that the cage was tucked into an alcove of a richly paneled hallway. "I have clothes for her; they'll need fitting. First, though, she'll have to have the barnyard washed off her. Go, clean her."

Tinker bristled. "I can speak low tongue quite well. And I'm fully capable of washing myself."

"Then do so. We have much to do before we arrive at Aum Renau. You must be fit to be brought before the queen." Sparrow bowed curtly and shot a hard look at Pony to collect a bow from him. Once Pony had paid his due to her, she flowed away, a shimmer of white and cerulean.

"This way, *domi*," Pony murmured to Tinker, indicating that they were to get out of the way of the arriving Wyverns. He led her down the hallway that cut through the center of the gondola. Behind them, the gossamer's crew prepared to cast off the moorings. There was an odd unpredictability to the floor that hadn't been that noticeable standing still; it shifted right and left, up and down minutely, so that each stride felt like a misstep.

Rooms were carefully balanced off either side of the hallway. The first door stood open, revealing an observation room, all done in creamy white and accents of red, with a bank of windows open to sky. Three elf females sat surrounded with bolts of Faire silk, laughing as they worked with the material. They looked up as Tinker paused to glance in at the view, and they went into stunned silence at her appearance.

"Pardon," Tinker stammered, and started to bow out of reflex. Again Pony caught her shoulder and shook his head. "Why do you keep doing that?" she whispered as she fled the doorway.

"You are higher caste than Sparrow and those females," Pony said. "There is no one on board that you should bow to."

"Oh." Tinker pointed to her forehead. "The *dau*?"

"Yes, the *dau*, and that you are now Windwolf's *domi*." Pony opened a door and stepped into a small room of hand-painted ceramic tiles. The motif was phoenix and flame flowers—a riot of reds and oranges on pristine white. "This is the bath. Do you wish to be attended?"

"No!" she cried, then eyed the room. Having been practically raised by Tooloo, she thought she knew how elves bathed—just like humans. The room certainly challenged her notion of this. She recognized the bathrobe hanging on a hook, but there were no faucets. There was what looked like a pull chain dangling next to a spout, but it was at knee level. "This is a bathroom?"

Pony considered the question carefully and then nodded. "Yes." He leaned into the room—he seemed loath to actually enter it—and lifted up a wooden disc sitting on a wide waist-high shelf. Beneath it was a large circular tank of steaming water. "This is the *pesh*." He replaced the lid. "*Bae*." This was a wide shallow bowl. "*Giree*." A dried hollow gourd. "*Safat*." A sponge-looking . . . thing.

"Soap?" she said hopefully.

Thankfully there was soap, heavenly scented, in a paste form close enough to bar soap that she could wing it. Pony handed the soap crock down off its shelf, then stood there, distressed. "I can get an attendant to help you."

"I can wash myself." *Yeah. Sure.* "Just—what's the pull chain for?"

Pony winced. "The wash water." He pointed to the low spout. "You fill the basin and pour it over you, then use the soap and the *safat*, and rinse again, then into the *pesh* to soak."

"Ah, I see." Seemed a damn uncomfortable way to wash, but she supposed it saved water. No wonder Tooloo stuck to human showers. "I can handle it from here."

* * *

The cold-water scrub was bracing—she'd rather never do that again. The tub's water seemed hot enough to melt her into a careless puddle, but she found herself worrying about everything. Why did the queen want to see her? Was Windwolf in some type of trouble for using the Skin Clan magic? How was she going to stand being so short and plain in a herd of high-caste elves? And why did Sparrow have a *dau* mark? Had the female been human in some distant past?

Pony tapped on the door. "*Domi*, pardon, but Sparrow does need you to fit your clothes."

It took every ounce of courage to climb out of the tub, tie on the bathrobe, and unlatch the door.

Pony looked as unhappy as she felt.

"What's wrong?" she asked him, trying not to clench the bathrobe tight around her. It covered her neck to ankles and then some, but still she felt naked in front of him.

"There is much for you to know before you meet the queen, what is proper and what would be unspeakably rude. It is not my . . . place to tell you these things, for I am just *sekasha*—but there is only Sparrow, and I'm afraid she's taking a *kaet*."

"A *kaet*?" She giggled; it was a purposely rude way of saying Sparrow was throwing a snit. "Why?"

"I suspect she's jealous of you."

"Of me?"

"She had ambitions to become Windwolf's wife." Seeing the look on her face, Pony added quickly. "No, no, they are not old lovers. There are some who make alliances with marriages, where two work together well, and they agree to make it a partnership. But that would not suit Windwolf."

"Are you sure?"

"I have known Windwolf all my life, and I believe I see him with clarity, whereas Sparrow—age only makes you wiser if you stay honest with yourself."

"Why does she have a *dau*?"

"Windwolf's father marked her when she was young to raise her out of the *kuetaun* caste, otherwise the *sekasha* would have never listened to her orders."

Ah, yes, the snobbery of elves. Like it or not, she was stuck dealing with it now. "What does the queen want with me anyhow?"

"She wishes to see you."

"Me? Why? I'm just a snot-nosed Pittsburgh teenager with an interesting ear job."

Pony nodded several times, as if ticking off her words in an effort to parse them. "Yes," he finally said, still nodding. "Exactly."

"What?"

"You are a young elf. All things elfin fall under the queen's power. Now that you are elfin, so you are now her subject."

"Automatically? I don't get any say?"

"No more than when you were born in Pittsburgh and fell under Maynard's power."

She wanted to say that was different, but she couldn't decide how. The fact that her conception was far from normal—perhaps paralleling her transformation into an elf—gave her a very unstable base to argue from. "Does she do this with every elf?"

"No. You are, however, now her cousin."

"What!"

"You are now her cousin," Pony repeated, more slowly.

"How did that happen?"

"You married Windwolf."

"He's her cousin?"

"Yes, which, by law, makes you her cousin too."

It was such a sane reason that Tinker found it comforting.

"Please." Pony indicated that she was to head back to the observation room. "Sparrow has a gown ready for you."

Tinker winced. "Oh, I don't like the sound of that."

"Why not?"

"In my own clothes, I'm still me. I can't see the change, so I don't notice it."

"I am sorry, but it will be better if you look your best."

Fortunately—in a manner of speaking—only Sparrow was in the Observation Lounge. The other females had been banished to another part of the ship, most likely because of the limited space in the room. Pony took up a post by the door and practiced at being invisible.

"We only have a few hours before arriving at Aum Renau," Sparrow told her. "We'll be going straight from the airfield to an audience with the queen. You must be ready." She handed Tinker a mass of fabrics. "This is a court gown."

Tinker fumbled with it for several minutes trying to make sense of it, until Pony finally took pity on her and reorganized the layers. He held it out then, by the shoulders, for her to see. It was a deep, rich, mottled bronze that looked lovely against her dusky skin, a silk soft as rose petals. While the skirt flared out full, the bodice seemed to be skin-tight, with long sleeves that ended in a fingerless glove arrangement. It wasn't something she'd pick out for herself—to start, there was no way to roll up the sleeves to keep them out of grease. Tinker wasn't even sure how you would get it on; she supposed you pulled it over your head and wriggled a lot. Over the bronze silk was another layer of fine, nearly invisible fabric with a green leaf design, so that when the bronze silk moved, it seemed like sunlight shimmering through forest leaves.

Sparrow waved toward a folding screen set up in the corner. "Step behind there and put it on."

"Just pull it over my head?"

"There are small hooks here that we'll close after you slip it on." Sparrow flipped the material up to show tiny hooks and eyes, oddly enough made of cling vine and ironwood instead of metal.

Pull and wriggle. She tried not to think of Pony standing on the other side of the mostly fabric wall as she gyrated half-naked.

"Wolf Who Rules sent footwear." Sparrow fastened the tiny hooks in the back of the dress. It fit nearly as snugly as Sparrow's gown. The female elf clucked and pinched it tighter. "It needs to be taken in more."

Sparrow handed slippers that matched the gown—tiny dainty things that Tinker loathed on first sight—but sitting on the floor were two pairs of stylish boots heavy enough to please her.

She tried one of the slippers on, hoping that they'd be too small, and found they fit perfectly. "How did you know my size?"

"Windwolf had your clothes measured," Pony said.

Tinker marveled at the slipper. "Truly? The high heels I was wearing were too wide."

Sparrow sniffed. "He asked me to measure your clothes, but I knew how humans make their clothes—standard sizes that fit no one well. I measured you while you were sleeping."

How utterly creepy.

"So, why is the queen here?" Tinker asked Sparrow to avoid thinking about it.

"I don't know." Sparrow smoothed away a hard, resentful look. "We no sooner arrived than the queen requested that you be sent for, and that triggered an argument over you—"

"Me?"

"You. Windwolf wanted to keep you in Pittsburgh until you adjusted, but Soulful Ember insisted that you be fetched, which resulted in my being sent back. I had to leave before learning why the queen has come to the Westernlands."

"Considering the speed at which the court moves," Pony said, "you may not have missed more than the formal greetings and exchange of gifts."

Sparrow fidgeted. "No, something has happened; I've never seen the court like this. The queen has her full guard with her and two dreadnoughts." She glanced sharply at Pony, as if she had said more than she intended. She picked up another gown. "Change into this one and give me that gown to have altered."

It was more difficult to wriggle out of the tight bronze silk than it had been putting it on. She handed it out to Sparrow and slipped the next one on. While she disliked the notion of *her* wearing a dress, she had to admit that the gown was a lovely mottled green. She came out from behind the screen, smoothing down the skirt, to find Sparrow gone.

"What are dreadnoughts?" Tinker asked Pony, glad she didn't have to look ignorant in front of Sparrow.

"Gunships," Pony told her. "Very big gunships."

"Here, hook me up in back."

He hesitated a moment before crossing the room to fasten the little hooks.

She found herself blushing as his fingers brushed her bare skin. In the full-length mirror, she could see their reflection, him leaning over her, the muscles of his arms rippling under his tattoos.

She looked away, for some reason embarrassed by the intimacy shown. She hunted for a safe subject to talk about. "The Wyvern female triggered her spell tattoo for some type of shielding. Do yours trigger defensive spells too?"

"Yes. The shield is to protect you from damage you can't avoid. They are a last resort; but they can not be taken away from us, short of removing the skin from our arms."

"The Wyverns' are red."

"Red is the Fire Clan's color."

"The queen is part of the Fire Clan?"

"She is head of the Fire Clan."

"And Windwolf is Wind Clan?" Getting a nod, she asked, "Does that make me Wind Clan too?"

Obviously this was a "why is the sky blue" question. Someone could tell her a reasonable answer, but it stumped Pony. "You were human, and humans don't have clans, so there was no other choice but for you to join the Wind Clan."

She looked down at her spill of mottled green silk and the tips of her bronze slippers peeking out from the edge of the skirt. "Why am I not wearing blue?"

Pony indicated her *dau* by touching his own forehead. "That speaks of your alliance. But it is not necessary for a *domana* to announce their clan; only the lesser castes do."

Tinker frowned, recalling all of the blue Sparrow was wearing, from the cerulean overdress to the ribbons woven in her hair.

"Why is Sparrow in blue then?"

Pony clicked his tongue in an elfin shrug. "Sparrow has issues of her own making."

They reached Aum Renau just before sunset, and the palace sprawled glorious in the shafts of deep gold sunlight. It crowned the steep hills along the river—white limestone with mullioned glass windows, partially obscured by towering trees and a riot of flowers.

"Aum Renau," Pony murmured beside Tinker as the gossamer closed on the palace.

"As viceroy, Windwolf usually stays here? Does the palace come with the appointment?"

Pony nodded to the first question, and then shook his head. "It is his, not the crown's."

Your boyfriend is rich, Tinker thought, and then winced as she remembered that—as far as the elves were concerned—Windwolf was her husband. *We're going to have a long talk about that.*

Typical of elfin design, the palace seemed to be a linked series of buildings incorporating the natural landscape. Beyond the structures that crowned the hill, more buildings stepped down the eastern exposure, tucked onto ledges and around a steep waterfall. In one wide flat area, jarring against the green and white, sat a courtyard filled with tall stark black stones.

"What are the stones?" Tinker asked, pointing them out.

"Nothing for you." Sparrow focused on storm clouds moving toward them. She made a slight hurt noise and headed toward the control cabin.

"They are the Wind Clan's spell stones," Pony told Tinker, glancing after Sparrow, and then he too focused on the storm clouds.

The dark forms converged in a manner not natural to clouds, although far too large and dark to be other gossamers.

"What are those?"

"Dreadnoughts," Pony said.

As the airships drew closer together, she saw that they were a product of elves' contact with man. Instead of a living ship like the gossamer, the dreadnoughts were fully mechanical, obviously a blend of airship and armored helicopter. The barrels of heavy guns bristled from the black hull, reminding Tinker of the spiked hide of a river shark. The two dreadnoughts blocked the airspace over the palace and flashed out a warning on a signal lamp. A few minutes later, having apparently received some communication back from the gossamer, the dreadnoughts pivoted and moved off.

"How odd," Pony murmured, his eyes narrowed in speculation. "I've never heard of the flagship being challenged before. Sparrow is right; something has happened."

The gossamer tethered at an airfield in a wide hilltop meadow, some distance from the palace. Horses and a coach waited. The Wyverns, still bruised and sulking, mounted the horses. The ground crew unrolled a carpet from the elevator to the carriage in order to save Tinker's hated slippers from harm. Pony had to help her mount the tall step up into the coach without entangling her long skirt. Inside one could hold a party; facing leather-upholstered bench seats allowed eight adults to sit comfortably.

"Slide over to the other side," Pony murmured as he made sure Tinker's gown didn't catch in the doorway.

Annoyance flickered over Sparrow's face as she stepped into the coach. She sat on the right side of the bench instead of making room for Pony. The bodyguard climbed in, latched the door, and settled on the bench opposite the females.

Minutes later, the reason for Pony's suggestion and Sparrow's annoyance became clear. They traveled along a wide avenue designed with views in mind. Around each curve was a new beautiful vista of the valley. The river ran wide as a lake, reflecting the sun. Stone walled enclaves sectioned up the west bank into orderly squares and rectangles. Virgin forest blanketed the far eastern bank. A ship was sailing upriver, the wind filling its sail colored Wind Clan blue, leaving a V-shaped wake behind it. A great white bird drifted over the water, giving desolate cries.

"What kind of bird is that?" Tinker asked.

Pony leaned forward to peer out the window. "A *chiipeshyosa*." He then directed her attention to the wooden docks lining the river. "Those smaller boats were built in *Pitsubaug*," he used the Elvish word for Pittsburgh, "and taken down river to the ocean, then around to here. They are steel-hulled, and use fuel-cell engines."

But then the palace came into sight, and Tinker lost all joy of the experience. The last few hours of Sparrow's and Pony's frantic tutoring had done nothing but reveal her ignorance of formal elfin culture, making her feel like a junkyard dog about to go on parade.

The front entrance had a portico of stone arches heavy with climbing roses. From there, they walked through a series of hallways— wide, airy, filled with sunlight, polished marble. Elves stood talking in small groups, all dressed in elegant splendor. Recognizing Sparrow, they would fall silent and bow, but their eyes fixed with curiosity on Tinker.

"Am I that odd looking?" Tinker whispered to Pony.

"They are merely curious to see who has captured Windwolf's heart."

"Me?"

"Yes, you."

And that gave her the courage to walk into the great gathering room full of beautiful females and males.

The room had been designed on a large scale, meant to be impressive. A grove of ironwood had been cultured into a straight row. The thick tree trunks vaulted hundreds of feet straight up before branching into a canopy of green. Polished granite formed the floor, and whatever made up the ceiling was lost somewhere overhead. Elf shines drifted in the shadows, gleaming motes of living light.

Large as it was, the room hadn't been designed to hold the number crowded into it now. Thankfully they were focused on the other side of the room, where a heated debate ranged. As Sparrow murmured something to a male in the queen's colors waiting at the door, Tinker recognized Windwolf's voice, and she edged sideways to see through the crowd to spot him.

He stood near the front of the hall, his hair unbound in a shimmering black cascade down his back. He wore a bronze that matched her underdress and a duster of the leaf pattern of her overdress. The sheath of his long ceremonial sword cut a slash of deep blue across his back.

"Earth Son, your proposals are like setting a forest fire to bring down one black willow," he was saying in High Elvish, in carefully chosen words. Between his clear, deep enunciation and slow pacing, Tinker easily followed what he said.

Earth Son was a male in a rich green, taller than Windwolf, but more slender. He was flanked by *sekasha* tattooed in Stone Clan colors. "You deny the Seer's Sight?"

"I am not saying that." Windwolf's voice filled the space with a deep grandeur that was unmatched by his opposition. "Certainly I have seen shadows of the oni against the wall. Even the humans are dreaming of tengu." At least that's what Tinker thought he said, although she didn't understand it fully. "Obviously their spies have reached Elfhome."

"We must take steps to protect ourselves."

"Slashing about madly will only take out our allies."

The press of bodies shifted and Tinker lost sight of the two speakers.

"Allies?" Earth Son's voice filled with scorn. "The humans? All evidence points that they are in league with the oni!"

"What evidence? Do you have proof that you are keeping hidden from me? If so, I demand that you bring it forward now. I represent the Wind Clan here; I will not be kept ignorant."

"The human Pathway is punching a hole through our defenses, leaving us open to attack! They are acting in conjunction with the oni."

Tinker shifted sideways just as Windwolf paced into view, in profile to her now. *My husband.* Gods, that sounded so weird.

"You are conjecturing that creating a tool is the same as gifting it?" Windwolf rolled his hand lazily, indicating one unsound statement following another. "Do you blame a smith for the crimes of a thief?"

"Ah!" Earth Son cried as if he won some great victory. "So you at least admit that the oni are using the human's Pathway?"

Windwolf sighed visibly and shook his head. "I do not deny that is possible, but I will also remind the court that the oni are as mythical to the humans as we were." He paced back out of sight. "It's undeniable that individuals or even groups of oni have reached Earth, why else the legends, but where are the screaming hordes? They are not on Earth."

"Do you think you've been told the truth? Do not be naïve in thinking humans understand honor."

Tinker shifted and caught sight of the two males again. They stood now only an arm reach apart, intent as duelists upon each other.

"I have found," Windwolf said with a dangerous rumble, "the percentage of honorable humans is the same as elves."

As Earth Son stood still, apparently considering whether he'd been insulted or not, Pony whispered to Tinker, "The Stone Clan have lost power since the Pathway to Pittsburgh opened. They have always advocated that the humans be forced to close the Pathway."

That helped clarify the situation! Now, why was she here?

Windwolf too took advantage of Earth Son's silence. "I have done all in my power to ensure that I know the truth. We of the Wind Clan have learned the human tongue and I have sent members of my household out to Earth proper to travel it extensively. If the oni are on Earth, they have concealed themselves well. They have passed out of the minds of humans, out of their nightmares, and nearly out of their language."

"But they are in Pittsburgh now."

Windwolf's face went bleak. "Yes. That is undeniable. How they came to be there, that is not known."

"The human Pathway opens to Onihida!" Earth Son cried.

"No!" Windwolf's denial rang through the hall. "If it opened to Onihida, the oni would have flooded out, unchecked, long ago. Look at this wilderness and think of their numbers. If they had clear passage, nothing would stop them! The only reason they would be using subversion would be because frontal attack is not possible."

"You speak as if you know this as truth."

"I know that the sun is hot, the stars are distant, and rules of warfare follow certain logic, regardless of the world."

"There is a door, open but not open." A female spoke in a cold, dispassionate tone, and all turned to look at her. In the shift of bodies, Tinker picked her out. She was willow-slender, dressed in pale moth white, with a glistening red ribbon tied over her eyes and trailing down over her gown like a trail of blood. "Darkness presses against the frame but can not pass through. The light beyond is too brilliant; it burns the beast."

"Can we keep the door from opening?" someone asked.

"No. It is only a matter of time. But if it is a time of our choosing, then the beast will be slain. If we do nothing and let the darkness come when it will, all will be lost to night."

The very lack of emotion was chilling. The room had stilled to utter silence, everyone straining to hear. Tinker caught Pony's shoulder and pulled him down to whisper in his ear, "Who is that?"

"The *intanyai seyosa*," Pony whispered. Literally it meant "one who sows and harvests the most favorable future of all," but what did that mean?

Sparrow hissed them to silence.

"How do we choose?" the same questioner asked.

"Bind the pivot," the *intanyai seyosa* said. "If the pivot be true, then the battle can be won. If the pivot proves false, all will be lost."

"Is the pivot here?" the questioner asked.

The female raised her hand and pointed. Elves parted like water, stepping back out of the way, and the finger did not waver. Where moments before Tinker could barely see the blindfolded elf, suddenly there was a clear path between them, and the female pointed straight at Tinker's chest.

Let there be someone behind me! Tinker shifted sideways as she glanced over her shoulder. No one stood behind her. When she looked back, the finger still pointed straight at her as if laser guided.

"Shit," she whispered.

Windwolf gave her a look of dismay and alarm. He turned back toward the front of the room. "What is the meaning of this?"

All other eyes remained on Tinker. The hard fixed interest was daunting. She wanted to hide, but there seemed to be no place to take cover. Pony must have sensed her fear; he stepped in front of Tinker to shield her with his body.

Gratefulness profound as love filled Tinker, and she reached out to lay her hand on Pony's back. He glanced over his shoulder at her touch and whispered, "Neither Windwolf nor I will let harm come to you."

"Calm yourself, cousin," the questioner commanded. "Let her come forth. We wish to see her for ourselves."

Pony gave Tinker a querying look, and she nodded, even though she still felt like bolting from the room. She couldn't hide behind him forever. He stepped smoothly to one side, and—as they practiced on the gossamer—they walked toward the queen. At least the seer had cleared them a path.

There was no mistaking Queen Soulful Ember. Not that one could truly mistake her, for she sat while everyone stood, crowned with a ruby-studded circlet. There seemed to be nearly visible power emanating off her, like the pulse of a heavy engine against the skin. Tinker expected her to be beautiful, but that was too meager a word for the queen. Soulful Ember was glorious: skin a radiant white, hair so gold it was metallic, eyes so blue they seemed neon.

Pony stopped and went down to one knee. Tinker carefully measured out the two extra steps beyond him that her rank allowed, and then gave a deep bow. Windwolf came to stand beside her, and she wished she could find his presence more comforting. He was at least a familiar face, but he obviously didn't know what he'd gotten her dragged into.

The queen studied Tinker for a moment, glanced to Windwolf as if puzzled by his choice, and asked, "How old are you?"

"Eighteen."

"You're only counting the days you've been an elf?"

Tinker frowned, trying to translate it, then shook her head. "I'm eighteen years old."

"You said nothing, cousin, as to how young she was. She's just a baby."

Tinker flushed with anger, and snapped, "I am not," out of habit, and then winced as she remembered to whom she was talking. "I'm an adult."

"Did you know she was the pivot when you had me summon her?" Windwolf growled.

"We suspected her," Queen Soulful Ember said without apology or anger in her voice. "The pivot would be marked with the Wind Clan *dau*. That is why we demanded that Lifted Sparrow By Wind accompany you originally. It was not known that you'd taken a wife."

"I don't understand. What is a pivot?" Tinker said.

"As there are layers of worlds, there are layers of future," the queen said. "Paths can be taken to lead to very different outcomes or just the same conclusion via a different route. Usually it is the action that chooses the path, not the person acting; any messenger can deliver the important message, and any sailor can lose the vital ship in a storm. When only one person can guide the future, they are a pivot."

"Are you serious?" Tinker looked to Windwolf. "How can you know the future?"

"It is the nature of magic to splinter things down to possibilities," Windwolf explained. "Spells merely guide the outcome to the desired path. In the presence of magic, the ability of humans and elves to guess the future becomes the ability to see possible futures."

"Lain says fortune telling is mumble-jumble," Tinker said.

Windwolf looked pained. "Yet Lain sees the future in her dreams."

"You brought me a tengu, and wanted me to bandage it," Lain had said the night Tinker brought her the wounded Windwolf. "I kept on telling you that it was dangerous, but you wouldn't listen to me. . . ."

And Tooloo had known too. "He'll swallow you up, and nothing will be left."

They had seen, in some fearful way, that Windwolf would unmake the human Tinker, leaving an elf in her place.

Tinker turned to the blindfolded elf, suddenly trembling. "What do I need to do?"

"You weave the ropes to bind yourself. Be true, and the battle can be won. Be false, all will be lost."

"What the hell does that mean?" Tinker whispered fiercely to Windwolf in English. "They're not going to tie me up, are they?"

"Dreams are the forerunners of visions," Windwolf said. "She does not have to be asleep to see, but they are still . . . difficult to determine their true meaning."

"So she could be wrong about me?"

"No." Windwolf put out his hand to her. Tinker hesitated a moment, Tooloo's words ringing in her mind, but then took his hand, lacing her fingers through his. It helped to have something to cling to in this sea of beautiful, dispassionate strangers.

"Let me send her off to rest," Windwolf asked the queen. "She has been through much the last few days."

"Is there anything we can do to influence the pivot?" the queen asked the seer.

"No. All is in place. The rest is of her own making."

11: SPELL STONES

TINKER wasn't sure if she was annoyed or relieved to be hustled off center stage. Certainly she didn't like being the focus of attention, but she would have liked to know more about what was going on. She had a feeling, though, that there was no way she could stay and not be the focus.

Sparrow seemed to take the escort duty as badly, though she did try to hide the fact that she was seething.

The sprawling layout of the palace translated into a maze of hallways, open courtyards, and short flights of stairs. Armed warriors stood guard everywhere. At first they only passed Fire Clan warriors who watched their passage in still silence, but at one intersection of hallways, they apparently moved into Wind Clan territory. From that point on the warriors all wore Wind Clan blue, and bowed low, their gazes curious although their expressions were neutral.

Finally they entered a large beautiful room with heavy mahogany furniture. Sparrow paused to state, "This is the private living quarters of Wolf Who Rules. You will be sleeping here until we leave for Pittsburgh," and continued walking through the room.

"What?"

"These are the *domou*'s and *domi*'s private quarters," Sparrow answered without stopping. "This way!" She entered a bedroom the size of a baseball field. "You will be sleeping here until the queen gives us permission to leave for Pittsburgh."

Tinker paused at the door, her attention caught and fixed by the large bed turned down to show off satin sheets. Did Windwolf plan to sleep with her in it? Surely in a place this large, there was another place he could sleep. Had he just assumed she agreed to it? Or would it be taken badly if she made him sleep elsewhere? How would anyone even know, if she did, in a place this big?

Did she want to sleep with him?

"Take off the gown," Sparrow stated briskly and Tinker realized that the female had already repeated herself several times. "You only wear that gown for formal occasions." Sparrow held out something white and flowing. "This is your nightgown here."

Automatically Tinker started to consider how to get off the gown before she found enough mental stability to realize that one, Pony and an unknown female warrior stood behind her and two, she didn't want to change into the diaphanous thing that Sparrow held. She crossed her arms and glared at Sparrow.

"I want my own clothes back."

"They are being washed. This is all you have to wear other than the gown."

Great. Tinker looked back at Pony.

He took that as permission to speak on a different matter entirely, "Forgiveness, *ze domi*. This female is Sun Lance; she is well known to me as brave and able. I have chosen her to attend you in the evening, and those places I can not join you."

Sun Lance bowed low. "I live to serve, *ze domi*."

Tinker felt like someone had kicked the legs out from under her. "You're leaving me alone?"

"Even a *sekasha* must sleep," Sparrow snapped. "He's staggering where he stands as it is."

Tinker realized guiltily that Pony was indeed exhausted. He must never really have slept since they left Windwolf's hunting lodge. "Of all the idiocy," she muttered in English, and then in Elvish said, "Go. Sleep." Tinker shooed Pony away.

Sparrow waited, nightgown in hand.

Now that they were down to just females, Tinker considered how to get out of her gown again, and decided that she couldn't do it alone. "Can you help me undo the hooks?"

It was interesting to note that elves made the same aspirated sounds when they were frustrated. Sparrow tossed the nightgown onto the bed, and came to undo the hooks. Her pale graceful hands were ice cold and trembling. Was she shaken by the news that she had been considered the pivot, or jealous that Tinker took her place once again? If she wanted the position, she could have it back.

Tinker carefully wriggled out of the gown and Sparrow took it to hang up in a vast empty closet. While not quite as tight, the nightgown of white fairy silk matched the gown in cut: long sleeves, tight bodice, and full flowing skirt. It slipped over her head too, like so much cool air, and spilled down over her body to swirl around her ankles. Despite being fully dressed, she felt naked. She glanced at herself in a mirror across the room and winced—the tight fabric left nothing to the imagination, looking like so much cream poured down over her.

"You don't have anything else for me to wear?"

"Nothing to lounge in." Sparrow came back with another pair of dainty slippers, these white to match the nightgown.

"Where're the boots you showed me earlier?" Tinker pulled off the bronze slippers and surrendered them to Sparrow's care.

"The boots are not appropriate to wear in the palace."

"Where are they?"

Sparrow looked at her levelly, whatever she felt carefully hidden away, but yet she seemed to radiate distaste. Were elves secretly psychic? After a minute of cold silence, Sparrow said, "They're in the closet with the other footwear."

Score one for the visiting team.

"Will that be all?" Sparrow asked.

"Yes," Tinker said, wanting rid of all elves, short-tempered Sparrow in particular.

Sparrow nodded, and Sun Lance bowed deeply, and at last, Tinker was alone.

Tinker went through the closet. Besides the gowns they fitted on the gossamer, there were several other elaborate gowns hanging— evidence that Windwolf must employ an army of seamstresses. What he didn't employ was common sense—she hated all of them. To be fair, the gowns were all very lovely; the only fault she found with them was that *she* was expected to wear them. Beside the dresses sat a rack of matching slippers. She found two pairs of boots, one of suede and the other of polished leather. Both had soles of hard leather, and a heel of ironwood. Not as hefty as her work boots, but they certainly were better than the slippers.

She also discovered a wonderful duster of painted silk that fit her perfectly. Made from a rich, mottled blue, subliminal images of wolves ran through wispy clouds of white.

Boots and duster made her feel dressed enough to take on the world. Avoiding the big bed and all its implications, she explored the bedroom. It seemed oddly sterile, like one of the Observatory dorm rooms, cleaned after the last scientist left and waiting for the next one to arrive. Just bigger with lots more doors. She worked clockwise from the walk-in closet: an updated toilet complete with imported toilet paper, a traditional bathing room done in Wind Clan blue tile, French doors that opened to a balcony.

Dusk had come and gone since the gossamer arrived at Aum Renau, and night covered the sky. The constellation of First Wolf was raising its bright shoulder star on the horizon. Roses, pine, and wood smoke scented the air. Below was another patio, nearly lost in the sea of darkness. Elf shines gathered like a living exit light around an open archway. Tinker glanced back to the big bed, the door to where Sun Lance stood guarding over her because she was Windwolf's *domi*, and the great hall filled with elves believing that the future pivoted around her.

It proved to be a quick scramble down off the balcony to the dark courtyard below.

So running away wasn't a bright idea. She could see that now. She really had to learn to plan three or four steps ahead instead of just one or two. Where the hell did she think she was going to go? Certainly she couldn't get back to Pittsburgh. One can't outrun the future. All she managed to do was get lost.

A figure stepped out of the darkness, barring her path. "Who are you?"

"I'm—I'm . . ." It grated to realize that her identity depended wholly on Windwolf's. "I'm Tinker *ze domi*."

He grunted in surprise and pulled out a spell light, activating it with a guttural keyword. The light flared to nearly painful white until he clasped the orb tightly, cutting down its intensity. A powerful ley line must run close by; now that she focused on it, she felt the invisible warmth running over her. Even in the darkness, squinting from the painful shafts of light escaping from between the elf's fingers, she could see the power roiling on the air around them, like moonlight on water.

The spell light revealed that the elf was a *sekasha* armed with longbow, pale feathered spell arrows, and a sword of ironwood. Considering the strength of the ley line, carrying steel weapons would be nearly impossible. His tattoos identified him as Wind Clan, which was oddly comforting. His shield spell was activated, though she hadn't heard him utter the spell; the intricate deep blue lines seemed to flow as magic followed the circuit, and an aura of dark blue outlined his body.

The warrior tilted the spell light to pick out her *dau* mark. "Ah, *ze domi!*" He flicked the light away from her eyes, but continued to block her way.

"Is something wrong?" she asked.

He hesitated and then whistled lowly. A moment later, a second warrior appeared silently out of the dark.

"What is it?" The newcomer eyed Tinker.

"It is Wolf Who Rules' new *domi*," the first said. It was interesting to note that he used the word "new" that denoted "first" instead of "newest." "I—I don't know—do I let her pass?"

The second one glanced back over his shoulder at whatever the darkness hid, and then clicked his tongue in a shrug. "She is Wind Clan *domana*." He bowed lowly to her. "Do you wish to continue this way, *domi?*"

Now they had her curious.

"Yes, please," Tinker said.

The first bowed too, and backed up to clear the path. "Forgiveness, *ze domi.*"

"Forgiveness." She started forward slowly, in case they changed their minds. *I'm harmless. I'm harmless.*

"So that is her?" the second murmured lowly. "They said she was small, but I did not expect her to be that tiny."

"It certainly puts her fight with the oni warriors in new light."

"The courage of dragons, they say."

She blushed hotly, embarrassed but pleased by their words. After her dealings with Sparrow, she was afraid that everyone except Pony disliked her. Perhaps it was just Sparrow. Certainly they seemed to think that she had a right to the mysterious stones.

She came to an open plaza and the guards and Sparrow were forgotten.

Monoliths stood in a massive circle, like silent giants. Elf shines drifted through the dark shadows cast by the stones. The air roiled with magic; it flushed her fever hot and made her feel so light she worried about drifting away. She stepped forward, and something thrummed underfoot, making her jerk backwards.

A channel for a ley line had been chiseled into the paving stone, slashing across her path. As she looked at it, her eyes slowly registered the nearly invisible purple of potential magic. Outside of the buildup on her electromagnet, she'd never seen magic in enough quantity to be visible. She backed up another step and considered what she was wearing. Suddenly the wood and leather fasteners on her clothes made sense. What about her boots? Sparrow had made some remark about them not being appropriate for the palace. She backed up a little more and pulled off her boots. The paving stones were polished smooth and toasty warm under her stocking feet.

Her boots in hand, she stepped over the channel and went out into the plaza for a closer look. Attracted by her movement, elf shines drifted to her in order to light the way. Without scale, she had mistaken the size of the monoliths, thinking they were only nine or ten feet tall. As she hiked across the wide flat plaza, they loomed taller and taller as she neared them, until they towered nearly twenty feet above her. The monoliths were made of polished granite, with spells permanently inlaid in their surfaces. She peered at the elaborate arcane design as the shines floated around her, reflected in the polished stone.

The spells inscribed into the rock were unlike anything she had worked with before, so much so she couldn't even guess their function. She found a jumper point sunk deep into the stone and realized that the monoliths were layers of inlaid slabs, in essence huge macro chips. They could trigger complex spells fueled by the massive amount of magic represented by the ley line—but to do what? And why hadn't Sparrow wanted her to know about them?

Someone was walking toward her, footsteps loud on stone. She turned to find Windwolf coming across the plaza, still in the matching bronze. As usual, all her emotions went tumbling so she wasn't sure what she really felt. Relief. Desire. Anger.

"Tink."

And she remembered him kissing her neck, whispering, *"Trust me, my little savage Tink."*

With a snarl, she flung her boots at his head, and immediately regretted it. What if she actually hit him in the face? She didn't want to hurt him—well, yes, she did—but not that bad.

Windwolf flinched his head aside so her boots sailed past him, not even ruffling his hair. "Is something wrong?"

"Yes! Look at me!"

"You look beautiful."

"Why did you do this to me?"

"I did not want you to die. You did not want to die."

"I thought you meant I was sick! I thought you were going to heal me of something." She pointed to one of her now-pointed ears. "You didn't tell me that you were going to make me an elf!"

"I thought you understood." He slipped his hand through her hair to run his fingertips over her ear point. "At least as far as you could."

His touch sent electric sparks all through her body. She wanted him, wanted him so badly it terrified her. She pulled away, trembling with more than desire. "Play fair. I'm not stupid, you know; I would have understood."

"It will take you a human's lifetime, and perhaps more, to understand what it is to be an elf. Can a wildflower tucked in the roots of an ironwood understand what it is like to tower over everything, face to the bare sky? Can the wildflower understand facing winter instead of going dormant underground? Can it imagine surviving lightning strikes and forest fires?"

She punched him in the shoulder, hard enough to knock him back. "Oh, don't go metaphysical on me. *'Do you want to be an elf?'* That's all you had to ask so that I knew what decision I was really making. I feel like you tricked me. I feel like you betrayed my trust!"

"I am sorry that you feel like I tricked you," he said in a low, sincere voice. "The timing was important, and I rushed things to meet the window of opportunity. I thought you understood as much as possible and consented fully. I would never betray you."

Much as she didn't want to, she believed him. Without malice or arrogance on his part, it seemed pointless to argue blame. She had, after all, given her consent, stupid as it was in hindsight.

"Can you change me back?"

"Is it so bad that to die a human is better?"

"Not to die human, to live a human."

"Is being an elf so bad?"

"No. Yes. I don't know. I don't like having someone follow me around." She didn't name Pony, feeling like she'd be betraying him. "And I don't like strangers showing up with swords and demanding that I drop everything to come with them. I don't like wearing these stupid clothes, and being looked at as if I'm some rude, ignorant thing. And I hate that saying even this makes me sound whiny."

"Ah."

He stood silent and still as she stalked away to retrieve her footwear. Tinker was too angry to be motionless, too civilized to scream like she desperately wanted to. After throwing her boots at him, she was too shamed to shout without provocation. If he had said something, anything, to let her vent, she would have happily latched on to it. He remained quiet as she pulled her boots back on; if he could wear his boots, she wasn't going to stand around in stocking feet.

"Tinker, I am sorry," he said finally. "I did not want to make you miserable."

"Well, you succeeded in doing just that."

He opened his arms, offering comfort without asking her forgiveness. She glared at him but her anger had run out, and all that remained was lonely hurt. She leaned against him, letting him wrap his arms around her and kiss her temple.

They stood unmoving and silent for several minutes until all the hurt was soothed away and curiosity took over.

"What are these monoliths?"

"They are the Wind Clan Spell Stones," Windwolf said. "It is from these that the Wind Clan *domana* derive their power."

"What do they do?"

"In the same manner that magic can allow travel *through* worlds, it can allow power to *cross* worlds."

"I don't understand."

"One calls for power, and it comes."

She shook her head, still not understanding.

"I will show you."

Windwolf stepped away from her, and held out his right hand, thumb and index finger rigid, middle fingers cocked oddly. "Daaaaaaaaae."

Tinker felt the tremor in the air around Windwolf, like a pulse of a bass amplifier, first against a sense she hadn't been aware of before, and then against her skin. She realized that she had felt the magic triggering. Windwolf's hand apparently was taking the place of a written spell, and his voice starting the resonance that would focus the magic into the pattern set up by the spell. Once triggered, the spell would continue until canceled or all magic was sucked out of the area.

Even as she realized that, the spell stones reacted. With the same "magic sense" she felt the sudden vast structure around them come alive. The invisible sluggish current that she had noticed before began to move faster, surging toward the standing giants. When it reached the monoliths, the violet gleam of magic crawled up the spell tracings. So close to the end of the visible spectrum, the effect was at first barely noticeable, and slowly grew to unmistakable. As she stared, the air around the monoliths started to distort, not from heat or light, but some other potential that echoed back on her "magic sense."

Allow travel through worlds . . . allow power to cross worlds.

He was talking about the quantum effects on a hyperphase level. Windwolf had the ability to *jump* magic from this point to his location. Judging by what she just felt, Windwolf would preform a trigger and it would bridge the gap between him and the spell stones, allowing the power to jump back, along the quantum level resonance.

Triggered and waiting, the massive power pressed invisibly against her.

Windwolf gestured and intoned another guttural vowel, and the power slowly collapsed. He indicated that she should be silent and still and, afraid that she might trigger something, she held motionless.

"You will be taught how to use these." Windwolf broke the silence when he deemed it safe to speak again.

Tinker let out the "oh wow" she'd been holding in. "I had no idea that elves could control magic like this! I've never seen anyone do anything like that in Pittsburgh."

"Only *domana* can summon magic. Only Wind Clan *domana* can call on these stones."

Somehow the monoliths were keyed to a specific genome, so the *domana* of one clan alone could set up the correct resonance to match the stones.

"Do other clans have their own stones?"

"Yes. Each clan normally has several. There are four other sets of Wind Clan stones. There is a range limit of one *mei*."

A *mei* was an odd number, nearly a thousand miles in length, and yet only rough in estimate, as if the exact distance wasn't important. It never made sense as a measurement before now.

She looked at her hands, the remembrance of the power still lingering like the memory of pain. "You made it so I can call magic?"

"Yes, but it takes a great deal of learning."

"Can I do it by mistake?"

He shook his head. "The triggers are quite complex on purpose."

That was comforting. Nothing like accidentally frying oneself in the middle of a deep yawn. Still it was mind boggling that Windwolf had gifted her with this type of power. Why her? Every female she'd seen, while maybe not her mental equal, certainly was young and beautiful. Why hadn't Windwolf fallen in love with one of them in the last hundred and ten years? Hell, Sparrow was right under his nose, and already marked with a *dau*.

It occurred to Tinker that while Sparrow was as beautiful as one of the high caste females, she was in fact still low caste. "Sparrow can't access the spell stones?"

"No. Genetically she is not *domana*."

"Why not?"

"That is no longer done." Windwolf reached out his hand. When Tinker took it, he started them toward the gate. "At one time, yes, we freely shifted lesser castes up to *domana* ability. But that was during a time of war. We no longer do it."

"What about me?"

"You were human and extremely mortal. The two cases are completely different, dire need versus convenience."

At the gate, they picked up shadows in the form of two *sekasha*. She realized with some mortification that one was Sun Lance. Had the female come with Windwolf, or climbed down the balcony and followed her silently from the very start? What in the world did the female think of her, fleeing into the dark and throwing boots at

Windwolf? Tinker winced and thought back through her conversation with Windwolf. What language had they been arguing in? English. Good.

"Will you please explain what you've done to me? Fully."

"Are you sure? It will be a very analytical discussion. You have been through so very much, it might be hard to hear."

"Yes, I want to know."

"Very well. I used a transformation spell, keyed via my sperm, with protections against any radical changes to the original. The spell is considered very safe; the base was developed by the Skin Clan millennia ago and improved since then. I took every precaution to make it failsafe."

"What precautions?"

"That you were a virgin was the ultimate insurance against possible contamination."

She blushed. "You're kidding!"

"No. When you do the spell, you use a source key. Sperm works best; it is, by its very nature, a template of life." What he said matched what Lain guessed. "However, having two sources could be dangerous."

"So I didn't need to be a virgin—just abstaining for a day or two would work."

Windwolf shook his head. "Human sperm stays active anywhere from three days to a week. Elfin sperm stays active up to a year."

"A year?"

"Half-elfin could range anywhere between the two."

"A year?"

"It is a sometimes problematic side effect of being immortal," Windwolf admitted. "It is one reason why we are not as promiscuous as humans."

"Yeah, that would do it."

"With you being a virgin, it wasn't a worry." He reached out and ran his finger lightly over her ear tip. "You are mine, and mine alone."

They had reached "their" living quarters.

She halted him before they could walk on to the bedroom. "Are you—we—there's just one bed."

He cocked his head. "In your bedroom, yes."

"And you have a bedroom too?"

Wordlessly, he showed her the second bedroom, undeniably Windwolf's. His scent hung in the air. A closet door stood open to show off his impressive wardrobe. All about the room were things to catch the eye, objects of beauty and interest, set down at the end of the day and not picked up again.

Two bedrooms? Didn't married people share one bedroom? Or was this whole marriage thing only a way for Windwolf to control the pivot? It certainly made more sense than him suddenly falling in love with her. Tooloo had been right; she didn't know her own heart. That he might not want her hurt more than she could imagine. She sat on a bench at the end of Windwolf's bed, confounded by herself.

Windwolf had shut the door, giving them privacy from the *sekasha*, and came to sit beside her. "I know that all this is difficult. I wanted to give you time to think and to adjust."

What do I want? What do I want?

I want him.

She reached out to touch his hair. If he had looked at her, she probably would have lost courage, but he didn't, so she stroked its softness. She gently brushed his hair away from his ear, and explored its outline.

He shifted, and she jerked her hand away.

"I wish you to continue," he murmured.

"Really?"

"I desire it very much."

She leaned against him and buried her face in his hair. She'd never really looked at someone's ear before. Were human ears less delicate and mysterious, with their odd little turns and curls? She kissed his lobe, and the pulse point beating under his ear, and then the strong column of his neck. She realized she was trembling, and wasn't sure if it was with fear or excitement.

She buried her face into his shoulder, and whispered, "Take me."

His arms encircled her lightly. "There is no rush, Tink. Let us learn together what pleases us most."

"You seemed to know what pleased me before." His shirt was bronze silk, warmed by his body, his muscles moving under it. He filled her senses, and she seemed so small.

"And yet you're afraid of me now."

Was it possible to shrink to nothing in his arms? "I'm afraid you don't want me."

"You are all that I want," he breathed against her neck, and even that warmth sent shivers through her. "My universe resides within you."

She peeked at his face, and found him watching her with tender regard. "Does that mean that you love me?"

"Love is such a small word to carry what I feel."

She would have to take that for a yes.

She never noticed her duster coming off, or when the hooks of her nightgown came undone. The nightgown was slipped down over her breasts, and bunched up high on her waist before she realized how undressed she was. By then Windwolf was lightly kissing his way up her inner thigh, and she didn't want him to stop. She raised her hips so he could slide off her underwear. He held her cupped in his hands, his thumbs opening her to him, his breathing the most intimate of touches. She shook with the need of something more, and whispered to him, "Please." He dipped his head, and pleasure seemed to pour liquid out of him, spilling from his tongue and into her.

It was only later, with his soft hair pooled over her bare legs, she realized it had been just like her dream.

12: AUM RENAU

THEY STAYED AT Aum Renau for three weeks.

Tinker tried to be happy there. Certainly it was a pleasant enough stay. She had the new universe of sex to explore. Outside of bed, Windwolf seemed genuinely in love with her, although why was as hard to fathom as how she felt about him. Her scientific mind wanted something to see and measure and quantify before she was willing to admit that she loved him.

Windwolf arranged things so she could avoid the queen, the court, and all things political—apparently needing only to cite her age and recent transformation to excuse her from those "duties." He, however, could not absent himself, and so needed to spend hours away. The first two days, she took apart everything remotely mechanical in the Wind Clan section of the palace: ten clocks, three music boxes, the kitchen dumbwaiter, and both master bathrooms. After that, Pony and a changing subset of the palace's twenty *sekasha* took her out exploring the countryside. They rode horses, sailed on a nearby lake, hiked in the mountains, visited the open market down by the river, practiced archery, and played a cutthroat, fast-paced cousin to lawn croquet. Eventually she bored of that, and nosed her way into the kitchen to carry on science experiments in the form of cooking, and spent a day in awe of the massive, steam-driven laundry facility, and finally talked her way onto the dreadnought (but only after promising that she'd take nothing apart).

The palace's staff took to her invasion well, their initial dismay and subservience thawing to open friendliness. At least she seemed to be meshing much better than Sparrow, especially among the *sekasha*, who seemed to treat Sparrow with quiet disdain.

"Sparrow is too self-centered," Pony explained. They were on the archery field, whiling away the long summer afternoon. "It is true that the *domana* rule the other castes, but it does not mean that it's more important. If the *seyosa* did not farm, and the *sepeshyosa* did not fish, and *selinsafa* did not do the laundry, or the *sefada* did not cook, where would we be?"

"Dirty and hungry." Tinker took aim at the warg target down field. (She refused to shoot at the disturbing humanoid targets.) The first arrow hit in the warg's hindquarters, but the next three grouped around the heart bull's-eye. The last actually landed in the red. "*Kiyau!*"

The *sekasha* laughed at her answer, and complimented her on her shots. One of the runners at the end of the field collected her arrows and ducked back to his shelter.

"Exactly. Pull!" Pony called, setting the warg whizzing around on its track in unpredictable starts and turns. "A body must have a brain, mouth, eyes, hands, bowels, and feet." He shot as he talked, loosing his five arrows nearly as fast as he could nock and pull, and yet they all grouped around the heart, three in the red.

"Oh, you flatter me so," Tinker said, meaning their compliments on her shots.

"You are doing well for someone who never handled a bow before," Pony said. "I've been practicing for nearly a century, the rest for millennia. Someday you'll be good as we are; your eye is good."

A century. That still put shivers through her. The *sekasha* seemed happy to spend an entire day on archery, but she was bored in an hour or two. Of course, they were honing their abilities while she saw it as a mere diversion, something to do while talking. She supposed that they didn't do math problems for fun. She wished she had been able to at least bring her datapad with her. Windwolf had given her several reams of fine paper and a score of pens, but it wasn't the same. He promised that he'd take her home soon, but needed the queen's permission. ("Is that elfin time or human?" she complained. "Elfin," he said sadly, "for I fear the human 'soon' has already passed.")

"Sparrow believes the brain to be all important." Pony drew her attention back to the conversation about Windwolf's assistant.

"Sparrow thinks nothing of making work for the rest of us," complained the female Stormsong—whose attitude toward clothes and boots delighted Tinker no end. "She demands fresh flowers in her quarters, special food from the *sefada*, and countless changes in her gowns. Pull!"

They fell silent the minute it took Stormsong to shoot. She carefully put all five arrows into the red, but Tinker had learned that the *sekasha* unofficially took points off for being too deliberate at aiming, and gave points for managing a discussion around one's shooting, as Pony had. It seemed a secret ego thing between them.

"Am I making extra work?" Tinker asked.

They laughed at Tinker's fear, belittling the idea that she was a nuisance.

"No, no, *domi*," Stormsong hurried to reassure her. "Pony's job is to guard you, and most of the time we merely include you on activities we normally do."

"Sparrow never says please or thank you." Skybolt made a sound of disgust as he shot, sending out his arrows in a show of graceful speed. "The other castes are beneath her politeness."

He too put all five arrows into the red; even Stormsong acknowledged his skill with "*Kiyau*."

Pony shook his head. "Sparrow does not see the clans' strength to be the cooperation of castes, but solely as the clan head in possession of spell stones. Since she can't access the stones, she grasps for other ways to show power: withholding politeness and petty demands."

The others nodded to this.

"We should call you Hawkeye," Skybolt said, "for your clear-sightedness."

The next day, it rained, trapping Tinker indoors. The grayness seemed to invade her soul, so after a Windwolf-less lunch she curled in the sunroom and watched the rainfall, fighting to keep in tears. It would be stupid to cry; everyone had been bending over backward to make her happy.

All the little seeds of fear, doubt, and unease, though, were growing into a wild, dark tangle. What was going to happen that made her the pivot? Beyond the cryptic warnings, there had been nothing more from the seer. At some point, all would depend on her, and she had an unspoken terror that the decision would have to be made when she was completely alone against a horde of oni, without so much as a datapad.

And what if the queen never let her go back to Pittsburgh? Certainly if the queen wanted to keep control of the pivot, she could insist that Tinker stay at Aum Renau, or take her back East. Windwolf told her that he asked permission daily, but for all Tinker knew, he could be lying to her. Surrounded by beauty and luxury, it seemed stupid to be so homesick for the squalid, half-abandoned steel town. She wanted her computers, tools, and hoverbike. She wished she could call Oilcan; just to know he was okay and not worrying about her. She desperately wanted to talk to Lain; since her grandfather died, Lain had been her guide through life's confusion. Lain could tell her what to do, make it all right.

"*Domi.*" Pony crouched down beside her. "The *sefada* know you are unhappy and say that you can come help them make *falotiki*. They are very simple to make, and the *sefada* promise to watch carefully so they will not catch fire, and afterward you decorate them with icing in bright colors."

"Um," her voice cracked, and his face blurred, so she scrubbed at her eyes. "Yeah, sure." And then to make them all stop worrying about her, "It sounds like fun."

And through sheer determination on her part, it actually was.

Windwolf came into the kitchen while she was icing. The little square *falotiki* cakes reminded her of the periodic table, so she had arranged them into the classic chart and was making each cake a different element. She was working on radium, and after telling the kitchen staff its radioactive properties, was reciting the "Little Willie" poem that featured his grandmother's tea. "Now Grandpa thinks it quite a lark, To see her shining in the dark."

"*Dama!*" cried Lemonseed, the head cook.

Tinker looked up to find Windwolf leaning in the doorframe, watching her with a grin. "You look pleased about something."

"The queen says we can leave for Pittsburgh in the morning."

Tinker squealed and flung herself at Windwolf. He swept her up and she kissed him until she realized that she was covering him with flour and that tears were running down her face. "Oh gods, I screamed, didn't I? Oh, that's so stupid. I'm not the type to scream."

"No," he agreed, resting his forehead on hers. "You are not the type to scream."

"Is she really letting me go home?" She saw the hurt go through his eyes. "I mean, back to Pittsburgh?"

"Yes. With provisions."

"Provisions?" She didn't like the sound of that. "Here, let me down, so I can wash my hands."

"The queen is concerned." Windwolf paused, obviously picking out the most politic way of putting things. "She sees you as a child with a child's grasp of the universe. She's not saying you're immature," Windwolf hastened to explain as Tinker made a rude noise. "By the time an elf reaches adult, he has had a hundred years of being steeped in our culture—which isn't always a good thing—but it does teach him about living for millennia. You can barely speak the high tongue, and you're not going to learn it, or any of the skills you need, by living daily with humans."

She froze, hands in the water. "What—what does that mean? That I can't go home? But you just said—I'm staying in Pittsburgh—or is this just a visit?"

"It is not a visit, but it will be a change in your living arrangement."

"What the hell does that mean?"

"We closed our Pathways on a land as pastoral as our own. The Dutch were a superpower. Latin was the tongue of the learned man, and the laundry you term 'prehistoric' would be a marvel of advanced technology." Windwolf pulled her hands out of the water and toweled them dry. "Most of the elves here at Aum Renau were alive during your Dark Ages. Many saw the fall of the Romans. There are even ones that saw the rise of the Egyptians."

She squeaked, as the weight of the ages seemed to compress down on her. "Really?"

"Lemonseed here is over nine thousand years old."

Tinker glanced to the sweet-tempered *sefada* who seemed no older than Lain. "Nine thousand?"

"By the very nature of humans and elves, the gate *will* close while you're alive," Windwolf said. "Currently you have the queen's protection. No one can call insult on you, or challenge you to a duel.

But that protection will not last forever. What is forgiven in a child will not be forgiven in an adult. You must know how to live with us—your people."

She became aware that everyone in the kitchen was trying hard to pretend that they weren't listening to the conversation. What language had they been arguing in this time? She winced as she realized that it had flowed almost seamlessly between English and Elvish, sometimes changing halfway through the sentence. Growling, she undid the mega apron protecting her dress, shoved it into the hamper for dirty linens, and stomped out of the kitchen.

Windwolf came after her, and a few steps behind him were Pony and Stormsong. She headed to their living quarters as one of the few places they could talk without the bodyguards overhearing.

"What are the provisions?" she asked once the door shut between them and the *sekasha*.

"I must establish a residence at Pittsburgh and move my household there."

"Move? For how long?"

He clicked his tongue in a shrug. "A couple of decades, maybe a century."

She winced, thinking of the close-knit community she'd found at the palace. "How many of the clanspeople here at the palace are part of your household?"

Windwolf looked slightly confused. "All of them."

"All!" Hope turned to ash; there was no way the entire palace staff would be shifted just because she was homesick. "There's like sixty people here!"

"Seventy-four, not counting Pony."

"Why not count Pony?" Tinker cried. Of all the *sekasha*, Pony was her favorite.

"Pony is yours, not mine."

"Mine?"

Windwolf paused, apparently considering his English. "Yours," he repeated, this time in Elvish. "Not mine."

Oh, shit, now what had she done? "How did Pony get to be mine?"

"Pony's parents are beholden to my father and I watched him grow up, which makes me protective of him. As he neared his majority, he wanted a chance to make a real decision about whom he looked to, and not just take his parents' path. I gave him refuge in my house, although he hadn't yet come of age. I expected him to offer to me, for we are fond of one another, but he was free to offer to you."

She dropped onto the bench before her bed, remembering then the conversation just before they left Pittsburgh, under watch of the queen's Wyverns. Once again, someone offered, and she accepted without realizing what strings were attached. "Oh, no."

Something on her face made Windwolf kneel down in front of her and take her hands. "I am pleased. I thought you two would suit well, that's why I left him with you. He brings you honor, since not everyone can hold a *sekasha*."

"I didn't realize what he was saying."

Windwolf looked dismayed and then sighed. "It is done now. Once accepted, even by mistake, the contract can not be unmade. It means you find the person unacceptable. No matter what you said, everyone would believe the worst of Pony, that he had acted in some way inappropriately."

She pressed the heels of her hands tight against her eyes. "Oh, gods, what a mess."

"I don't understand why you're so upset. You obviously love Pony well, and we're returning to Pittsburgh."

She peeked at him through her fingers. "We are?"

"I told the queen that the provisions were acceptable."

The hands came off her face completely. "You did!"

"It is only for a short time."

Of course.

Yet, she felt guilty that so many people were having their life turned upside down because she didn't want to change. Windwolf, though, had volunteered knowing full well who would be affected and how. She hadn't known. She hadn't known when she saved him from the saurus and he marked her to be part of his household. She hadn't known when he offered his betrothal gift. Or when he asked if she wanted to be immortal. Or when Pony offered himself. Again and again, she was lost in ignorance, while others acted with full knowledge. Why should she feel guilty?

Because they thought she'd understood. Because she didn't admit to her ignorance. It was bad enough when it was just her suffering the consequences, but others were now being dragged in.

* * *

Tinker leaned against the glass, eager for her first sight of Pittsburgh. For hours they had sailed over the unending green of elfin forest, gently rocked as the gossamer swam against the headwind. The crew had said that it would take six hours, and now at noon, the time of arrival was nearing.

Beside her the navigator had been peering intently through a spyglass, picking out familiar landmarks. "We're here."

She scanned the horizon, finding the glitter of a river, guessed it to be the Monongahela and watched it unravel westward through the forest. There was a clearing in the forest with a cluster of enclaves and a wide field thick with colorful tents, and then more forest, and another river. "What's that?"

"Oakland," the navigator said. "Bring her to a slow speed!"

Oakland? Tinker frowned, studying the onrushing buildings. Faintly she could see the Rim, its barren strip of no-mans-land, arcing through the forest. Yes, it was the elfin Oakland, but Pittsburgh wasn't there. No human streets, half-empty buildings, skyscrapers, or bridges. Just unending forest. "Oh no, it's Shutdown!"

"Of course it is," Sparrow said. "We've always thought it as an odd and awkward way of doing a Pathway, but that's humans for you."

Windwolf shot Sparrow a hard look, which gained a contrite half-bow and his assistant fleeing. "I am sorry. I had forgotten to check."

"It will be back tomorrow." Tinker shoved away her disappointment. They were all but home now. "The enclaves will be full tonight."

"Room will be found." Windwolf hugged her.

His presence distracted her from Pittsburgh's absence, to a realization of the date. "We met last Shutdown. Just twenty-eight days ago." Oh gods, the last three weeks had been the longest in her life. Immortality at this speed was going to drive her nuts.

"Time expands and contracts." Windwolf kissed her hair. "Sometimes a day can seem like a second, and sometimes it lasts forever. Certainly the hours that I lay helpless on Earth were the longest I've ever lived."

"Then we're even."

Prior to Shutdown, all the elves living in Pittsburgh shifted temporarily to either the enclaves or camps at the Faire Grounds, thus the collection of bright-colored tents crowding the meadow. Since the Faire Grounds doubled as the airfield for the massive airship, it took shouted negotiations, followed by careful maneuvering to accomplish a tethering.

While this was being accomplished, Tinker studied the flip side of Pittsburgh, the great circle of forest sent to Earth with Startup. Here on Elfhome there was nothing at the Rim but barren land. Back on Earth was a chain-link fence surrounding the forest—a great wall of China done in steel—to keep in dangerous elfin wildlife, and more importantly, keep out unwanted human immigrants. On Earth and in Pittsburgh, EIA patrolled the Rim. From the Observation lounge (having been politely scooted out for the already complicated tethering) Tinker could see elfin rangers moving through the trees, keeping close to the Rim but scouting for trespassers. The sole building within the forest was the legendary EIA lockup, an ugly squat cinderblock building whose only function was to hold prisoners until Startup returned them to Earth. At one time, Tinker lived in fear of it and its polar opposite, the glass castle of EIA headquarters in Pittsburgh.

Also from her high vantage point, Tinker could see that someone had managed to do some illegal logging of the virgin forest. The south shore of the Ohio, approximately where the West End Bridge crossed in Pittsburgh, had been stripped bare, although she couldn't imagine how anyone could cut down the trees and get them into the river without heavy equipment. Apparently the EIA's watch on Earth wasn't as legendary as she'd always heard.

Movement directly below caught her eye and she looked downward. Someone was waving at the gossamer, a short and plain figure among the tall, elegantly dressed elves.

"Oilcan!" she cried. "Oh gods, what is he doing here?"

After waving at her cousin to let him know she saw him, she went to beat on anyone who could get her down to the ground. Minutes later the elevator dropped her down, the door opened and he was there, waiting, and she pounced on him.

"What are you doing here?" She hugged him tightly.

"Waiting for you," he said. "Gods, look at you. You look wonderful."

"I still feel a little dorky in these clothes." She plucked at her skirt.

"I had to be 'acceptable' at Aum Renau in case I ran into the queen in some dark hallway." She realized that she was rambling and hugged him again. "What are you doing here?"

He grinned. "I just had this feeling that you'd be coming back during Shutdown, and I'd been kicking myself for not going with you, so I asked Maynard to get me permission to ride out Shutdown on Elfhome." He glanced back at the wall of trees beyond the Rim. "It was weird watching Pittsburgh vanish, though. I've had this creepy feeling all morning, like it wasn't coming back and I'd be stuck here. I was starting to think I'd made a big mistake."

"By the very nature of humans and elves, the gate will close while you're alive."

She glanced around at the single cluster of enclaves and the handful of tents—no electricity, no computers, and no phones. Oh gods protect her, she'd go mad.

13: CROW BLACK SHROUD

"TINKER! Tinker!"

Tinker had learned to ignore her own name, since anyone not calling her "*domi*" only wanted to interrupt her with stupid questions. She wasn't listening: 546879 divided by 3 equaled 182293.

"Alexander Graham Bell!"

Tooloo was right; anyone knowing your real name gained power over you. Tinker flipped up her welding visor and looked down through the tower's trusses to the ground far below. Lain glared back up at her. A quick check showed Lain's hoverbike parked alongside Tinker's and Pony's, which explained how the xenobiologist got to the remote building site, but not why.

"What?" Tinker shouted down.

"Come down here." Lain tapped the ground with her right crutch.

"Why?"

"Young lady, get your butt down here now! I am not going to scream at you like a howler monkey."

Sighing, Tinker turned off the welder. "Pony, will you kill the generator?"

He paused, sword half-drawn. "Kill what?"

"Hit the big red switch." She pointed at the purring generator.

"Ah." He slid his sword back into its sheath. "Yes, *domi*."

She stripped off her welding visor, and pulled off the heavy gloves.

The carpenters' foreman realized that she was leaving, and hesitantly asked, "*Domi*, what should we do next?"

Good thing she'd planned for this. She searched her blue jean pockets until she found her printouts for the current phase of work. "Please, do as much as you can of this and then take a break. Thank you."

She climbed down the tower calling out instructions to work crews as she spotted problems.

The cutting crew waited for her at the foot of the ladder. "We cut to the survey marks, *domi*."

"Good, good, thank you." She scanned the ten acres of cleared hilltop. "The stumps in the area of the foundation need to be removed. I'm not sure how that's done. I suppose we could blast them out."

"No, no, no." Strangely, they seemed anxious for her not to use explosives. Too bad—it would have been fun. "There is magic to excise roots. We'll see it done."

"Thank you, thank you."

Lain stood beside the board tacked heavy with technical drawings, floor plans, and concept pictures. "What do you think you're doing?"

Was that a trick question? "I'm creating infrastructure." Tinker drew Lain's attention to the board. "Phase One was to choose an appropriate building site. Phase Two was to commandeer a work crew. Phase Three is to clear the building site." She waved a hand at the denuded ridgeline. The topology maps were correct—this was one of the highest hills in the area. "Phase Four is to secure the building site." She paused to check off item one of the Phase Three schedule posted on the board. "Phase Five is to create an energy source. Based on an article I read once, I've designed a wind turbine using rear brake drums from Ford F250 trucks. See." She found the concept drawing. "This is really beauty in simplicity. I can adapt old electric motors into these 'inside out' alternators common on small wind turbines—which eliminates the need to build a complicated hub that attaches the blades to a small-diameter shaft. See, this simple plywood sandwich holds the blades tightly in the rotor and the entire assembly is mounted directly to the generator housing: the brake drum. It should churn out three hundred to five hundred watts per turbine."

"Per turbine?"

"Roughly." Tinker realized watt output wasn't Lain's question. "Oh, I'm hoping for at least five to start with along this ridge. I originally thought I could install them near the Faire Ground and then realized since it doubled as the airfield that wouldn't work."

"Tinker . . ."

Tinker held up her hand, as she hadn't really come to the heart of the plan. "Phase Six will be to create telecommunication abilities not relying on Pittsburgh resources. Phase Seven will be to develop the Tinker Computing Center. Scratch that. Tinker *domi* Computing and Research Center."

Tinker paused to note the name change and Lain snatched the pen from her hand. She eyed Lain, tapping her pen-less fingers. "What are you doing here?"

"It is the sad truth that anyone that knows you well also knows that I have some influence with you. I have had Oilcan, Nathan, Riki, Director Maynard, four human agencies, and five elfin household heads call me in the last hour. I even had my first ever telephone conversation with Tooloo, not something I ever want to repeat again. Honestly Tinker, what in the world do you think you're doing?"

Tinker glanced at the plan-covered board and back to Lain. Strange. She thought Lain was fairly intelligent. "I told you. Creating infrastructure."

"You've commandeered workers from all the enclaves, and I'm sure you're working them without pay. The EIA director is in a froth about missing evidence, the department of transportation supervisor complained that you've hijacked one of their dump trucks, and the police say you've taken a Peterbilt truck from the impound."

"I needed a lot of stuff."

"Why are you doing this?"

Tinker jabbed a finger at her plans. "I'm creating *infrastructure*!"

Lain caught her hands, held them tight. "Why?"

"Because it's not there. Twenty years of Pittsburgh being on Elfhome, and everything is still in Pittsburgh. Elfhome has the train and some boats, and that's it."

"That is not why. Why are *you* doing it, in this manner?"

"Because obviously no one else is going to do it, or it would already be done."

"Have you considered that the reason why might be because the elves don't want it on Elfhome?"

"I don't care what they want. I want it. I'm not going to spend another day without a computer, let alone three weeks, or a century, or millennia. Maybe this is why I'm the damn pivot. I say 'enough already, get with the program' and when the oni comes, my Elfhome Internet saves the day."

"Tinker, you just can't do this."

"Actually, yes I can. See, I've learned something in the last three weeks. When the queen says 'you're dropping everything and flying to Aum Renau,' you go. And when the queen says 'you're staying at Aum Renau,' you stay. And when the head of household says 'we're all moving to Pittsburgh,' you move. And when the clan head says 'I need all the rooms in this enclave, please find other lodgings,' you do. Well, I'm Tinker *domi*! I can make a computing and research center."

"Where is your husband?"

"Oh gods, don't say that." Tinker fled her, ducking into the commandeered tent of Wind Clan blue.

Lain followed close behind, despite the deep ruts churned up by the heavy equipment. "Don't say what?"

"Husband." Tinker peeked into the wicker lunch boxes sent from the enclaves until she found some *mauzouan*. "You want something to eat?"

"No, thank you."

Tinker scowled at Pony until he got himself some food. "A male gives you a bowl and suddenly you're married? Please. Okay, the sex is fantastic, but is that any basis for a relationship?"

"Of course not." Lain sat down in one of the folding chairs purloined out of the gossamer. "But I can't imagine Windwolf committing himself to marriage solely for sex."

"He says he loves me." Tinker settled herself at the teak table, also from the airship. "I don't know why."

"Tinker!"

"I mean . . . he didn't know me. I still barely know him. We spent the twenty-four hours of Shutdown together. I saw him once the next morning—oh, wait, make that twice—and then he proposed to me. Elves don't fall in love that fast—do they?"

"I suppose it could be a case of transference."

"Mmm?" She mumbled around a hot *mauzouan*.

"It's not uncommon for patients to fall in love with their doctor."

"You stitched him up."

"Yes, but you moved houses and fought monsters to keep him alive."

"Is this supposed to make me feel better?"

"Tinker, we can't know other people's hearts. Humans fall in love at first sight, and only time tells if that love is true. There is no reason that elves can't do the same. Certainly while Shutdown was only twenty-four hours, they were quite intense ones."

"Yeah, I suppose," Tinker murmured, remembering what Windwolf had said to her. "Certainly the hours that I lay helpless on Earth were the longest I've ever lived."

"If nothing else," Lain continued, "you showed the depth of your intelligence and grit."

"Grit?" She popped another *mauzouan* into her mouth. "What does sand have to do with it?"

"It's a way of saying your strength of character; your courage under fire."

Tinker snorted at that. "Lain, how do you know when you're in love? How do you recognize it?"

"Sometimes you don't. Sometimes you mistake lust as love. And sometimes you only know after you've thrown love away."

Trust Lain to say anything but words of comfort. Tinker dropped her head on the table and considered banging it a couple of times. "Argh," she groaned into the wood.

"Give it time," Lain said.

"If someone says that one more time, I think I'll scream."

She hated this feeling of being out of control. Last night, they had sat up waiting for Startup. Elves had little need for wristwatches, so it was without warning that Pittsburgh had flashed into existence, a dark sprawl of buildings washed in moonlight. From the enclaves up and down the street had come shouts of approval, as the elves cheered the return like a magician's trick. And in that moment, Tinker had realized that she would probably never see Earth again; elves stayed on Elfhome during Shutdown.

Like a cascade, realizations spilled down on her. She wasn't going back to her loft—Windwolf and Pony wouldn't fit, let alone the rest of the household. There was no reason for the viceroy's wife to work. Leaving Pittsburgh now wasn't just a matter of convincing Oilcan to come with her, but also leaving Windwolf and Pony behind.

It wasn't that Windwolf had taken away *all* her choices, but the ones left were dubious. Insist on living alone? Continue to spend inventing time on the scrap yard when Windwolf had money to burn? Betray the elves who loved her to leave everyone and everything she knew?

Desperate to snatch control of her life back—and yet not totally wreck everyone's lives with stupid decisions—she came up with the computing center. So maybe she went a little overboard.

Tinker sighed. "Let's get it over with. Give me my lecture."

"I don't know what to say," Lain stated, getting up. "And I'm not sure it's my place to say anything. I suggest you go talk to Windwolf."

"Run to my husband and get permission for what to do with my life?"

"No, go discuss with the viceroy what future the two of you are going to build for your people."

"Ouch," Tinker said.

"I never said being an adult is easy." Lain squeezed Tinker's shoulder. "But I have faith in you. And I'm fairly sure Windwolf does too."

After Lain left, Tinker glumly finished her lunch. She had no idea how Windwolf might take this scheme of hers. Would he think she overstepped her bounds, as Lain obviously did? Or would he be pleased at her initiative? Oilcan had gifted her with her datapad the evening before and she'd spent the night communing with it, laying plans, and barely noticed when Windwolf left in the morning. She eyed the denuded hillside, the conscripted elves, and the commandeered equipment; wherever Windwolf was, it couldn't be nearby.

"Pony, where is Wolf Who Rules?"

"He and Sparrow are looking for oni. The queen wished verification that the oni are not using Pittsburgh to access Elfhome."

A jolt of fear went through her. "They went out alone?"

"No, they have the *sekasha*, the EIA, and the rangers with them."

It sounded like a small army. She had been more wrapped up in her own plans than she realized. If the EIA were with them, then finding them would only be a matter of a phone call. Of course there was the problem that she'd apparently ticked off Maynard by misappropriating the smugglers' high-tech goods.

Then again, a small army shouldn't be too hard to spot.

The road up to the work site was just raw dirt, already growing deep ruts. She'd have to get it properly graded and graveled before it turned into a mud slalom. There was no way they could drive the Rolls up and down it without fear of tearing out the undercarriage. She'd pulled her old Gamma out of storage early that morning and coaxed Pony into trying the hoverbike.

He'd been dubious at first, but he smiled now as she headed for the bikes. "Ah, good, we're going flying again."

"Yeah." She swung her leg over her Delta's saddle. "I want to find Wolf Who Rules. Do you have any idea where he might be?"

"Sparrow was to search between the Rim and the rivers." Pony pointed down the Ohio River. The Rim arced along the Ohio's bank, clipped above the confluence of the Allegheny and the Monongahela, and then ran roughly parallel to the Mon, leaving odd slices of Pittsburgh without bridges. "Wolf Who Rules chose to search the bulk of the area, beyond Mount Washington."

Yes, Windwolf had more land to cover, but Sparrow actually had the thankless job. Between the three major rivers, the numerous smaller rivers and larger streams, Sparrow's team would be backtracking often to navigate over water or sheer hillsides. Pittsburgh had been the city of bridges—unfortunately, most stayed on Earth.

"You up to a long ride?"

"Very much so." Pony mounted up, thumbprinted the lock, and hit the ignition button of the Gamma. The bike's lift drive rumbled to life. Pony eased down on the throttle until he was at cruise level, and retracted his parking studs. "Come, *domi*, let's find Wolf Who Rules."

They went down the steep muddy road hacked through the forest until they hit the Rim. There, they crossed onto the abrupt start of I-279 North—six lanes heading into downtown with no traffic. There, to Pony's delight, she opened up the throttle and soared along the wide even pavement, gaining altitude. He was a good mix of fast learner and yet still cautious.

Confident that Pony could take care of himself, she focused on finding Windwolf. The South Hills continued the Pittsburgh tradition of houses clinging to steep hillsides, narrow valleys, and winding roads. She and Pony could miss Windwolf by a hundred feet and never realize it.

Maybe I should make nice with Maynard first, she thought, and bypassed the Veterans Bridge on-ramp to head for the Fort Duquesne Bridge; that would drop her closer to the EIA castle.

Two car-lengths behind her, Pony suddenly veered off onto the steep on-ramp, followed close behind by a blue sedan. Focused on Windwolf, Tinker had missed whatever caused him to swerve onto the ramp. Had the car cut Pony off? Tinker couldn't see how; it wasn't that close to Pony. Strangely, Pony wasn't watching to see what she was doing. She glanced up to check if she was cleared for pop-up onto the road, but there were signs and streetlamps in the way. A second later, she was under the sudden tangle of Route 28 crossing over 279, and the Veterans Bridge's on-ramps and exits vaulting over it all.

That neatly, a trap was sprung. Hoverbikes surged out from around bridge supports and down off of Route 28, converging on her. Even as she did a pop-up to miss the first one, she recognized at least three of the riders. The oni.

She nailed the throttle, ducking as the pop-up threatened to smack her into the I-beams of the Route 28 overpass. Even at maximum lift, she didn't have the clearance to make it up onto the Veterans Bridge, now two street levels above her. She shifted power into the torque spell chain, sacrificing height for speed.

She glanced in her mirrors, seeing the oni scramble to chase after her. *Nyah, nyah, eat my dust.*

But there were more combatants than she had counted on; a red Corvette came snarling down the on-ramp from Nash Street. There had to be an ancient V8 under the hood as the Corvette matched her speed, crowding her to the left side of the road, forcing her to take the lower deck of the Fort Duquesne Bridge. The bridge closed in around them like a tunnel, and the Corvette herded her across the river, with the other bikes following. They flashed across the bridge and down into the chute of the Tenth Street Bypass that ran along the river. The surface tension of water wasn't enough to support a bike, or she'd skip off across the river.

As they rushed toward the overpass of the Sixth Street Bridge, she popped up—slewing sideways in mid-air as she scraped over the railing—and landed hard on the overpass. She skidded across the road, momentum carrying her in a straight line toward the far railing.

Sometimes she really hated the laws of physics. She leaned hard to redirect the lift drive to check her slide.

There were two hoverbikes coming across the bridge, the riders nearly dwarfing their machines. She had to keep moving. If she stopped, they would have her. The city was to their advantage—the short runs and sudden dead-ends would let them pen her in with sheer numbers. The long stretches gave her, on the faster bike, the advantage.

She nailed the throttle open—the torque spell shooting her forward—and threw her mass far out, nearly kissing pavement, as she muscled the bike through a sharp right turn onto Fort Duquesne Boulevard, heading back to the bridge. All three lanes of traffic were slowing for a red light, too tight for her to weave through. A single tractor-trailer truck occupied the rightmost lane. She popped up to race the trailer's length, skipping her lift drive off its roof. She shot out over its cab, lost lift, and smacked down hard on the pavement in a bone-jarring impact. The truck horn blasted behind her, a wall of metal filling her peripheral vision.

Cursing, she flung all power into the torque. The bike leaped forward and she ran it up the gears as she whipped back over the bridge, this time on the top deck. Mid-bridge, she took the fork toward 279. She didn't know what they'd done to Pony, but they'd gotten him away from her somehow. She had no idea what she was going to do when she caught up with them, but there was no way she was leaving Pony in their power.

She came to the snarl of on-ramps to the bridge. None actually connected the road she was on to the bridge, but she skipped over jersey barriers to catch the Route 28 on-ramp.

Veterans Bridge crossed the Allegheny in eight lanes of broad plainness, crossing first the Allegheny River and then the Strip District. At the far end it splintered into mad twistings, each exit heading in a radically different direction. She roared across the bridge, sick at the thought of reaching its end and not spotting Pony. Did they take him downtown, intending to hold him in whatever trap they had tried to maneuver her into? That didn't make sense. Why hadn't they caught her the same way they had caught Pony? Was it because she was *domana*?

Movement caught her eye, and she glanced into her mirrors. Oni were skipping up from the Strip District to land on the bridge behind her.

Shit. She ignored the first exit off the bridge that would have funneled her back into the city. Beyond it the roadway carved through the foot of the Hill, creating a cement canyon of pavement and bridge supports. She shot into the canyon, six hoverbikes trailing behind her, and the Corvette joining the fray from the downtown on-ramp. Straight would take her over the Liberty Bridge arching over the Monongahela River, through the tunnel to the South Hills maze and Windwolf somewhere searching for oni with a small army.

"Look what I found, sweetheart," Tinker muttered, but the Corvette was attempting to herd her that direction. No, if that was the way they *wanted* her to go, she'd better not.

As the Corvette crowded close, she popped up, and then kissed off his hood before he could correct, leaning hard to angle the lift into a sideways skip. She touched down on the exit ramp for the Boulevard, the scream of brakes behind her as the Corvette tried to stop, followed by the unmistakable thud of him hitting something.

Yeah, bring a car to a hoverbike chase. Loser!

She lost speed in the jump, though, and the pack of hoverbikes closed like a pack of wargs scenting blood. She put everything into torque, and whispered sweet things to her Delta. The ramp leaped from the canyon to the clifftop Boulevard of the Allies in one mid-air arc. Dropping down to the Parkway that ran parallel to the Boulevard at the foot of the cliff would be insane; even with the lift drive at max, she'd drop like a stone and—from that height—splatter.

If she could keep ahead of them, it was only a quick run to the Rim, and the EIA border patrol. She'd get them and the cops and find Pony.

The lead oni hoverbike, though, was one of her custom Deltas— talk about a mistake coming back to haunt you. For an oni, the rider was a little shit, grinning viciously at her with a mouthful of sharpened teeth. He matched her speed, smacking her closer and closer to the edge of the cliff. She ground her teeth, fighting to control her bike, but he had the mass on her. A pop-up might lose him, but that would cost her speed, and put her in the middle of the pack. His bike looked like Czerneda's, done in aquamarine fish scales. He had to have stolen it, since Czerneda would rather sell his soul than give the bike up. She braced herself against the battering and risked a look down at the thumblock. In its place dangled a mass of wires, bypassing the bike security system. *Ha, well, bye-bye Mr. Oni.*

She reached to yank loose the wires. He realized what she was doing and swung away from her. She risked overextending herself in a desperate grab. He came back at her, grabbing for her outstretched arm.

Shit, she had forgotten that their goal was *her*! She jerked away, and the motion rode her bike up the retaining wall and left her teetering on the narrow lip. Before she could push her bike back down to safety, the oni hit her again. As her bike tipped over the edge, he realized what he'd done—eyes going wide in panic, he grabbed hold of her bike instead of her and yanked it hard.

Instantly she was airborne, screaming as she went over the cliff and rushed toward the ground with nothing, nothing, to grab.

And then something grabbed her.

Riki had her by the back of her shirt.

She flailed backward, got hold of him, and swarmed up his body to cling deathly tight to him. "Oh, gods, oh gods, thank you, thank you."

Far below their feet, her Delta struck the riverbank and was instantly reduced to a mass of twisted wreckage.

Feet?

She jerked her gaze upward.

Massive wings, crow black, sprouted from Riki's back. She could feel soft down on his back and the start of wing structure and the movement of muscle as the wings beat the air. She could only stare in amazement as feathers shrouded the sky with black.

"Don't thank me," he snarled, shifting his hold on her so he had her by the back of the neck.

"I would have been dead if you hadn't caught me," she said, for the first time in her life only able to think "what—what—what—?"

"I shouldn't have had to." He twisted her in his hold, bringing up something to her face. "They weren't supposed to hurt you."

It all sank in as she recognized the flower in his hand. He was one of them. He was a tengu. He was there to catch her because he'd helped to design the trap in the first place. She tried to twist away from the flower, but he tightened his hold on her neck until she thought he would snap it. He pressed the *saijin* to her face, crushing soft fragrant petals to her nose. The heat and goldness of the sun filled her senses.

"No!" She struck out. Her fist slammed into his nose, snapping back his head and instantly bloodying him. He straightened out his arms, keeping out of her reach as he kept the flower tight against her.

She tried to squirm out of his hold, turn her head away.

He forced her still, watching her with furrowed brow. Without his sunglasses his eyes were a stunning blue—not the blue of Windwolf's, whose eyes were the dark, rich blue of expensive sapphires, but the cerulean blue of an electric spark. She could see that they weren't human eyes now, too vivid a color, the shape faintly almond, the lashes thick and long, viewing her with the same deadly detachment as electricity . . .

14: ONI MOON

TINKER WOKE with her head pounding and stared in confusion at the strange ceiling above her. For several minutes it seemed like a normal white plaster ceiling. Then she felt as if a long, thin-limbed spider was picking its way across her forehead. She bolted upright, swatting at her brow. Her fingers found nothing to kill, nor was there anything now on her lap except a spill of fine linen sheets. She sat on a futon mattress, level on the floor, with a nest of sheets, blankets, and pillows so comforting to look at that she nearly sank back into them. Things were wrong, though, and she dragged her eyes back to the ceiling. Same plain white ceiling, or was it? She got the vague impression that something had changed, only she couldn't put a finger on what.

A few feet from the end of the mattress was a stone wall with a deep-set window. Sitting on the floor, she could only see a slice of blue sky. She crawled to the wall, having difficulty controlling her overly light limbs. She looked out the window and gasped.

A city rolled out to the horizon, endless heavy stone buildings with red clay roof tiles. It reminded her of martial arts vids. As she stared hard at it, she finally made out the Allegheny and Monongahela rivers, converging to make the Ohio, meaning she was on Mount Washington, not far from Oilcan's apartment—only at least one reality removed. Whatever they called the city below, it wasn't Pittsburgh.

"Wondering where you are?"

She turned and discovered that a female dressed in a kimono, feet tucked under her, sat in the far corner of the room, watching her. Had she always been there? Tinker's mind was too drug-clouded for her to remember.

"No," Tinker said, not because it was the truth—she was dying to know—but mostly because it was the opposite of what the female wanted her to say.

"Obstinacy will get you nowhere," the female said.

"It's all I have at the moment, so I'll stick with it."

Tinker went back to staring out the window. This wasn't Earth, nor Elfhome, but something beyond Elfhome. Judging by the room she was in, the narrow twisting roads, and the lack of any outward sign of machinery, the technology level of the reality was on par with Elfhome. Unlike the elf world, though, it seemed as if this place staggered under Earth's population problems.

"You're on Onihida," the female said. "There is no escape."

No need for bars on the window; the whole world was a prison. Still Tinker examined the possibilities for escape. The building she was in continued the Oriental theme, only on fortress scale. The outside wall was of massive stones and was mortared tightly, presenting seriously scary rock-climbing potential. The drop down to the ground was thirty or forty feet. A misstep would put her down over the cliff edge too, adding two hundred feet to the fall.

All things considered, she should find another escape route.

Tinker turned her attention finally to the female. She seemed familiar. While lacking the elfin ears, she was beautiful in the way of elves, perfection in the small-pored, unblemished skin, symmetrical features, a cascade of red-gold hair, and eyes of a vivid reddish-brown. "Who are you?"

"I am Taji Chiyo."

"What did you do to Pony?"

"The little horsie betrayed you," Taji said casually, but her eyes sharpened with interest, as if she wanted to see the pain her words caused.

"No he didn't. Riki did."

"You will call me Lady Chiyo. And yes, he did, he drove off and left you. Ta ta."

"I don't know how you did it, but he didn't betray me," Tinker growled. "Pony wouldn't do that, and you have no reason to tell me the truth, Chewie."

"Chi-yo. Lady Chiyo."

"Look, bitch, you snared me this way because you needed to get around Pony." Tinker scrambled for facts to support her gut feeling. "If he was one of you, he could have delivered me up in the Rolls at any time. The first day Windwolf left me at the lodge, or all the next day while I was running all around Pittsburgh—hell, Riki talked me into ditching Pony at the scrap yard just before the Wyverns nabbed me. That probably pissed you all off—didn't it? You got me all by myself and the Wyverns showed up unannounced." Chiyo's eyes went wide and the startled look fit another piece of the puzzle together. "You're Maynard's secretary."

"Was." Chiyo rose out of the awkward-looking sitting position with grace and poise. "Someone else does that petty work now. If you want to know what happened to your warrior, come with me."

Chiyo glided to the door with little delicate footsteps nearly completely masked by her flowing kimono. Tinker thumped after her, annoyed with the way her feet seemed enormous. Had they always been that big, or was it a side effect of the drug that Riki had given her, making them look bigger?

Chiyo had paused at the door; she noticed Tinker's inspection of her feet and gave a small smug smile. Tinker decided at the first possible point to step on those delicate lady points with her steel-shod feet, hard. Lady Chiyo frowned slightly, slid open the door, and hurried down the hall in tiny little steps.

There were two burly armed guards outside the door, bracketing it. Tinker slipped between them, trying blithely to ignore them. *I'm not scared of you. I'm not scared.*

Oh, gods, she wished she and Pony were home safe.

Lady Chiyo led, and a step behind Tinker, the guards followed.

Tinker forced herself to amble, trying to stay oriented despite the drug. Except for occasional windows looking out over the sprawling city, the stone passages were maddeningly the same, like a computer-generated video screen with a limited algorithm. Abruptly they were in a garden courtyard, all done in Oriental style. A stream meandered through the heart of it, through a bed of mossy rocks. A ribbon of silver here, murmuring over a slight falls. A widening and deepening there, to make a still dark pool full of darting fish. Chimes rang in the wind with stunningly clear tones, and yet, yet, there was something hazy about the whole thing, like a dream.

It's the drugs, isn't it? Tinker wasn't sure.

Lady Chiyo led her to a gazebo overlooking one of the still ponds.

Riki sat in the gazebo, wearing an over-large muscle shirt and loose black pants, with bare feet. Despite the casual clothes, he perched in the gazebo window, looking as unhappy as a caged bird. He wore earbuds trailing wires down to an old MP3 player. Surprisingly, he was smoking, something an elf could never do.

He was alone.

"Where's Pony?" Tinker said.

Riki sighed, and pulled the earbud from his right ear, letting the music play on in his left. "Hopefully, your guard is even now reporting your untimely death, a mid-air stunt resulting in a fall into the river. Of course the river will be dredged, but that will prove nothing."

"You're lying. Pony wouldn't betray me."

"He's not betraying you; we've deceived him." Riki took a deep drag on his cigarette, and breathed it out his nose in a twin column of smoke. "We have magic that the elves do not, the bending of light and sound to make illusions."

Chiyo complained in a foreign language made harsh by her sharp tones.

Riki gazed at Chiyo unrepentant. "Stop your barking. I'm in charge. I tell her what I want."

"Lord Tomtom gave orders for . . ."

"He wants her to work. She won't work if she thinks we killed her warrior." Riki stared Chiyo into silence. "The magic works on the lesser elves, but not on you greater bloods," he explained, meaning the *domana*. "We didn't want to expose the people we have in Pittsburgh. If the elves knew you were kidnapped, they would tear the city apart looking for you. They're already searching; the fewer clues we give them the better. So we split your guard away and fed him what we wanted him to see. You got increasingly daring with your flying until you fell and the hoverbike crashed. Oh so tragic, but accidents happen, and your warrior provides the incontestable witness."

Strange how she could be relieved and increasingly terrified at the same time. Pony was utterly loyal, and safe and oh so far away. Windwolf would never question her "death" with Pony witnessing it. She clung to hope. "What about all the people that saw me being chased?"

"We oni know that what is seen is not always correctly perceived."

Riki took one last drag of his cigarette, and ground the tiny ember out. "Think of the difference of being in a race and watching it from the pits. To you, it was clear that you were being chased. What did the average person see? You going fast and dangerous—that matches Pony's story. A hoverbike chasing you? That would be Pony. Did they even see a second or third hoverbike? If they looked away for an instant, probably not. And what if they did? If Pony says no one was chasing you, they must have been mistaken—that must have been another group of hoverbikes racing."

She tried to resist the logic, but it was too sound. There would be no rescue.

Chiyo murmured something to Riki in the foreign language.

He nodded, flicking the dead butt out into the garden. "So, you understand your situation."

"I've been knifed in the back by a man I thought was my friend."

"I am not a man, nor, regrettably, have I ever been free to be your friend," Riki corrected her almost gently. "I was under orders, penalty for failure greater than you can imagine, although you will soon be educated in that regard."

It hurt to think she had been so wrong. "You're a tengu."

"Yes."

The wings she remembered were massive, but there were no signs of them now, as he sat in the window, even as he flicked away the cigarette butt.

"Where are your wings?"

Wordlessly, he turned around. The muscle shirt covered only his front, leaving his muscled back exposed. An elaborate spell had been tattooed onto his skin, from shoulder to waistline, in black. He whispered a word, and magic poured through the tracings, making them shimmer like fresh ink. The air hazed around him, and the wings unfolded out of the distortion, at first holographic in appearance, ghosts of crow wings hovering behind him, fully extended. Then they solidified into reality, skin and bone merged into the musculature of his back, glistening black feathers longer than her arm.

She couldn't help herself. She reached out and touched one of the primary feathers. It was stiff and unyielding under her fingers. The wings were real, down to the tiny barbs of the feather's web. "How—how can they come and go and yet be part of you?"

"They aren't truly real, but solid illusions, crafted out of magic."

"You should not be telling her this," Chiyo snapped.

"Go play with the dogs," Riki said.

"Shut up," Chiyo cried.

Riki spoke another word, and the wings vanished, and only the tattoo remained as evidence.

This close to him—and without the distraction of the wings—she could now recognize the song leaking out of the one earbud; it was one of Oilcan's favorite elf rock groups. With a jolt, she recognized the MP3 player as Oilcan's old system.

"Where did you get that?"

"Your cousin gave it to me when I told him that I had nothing to play music on." Riki gazed at the thumb-sized player. "It was kind of him."

"Have you hurt him?" she asked fearfully.

"No, of course not." Riki glanced toward Chiyo and added, "It would endanger my cover."

Chiyo said something that earned her a glare of disgust from Riki.

"What did she say?" Tinker asked.

"Something stupid. It's stunning that her kind is considered clever. She must be a throwback to the original bitch."

Chiyo curled back her lip in a snarl. "At least I'm not from blood stock of scavengers easily distracted by bright and shiny toys."

"Yes." Riki seemed only amused by Chiyo's retort. He gave a suddenly birdlike cock of his head, and another verbal poke. "But your blood stock has a tendency to run mad, frothing at the mouth."

Tinker took a step back in sudden horror. "Your people interbred with animals?"

No wonder the elves fled back across the worlds, closing gates behind them; the oni had crossed moral lines that even the Skin Clan hadn't. The two oni turned to look at her as if they'd forgotten she was listening.

"Shut up!" Chiyo snapped and sulked to the other side of the gazebo.

"The greater bloods are still pure." Bitterness tainted Riki's expression. "They mixed their servants with animals at the genetic level to create us lesser bloods. We tengu have the crow's ability to fly at an instinctual level."

Chiyo responded to Tinker's questioning gaze with, "Don't look at me that way, little fake elf. You're a dirty little human girl in a fancy skin."

"Thank you, you don't know how good that makes me feel."

Riki gave a squawk of surprised laughter.

"So why did you kidnap me?" Tinker asked.

Riki sobered. "Lord Tomawaritomo wants you to build him a gate."

"Who?"

"To-ma-wa-ri-to-mo." Riki sounded out the syllables. "He is Windwolf's counterpart among the oni."

Remembering Chiyo's comment earlier, Tinker asked, "Lord Tomtom?"

Riki gave a very human shrug. "That's what those of us born on Earth tend to call him."

No wonder he passed so easily for human if he grew up around them. "That's why you speak English so well?"

"Yes. I was born in Berkeley, California."

"Hatched! Hatched!" Chiyo barked. "If you're going to go all truthful with her, then tell it all. Your mother popped out an egg." Chiyo measured out a stunningly large sphere with her fingers. "And brooded on it to keep it warm, and when the time came, listened all so close so she could break you out of your shell, and as a child they kept jesses on your feet to keep you from picking your nose with your toes."

Tinker glanced downwards and noticed for the first time that Riki's toes were stunningly long, thin, agile-looking and only three in number. "Your mother wasn't the woman killed when Lain was crippled; she couldn't have passed the physicals as human."

Riki looked at Chiyo in cold rage, and said, "I hope you are keeping your focus. You know how angry Lord Tomtom would be if this failed."

Chiyo went white and silent. For a minute only the tinny music from Riki's earbud could be heard, and then like a bubble breaking, the background noise from the garden started again. Chiyo stared at the ground, panting like a frightened animal.

"I don't understand," Tinker said. "If you can get to Earth, Elfhome, and back again, why does he need me to build a gate?"

Chiyo giggled and murmured something in their own tongue.

Riki shot her an irritated look and explained, "When the elves destroyed the door from our world to Earth, they stranded a large group of tengu and others in China. We've lived in secret among humans, hiding our differences."

He lifted his foot up, flexing his toes to demonstrate what differences he meant. "Like the elves, we're immortal on our own world, and long lived on Earth. We waited for our chance to return to our own land, our own people. When the gate opened the door between Earth and Elfhome, it also opened a door to Onihida, but it's inconveniently placed. We don't have the ability to move an army through it."

The seer's words went through her mind. *There is a door, open but not open . . . darkness presses against the frame but can not pass through.* The seer must have been talking about the unusable door. But what the hell did the rest mean? *The light beyond is too brilliant; it burns the beast.*

Chiyo murmured something to Riki which surprised him.

Tinker was tempted to kick her. "I don't like it when people talk about me in front of me."

"It's better you don't understand her poison," Riki said.

So, the seer was right. She was going to be the pivot. "You want me to betray Elfhome?"

"I know what they've done to you. They took you and changed you to make you loyal to them. All the while they held you at the palace, I was with your cousin, watching him go quietly insane with worry whether they'd bring you back or just decide that you were too dangerous to allow to live."

"Windwolf would never—" She bit off the retort. Riki had no reason to tell her the truth and every reason to lie. "Oilcan didn't say anything to me last night."

"He's a fair man. He wouldn't try to poison you against your husband, not even if what he had to say was the truth."

Tinker backed away from him, shaking her head. "You've lied to me since the first moment I met you. You're probably lying to me now. You'll say anything to get me to help you."

Riki lunged and caught hold of her tightly. "Yes, I would!" he cried, looking pained. "I'd say anything because I know what Lord Tomtom will do to get his way—and I'd rather not see you go through that."

"I believe Lord Tomawaritomo has arranged a demonstration." Chiyo turned to speak to one of the guards.

With a thin shriek of terror, the little oni who had knocked her over the cliff was brought forward between two of the massive guards. He begged in the oni tongue, sobbing.

"They're going to remove the bones from his left arm," Chiyo told Tinker in a casual tone, as if what was about to happen had no more import than picking wildflowers. Tinker had a sudden sympathy for black-eyed susans. "All of them. While he's awake."

While the guards pinned the oni down, a third, wizened-dwarf of an oni with a bloodstained leather apron and bright sharp knives started to cut.

After putting the earbud back in his ear, Riki held her still, made her watch.

Tinker curled her arms up tight against her chest, trying hard not to cry. If she had still been on Elfhome, she might have been able to defy them, clinging to the hope that Windwolf and Oilcan would be there to rescue her, or even that she could escape. All alone on this strange world, every hand upraised against her, she couldn't find the courage.

When it was done, Riki said, "Lord Tomtom expects results."

Tinker was still numb as they escorted her to the workshop. Riki tried to guide her with a hand to her elbow. The touch made her aware of the bones within her arm, and she jerked away from him. Something in her face—either her initial fear or the anger that followed it—made him look unhappy. Good. She stomped after Chiyo, who minced down the hallways at a surprising speed.

Riki noticed it too. "Why are you going so fast, Taji?"

A sharp retort in the oni tongue from the female made Riki laugh.

"What?" Tinker demanded, angry now. Angry that they were talking in a language she couldn't understand. Angry that Riki could laugh after watching *that*. Angry that she had been too scared to tell them no.

Riki grinned but would not say.

After all she had seen since she woke up—the castle they were in and the city outside it—Tinker was surprised by the workshop. It was a vast Earth-like warehouse, not much different from the one that the EIA had used to store the smugglers' goods. The one massive room was five hundred feet long, three hundred wide, and perhaps three stories tall. High above were sunlit windows, but the lower windows were all painted black; great floodlights fought the resulting gloom. What was it that they didn't want her to see? All the windows up to this point had looked out over the cliff with the oni city far below. Perhaps the painted windows were at ground level.

The only outside door was padlocked shut and wired with an alarm.

The floor was an oil-treated wood, swept spotless. Workbenches lined the outside walls, leaving the center of the huge room open for large equipment to be assembled. As she toured through the various workstations, she found that all the tools were human-made.

She picked up a cordless screwdriver. "This stuff is all from Earth."

"Unfortunately, your technology is far in advance of ours."

"How did you get it here?"

"One piece at a time," Riki said. "We've had twenty years to put together this workshop."

"All assuming that you'd find a genius to put it all together?"

"We're patient; humans are creative. Sooner or later, we'd find someone to suit our needs."

Tinker flipped the on switch on the drill press, and it roared to life. She glanced behind the machine to see that it was plugged into a standard 220 outlet. "Where is the power coming from?"

"We've got a power plant," Riki said after a moment. "It runs everything in here. Lord Tomtom is quite thorough and gets results. Everything has been well tested, and that's all you need to know."

"So I'm supposed to build a gate out of scratch, something I've never tried, that no one else on the planet has managed. Am I to spin straw into gold too?"

"According to the CMU entrance test, you understand the gate theory well enough to create a functioning gate."

So much for the NSA keeping that news from leaking out. "Theoretical design and actual working prototype can be years apart."

"You don't understand. Lord Tomtom is immortal, and now, so are you."

So she could be here forever, building until she got it right, or Lord Tomtom got impatient.

At the back of the shop, a skylight threw a shaft of sunshine down into an office area, complete with drafting table, desk, and computer equipment. There were designs already laid out on the table: blueprints for the orbital gate. She glanced to the legend. Her father's name was printed there in neat drafting print. "Your people killed my father and gave his work to the Chinese."

"He wasn't supposed to be killed," Riki said. "They were just trying to kidnap him. The car was truly an accident."

"Were you there?"

"No. I was in high school, being a geek: playing on the Internet, learning basic physics, and sitting out gym class on a doctor's excuse."

"So you don't know what really happened."

"Lord Tomtom wanted him alive. You've seen how he punished the oni that merely put you at risk. I won't upset you with the details of what he does to those who utterly fail him."

"Your people killed my father while trying to kidnap him—just to get back to a world you'd never seen which is ruled by immortal sadistic madmen?"

"That's about the size of it."

"You're all insane."

"Perhaps," Riki said.

She was hoping for a less unsettling answer. On the desk was a datapad with a complete download from her pad. She glanced at the computer system, identical to her own, down to style of printer, scanner, and holo projector. "Sparks?"

"Yes, Boss?"

"Fuck." She whirled on Riki. "You copied everything while I was gone! I trusted you. Oilcan trusted you! But you just used him to break into my security and steal my thoughts."

"I had to," Riki said.

She hit him, a stupid girlie smack the first time, and then, realizing that he wouldn't dare hurt her, she hauled back and punched him right. Then did it again, and again. All her fear became rage and she funneled it at him. He grabbed her right wrist, so she stomped down on his bare foot, and jerked out of his hold as he fell. There were tools lying on the table beside her; she snatched up a heavy monkey wrench and laid into him. He managed to block most of her hits, so she flung the wrench away and grabbed a crowbar off the table.

Riki scrambled backward, holding out his hand. "Tinker, I'm sorry! I'm sorry! I really am. But the moment I came to Pittsburgh, it was do it, or die horribly."

Tinker stopped, crowbar cocked back over her shoulder, panting. His words hadn't checked her—it was the sudden knowledge that she wanted to kill him, and had the means tight in her hands. Already he was bleeding from his nose and mouth and a cut along his cheek. She'd caught him in one eye with something, and the white was now a shocking red. There were bruises on his arms from fending her off. From the odd look of his foot, she'd broken at least one of the bones. She could beat him to death—but what would that gain her? Certainly not her freedom. And she was in his shoes now; do or be tortured, with an entire world staked on the outcome of her intelligence.

Think, you idiot, don't react.

"Okay, I forgive you." Tinker lowered the crowbar, but didn't put it down.

The NSA agents Durrack and Briggs said that someone had kidnapped several scientists. Obviously it was the oni. Obviously the scientists refused to work on the gate, or tried to escape, or just hit the end of Tomtom's patience. She was just the most recent victim. The seer said that there was no stopping the door from being opened. Tinker was the pivot. If she said "fuck off" then they'd just kill her and get someone else. She had the means, somehow, to stop them cold. Why hadn't the damn bitch just told her how?

Chiyo was talking to Riki in Oni again. Tinker glanced at her, irritated, and considered whacking the female a couple of times with the crowbar instead. She might even be able to get the guards to hold the little bitch down for her, just like they'd done with the tortured oni. Tinker's look was enough to make Chiyo yelp in fear and dart out of range, crying, "No, no, I'll stop!"

"Good." Tinker put aside the crowbar. "We all understand each other now."

"Yes." Riki wiped the blood from his mouth. "I think we do."

"Don't you ever sleep?" Chiyo asked peevishly.

"Sometimes, I do." Tinker squirmed around on her futon bed to put her feet on the wall without taking her eyes from her datapad. "Sometimes, I don't."

Chiyo whimpered.

With the exception of the skylight, the warehouse office hadn't been set up with comfort in mind. After a few hours on the padded stool that was the office's only seat, Tinker moved back to her bedroom. Annoyingly, everything that the oni missed when they killed her father, Riki had copied off her home system. He had made notes in a separate file, obviously trying to design a land-based gate himself. He'd gotten far enough to confirm that he had a degree of physics from Caltech, and that while gifted, was seriously out of his league.

Riki had also added everything ever published on the gate since the Chinese received her father's plans from the oni. Some of them were in original Chinese, and others had been translated, hopefully accurately. There was an entire folder on as-built drawings for the space station, the hyperphase gate, and the power systems for both. Reading over the files, it became obvious that some of her father's obscure notes relating to the Dufae Codex had been translated by an oni familiar with both physics and magic.

She was familiar with everything published after the gate was built, as Western scientists scrambled to reverse engineer the device that the Chinese seemed to produce out of thin air. She skipped them, reading only papers published in the last three months and making notes in a scratch file.

Of the missing scientists, there was frighteningly little. She checked to see if maybe Riki loaded files and then deleted them without doing a deep scrub. She found Harry Russell's journal of his captivity. In a stunning display of iron will, he'd resisted the oni while they whittled him down, first finger by finger of his left hand, then the hand itself, and finally his arm. They broke him too completely, and after a brief stuttering dictation as Russell fell into shock from pain, the journal ended abruptly. She scrubbed the file completely off her datapad.

All the while, she pondered the seer's words, or lack of them. For the first time she saw a certain Heisenbergian logic to the seer's silence: the act of seeing the future—thus able to avoid it—made it more unlikely that path would be taken. The seer didn't want her to deviate from some path she'd naturally take—perhaps. It would be nice, if she had some clue as to what she was supposed to be doing. Just as a straight "no" to the oni wasn't the answer—as Harry Russell found out—fully cooperating with them surely couldn't be either.

Finally sick of the whole mess, she dropped her pad onto the futon and went to the window to stargaze. The moon was out and full, looking the same as Earth's or Elfhome's. She looked for the planets that had been in conjunction the month before on Elfhome.

"Stop looking out there," Chiyo moaned from her corner.

"Why?"

"Because it gives me a headache."

"Why does my looking out a window make your head hurt?"

"Because you are a stupid little fake elf, and this is a stupid waste of my abilities. I was meant for greater things than being your jailer. You'll never figure out this gate, and all my time and effort will be wasted."

"Well, then let me go."

Chiyo gave her a dark look. "They should just shackle you in a dank little hole and be done with it. Throw in scraps of moldy bread and let you eat cockroaches for protein. There is no reason you need to live like a princess."

"Except the whole plan depends on her," Riki said, standing at the door, his arms full of clothing. Chiyo barked something in Oni, which got a sputtering laugh from Riki. "Dream on, little kitsune. It's not going to happen. We're never going to be more to them than what we were created to be: tools. You don't turn a hammer into a noble just because it hammered down a stubborn but vital nail. You either whack another nail with it, or shove it away and enjoy what you've made using it."

"A noble?" Tinker asked. So the whole "Lady Chiyo" was the female's desired reward for spying on Maynard and guarding her.

"Onihida is mostly feudal, with a few small bright sparks." Riki had healing spells inked over his foot, and it looked normal—for him—but he limped as he walked, wincing in pain. "We seem forever stuck in the dark ages. Nobles are usually greater blood, but occasionally a lesser blood can work its way up to a minor lord by being brutal and meticulous. Lord Tomtom is one. Mostly, though, lesser are tools made by the greater bloods, just like Windwolf made you."

"Windwolf changed me, but he didn't make me."

"Make, change, twist, mold; it's all the same. Here are your clothes."

He handed her the clothing. The stack contained five changes of panties, socks, shirts, and jeans. The underwear were silk, and the jeans were Levi's, all in her size. Behind a mask of vivid bruises, Riki's eyes were dilated into wide cerulean blue discs. If she hadn't read Russell's journal, she might have felt guilty.

"I'd tell Windwolf to piss off before I'd betray a friend."

"Sometimes you get stuck in a trap of your own design." He limped to the window to collapse onto the deep sill. "I didn't know what Tomtom had done to the other scientists, just that they were dead, and they needed someone that could pass to find Dufae's son."

"Why the hell did you even get involved with them? You nearly have a doctorate of physics, why the hell would you give it all up to be a tool on some backass world?"

"You wouldn't understand." Riki fumbled through his pockets, found the MP3 player, gazed at it sadly, and put it away to pull out cigarettes.

"No, I don't. Nothing could make me do what you're doing."

"Really?" He tapped out a cigarette, his motions slow, like he was moving through deep water. "What if someone sealed away your intelligence? Made you an idiot but left the memories of your brilliance? At night you'd dream that you were smart again, creating clever gadgets, having that wildfire of creativity, and wake up to find it all ashes. What would you do to get it back?"

She swallowed down sudden terror. "I wouldn't do this."

"Liar," Riki whispered. He clicked his tongue and the cigarette lit.

"What is it that you get out of this deal?"

"I'm a tengu." He took a deep drag off the cigarette, and languidly raised the hand to rest against his temple. "Hard wired in this brain is the instinct of flight. Millions of years of evolution focused on that one thing, tightly packed away," he held out his hand, showing it innocent of feathers, "in a body that can't fly. You can't imagine— even with your marvelous brain—what an endless torture it is. Tengu don't die of old age on Earth—sooner or later, they just climb the tallest mountain and throw themselves off, just to feel that oneness with the sky."

"There's hang gliding."

Riki's shoulder shook with a short, silent laugh. "Hang gliding, parachuting, high diving . . . I could name them all, but the thing is, you only go down, you never come back up."

"You could have just gone to Elfhome. Obviously the spell works there."

"When people throw themselves off mountains, normally there's not much left to salvage." He took another long drag on his cigarette. "But we tried. We skinned the bodies of the old ones who had the tattoo, preserving them for centuries, waiting for a chance to have our wings and our freedom at the same time, slowly going mad."

"But it didn't work, so you sold yourself back into slavery."

"Yes," he murmured and then looked sharply at Chiyo. "Hey! Chiyo! You can't go to sleep!"

"I'm so tired," Chiyo moaned.

Riki sighed, and gave a sharp whistle. The guard from the hall opened the door and looked in. Riki flicked the hand with the cigarette, giving a command in rapid Oni. The guard glanced at Chiyo, then to Tinker, nodded and went out.

"What?" Tinker asked.

"We have a slight personnel problem. One of Chiyo's cousins was killed in a car accident the Shutdown we missed our kill on Windwolf. It leaves us shorthanded."

Things suddenly clicked for Tinker. The oni were the smugglers; the high-tech goods were for building the gate. Chiyo's cousin must have been the pinned driver who had been shot by the other oni, rather than let him fall into EIA hands and be questioned. Tinker looked sharply at the female; if someone had killed Oilcan, she would—she would . . . She couldn't finish the thought, the possibilities of Oilcan being caught and hurt in all this was all too real for idle speculation.

"So." Tinker distracted herself with details. "We're missing materials for the gate?"

"No. Lord Tomtom is quite methodical. We have a surplus of everything."

The door opened and the guard came back, carrying a *saijin* flower.

"What's that for?" Tinker scrambled backward, away from the guard.

"It's time for you to sleep." Riki took another drag on his cigarette, and breathed the smoke out his long sharp nose.

"I don't need that. I'll sleep without it."

"We have to be sure. Please, just take it nicely. With what I'm buzzing on for the pain—" he lifted his foot that she had broken "—I don't trust myself not to hurt you."

Sullenly, she held her hand for the flower, and with everyone watching closely, breathed deeply of its false comfort.

Tinker drifted out of the white fog of drugged slumber, opening her eyes to an unfamiliar ceiling. Where was she? Sleep still clung to her with pulled taffy strength, making it hard to think. She dragged her hand free of the blankets to rub at her eyes, trying to force herself awake. As she moved, she felt the spider again, picking its way carefully across her forehead. She smeared her hand up, over her brow, and combed her fingers on through her hair, finding nothing. *What the hell?*

The ceiling had changed.

She frowned at the expanse of white, now recognizable as the one above her futon on Onihida. Wait, the ceiling hadn't changed—or had it? Both ceilings had been featureless white; she couldn't say how one was strange and the other familiar. And why would anyone swap ceilings? That didn't make sense. Maybe it had been a trick of lighting. She sat up, knowing that something was wrong, but still not sure what.

Chiyo sat in her corner wearing a fresh kimono and a smug smile.

Tinker fumbled her way into the clothes Riki had brought her the night before, trying to think past the fog banks rolling through her mind. The Levi jeans distracted her from the ceiling mystery. The blue jeans were men's thirty-by-thirty carpenters, which she usually wore, but brand-new. She puzzled over them a moment—wondering how they had gotten the correct size and type—before realizing that Riki probably had just checked the dresser in her workshop. Oilcan might have noticed missing clothes, so the oni bought her a new wardrobe. The oni's thoroughness depressed her.

Riki arrived as she was putting on her boots. Annoyingly, his bruises had faded during the night to almost nothing.

"It wasn't an elf," Tinker said to him.

"What?"

"You said it was an elf that beat you up at the Faire the night

Windwolf changed me. It couldn't have been—you would have been healed by the time I got back three days later."

"Tomtom had me beaten," Riki admitted. "He didn't think you were coming back. I convinced him that you'd come back eventually for your cousin's sake, so he let me off lightly."

Tinker grunted at the oni's idea of "lightly." "I want something to eat, and then we can talk about this gate you want me to build."

At least they had good food: smoked trout, eggs poached in heavily salted water, and a sweet, orange-yellow, soft fruit peeled and sliced, all dumped on top of a huge bowl of nutty-flavored, dark brown rice. The only thing she didn't like were oddly pickled vegetables. Chiyo and Riki ate them in a resigned manner.

Riki explained that they were traditional staples from Lord Tomtom's region; apparently in the warmer climates, pickling was the easiest way to preserve food. "And the cook is a seven-foot-tall *shankpa* whose family died in a famine. He takes wasted food personally."

Shankpa? Tinker refused to ask on the grounds that at some point ignorance started to sound like idiocy. She'd find out later.

"You don't send plates back with food on them." Chiyo tipped her bowl to show it was empty.

"I see." Tinker picked up her pickles and dumped them into Chiyo's bowl.

Chiyo looked laughably stunned for a moment, and then her lip curled back into a snarl. The look vanished away with one murmured word from Riki.

"What's the magic word?" Tinker asked him as they walked the maze of identical stone hallways.

"Which one?"

She attempted to reproduce the word; apparently she didn't come close because Riki puzzled a moment.

"Ah," he said. "That's the act of being deboned."

At the workshop, she found a distance measurer and a piece of chalk. She walked around the vast room, pointing the instrument at the distant walls.

"What are you doing?" Riki perched on a workbench. He'd sent Chiyo off on some errand, much to everyone's relief.

"I'm measuring the room to find its exact size so we can model it on the computer." Tinker tapped the button, called the measurement to Sparks, marked the floor and moved down roughly a foot. "If we're building the gate in this room, then we need to know the maximum size it can be." She paused. "You do want it built in here, don't you?"

"Yes."

"I thought so, judging by your notes and what you told Russell."

"You found that?"

"Yes."

Riki winced but said nothing.

"The gate in orbit is just over twenty-six hundred feet in diameter, basically half a mile." She finished the width measurement and started on length. "The ceiling is going to be the prime determiner. Depending on the slope of the ceiling and the various support beams, it's going to be somewhere between twenty and thirty feet in diameter."

"Russell maintained that it couldn't be scaled down."

"It was only designed that size to allow for spaceships to pass through it. Didn't you show him my father's notes?"

"There's nothing on how Dufae decided on its size."

Gods save her from idiots. "What do you think all the technical specs on the space shuttle were about? He was trying to plot out the minimum size of a colony ship. At minimum, a colony would need something that could safely land people on a planet. He thought that anything going out should be able to have a shuttle riding piggyback on it and still fit through the gate."

"Doh!" Riki said, sounding very human.

Scaling it down presented a host of problems. With the large surface to play with, her father hadn't bothered to economize his design, and the Chinese apparently hadn't dared to deviate from the stolen plans. She'd have to use every trick she knew to compact the circuits. "Where is the ceramic coming from? You said we have surplus of everything."

"We've been stockpiling ceramic tiles for nearly fifteen years. They decided early on, though, that the shield material wasn't needed."

"Yeah, that's just to protect the gate from micrometeor impacts and solar wind." Tinker finished up her measurements by taking the ceiling readings at every grid point that she had chalked on the floor. "Sparks, render that for me."

"Okay, Boss."

While she waited she considered the scale ratio. The easiest might be a simple one to a hundred ratio: 2640 feet shrinking to 26.4.

"Done, Boss." The AI projected it onto the screen.

She snapped out a circle to represent the scaled down gate and moved it around the workshop. Gods, manufacturing the damn framework was going to be a bitch. The nonconductive material used in space wouldn't stand up to gravity. While steel could take the stress load, the amount of metal needed to make the gate would play havoc with the system.

A good fit on the model drew her attention back to it. She locked the circle down. "Let's see if this works."

As Sparks read off the gird coordinates, she found the matching points on the workshop floor and circled them in chalk.

"Is that it?" Riki asked with quiet awe.

She snorted in disgust. "That's the easy part. Of course if I make a mistake now, we might not know until the last moment. Let me think on this for a while. Get me a list of supplies that we have, and see if you can find some more comfortable chairs."

She'd shifted the locations three times including rotating the gate half a turn as she considered factors from height clearance, use of the overhead crane during construction, the ease of getting large materials into place, and finally the local ley lines, faint as they might be. Riki reappeared with the materials list and a surprising array of office chairs just as she was spray-painting the final location onto the workshop floor. He also had a lunch of steamed fish, brown rice, and more pickles.

She took the list and studied it as she ate. Again, she found the oni depressingly efficient, though noncreative; they had slavishly gathered what had been used to build the orbital gate and nothing else. "We need something for the superstructure of the gate, something inert and nonmetallic. If we were on Elfhome, I'd use ironwood. I don't suppose you have something similar?"

"Ironwood?"

"Yeah."

"You want to use ironwood?"

She flicked her pickles at him. "Hello! That's what I said. I know you understand English, Mr. Born-and-raised in Berkeley."

"It's just using wood is so low tech."

"To quote you—doh! From little minds come no solutions. Ironwood is stunningly strong, renewable, non-toxic, recyclable, and easy to work with. Do the oni have anything like it or not?"

"We can get ironwood."

She waited for explanations but they weren't forthcoming.

"I'm talking massive timbers." She held out her hands to show the beam size.

Riki nodded. "Just tell me how much, and I'll get it."

"Okay. We're in business then."

Time blurred for the rest of the day, as she designed the wood framework. Riki came and went, searching out samples of the ceramic tiles and other materials stockpiled elsewhere. Each item fired new ideas, and she branched out to how to affix the tiles, a ramp over the threshold to protect the gate, and a preliminary sketch of the power supply grid.

Night fell, and shadows in the warehouse grew deeper. Chiyo brought dinner and almost instantly the female and Riki started bickering in Oni. Tinker sighed, leaning back in her chair to look up through the skylight. She expected the stars to be strange and unfamiliar, like the sky of Earth. First Wolf, though, was right overhead, his shoulder star the brightest thing in the sky as always. It was comforting to see it, so very familiar. Then it struck her—it was too familiar. She leaned from side to side to see more through the overhead rectangle of Plexiglas, studying the constellations. The moon spinners. The dark-eyed widow.

It was the sky of Elfhome overhead.

And suddenly it was all clear to her.

You have a prisoner, extremely intelligent, to whom you need to give great freedom and entrust with a great deal of material that could easily be twisted into weapons. Wouldn't the simplest method of holding said prisoner be simply to convince her that she is in another dimension? Even if she fled the building, the whole world would act as a prison. Escape would seem impossible.

She had to still be on Elfhome. Why else would they paint the warehouse windows to keep her from seeing outside? How else could Riki be on Elfhome prior to Shutdown and after Startup and yet have a copy of her computer system up and running? How he had access to office chairs and ironwood? How he got her to the "castle?" If Riki could pop back and forth freely between Elfhome and Onihida, carrying kidnapped girls, ergonomic workstations, and large trees, the oni had no need of a gate.

And yet, she couldn't completely explain away the city outside the windows. How had they tricked her so completely?

"Kitsune are the fox spirits," Lain had told her. "They usually appear to be beautiful women, but they really are just foxes that can throw illusions into their victim's mind."

Was the spider she felt every morning Chiyo stepping into her mind, reading it and planting illusions? When she considered it, she could find a dozen times Chiyo had reacted to her thoughts.

Chiyo could read her mind.

Tinker glanced over at Chiyo, who was still arguing with Riki. Her greatest weapon was her enemies' ignorance. As long as they didn't realize she had discovered the truth, they would continue to allow her the freedom of the workshop. And with the workshop, she could build tools to escape. But Chiyo mustn't discover that she knew . . .

The fight finished up when an oni guard came into the warehouse to fetch Riki away, leaving behind Chiyo to guard Tinker. To distract herself, Tinker started to factor out large numbers, looking for primes.

Chiyo winced at her. "What are you doing?"

"Factoring numbers," Tinker said truthfully.

Chiyo rubbed her forehead. "You're a hideously ugly little creation."

Tinker gathered together all the cordless screwdrivers and started to remove the battery packs. The joy of being a genius was that you could do complex math in your head while assembling simple but effective weapons almost thoughtlessly.

Trying not to grin, Tinker switched to determining escape velocities, which reduced Chiyo to quiet whimpers of pain.

Tinker would have liked to create more of a plan, but she didn't dare plan anything with Chiyo prying into her mind. She finished the simple stun baton and tested it by pressing it against Chiyo. The kitsune collapsed into a satisfying heap of silk. Tinker bound and gagged her quickly, surprised to discover Chiyo had very sharp canine teeth, small furry dog-ears, and a foxtail hidden under the kimono.

Tinker swapped fresh batteries into the stun baton, glancing around. The warehouse had changed little, but that would almost be expected. The low windows had been painted black so Chiyo wouldn't have to disguise anything outside.

She bypassed the alarm on the outside door, cut off the padlock with a welding torch, and opened the door.

She expected to be on Mount Washington—it was the view out her bedroom window, only from the Onihida perspective. Looking at the moonlit hills rising all around her, she realized that the view had been a complete sham. They were in a river valley someplace far from downtown. As she scurried down the alley, she decided that it was logical. The oni would want to be as far out of the public eye as possible. Mount Washington, being far above the floodplain and yet close to downtown and the Rim, was still heavily populated.

She paused at the mouth of the alley, trying to get her bearings. She was in an industrial park of some sort, the long tall warehouses standing dark all around her. Nothing looked like a stone castle, so her bedroom and the rest of the living spaces were probably in one of the warehouses, hidden from prying eyes.

Fake, all of it.

She peered around the corner. Surely there would be guards—unless they were afraid of advertising their presence. She dashed across the street to the cover of the next alley. It took her to the water's edge.

Only twenty feet across with high cement retaining walls for banks, the waterway was too narrow to be a river. Most streams in the area, though, flowed into the Ohio River eventually. A silvery leaf tossed down to the dark water pointed out which direction the creek flowed. Following the creek would take longer than striking off across country, but heading in a random direction might only take her deep into Elfhome wilderness. Hopefully Riki wouldn't be back soon.

After five minutes of walking with the warehouse to her right, she realized how large the oni complex was. The long building was easily a quarter mile or more long. There was a wide break, and then another long warehouse running alongside the creek. At the end of the second warehouse, a thick column of white limestone lit by moonlight drew her eyes upwards. A massive bridge spanned the valley in several graceful arches, totaling sixteen hundred feet long with a deck two hundred feet above the creek. Even in the city of bridges, it was quite singular, and she recognized it.

The bridge was the Westinghouse Bridge, which meant the oni base was the old Westinghouse Electric Airbrake plant. By blind luck she had gone in the right direction, because the Rim cut through just feet north of the plant. The erratic path of the Monongahela River and the Rim effectively isolated this small slice of Pittsburgh. The elfin forest deeply encroached on the area, slowly whittling it down. Last she'd heard, something had killed and eaten the last human inhabitants; now she wondered how much the oni had had to do with that.

No matter; now she knew where she was, she knew where to go for help. She sold scrap to the converted USX steel mill just downriver. The mini mill operated twenty-four hours a day, melting down old steel to reforge it to slabs which were sent upriver via barge to the rolling mill at Dravosburg. It was less than three miles. Unfortunately, most of the steelworkers now lived across the river, where miles of transplanted Pittsburgh buffered them from Elfhome wilderness, but there were plenty of bars.

Sticking to the water's edge would be slow, and considering the black willows and jumpfishes, far from safe. She decided to take a risk and follow the street.

She heard the car engine and saw the headlights running on the power lines overhead moments before the car swept into view. She had ducked back into the shadows, and then recognized the car. It was one of Windwolf's Rolls-Royces.

"Hey!" she cried, stepping into the light. "Stop!"

The car squealed to a stop and the driver's door flung open. Surprisingly, it was Sparrow who got out. The female was in mourning black, with her pale hair simply braided. It was the most unadorned that Tinker had ever seen her. "Tinker? What are you doing here?"

"Escaping!" Tinker laughed, crossing to touch the marvelous, beautiful car. "Is Windwolf with you? Pony?"

"It's in the middle of night," Sparrow said. "They were searching the river for the last two days. I believe they're sleeping now. How did you get away?"

"With this!" Tinker proudly held out her homemade stun baton.

"That tiny thing?" Sparrow held out her hand. "What is it?"

Without thinking, Tinker handed the weapon to Sparrow. "It's a stun baton. You just press against someone, hit the trigger and the person is stunned."

"Like this?" Sparrow pointed the baton toward her, thumb on the trigger.

"Careful." Tinker reached to take it back.

Sparrow pressed the tip into Tinker's outreached hand.

The pain was instant and intense, and she started to fall as all her muscles spasmed.

Sparrow caught her. "Ah, yes, how clever of you. I must tell Tomtom to keep a closer eye on you."

By the time she recovered, Sparrow had her bound and inside the car.

"Are you mad? Why are you working with them?"

"Sometimes the best tool is a very big stick."

"What the hell does that mean?"

"I'm using the oni to fix what is wrong," Sparrow said. "I'm going to take things back to the way they should be."

"How should they be?"

"If you repeat a lie long enough it doesn't become a truth, but everyone will act like it has. I'm sure you've been told how evil the Skin Clan was and how the *domana* nobly dispatched them. The truth is that the Skin Clan took our race from one step above apes and made them one step below gods. As we were when the Skin Clan toppled, we still are. Under the *domana* we're stagnating. It's time to go back to the old ways."

"How could you do this to your honor?"

Sparrow gave a slight laugh. "Honor is nothing but convenient ropes that the *domana* use to bind the lower castes helpless. They are slave lords with invisible chains."

"How can you say that? They made you one of them."

"They've made a mockery of the *dau*. I should have undergone the same transformation as you, to be wholly *domana*, but that would have weakened their power base. So they call me *domana*, and expect the lower castes to bow to me, but everyone knows the truth. I'm no more *domana* than I was at birth."

"You're going to destroy your people because the lower castes never groveled to you? The *domana* are evil because they wouldn't make you one of them?"

Sparrow stopped the car to look down at her. "I can kill you. Doing this now is convenient, but if it proves too annoying, I can easily wait another hundred years for my chance. And so can the oni."

Tinker shrank away from the cold, impartial stare, barely able to breathe.

"Good." Sparrow started the car. "You really must start thinking like an elf. Look at the long-term future."

Like she had one.

Tinker found no comfort that Sparrow, after several minutes of silence, felt the need to justify her actions with, "My case only illustrated the hypocrisy of the *domana*; even when they lift up one of the lower castes, they still suppress us."

15: WHIPPING BOY

THE BACK DOOR of the Rolls opened and an oni warrior, face painted for war, gazed down at her—bound hand and foot—as Sparrow murmured something in the Oni tongue. The warrior grunted, took out a whistle, and blew a single long note that jumped from shrill to inaudible. Somewhere close by, small dogs broke into excited barking.

Sparrow said something about Tomawaritomo, and the warrior pointed off into the darkness. She walked away without looking back.

The warrior reached into the Rolls with huge gnarled hands and lifted Tinker out, passing her like a hissing kitten to another guard. Oni warriors were emerging out of the night, faces painted and heavily armed. Apparently her escape had been noticed, and the oni had been on the hunt, now called back by the silent whistle.

Without the kitsune's deception, the airbrake plant was a collection of massive, old buildings, heavy with the sense of otherworldliness where men did the works of gods and sneered at the concept of magic. Yet rising up in the moonlight beyond the great buildings was the wild primal forest of Elfhome, and all around Tinker, smelling like wet dogs, were the brutish oni warriors.

Tinker was carried into one of the mile-long buildings. The first section was a garage, holding a host of hoverbikes and cars; Riki's motorcycle sat to one side, as singular as the tengu. The second section was a kennel, filled with steel cages. Many of the cages held yapping little pug dogs. In one cage was a muzzled warg, its glowing eyes lighting its corner with icy rage, its bulk filling the cage.

Beyond was empty warehouse. A shallow, narrow channel cut

down the center of the vast room; oily water flowed in the cement drain. On one side was the bare skeleton of a freight elevator. There was something disturbingly familiar about the space. They passed a dark stain of old blood on the floor, and there, in the dust on the floor, were her bootprints and Riki's footprints, where he had held her still and made her watch the deboning that first morning. This was the true appearance of the courtyard garden with the gazebo.

At the far end, they caught up with Sparrow. The elf female was coming to a stop beside an oni male. Riki knelt on the ground in front of the male, head bowed until his forehead nearly touched the dusty floor. To one side, the wizened-dwarf torturer sharpened his boning knives.

"I caught her before she could do harm," Sparrow was saying to the oni. The guard dropped Tinker onto the ground, knocking the breath out of her. "Really, Lord Tomawaritomo, I had hoped you could contain her more than three days."

"The kitsune let her slip away." The oni male reached down to catch Tinker by a handful of shirt and bra and lifted her up to dangle in mid-air as he inspected her.

So this was Lord Tomawaritomo. Tall and lean, he towered over Tinker; even the long thin sword strapped to his side was taller than her. He was striking in appearance, but not beautiful; his cheekbones and chin were too sharp, and his nose too flat. The gold of his pupil filled his eyes, with an iris a dark vertical slit. He had a mane of white that spilled down over his back. His ears were more than just pointed: they were white-furred, and cupped forward, like a cat's. He wore a kimono of vivid purples and greens, and a fur of pristine white that matched his snow-white hair. The pelt was wrapped over one shoulder and pinned in place by his shoulder guard of ridged bone. The fur looked to be white wolf or warg, though larger than either species. The origin of the bone, however, Tinker couldn't guess, except that the body part involved was the jawbone, hinged midpoint at the oni's chest.

After inspecting Tinker closely, Tomtom grunted. "Such trouble in a little package."

"It seems to be a universal constant that keys to doorways are usually small." Sparrow smiled at her own wit.

Tomtom grunted again. "Perhaps I should put this one on a chain to keep it from being lost."

"Whatever it takes," Sparrow said.

Perhaps it was just as well that Tinker didn't have breath to talk; she had a feeling that she would be saying things that she'd regret later. She comforted herself by thinking choice insults.

Tomtom clicked his tongue and Riki looked up. "Take this." The oni lord held Tinker out to Riki. "See that it doesn't slip away again."

So Tinker found herself handed off again like a child's doll. Annoyingly, she couldn't help but feel somewhat safer with Riki, perhaps just because he was familiar. He, at least, balanced her upright and stooped to undo the ties around her ankles. "Stay still. Stay silent," he whispered to her without meeting her eyes. *Yeah, right.*

Tomtom's cat ears flickered from Riki to a distant wail. "Ah, my warriors have found the vixen."

"You'll have the kitsune killed." Sparrow said it as a disinterested statement, not a question.

"One normally has to be diplomatic with the kitsune," Tomtom said. "This presents possibilities . . ."

A moment later frantic cries became audible, growing louder. Chiyo was dragged into the vast room, struggling in the hold of two oni warriors. Her fox tail stuck out of a tear in her kimono, and her doglike ears were laid back in distress. At a signal from Lord Tomtom, the warriors released Chiyo and she flung herself at Tomtom's feet. As the kitsune begged in frantic Oni, the corners of the oni lord's mouth curled up into a grin.

"Her Oni is worse than mine," Sparrow said. "What is she saying?"

"She says she'll do anything to avoid the knives." Lord Tomtom motioned to one of the waiting oni. "This will interest you."

Sparrow gave an exasperated sigh. "My time is limited."

Tomtom gazed at Sparrow hard. "Stay and be instructed."

He put out his hand and one of the warriors gave him a leather lead and slipknot collar. Tomtom dangled out the lead, clucking as one would to a dog. Chiyo cringed but sat up, canting back her head to lay bare her throat.

"Many of the lesser bloods have the spells to manipulate them threaded through their genetic pattern," Tomtom explained to Sparrow as he slipped the collar over Chiyo's head. He pulled the slipknot tight, winding the lead around his fist. "I could reduce her back to fox if I wanted."

Chiyo whimpered in fear.

"What use would a fox be to me, little kitsune?" Tomtom purred, wiping away Chiyo's tears. "I've decided to breed you. No, no, no." He murmured as Chiyo glanced at the surrounding warriors. "Your mate will have to be fetched. Now hold still."

He growled out a word, and strange runes gleamed to life on Chiyo's skin. In a low dull drone, Tomtom chanted out a spell, and her very skin began to glow. After a minute, he fell silent and the light vanished, and Chiyo panted quietly.

"I've put her into season." He loosened the lead and handed it to one of his warriors, pointing back across the warehouse and saying something in Oni.

Chiyo cried out as if struck. "Warg?"

Sparrow made a face of distaste. "Oh, beat her and be done with it."

"The lesser bloods are socketed so they can breed with anything," Tomtom said. "I want to introduce the warg abilities into the kitsune line."

Sparrow scoffed at this. "You don't change the genome directly?"

"Breeding for pups is a simpler method," Tomtom said.

"This is a waste of my time," Sparrow said. "I must be gone before I'm missed."

"Speak then," Tomtom said absently, watching the kitsune be stripped of her kimono, bent over a bale of bedding, and tied into position.

Tinker turned away as warriors took advantage of Chiyo's helplessness; the males laughed as their manipulations made the kitsune in heat moan wantonly. *Remember what she's done to me. I hate her. I should be glad she's being punished.*

Sparrow took no notice of the events with the kitsune. "I told you at the start of this that Wolf Who Rules needs to be eliminated."

Riki caught Tinker before she could launch herself at Sparrow, muffling her stream of curses at the elf.

Tomtom glanced at Tinker struggling in Riki's arms and a smile quirked at his mouth. "I have done all I will do in that regard."

"You failed miserably," Sparrow said.

Damn right, bitch, Tinker thought fiercely, still muted by Riki's hand.

"Exactly," Tomtom said. "I will not endanger my position by

fruitlessly striking at him. The dogs were expendable, but I will not risk my warriors."

"He suspects that his *domi*'s disappearance is not an untimely accident," Sparrow said. "He plans to return to the citywide search."

"And you will take the river edge as before," Tomtom waved aside her concern. "Avoid this valley as planned. If you can not, call your contact first and we'll trigger the greater cloaking spells."

"Wolf Who Rules loves this little piece of trash!" Sparrow cried, making Tinker's heart do a strange little flip in her chest. "He's not being swayed from the truth. He knows we took her, he just doesn't know how or where we're hiding her."

Tomtom turned to look at Sparrow full on, wordlessly.

Sparrow visibly needed to steel herself against his cold look. "You are failing to see how dangerous he is."

"And you are overestimating him," Tomtom said flatly.

"Your people have never dealt with a *domana* lord on his own land," Sparrow said.

"A knife in the spine," Tomtom said. "An arrow through the eye, or a sword through the heart, and he will die like everything else in this universe."

"No!" Tinker cried into Riki's palm, and the tengu held her tighter still.

Tomtom turned away dismissively as the massive warg was brought in, muzzled, on a stout stick lead. The beast strained against the handler, heading for Chiyo.

"So arrange the knife!" Sparrow refused to be ignored. "Or the arrow or the sword! Kill him!"

Tinker wriggled in Riki's hold. *Shut up, bitch! Shut up!*

Tomtom's tone grew flatter, colder. "I will not stand here, repeating myself, or do you wish to go after the kitsune?"

Sparrow looked then, as did Tinker. The warg loomed over the kitsune, erect, proportionally wrong for the female, seeking an entrance in her slight body. Tinker looked away, desperately concentrating on anything but Chiyo and her sharpening whimpers. Sparrow watched, not even flinching as the kitsune gave a scream of agony. Tinker hunched against the sound of the big animal laboring, and Chiyo's now endless, shrill barks of terror and pain. She wanted to cover her ears, but Riki wasn't loosening his hold.

Sparrow tore her gaze away from the godless union. "So be it then. Let Wolf Who Rules be the *domana* you cut your teeth on. If you're to take this land, you'll need to face them eventually."

"Ah, good, he's tied with her." Tomtom ignored Sparrow in favor of the breeding. "If she brings a litter to term in two months, I'll breed her again next season." Tomtom glanced down at Tinker. "This one has the *domana* genome? Perhaps I'll get my own litter on her. She's tiny, but I suppose that gives her a certain childlike allure."

Tinker shrank away from his clinical gaze.

"You can breed her later," Sparrow said. "The queen's seer says she's the key to our plans regarding the gate."

"So it was reported to me." Tomtom knowing obviously threw Sparrow; Chiyo must have told him earlier, after reading Tinker's mind.

"The seer said," Sparrow continued, "that the only way to bind her was with ties of her own making."

"Which means?" Tomtom asked.

"You'll only be able to hold her with promises freely given," Sparrow explained. "How you'll manage that, I do not know, nor do I care. Torture her if you must, but bind her. Obviously she'll slip away if you do not."

Sparrow nodded then and swept away, leaving Tinker with her enemies without so much as a glance. Tinker had thought she hated Riki and Chiyo; she understood now what a shadow of hate that had been.

With a look from Lord Tomawaritomo, Riki released his hold on Tinker.

"You were human, the weakest of us." Tomtom studied her with his cat eyes. "If the elves had left the gate between our worlds open, we would have long since enslaved the humans. Weaklings, all."

"You don't need muscles when you have brains," Tinker snapped.

"The question is, how elfin are you now?" Lord Tomawaritomo said. "If I have you punished as you should be, will you survive it? The human didn't."

He meant Russell, whittled down by inches. Her arms tucked tight to her chest, and he laughed. She tried not to think of those bright sharp knives, the blood, and the white of bone.

"The risk would be great that she wouldn't survive," Riki murmured.

Lord Tomawaritomo glanced at Riki, eyes narrowing in speculation. "If you helped it escape, death would be preferable. You are being spared right now only because I myself called you away."

It took Tinker a moment to realize that Tomtom was referring to her as "it" as if she was a thing, not an intelligent being. Only a warning look from Riki kept her silent.

"Chiyo doesn't have the brain to keep her deluded," Riki explained.

"See that this is secure," Tomawaritomo growled softly, pointing at Tinker. "Then get me a whipping boy to use against it."

Riki bowed low, caught Tinker, and hurried her from the room, while Tomtom turned back to supervise the end of Chiyo's breeding.

They locked Tinker in a broom closet. It was only wide enough for her to sit down, knees tucked under her chin. No air ducts or even electrical outlets. After Riki untied her, four of the oni warriors, the shortest clearing seven feet, put her firmly into it, shut the door, and locked it, leaving her in darkness.

Hours crawled by.

A whipping boy. Who would they bring to torture in her place? Oilcan? *No, no, please not him!* Lain? That would be unbearable too. Windwolf? Unlikely—for all the reasons why Tomtom was refusing to kill him—Windwolf was too visible, too well guarded. Nathan? It would be the ultimate irony if he died for her.

Oilcan made the most sense, though, and the realization made her start crying. Damn it, she hated to cry. She rocked in place as tears burned in her eyes. Oh, please, please, anyone but Oilcan.

She heard footsteps approach the door and an exchange in Oni. One of the guards unlocked the door in a jangle of keys, and they opened it up, all poised to grab her if she tried to put up a fight. Ha! She was tempted to snarl at them, and make them flinch, but something about coming only to mid-stomach on them kept her from taunting them.

They took her to Tomtom's suite. Whereas most of the place was run-down offices and warehouses, the suite had been remodeled to opulence. The ceiling was a design of blocks within blocks, the walls a deep rich red, and the polished wood floor strewn with the pelts of large white animals.

Tomtom, Riki, and the torturer waited there with a host of armed, tense, and bloody warriors. Their focus had been on a body lying still on the floor in front of Tomtom. They shifted their feral interest to her as her guard checked her just inside the door. The body lay curled into a fetal position so that she could see only the curve of the spine.

Tinker trembled. Who was it? What had Tomtom's people done to the person to make him or her lie so still? Please, not Oilcan.

The body shifted, revealing the spill of long elfin hair, and she felt a wave of relief. Not Oilcan. Oh, thank God. And then she recognized the elf: Pony.

On the slight wave of Tomtom's hand, the guard let go of her, and she went to Pony without thinking. They had stripped him down to his loose black pants and beat him soundly. He flinched violently when she touched him.

"Easy. It's me, Pony."

He slit open his blackened eyes, and looked at her in first confusion and then in dismay. He groaned and tried to get up, to get her behind him, to protect her. He only managed to sit up, and she caught him before he collapsed.

Lord Tomawaritomo came and stood over them, gazing down at her with his cat eyes. "Good. You care for this whipping boy."

She realized then that she had made a mistake. She shouldn't have put her arms around Pony. She should have ignored his presence, refusing to acknowledge him. Lord Tomawaritomo knew now that he could affect her by hurting Pony.

"You didn't have to beat him," she snapped.

"One does not lightly take a warrior prisoner," Tomtom said. "They are made sturdily. One can cut them down to almost nothing before their life force gives out."

Tomtom lifted his hand and the squat torturer scurried forward wearing his bloodstained leather apron, boning knife glittering in his hand.

"You don't have to hurt him," Tinker cried, tightening her hold on Pony. "I'll make a gate."

"I am not afraid." Pony pulled out of her arms and managed to get to his feet. "Go ahead. Torture me. Kill me. She will not do what you ask of her."

Tomtom stepped back. "We will take only his sword arm first."

"No!" Tinker shouted, stepping between the oni and Pony, spreading wide her arms to shield him. "Don't hurt him! I'll do it! Just don't hurt him."

"Tinker *domi!*" Pony caught hold of her, pulled her back. "Do not do what they ask of you."

Tinker wriggled in his hold. "I can't watch them kill you little by little."

"I do not care what they do to me," Pony said.

"Pony, I can't." She swung around to focus on him. "I know myself too well. I can't sit and watch you scream your life away. I'll break. Maybe I can last until you've been tortured to death. But then they'll go find someone else to hold against me, and I won't be able to say no again, especially not after watching them cut you to pieces. I *will* break. I would rather break *now*, without having to take your screams to my grave, than after you're dead."

"I see," Pony said quietly. "Forgive me my selfishness."

"You do not understand." Tomtom's voice was a dangerous low rumble. "They will take his bones just so you know how serious I am. For any disobedience, the punishment will be worse."

Tinker could not imagine worse, but she was sure that Tomtom could. "No. No. Don't hurt him. I'll do what you want."

"Yes. You will." Tomtom gave an order. One of the warriors bent down and caught her by the waist, lifting her off the ground, while the other two caught hold of Pony.

"No! No!" Tinker cried. "If he's hurt, I will do nothing!"

"If torturing him does not work, we'll get another. One that works better."

Oilcan! She cried out as if struck, and then thought quickly. Did she have any leverage point beyond her ability? "Leave him alone, and I'll finish in a month!"

Tomtom whipped around and had her by the throat before she could react. "A month? That is twenty-eight days?"

He was going by the moon cycle, instead of Earth's calendar, but she wasn't going to argue schematics with him.

"Yes, twenty-eight days," she whispered. "Hurt him, and I'll do nothing! No matter who you get to replace him."

"You're lying," Tomtom said, making her stomach turn to lead and sink. "You cannot do it in a month."

"Yes, I can!" she cried. "The process is easier than I thought. I'll make a gate in a month, but only if you torture no one—I'd rather die than reward those who harmed ones I love."

Tomtom cocked his head, considering her. "Twenty-one days."

"What? Three weeks?"

"Twenty-one days or I'll have the bones removed."

She glanced at Pony, and wet her mouth. "Fine, I'll do it in twenty-one. But I'll need work crews: carpenters, electricians, and Riki."

"So be it." Tomtom gave an order, and the guards started to separate them again.

"Wait!" Tinker cried. "No! We had a deal!"

"He is spell-marked," Tomtom said. "The skin will have to be flayed."

"No!" Tinker said. "He's not to be hurt in any way."

"I'd be a fool to let him keep the spells," Tomtom said. "You could use them to escape."

"I promise I won't!" She beat on the massive arms holding her, trying to get to Pony. "On my honor, and the honor of my house, I will stay here without escaping and build your gate. Harm him, and I will do nothing."

Tomtom shook his head. "What is it with you *domana* and your sentimentalism for your underlings? It must be genetic. It makes you weak."

"Fine. I'm weak." She kicked her feet, dangling as she was in the guard's hold, emphasizing that she was small and scrawny. "I'll give my word and stay without trying to escape and build your gate within twenty-one days *only* if he's completely unharmed."

Tomtom came to grip her chin and gaze deep into her eyes. "Say it again."

So she repeated it. Carefully.

"Sparrow said that we'll only be able to hold her with promises freely given," Riki said. "If she can hold a warrior, then her word must be binding: she can't lie when giving her word."

"Very well." Tomtom released Tinker's chin and growled a command. She found herself on her feet, Pony supporting her. "Take them back to her room. She'll start working tomorrow at first light."

Riki helped her support Pony on the long walk to her bedroom, through dusty warehouses and barren offices. The *sekasha* concentrated on putting one foot in front of the other, only flinches of pain on his face showing how badly he was hurt. Tinker wanted to scream accusations at Riki, but Chiyo's punishment was still stark in her mind. Even the kitsune considered the breeding as the kindest of her possible punishments.

"I'm sorry," Riki said as he delivered them to the bedroom that proved—without Chiyo's presence—to be windowless.

"Why?"

He took her to mean "why Pony," although she wasn't sure herself which of the many whys she meant. Why did he continue serving such a monster? Why had he kept her silent—thus, and in hindsight, safe from Tomtom's anger? Why hadn't he chosen one of the many humans she loved?

"I find that I actually think of myself as human more than I thought," Riki said. "It was easier to pick an elf; I was taught to hate them."

"I'm an elf."

"You'll always be a human to me."

Only humans said things like that, so maybe he was telling the truth. Still, she couldn't find any room to forgive him.

"Go away," she said, and shut the door on his face.

She wanted to press Pony for details about what Windwolf was doing, how Oilcan was coping with her supposed death, if work had continued on her research center . . . but Pony looked like hell. She cleaned the blood from Pony's face, and nearly cried over the heel print bruised into the back of his right hand, his fingers swollen and broken.

"It is nothing," he mumbled. "I heal quickly. I will be better in no time."

Unfortunately, until he was functioning better, there would be no escaping.

She fingered where the power beads had been worked into his hair; the oni had cut his braids off, leaving little tufts of hair. Spell-marked or not, without the stored magical power, Pony's shields would quickly fail. The oni's ability to create "permanent" constructs—like Riki's wings and the Foo dogs—outclassed the elves' magic that normally required a ley line or it exhausted local ambient magic.

Pony took the lack of weapons and shields personally. "I'm sorry that I have failed you."

"Don't be an idiot. You haven't failed me." And then, because he didn't seem to believe her, she added truthfully, "I'm glad not to be all alone."

"Ah. I see. Then I'm glad to be here."

She couldn't bring herself to scorn him, despite it being silly for him to be happy to be stuck in such a situation. "What are you doing?"

Pony had started to stretch cautiously out on the floor. "I am going to sleep."

"Oh, get in the bed."

"You should sleep in the bed. I can sleep on the floor."

"Don't make me hit you." Tinker pushed him toward the bed. "The bed is huge, and I'm quite small, as everyone keeps pointing out. We can both share it without even noticing the other is in it."

"It wouldn't be proper."

"Get in the bed or I'll sleep on the floor too."

He actually agonized over it before giving in.

What the hell had she been thinking?

Fully awake in the darkened room, Tinker listened to the whisper of Pony's breathing. He lay so close she could feel the warmth from his body. His well-defined, muscled body. If she put out her hand, she could touch his hard stomach. Run her hand down his lean flank.

Why had she thought sharing a bed would be a good idea?

She had been scared and angry and frustrated when she went to bed. Now, for some inexplicable reason, she wanted to be held. No, more than held. All too easily, she could imagine being cradled naked in Pony's arms, his mouth on the nape of her neck, his strong hands cupping her breasts, their bodies thrusting together as his . . .

That was a truly dangerous line of thought. *You're a married woman, idiot!* She loved Windwolf, so why was she suddenly lusting for Pony?

Even pretending to be asleep became impossible. She opened her eyes and found that she could make out Pony's face: the shape of his mouth, the line of his nose, and the soft curve of his brow. Among the elves, she had taken his good looks for granted. After being surrounded by the oni and their alien ideals of beauty, she saw him with new eyes. Looking at him shot something akin to a low-voltage current down through her body to her groin. What would it be like to kiss him? Would he taste like Windwolf? She turned over to resist the temptation to find out.

Why was she feeling this way? She loved Windwolf. Didn't she? Certainly, if she could choose, she would want Windwolf beside her. Did she desire Pony only as a stand in for her husband? Did she only want someone bigger and stronger to make her feel safe and protected? Or did she love Windwolf only because of the sex? Would any sexy elf male do?

What a stupid time to be worrying about it. Pony's honor would never allow anything to happen, and besides, she'd probably never see Windwolf again. The oni were going to kill both of them as soon as the gate was done. There was no point pretending that Tomtom wouldn't dispose of them in some cruel yet offhandedly casual method. The white of exposed bone flashed into her mind. She curled against the flare of fear and misery.

I got away once, she reminded herself. *I can do it again.*

What was the point of being a genius, if she couldn't outthink her enemies?

Pony was doing exercises when Tinker woke the next morning. Stripped to the waist, he worked through a series of lightning-fast moves that would end suddenly in a perfect pose. Movement. Stillness. An attack. A block. A kick. A parry. Fluid. Precise. Soundless. Muscles upon muscles shifting under sleek skin, he was beautiful to watch. She felt the ache of desire flare up again. She moaned, rolling over to bury her head under pillows. Could this get any more embarrassing?

She realized then that she needed to pee.

She sat up and discovered that in that position, the need was greater.

"Good morning." Pony pressed his fist against his palm and bowed.

"Morning." She eyed the chamber pot in the corner. There was a real toilet off the workshop—could she reach that? No. She felt like she was about to burst. "Could you, um, turn around?"

She tried to pee quietly, but failed due to the acoustic properties of ceramic and the amplifying curvature of the bowl. Horses pissed quieter. Was it possible to die of humiliation? Mark up another difference between Pony and Windwolf—she hadn't been self-conscious the first time she used the toilet in front of Windwolf. She tried to act nonchalant, but she could feel the burn of embarrassment on her face as she washed her hands.

"Do you train every morning like that?" she asked to distract both of them.

"Yes. The *sekasha* were made to be living weapons. We hone our bodies to perfection."

"You embrace being a weapon?"

"I take joy in my strength." He high-kicked and locked into place, balanced on one foot. "And I like to fight."

He grinned, and suddenly he didn't seem like the mild Pony she knew, but someone wilder, and fiercer, more aptly named Stormhorse. She tried to study him clinically, taking note only of his injuries. His bruises looked days old, mottled purple and faded yellow.

"How do you feel?"

"Whole, except for my hand." He held it out for her inspection. The middle and ring fingers were still swollen and stiff. He flexed them carefully, wincing. "It will be another day or two before I'll be able to hold a sword, perhaps as much as four before I can strike with this hand without fear of causing more pain to myself than my opponent."

"Good. We have to get out of here."

"Out?"

"We need to escape."

Pony looked at her with utter surprise. "But you gave your word."

Tinker winced: She had suspected that this was how the conversation would go, but she hated to have her fears confirmed. "Pony, these are bad, nasty people with not a fleck of honor among them."

"In giving your word, it is only your honor that matters, not the receiver. If you think the person is not worth your honor, you don't extend it."

She checked the impulse to stick her tongue out at him. "Would you rather I break my word or let these monsters take over our world?"

"I would rather die than be the reason you broke your word."

Elves! "This is not about you, this is about them doing whatever they could to break me."

"That's because you are the pivot."

"Yeah, yeah, so everyone keeps reminding me." But, actually, she had kind of forgotten all that between Sparrow's betrayal, Chiyo's breeding, and Pony's capture. Tinker thought she understood the mess until Sparrow waltzed in and clued the oni. How did their knowledge and her promise change things? The seer had said that it was only a matter of time before the oni opened a gate—certainly if Tinker refused to cooperate, they could bide their time; they were immortal and humans made advances in technology daily. That equation had a zero sum—which was why she was cooperating until she could escape. But the seer also indicated that they could only defeat the oni by choosing when the gate was opened, and indicated that the pivot picked the time. If she was in the oni's control, did it mean that the oni controlled the choice?

She decided to bounce her questions off of Pony, who probably had more experience in these seer-type of things. "Sparrow told the oni that the only way to bind me was with ties of my own making . . ."

"Sparrow?"

Oops, she forgot Pony didn't know that little piece of nastiness. "She's working with them. They had me fooled into thinking I was on Onihida, but I figured it out and got away last night. Sparrow recaptured me and brought me back to them."

Pony darkened with anger, and he stalked about the room as if looking for something to vent his rage on. He growled out Elvish she didn't recognize, but they sounded like obscenities.

"Pony, I'm trying to figure out what the seer meant."

"Forgiveness." He fell silent, but he continued to stalk about the room.

"Do you know if the seer said anything more about me being the pivot?"

"She did not, although closely pressed by all. 'Bind the pivot,' was all she said. 'If the pivot be true, then the battle can be won. If the pivot proves false, all will be lost.' "

Tinker tried to wrap her mind around it, but Sparrow's translation was making it difficult. "Sparrow told the oni that they'll only be able to hold me with promises freely given. Has the oni won merely by making me promise? Is it just the words, or . . ."

"Sparrow often hears what she wants to hear," Pony interrupted her. "The seer isn't saying that getting you to make promises will win the battle. The seer said 'if the pivot be *true*' which means you must keep all your promises, no matter to whom."

"Oh, you must be kidding."

"No."

"I can't make them a gate."

"You must. You promised."

"Th-that doesn't follow logic," Tinker protested.

"Seeing into the future is like having a gleaming thread appear in the darkness. You must walk that path, no matter how treacherous, to reach the foreseen outcome. If you step off it, you're lost from sight, and both you and your goal become unknown again."

"So, although it flies into the face of everything sensible, the only way to stop the oni . . . is to do . . . what they want."

"What they forced you to promise."

She shook her head. No. It didn't make any more sense out loud or stood on its head. "What if being 'true,' is just 'loyal'? I can't be 'loyal' to the elves if I'm making a gate for the oni."

"No. You're confusing words. Those don't mean the same thing."

She winced. "They're synonyms, right? Close to the same meaning."

"True only means that one keeps their word of honor. It is a word applied to head of households and clan leaders as they interact with equals or enemies."

If she got out of this, she had to smack Tooloo a good one. Obviously when the half-elf taught her Elvish, any approximate English word would work, to hell with confusion that other meanings of the English word might cause.

"*Domi*, you swore not only on your honor but on the honor of your house. For an elf, there is no stronger oath."

Yeah, that was why she used it. She wanted to scream. What an irrational mess. "I'm not really an elf! I'm a human with funny ears. I didn't know what Windwolf intended with the spell. I'm not even sure why Windwolf made me this way. If you love someone, don't you take them as they are?"

"*Domi*, I am young for an elf, but I am over a hundred. I grew up in a large city in the Easternlands. Many elves live there, but in a hundred years, one meets most of them. And in all that time, I have never met anyone like you. Not a single person, having met you, has questioned Windwolf's desire to prolong your life. You blaze like a star. You don't seem to see that, but then you surround yourself with people nearly as bright as yourself. You raise people up to your heights. Even if Windwolf did not love you, he would not want to see your brilliance put out."

She burned in embarrassment. "Me? Blaze?"

"From your wit to your confidence to your compassion, you are an amazing person."

"Windwolf barely knew me when he proposed."

"After living so many years, if you're wise, you learn your own heart. You know when you meet someone that 'this person I can be friends with,' or 'this person I can build a friendship with—it will be difficult work—but it *may be* very sound,' or 'this person I will never be friends with.' There are times, though, where it seems like magic; you look at a person and your soul opens up and recognizes a true love. Windwolf looked at you and believed you are one he could live forever with. And in some ways, I am the same."

She looked at him. "What?"

He dropped to one knee and took her hand. "*Domi*, do you think I would pledge my life to you, be willing to die for you, if I did not in some way, love you?"

"You love me?" she repeated, stunned.

"You are my *domi*. And in all ways, you have proved the worth of my decision. You have protected me, as I have protected you. A holding is like a marriage, where trust runs deep. And in only a few days, I knew that to be beholden to you would be a good thing."

That threw her into a whirlwind of emotions, but the door opened behind Pony, saving her from discovering what dangerous thing might arise from that chaos. A gale force of alarm blasted through her, scouring away everything else.

There was an entire squad of oni warriors with Riki to escort her and Pony back to the workshop. Ironwood timbers sat stacked just inside the side door, which was padlocked shut again. A crew of humans sat waiting. They were Asians in blue jeans, T-shirts, and work boots.

Tinker checked in confusion. "Who are they?"

"They're the carpenters to make the frame out of the ironwood," Riki explained. "I thought since you designed the framework yesterday, that you'd want to get started on building it. We've got a tight deadline."

"Wait, isn't this like your ultra-secret hideout? What the fuck are they doing here? Did you kidnap them all? Are you going to kill them when they're done?"

Riki blinked and glanced again at the carpenters. "Oh, no, they're not humans. They're oni permanently disguised as humans, sort of like how the yap dogs were those big monster things. We had to immigrate them into Pittsburgh under Chinese visas."

Tinker thought of the sprawling Chinatown on the Northside. "Oh shit, don't tell me all the Chinese are oni."

"Okay." Riki walked away.

She was growing sure that Riki had told her one truth—a gate had only recently opened from Earth to Onihida. Too many little things were pointing at it: the throwaway comments about Earth-born oni, the carpenter's obvious awkwardness with the most basic of power tools, the famine-obsessed cook, the brown rice which turned out to be a luxury item not served to the carpenters, to their dismay. The list grew the entire morning. When she believed she was on Onihida, she hadn't paid attention—that she was no longer on Elfhome had been proof enough for her. Now she couldn't stop wondering about it.

She had delegated building the framework to Riki so she could concentrate on limiting the veil effect and making it the primary function of the new gate. Her biggest fear was she'd only swap the dimensional side effect with the jump capabilities of the gate and accidentally send Pittsburgh to Alpha Centauri. An hour of running models reassured her that if she did, it would be a very small chunk, most likely only the oni compound itself. Small loss there.

Her mind, however, kept trotting back to the oni's door to Onihida. Riki had said it was in an inconvenient spot; obviously it was located outside of the U.S., or the Chinese visas wouldn't be needed. Certainly, if the two doors were on opposite sides of the planet, it could be called inconvenient.

She jerked to a halt. Luckily only Pony noticed.

"What is it?"

"I think I know where their stupid door is," she murmured, wheeling her chair away from the drafting table to her desktop screen and calling up a world map. "I just can't believe no one's noticed before now."

Like all the information on the gate, she had the location where the gate was in geosynchronous orbit over the Earth's equator. She found the point and zoomed in. "It's so simple. Pittsburgh is on Elfhome because the gate projects the veil effect down through the Earth, where the magnetic core bends it, kind of like a prism bends light, thus hitting Pittsburgh on the other side of the planet."

Only partially under the gate was a tiny island surrounded by ocean. She laughed. "Of all the dumb luck, a few more feet and their gate would have been totally in open water."

Pony peered at the island for several minutes before saying, "I don't understand. How can this open to Onihida, and this," he pointed to the other side of the world, "open to Elfhome?"

"That's the simple part. The Earth core is acting as a lens."

"Pardon?"

She closed the incriminating map and opened a scratch file. "Look, here's Earth with the core in the center. This side is the China Sea, and the other side, up here, is Pittsburgh. The gate orbits over the sea. The veil effect comes down a cylindrical shape, but the core acts like a lens. That means the veil is 'flipped.'" Seeing Pony's blank look, "You see things because light comes down and reflects off it. So if you have a tree, the light comes from the sun, hits the trees, and reflects to your eye."

He nodded. "Yes, I know this."

"But if you hold a glass lens up between you and the tree, the light is bent by the lens. The top of the tree is bent to the bottom, and the bottom is bent to the top, so the image is flipped."

Pony pointed to the tree. "Onihida." And tapped the upside-down image. "Elfhome."

"Yes. That simple. For twenty years, every Shutdown and Startup, that tropical island has been going to Onihida and back, and no one has noticed."

"Or noticed and the oni killed them."

"Yes, that too."

Pony pointed then to the gate in orbit. "Whatever you do—build the oni a gate or not—means little while that exists. That is the true prison door hanging open."

* * *

The carpenters tried to quit after dinner, but she tracked Riki down in the ocean of sawdust with shoals of massive timbers and littered with the flotsam of cut ends.

"Tell them that they can't leave," she said.

"They've been working for like ten hours."

"They can work until they drop," Tinker growled. "Tell them to get back to work."

"They're tired."

"I don't care! If I'm going to meet Tomtom's deadline, then *everyone* is going to have to work until they drop."

"Be reasonable."

"Your people started this. I'm just going to finish it. Tell them to go back to work or I'll take a crowbar to them."

Riki winced. "Okay, okay, I'll get them back to work."

Only Tomtom's appearance at midnight kept the carpenters from revolting. The carpenters would jerk to a stop, bow low, and get waved back to work, which they did with stunning enthusiasm. No, no—no slackers here. Tinker shut files on her desktop as he closed in on her office.

"It looks nearly complete." Tomtom motioned to the massive circle of wood taking form.

"The framework is getting there," Tinker said. "It's still a long way to go on this gate. Once we finish here, the carpenters can start work on the second gate. The frame itself will be identical, so the crew will need less guidance—I need Riki here with me."

"*Hanno.*" Tomtom cocked his head. "Second gate?"

Tinker picked up evidence A. "Well, you've got enough material here for two gates, maybe three. I just assumed that you were building more than one—since the gate size is limited by the roof."

"A second gate," Tomtom said slowly.

"I haven't had a chance to look over the area." Tinker indicated the buildings around them. "I recommend you keep the two gates as far apart as possible; there might be possible interference between the two. Besides, it would prevent bottleneck."

"Bottleneck?"

"Traffic jams." Tinker turned to Riki as he arrived from the other side of the warehouse. "Riki, can you explain 'bottleneck' to him?"

Riki looked puzzled, but launched into Oni, pushing his hands together to illustrate two forces colliding together. Tomtom's reply made Riki jerk around to stare at her. "A second gate?"

"Doh!" she said.

Riki looked at her in blank confusion.

"The framework for a second gate might go faster." She ignored Riki to focus on Tomtom. "But the rest of it will take the same amount of time, and I won't be able to start it until after this one is done. The schematics will need to be tailored to the location and orientation and various other deciding factors."

"Riki can not do them?" Tomtom said.

Tinker shook her head. "No more than he can do this one."

Tomtom turned to Riki for verification.

Riki looked at her strangely. "No. I can't. I'm still not grasping how the gate works. I have no clue what the next step will even be."

Tomtom accepted the truth. "Fine, we will have a second gate, on the other side of the compound."

The carpenter foreman came up to grovel and beg.

Tomtom laughed, showing sharp cat teeth. "As eager as you are, I can not have you slave-driving my people. It would reflect poorly on me. Everyone quits for the night. Even you."

Twenty days left.

Just stay focused, Tinker told herself but found she eyed the clock often as the numbers jumped through the hours of the day at despairing speed.

Chiyo appeared at the workshop late in the morning, with head high and hard stares at anyone glancing at her. Of the mating, there was no outward sign. The kitsune, however, radiated hostility like a steel blast furnace. The looks she gave Tinker shifted Pony from nearly invisible behind Tinker to between the two females. Unfortunately, he could do nothing about Chiyo's illusions; since the kitsune no longer needed to keep her mental abilities secret, she began torturing Tinker with them.

"Does she have to be here?" Tinker asked Riki later after reacting to the third giant illusionary spider.

"She's the only one besides me and Tomtom that speaks English, Elvish, and Oni."

"Fine." Tinker resolved herself to factoring numbers, and occasional remembrances of a nasty brush with a steel spinner—anyone that could do spiders that creepy had to be scared of them. "I've done some research. Normally you'd lay down ceramic tiles onto a backer board, but we can't do this here. In space they used these brackets. We're going to have to modify the brackets, since they were designed to connect to the framing with these connectors." Tinker showed him the hooks, and then tossed them over her shoulder. "Can't use those."

There was a yelp behind her, which she ignored.

"I want a wooden mounting plate made, then holes drilled into the brackets here, here, and here." Tinker marked the points. "Then we got these cool plastic bolts here, which were actually part of the shielding. Fasten the brackets to the mounting plate, but first, have the carpenters figure out how to attach the plate to the framing. I'm thinking to cut grooves—" she did a quick sketch to illustrate "—and slide them in and attach a piece of molding to lock them in. We can't use nails, but they should be used to that. The end result needs to have the tiles separated by no more than an eighth of an inch, but not much less since we have to allow for heat expansion."

Riki took out a handheld and jotted down notes. "Okay."

"Once we get the mounting plate designed, we need to run the power cables, so have them moved into the workshop. Remind the carpenters that we're going to be running power to the tiles up through this point in the bracket."

Riki made a face and scribbled more notes.

"Also we need the station for the tiles set up eventually." Tinker picked up the specially made ceramic tile. "Once I get the circuits designed, we can start masking them. You know, if your goons had held off just five or six years, my father would have done all this work himself on a Home Chip Lab."

If she had more than twenty days she could translate the entire thing down to integrated circuit level, shrinking the whole process down to something the size of . . . a wedding ring. That thought put shivers down her spine.

"Things were right for us to make a move," Riki said simply.

"Keep riding herd on the carpenters," Tinker turned back to her computer, trying to ignore the end of the conversation. *Twenty days.*

Focus. "I want the framework done today and the mounting plates ready to go by tomorrow."

Ten days.

Tinker was growing frightened that she wasn't going to make the deadline.

True, the carpentry finished the first week, and the carpenters moved to the second gate to leisurely work there. After a week of hammering, the silence had seemed a blessing, but now the quiet seemed only to make the approaching deadline more ominous.

She hadn't counted on the fact that the oni had no electricians, and that those oni working with her were so unfamiliar with electricity that they were clueless. What could be so hard about running cables? She thought monkeys could do it. She had been interrupted time and time again to check their work. Wiring out of phase. Miswiring the grounds. Hooking the grounds in sequence into the main 240 line. The oni didn't miss a single way to screw up something so simple. More than once she had them rip several hours of work out. At least the confusion allowed her to slip in modifications unnoticed by Riki or Chiyo.

Speaking of the kitsune, she was going to kill Chiyo soon.

After a battle of spiders—which she won with the steel spinner incident—snakes began to infest her thoughts. Unfortunately, all the bits of cable littering the warehouse lent themselves to Chiyo's illusions. The kitsune apparently couldn't find room in Tinker's head while she was locked on circuit design, but the moment she was called away, she'd find the nearest cable suddenly slithering around. Annoying as it was—Tinker was more frightened that Chiyo would report Tinker's concerns of missing the deadline.

Only ten days remained. She had carefully reshaped the original gate's specs so that her gate opened a dimensional door only within its limits. She was still struggling with compressing the design down to the hundred-to-one ratio. There was still the masking, dipping, fitting . . . the list went on and on. And that assumed everything worked the first time. In danger of losing track of details, she'd sacrificed an hour to creating a schedule, copied it to her datapad, and printed up a copy for the wall. She found herself, however, now glancing at the schedule instead of the clock. Ten heavily loaded days.

"Stay focused," she murmured, and jumped slightly as Pony set a bowl down in front of her.

"Forgiveness."

"Oh, it's just Chiyo with her damn snakes and prying thoughts keeping me on edge on top of everything else. Rice and fish again? Bleah."

Pony grunted slightly. She looked up, and noticed that he was focused across the warehouse. A patrolling oni warrior had come into the warehouse, strolling around the massive wooden ring.

"A new one?" she asked, returning to her food and diagrams. Non-workers wanting to see the imposing gate were an annoyance she suffered for Pony's sake; he used the opportunity to track the onis' numbers.

"Sixty-one," Pony whispered. "Small, rifle and sword, no pistol."

Tinker winced at the number, which climbed daily. Already the oni warriors outnumbered Windwolf's *sekasha* three to one. Pony was of the opinion, though, that oni weren't as skilled fighters. *"The ones in charge are always the biggest and loudest, they run toward fat, and I haven't seen any sign of weapon practice."*

Riki came up, checking things off his datapad. "I think we finally nailed down the wiring. How's the circuit coming?"

"I'm just finishing—I think. I want to run them through a simulator before committing them to tile."

Riki nodded to the wisdom of this.

Tinker sensed Pony tensing, which probably meant Chiyo was closing on them. She spared a glance to check. The kitsune had paused, standing in profile to them to talk to one of the oni doing the wiring. Already the kitsune looked like she had a small pumpkin under her kimono. Riki had mentioned that a kitsune gestation was only fifty days; at ten days she was nearly the equivalent of three months in human pregnancy.

I can't let the oni into my world, Tinker thought for the thousandth time, and then firmly locked away her thoughts. "What is your plan? Do you have an army sitting on the other side of this gate?"

"Yes," Riki said.

"It started to amass last year." Chiyo joined the conversation. "I'm told it numbers in the tens of thousands."

"This gate is only good while Pittsburgh is on Elfhome," Tinker pointed out. "Even if you wait until after Shutdown to start bringing over your army—to maximize your time before the humans can react—you only have twenty-eight days until the next Shutdown. Then Pittsburgh goes back to Earth, either fully loaded with oni, or a war-torn ghost town. What little I know of the United States, they usually don't take kindly to that kind of shit."

"We'll ride this Shutdown out," Riki said, unconsciously echoing Oilcan's phrase. "And after that, there won't be another Shutdown."

"What?" Tinker yelped. "How can you stop Shutdown?"

"Shutdown is just flipping a switch," Riki said.

Chiyo laughed. "Oh, stupid fake elf, if we had the station built, don't you think we can control when it turns on and off?"

"The oni are working *with* the Chinese?" Somehow Tinker thought the oni had merely been feeding the Chinese information. But even as she said it, she realized that the cooperation would have to go deeper than that.

"I told you that some of us were stranded on Earth for hundreds of years," Riki said quietly. "Many of the kitsune's mental powers, like the mind reading, do not need magic to work. They have infiltrated the Chinese government to the highest levels. They're the ones that pushed through the building of the gate."

Tinker frowned. "The gate was wholly an oni's project? What about the colony at Alpha Centauri?"

"There is no colony," Riki said. "It's an elaborate sham that the tengu and the kitsune dreamed up. The gate is nothing more than a huge magician's box that we pull rabbits out of."

The problem with liars was knowing when they were telling the truth. Tinker couldn't believe that the entire twenty-year colonization program had been a sham. "Where the hell are the colony ships going?"

"Don't know." Riki shrugged. "We were hoping that they would go to Elfhome, or, failing that, Onihida, but they didn't go to either. We don't know what star system your father calibrated the gate for, so we picked one for the media. As far as we know, the ships could be on the other side of the galaxy, or a fourth dimension of Earth. Wherever they are, they've got a lot of empty cargo pods—we had to keep pushing stuff through the gate to justify leaving it on."

"They've been without supplies for twenty years?" Tinker stared at him, stunned. Lain and the astronomers had filled her life with information on the colonists until they were intimate strangers. "How could you do that?"

"We don't even know if they've survived the jump. If they came out next to a black hole, or any exotic star system—like a red nova or white dwarf—all the supplies in the world couldn't keep them alive."

"But—but—but all the progress reports from the colony?"

"We didn't have to worry about reports immediately, as Alpha Centauri is light years away. Eventually we put up a satellite in an extreme orbit with correctors to fake a signal from the colony. Beijing beams the feed up to the satellite that bounces it back in a wide enough spread that you can pick it up anywhere on Earth."

She noticed Chiyo's gaze fixated on her, like a hunter seeing prey, and concentrated on factoring numbers. "Stay out of my mind, you little bitch."

Riki picked up the dirty dishes and handed them to the kitsune. "Make yourself useful." They watched Chiyo carry the plates away. "If it makes you feel any better, all the first colonists were tengu and kitsune. They knew the risks. And we did send supplies for the first few years—they were our family—but Tomtom decided it was a waste of food and goods. He diverted the cargo to Onihida, where starvation is common."

"There's been ships full of people every five years since then!"

Riki nodded, bleak. "Yes. There have."

16: END GAME

TINKER WAS SICK of keeping Chiyo out of her head. Working on the various mathematical and mechanical problems of the gate had provided automatic protection for the first two weeks, but the last few days—as much of the work resolved down to grunt work, little fiddles and small fixes—she had to switch to solving random math problems. More annoying was that she hadn't been able to share with Pony anything she didn't want Chiyo to pick out of his head. The level of trust that her bodyguard had in her was unnerving; if their places were swapped, she'd be climbing the wall to know "the plan." Pony, however, seemed content to wait and see what she pulled out of the hat.

The first step of "the plan" was simply to finish early. Tomtom would be on hand during the twenty-first day, so she slaved everyone unmercifully to hit the twentieth. Stunningly, they actually managed to finish early in the morning, but she dawdled, going so far as creating minor glitches. She wanted the cover of night—and confusion on both ends of the gate—when they activated it.

But what if it didn't work?

She tried to ignore that worry. Dusk grayed the sky as the dinner bowls arrived. As usual, afterward it fell to Chiyo to clear the dishes. Sexism, got to love it sometimes. Tinker gave Riki the chore to start moving the heavier tools and equipment to the second gate site.

For a few spare seconds, she and Pony were alone with a handful of guards that didn't speak Elvish.

"I've finished the gate, and I think it works," she murmured to Pony. "We'll see in a few minutes. I kept my promise. We go as soon as I turn it on and we can slip away."

"The other gate?" He nodded his head in the direction of the second gate, currently being wired without her guidance.

"If we don't get away, it's what will keep us alive." *But not intact.* She shoved the thought away, and pulled him over to the rack that used to hold the wiring spools. "These." She twisted and pulled the middle pole far enough out to show that it wasn't attached. "They're a weapon for you. It's the best I could do."

The poles lacked the magically sharp edge of the *sekasha*'s ironwood swords, but they matched the blades in size and, probably, weight.

Pony's eyes widened at the long stout poles of ironwood. "They will do nicely. Very clever."

"We'll see how clever I really am."

With her stomach squirming like a nest of snakes, she walked to the huge red-painted switch and threw it. It started the sound and light show on the gate, drawing the guard's eyes while she moved back and kicked the secret power switch on. If she was right, the gate would exist *between* both dimensions while operating, and thus be impossible to damage. Hopefully no one would discover how to turn off the power until too late.

Oh merciful gods in heaven, and the five spirits of the world, let this work.

The air around the gate shimmered and distorted, a massive confusion of particles as space was folded. Almost immediately she could feel the feedback pulses, but still so slight that she hoped no one would be able to notice them. Visibly, the area *through* the center of the ring looked no different, just oddly distorted, like water over glass, with the back of the workshop still discernible. No wonder natural gates were so hard to find. One might think the gate wasn't working, except the entire structure—including the ironwood framework but luckily not the ramp—had also phased out, becoming ghostlike.

The sudden blaze of lights brought Riki and the guards with him back.

"You turned it on?" Riki cried.

"It's the only way to see if it works." Tinker stood with her hand on the big red button, hoping to implant the wrong impression in the tengu's mind.

"Does it work?" Riki peered at the shimmering area inside the gate, keeping well back of it.

"I merely build these things, I don't test them." Tinker raised her hands, warding off any attempt to send her through. That would totally mess up her plans. "But it looks like it works to me. Why don't you get one of the guards to test it?"

That triggered the debate she hoped for. Trying to be all-so-unnoticeable, she walked back to the wire rack, took down the dinner-plate-sized spool of lead wire, and pulled free the pole. That she handed Pony, and removed another for herself. *Us? Just moving wire. Nothing to see here.*

The smallest of the construction workers was drafted to be first through the gate. Every eye was on him as he crept nervously up the ramp. The poor thing was trembling violently as he scanned the entire gate, arching around him. The others shouted at him in Oni, encouragements, commands, and curses.

As the oni stepped forward, vanishing into another world, Tinker and Pony slipped out the side door into the darkness.

The oni warriors were too well trained to let the gate totally distract them. The four assigned to Tinker tore themselves away, and the one who spoke crude English said, "Where go you?"

"The other gate." Tinker motioned with the spool of wire. *See, harmless.* "Build next door?"

He glanced back to the brightly lit workshop, where everyone waited for the vanished worker.

Tinker didn't wait for him to decide, but headed slowly into the darkness.

Twenty days of playing construction demon goddess paid off; the guard followed without trying to stop her.

She had made only one trip to the second site, early last week, learning its location under the disguise of having to sign off on the exact orientation of the gate. Tomtom had taken her at her word and placed it at the complete opposite end of the mile-long warehouse, where the garage had once been. They passed through the gazebo room, and then through the kennel. The little dogs instantly launched into barking fits, but the warg merely eyed them as they passed.

Oh, gods, let this work.

The second workshop was empty of oni; the work crews had

already left for the night. A handful of low-wattage bulbs threw pools of light down into the cave dark. Their footsteps echoed as they walked toward the gate; wrapped in shadows, it loomed over them—their insurance plan in ironwood.

"This part of the plan is nebulous," Tinker whispered to Pony in High Elvish, while pretending to examine work done. Without her slave driving, only the wood framing had been completed. Table-sized and smaller spools of wire—like the one she carried—sat waiting for the wiring to begin. "Do you think you can kill our escort?"

"Yes, *domi zae*," Pony said, paused, considered, and then asked, "Now?"

"Yes." She stepped behind him to give him room to work. "Now."

Pony took out the first two oni before the guards even realized he was attacking. One moment he was standing with the pole in his right hand, and the next he was driving the pole through the eye of the oni to the left with a motion that had his full body strength behind it. He shifted his grip, and swung the pole back to the right, like a baseball player hitting a line drive. The pole hit the oni's nose with a crack of shattering bone; the guard crumpled to the ground and lay still as death.

The third oni actually managed to dodge Pony's lightning swing, as the fourth pulled out his sword.

"Shit!" Tinker flung her spool of wire underhand—like a horseshoe—at the dodging oni. The spool hit him mid-chest, knocking him off balance, and Pony's pole struck him hard. The oni continued to move, though, while the last oni charged Pony with his sword ready. "Get the sword warrior, Pony, I'll deal with that one."

Yeah, right. But Pony was already engaging the last oni, meaning she'd better act. She gave the two fighters a wide berth as she dashed toward the crawling oni. She'd kicked a lot of people, and punched, and hit, but she never struck to kill. It'd been so easy to tell Pony to do it. The oni looked up, read her intent, and lunged at her—and she stopped being afraid to hurt him. She jerked backward, out of his reach, and swung at him as hard as she could. He threw up his arm, caught her pole and, laughing, wrenched it out of her hands. Cursing, she stomped down on his foot. He backhanded her and it was like being hit by a truck. The blow knocked her across the floor and up against the tanks of the acetylene torch. The taste of blood filled her mouth. Growling something in Oni, the guard flung aside the wood pole and came after her.

She twisted both gas lines wide open, snagged the torch, aimed it at the oni, and hit the igniter button. A foot-long lance of white-hot flame shot out in a deep "woof" of rapidly expanding air. It struck the oni full in the face.

He screamed in agony, stumbling back—and then went suddenly quiet as Pony cut his throat.

"*Domi*, are you hurt?" Pony asked, dropping the oni's body.

She shook her head, panting, staring at the blood rushing out of the still body. *This was soooo not her.*

"We should go." Pony came to lift her up, making sure for himself that she wasn't hurt. "Can you shoot a gun?"

"I've done it once." To save Windwolf from the oni to be exact. "It's not that hard. Point and pull the trigger."

He held out one of the onis' guns. "This is an Uzi. This is the safety; it will not fire with the safety on. This is a single shot. This is a three-bullet burst. This is rapid fire." He left the safety on, the gun set on rapid fire. He demonstrated holding it while firing it. "Brace yourself, it jumps in your hand and you quickly find yourself shooting into the sky. The bullets go until they hit something, so never fire with someone you don't want to hit standing anywhere in front of you."

"Good safety tip." Especially since it would most likely be Pony.

"It eats bullets fast." He showed her that the ammo clip slid out and another could be locked into place. "It takes about three seconds of continuous fire to go through a clip, so be selective."

He let her pocket the three extra clips before handing her the gun. It was cold and heavy. It felt like death in her hands, and she didn't like it, but there was no way she was going to stay helpless.

Pony took one of every weapon available; tucking away knives and guns, here and there, making them vanish on his solid frame.

Still shaky, she crossed to the windows and peered out. During her visit the week before to select the building site, the oni hoverbikes and cars were still parked in this section of the warehouse. She had hoped that the oni hadn't moved them, but the vehicles were gone. Damn, they weren't even outside. Much as she'd love to steal a pair of hoverbikes, they didn't have time to search blindly for them. Change of plans.

"Where might Windwolf and the other *sekasha* be at this time of night?" Tinker headed for the door. "At the hunting lodge?"

"Unlikely." Pony followed, her second shadow. "We were staying at one of the enclaves while the site for the new palace was cleared, and then we were to move into tents at the work site until temporary housing could be made."

"Where is that?"

"Between here and the enclaves, but much closer to the enclaves."

The steel mills were closer, but it didn't make sense to bring the oni down on unarmed humans. She'd love to call the EIA, but the oni had infiltrated it. A call for help might only bring disguised oni down on them. Windwolf and his bodyguards were the only ones that probably could deal with the oni.

"Let's head there." She bypassed the security alarm on the door and cracked it open. One would think that the oni would have gotten a better security system after the last time. Oh well, their loss, her gain.

There were no guards in sight. Quietly, they slipped out into the night. They moved cautiously through the compound, listening carefully and moving slowly to keep quiet. In the stillness, she could once again feel the feedback from the gate. Good, her gate was still on. Perhaps the oni couldn't feel the faint pulse; maybe she could only feel it because she was *domana*.

Minutes later, they made the safety of the forest and started to run.

"*Domi*, what is wrong with the air?" Pony matched her stride despite the fact he probably could outrun her.

Okay, it wasn't just her then. "I realized that the veil effect would link this gate with the one in orbit. By designing this one to be on the same proportions, I set it up to be a harmonic, in order to amplify the resonance."

"I don't understand."

"Every object has a frequency at which it will vibrate if disturbed. When an outside force with the same frequency as the natural frequency of the object causes the object to vibrate, it's called resonance, or sympathetic vibration. I can't believe Riki didn't realize what I was doing—although I kept him as busy as I could."

"I still don't understand."

Tinker had to check the impulse to stop and explain—with little pictures and lots of hand waving. "Oh, sweet lords, Pony, it's not easy to give physics lessons at a full run! When you have resonance, a small force can increase the amplitude of the object's vibration substantially."

"Talk plain Elvish," Pony groaned.

"Do you know that if a singer hits a certain note loud enough it can break a crystal goblet?"

"Yes."

"That's resonance. The note the singer is singing is the same frequency as the glass, which makes it literally vibrate itself apart. The gate I made is on the same frequency as the orbital one."

"The orbital gate will shake itself apart?"

"It should, as long as the as-built drawings are correct. Structurally, the one on the ground is much sturdier. Either my father wasn't much of a structural engineer, or he never had time to go back and add supports—and the oni never corrected the design weaknesses."

Pony checked at that point.

"What?" Tinker glanced back into the valley. The second workshop was now lit up as brightly as the first—someone had found the dead guards.

"We should go back," Pony said. "Make sure that they don't turn off the land-based gate."

"I rigged it so it's not easy to turn off, and we're now escaping, which hopefully—I think—will distract them long enough."

"Ah, yes. I see. We should hurry then."

Minutes later, a flare of magic behind Tinker made her stop and look back. The valley was now out of sight; there was nothing but trees and moonlight. For the first time she realized that, while the woods were dark, she was seeing quite well. Ah, built-in night vision—how handy.

"What is it?" Pony stopped beside her. He wasn't even breathing hard to her panting.

"I don't know. I felt something. Magic, I think."

"A powerful spell then."

"There it is again."

"We've got another mile to go. Come."

She was starting to wonder if everything she'd experienced at the palace had been by design. Certainly if the oni had captured her three weeks earlier, then she wouldn't have risked everything to save Pony, who was nearly a stranger at that point. Obviously she needed someone of his abilities to make an escape attempt feasible. And the exercise—all the hiking, jogging, and horseback riding she did keeping up with the bodyguards—was the only reason she was able to run as far as she had. But she was slowing down, and she didn't think she could run for more than another mile.

Oh, Windwolf, please be there.

"Run," Pony commanded suddenly, although he dropped a step behind her.

"I *am* running."

"Something is coming."

"What?" She risked looking back, but there was only forest behind her.

"Something large. Run."

She could hear it then, something big, coming through the forest; padded feet beat a fast cadence, and the harsh breathing of a big animal grew louder as it closed.

Oh god, not a saurus, was her first thought, *not now.* And then she realized what it had to be—the Foo dogs. Riki had told her that they kept the dogs small to make them easier to hide and to handle. He also mentioned that they could be expanded as easily as his wings.

"Shit! We should have killed the dogs."

"We didn't have time," Pony said.

"You have to hit the dog inside the construct." What else should she tell him? How did her Uzi work again? "The spell form protects them from sword swings; it will also affect the speed and path of bullets."

The forest ended and they were suddenly in a clearing of torn earth. Thirty acres had been thinned down to a scattering of trees on a wide hilltop. The trees left seemed to be all elfin oak, squat toadstools against the tall ironwoods, but still the lowest branches were at least twenty feet up. Stacked logs, survey markers, foundation stones, and large tents of white canvas cluttered the building site, but it was without activity or light. No one seemed to be there.

She stumbled to a stop, panting. "Oh shit."

There were two roads cut into the surrounding forest, but she was too disoriented by the shortcut through the trees to know where the roads might lead.

"Here it comes," Pony warned.

She whirled to face the oncoming animal. It was twice as massive as the constructs she had fought with Windwolf. Somehow the flattened face and mane were more recognizable as a lion's, although the body still seemed built on a bulldog design with the same odd poof tail arched over its back. As big as a horse, the Foo dog—no, make that Foo lion—rushed toward them.

She yanked up her Uzi, flicked the safety off with her thumb, and braced herself against the reported kick. When she pulled the trigger, it seemed like she was suddenly holding a living thing, intent on getting out of her hands, spitting smoke and fire. The noise of each bullet firing blurred into a prolonged rolling thunder. If the damn Foo lion hadn't been nearly on top of her, she might have missed the beast completely. As it was, though, hitting a barn would have been as easy.

As the first bullet struck the lion, its appearance transformed to the deep violet spell form, a polygon rendering of a lion done in magic. The runes flared with each rapid hit, flashing like a strobe light, the small dog writhing inside the monster puppet. The spell form slowed the bullets until she could actually see them flying through the magic like a swarm of angry bees. The first bullets missed the important dog core, but they acted like tracers for her aim, even with the kicking gun. The construct was smashed backward, and at least three bullets struck home. Once dead, she expected the lion to revert back down to lap dog, but the massive body remained, showing no sign of what killed it.

Three seconds. Her gun was empty, her ears were ringing, and the beast was dead.

Then the second Foo lion hit her from behind, bowling her over.

Its massive jaws closed on her shoulder and she was jerked upward, off her feet. She screamed in surprise and fear. With her dangling in its mouth, the lion bounded back toward the oni compound. Shit, it was *fetching* her like some rubber play toy!

"Pony!" she cried as she thrashed, trying to squirm free. The teeth didn't seem to be piercing her skin, but it had a firm hold on her. She clawed at its face, but it didn't seem to be feeling pain from her flailing at it. How was it seeing, she wondered, and clamped both hands over its eyes.

The Foo lion stumbled to a stop and shook her hard; its teeth sank into her shoulder, and she screamed in pain and sudden fear of being mauled.

The construct's pause, though, had given Pony a chance to catch up. He slammed the oni sword deep into the lion's side. The length of steel shifted the lion into spell form and revealed the dog within. The blade struck not where the real heart of a lion would lie, but farther back, to unerringly pierce the dog. The lion roared with pain, dropping her, and then collapsed.

"*Domi*, are you hurt?" Pony crouched beside her as she crabbed backward away from the unmoving lion.

"No." With him between her and the beast, she felt safe enough to stop crawling and actually consider if she was hurt. "At least not badly, but I'm getting tired of hearing that question."

"Forgiveness," Pony murmured, and lifted up her shirt to examine the puncture wounds.

"Pony!" she whined.

"Sometimes one is wounded more than one knows." Pony eyed the puncture wounds, then glanced about, as if looking for a light source. "I can not tell how deep they are. We need to stop the bleeding. Come, there will be supplies in one of the tents."

"I'm fine." She stood by herself to prove it. "I just want to get someplace safe. And I want my gun." She swayed as she looked down, trying to see the matte black Uzi on the ground, but the dark was making it impossible to see.

"I'll look, you just walk to the tents."

So she teetered off ahead of him as he went slowly, searching the ground that the Foo lion had covered while carrying her. It was a surprising amount. If she'd been feeling up to a faster pace, she would have told him to forget the gun. As she reached the tents, delayed reaction was setting in and she came to a complete, trembling halt. Why couldn't she get her breath? Was her lung collapsing? Oh, no, that's right, she'd just run like three miles.

Oh gods, oh gods. She desperately wanted Windwolf, a hot shower, and a comfy bed with him in it.

"Here it is, *domi*." Pony handed her the Uzi, considered her, took it back, searched her pockets for a fresh clip, reloaded the gun, put the safety back on, and slung its strap over her head, settling it on her back. "I'll find a first-aid kit. Sit down."

She sat on a pile of massive foundation stones between two tents, panting and shaking, as he went off. Now that she was still, she could feel the feedback again. It seemed stronger.

Okay, get a grip. Two roads. Which one should we take?

When built, the palace was going to have a great view of Pittsburgh. From where she sat, she could see out over the top of the surrounding elfin forest to the barren cut of the Rim and the bright human city beyond it. Both roads, however, led downhill into dark unknown. The left road would be the more direct way—but in Pittsburgh, that usually meant a need for a bridge. She doubted that three weeks had been enough time for something as ambitious as a bridge to be built—but hey, she built a gate that folded dimensions during that period. Still, if said bridge was unfinished, they'd lose valuable time backtracking.

On the left-most road, a shadow moved against the blackness, perceivable only as motion. Tinker froze in sudden fear that it was another Foo lion, and then realized it was humanoid. Friend or foe? Human, elf, or oni? Tinker got the impression of tall, slender, and graceful, realized it was an elf, and had started forward to greet the elf when she suddenly recognized the female. By then it was too late. Suddenly the tents and stones became sides of a trap.

Sparrow was in black leather pants and a black shirt, only her white skin and long pale braid glinting in the moonlight. The elf pointed a pistol at Tinker, the barrel hole seeming massive. "They must be complete twits not to be able to keep track of one little girl. Where is Stormhorse?"

"The oni sent Foo lions after me." Tinker indicated the nearest dead lion and the dark forest beyond. She could feel the Uzi heavy on her back. Could she get it swung forward and the safety off before Sparrow shot her? She let all the weariness and heartache of the last three weeks bleed into her voice. "He told me to run . . ."

"How convenient. Tomtom wants you back. Make no mistake, you're too dangerous for me to let wander back to Windwolf. One false move, and I will kill you."

"You've already lost, Sparrow. I'm the pivot. I've made my choice. There's nothing anyone can do about it."

"You're still thinking like a human," Sparrow tsked. "I've got the rest of time to figure out another way of doing this. The beauty of all this is that I only lose if you live to tell Windwolf what I've done."

Guessing what was coming next, Tinker threw herself sideways, but still Sparrow's bullet smashed into her side, knocking her off her feet in a violent half turn. Pony was suddenly there, catching Tinker before she fell against the stone. He shouted something and Tinker felt magic surge up, rushing like hot floodwaters. The blueness of his magical shields flared around them.

Sparrow's gun thundered again and again, the muzzle spitting flame and smoke.

Tinker felt the bullets strike Pony's shields—expending energy into the system with a hard kick that transmitted through the spell and Pony's body to her—and then ricochet harmlessly away.

When Sparrow hit the end of her clip, Pony drew his oni sword— the steel blade disrupting his shields—and thrust the sword deep into Sparrow's chest. "Die, you traitorous bitch," he growled and shoved it on through her.

Sparrow had cried out when the sword first penetrated her. She looked surprised at the blade buried in her own body, and then concerned as she tried to gasp for breath that wouldn't come. Sparrow slumped backwards against the tent wall even as Pony yanked the sword back out of her chest, her eyes going unfocused. The canvas cradled Sparrow gently, bowing under her falling weight so she slid elegantly downward, leaving a smear of blood on the white canvas.

Tinker stared at the dead elf. She thought she'd be happy to see Sparrow dead, but she could feel no joy in the killing. Maybe she hadn't hated the female as much as she thought.

"Tinker *domi*! Where did she hit you?"

"In the side." Tinker realized she was holding her side. She lifted up her hand and found it covered with blood. "Oh shit."

Pony sat her back on the stones, activated a light sphere, and examined the wound. "It is not bad. The bullet merely grazed you. I feared the worst; I thought she had killed you."

"I'm still alive and kicking."

"We must stop the bleeding. Then we must get out of here." He took his hands away as if he expected her to topple without his support. When he saw she could actually sit by herself, he went to fetch the abandoned first-aid kit.

"Sparrow came up the left road," Tinker told him when he'd returned. "She probably left the Rolls somewhere close by."

Pony sprayed the wound with a cool antibiotic and then pressed three large artificial skin patches into place. "You need a healing spell."

The kit was human-made, so there would be no spells in it. She was surprised he knew how to use the skin patches, but she supposed that knowing all sorts of first aid would be handy in a bodyguard.

"That looks good," Tinker lied. "Let's go."

Pony raided Sparrow's body for weapons, coming away with a pistol, two clips, a light bow, a quiver of white fletched spell arrows, and a sword and dagger of ironwood, which would allow him to keep his shields up. He left the oni sword where it lay, covered with Sparrow's blood.

Tinker felt light-headed and odd as Pony guided her to the road, saying, "We need to get to the enclaves or the hospice."

The road cut a narrow path through the forest, only twelve feet or so wide. It went straight down to a gorge; wooden scaffolding provided a temporary footbridge across while stone buttresses indicated that the future bridge would be built on an impressive scale. On the other side of the bridge were the enclaves and human civilization gleaming just beyond.

Pony, however, pulled her to a halt, and drew his sword. The shadows moved all around them, and oni warriors emerged out of the darkness.

"Oh, fuck," Tinker whispered.

Magic surged in around them as Pony activated his shields, a scant comfort in the face of so many guns pointed their way. How much could the spell stop? Five bullets? Ten?

"I have played lightly with you." Tomtom's voice came out of the night, and he shifted into view directly in front of them, flanked by two of his largest warriors. Gone were the kimono and any pretense of being anything but a large dangerous animal. Spell tattoos covered his skin, starting at his collarbone and flowing downward over muscled thighs and calves. He wore only a loincloth of black silk hung on a diagonal cut from right hip to left shin and a sword belt. Like Chiyo, he had a tail to match the inhuman ears; it flickered behind him in agitation. "My claws are out." He lifted his left hand to show that indeed his claws were extended, showing off three inches of needle-sharp points. "One false step, and I'll content myself with whatever the tengu can do to salvage your work. This is not your battle, female—you are truly human under that skin. You owe them no alliance. My people are crowded and starving while the elves greedily hoard this vast wilderness. We only want what they do not use."

"I'm not going back with you. I'm not going to betray them."

"Submit now, and I will show mercy."

"I've seen your mercy with Chiyo." She was surprised that he was even bothering to talk to her. By oni mentality, she needed to be punished, something she was highly resistant to submitting to. There was no way she'd agree—so why wasn't he just ordering an attack? She glanced to the right at Pony, sword ready, his shields gleaming softly blue like an aura around him.

Of course. Pony's shields sucked down large amounts of ambient magic. On a ley line, he could maintain them indefinitely. Where they stood now, though, it was only a matter of time before the shields drained the area and failed. Tomtom was stalling.

"I gave the kitsune a choice of punishments," Tomtom was saying. "Drop your weapons, surrender yourself, and I will go lightly on you too."

Screw this. Tinker leveled her Uzi, flicked off the safety, and emptied the machine gun at Tomtom. Even as she pulled the trigger, though, the oni lord flicked up his left palm, growling out a spell, and the tattoos along his left arm flared and a haze appeared between them. The bullets spat out of the muzzle of the machine gun, struck the magic barrier, making it flare and, weirdly enough, gleam brighter. She actually felt it sparking up levels with each bullet hit. The bullets didn't pass through, nor ricochet, but instead dropped to the ground, inert. Damn, somehow the oni shield translated the kinetic energy of bullet back into the spell, fueling it.

Too late she thought to spray the warriors to either side of Tomtom; she'd already run through the clip and now worked the trigger to be rewarded only with a series of clicks.

Tomtom pointed at Pony and uttered a word, and then indicated Tinker, and gave a longer command. Tinker didn't need to know Oni to know what he'd said. *Kill him, take her alive.*

"No!" she shouted as the oni warriors surged forward, some with swords and others with hands outreached.

She tried to reload the Uzi only to have clip and gun wrenched from her hands, and then her arms held and she was lifted off the ground. She screamed wordlessly this time, kicking at the oni holding her, and her legs were caught. Hoisted upwards by the four oni, she saw Pony, shields blazing blue, desperately fending off eight oni warriors with sword and knife.

He was never going to be able to hold them off. They were going to kill him.

"No! No!" she cried, trying to wriggle free of the warriors' hold, but it was like being held by steel bands.

With a deep roaring sound—like an oncoming train—the wind suddenly blasted across the bridge and up the road, pouring over them, strangely hot. Her skin seemed to crawl as all her hair stood on end. She recognized the massive influx of active magic, but there was more—something like static electricity—that rode piggyback upon the magic. Judging by the startled outcries around her, the oni felt it too.

"To me! To me!" Pony shouted and went down to his knees, crossing sword and dagger over his head.

"Pony!" she screamed as he dropped his guard.

With blinding whiteness, lightning struck.

She'd never been this close to lightning before. It split the air with a deafening crack, and the boom of thunder was instantaneous in a wave of heat and pressure that vibrated clear through her bones. It was there, and then not there, but its brilliance remained burned into her sight. The bolt had splintered, forking all around Pony, striking the eight oni attacking him. The warriors flew backward to land dead—blackened and smoking from the lightning.

It seemed an impossible miracle, and then she realized the truth.

Windwolf had arrived, summoning the magic of the Wind Clan spell stones to call down lightning.

Pony came off the ground now, blades flashing, and launched himself at the oni holding Tinker. Tinker struggled harder to get free, cursing at her captors. Tomtom shouted in Oni, pointing toward the bridge, correctly identifying which of the three elves was the most dangerous. Another lightning bolt hit close at hand, striking into a knot of oni warriors attempting to attack Pony from the rear.

Two of the oni holding her decided to face Pony rather than die keeping her captive—and a hard kick into the face of the third left her dangling in one warrior's hold. There was a knife in his belt; she yanked it free and stabbed him in the stomach with it. The blade slid in to the hilt with stunning ease, and blood poured hot over her hand. The oni howled and punched her in the face.

Darkness washed in, and when it retreated Pony had her over his shoulder and was running for the bridge.

Had they won?

The crack of rifles and whine of bullets verified that no, they hadn't.

Lightning struck—and as it flashed all vision to white—Pony stumbled and fell. It seemed as if he'd tripped over something. He started to fall to the left, which would have smashed Tinker under him. He dropped his sword, tucked her close, and rolled in mid-air to hit his right shoulder first. They tumbled through the mud of the road, Pony taking the brunt of the damage, as he protected her with his own body. They stopped when Pony slammed against the stone abutment at the end of the bridge.

As Pony lay unmoving, Tinker glanced back toward the pursuing oni.

She had one glimpse of Tomtom standing approximately where Pony had stumbled, a vicious grin on his face, before the oni lord stepped back into the shadows, completely vanishing from sight. She flashed to his first appearance on the road, he and his guard suddenly appearing as if teleporting. How was he doing it? Was he actually teleporting? Was he going invisible? Or like Chiyo, was he projecting what he wanted them to see into their minds?

Maybe the reason Chiyo had been so sure she could become a noble was because Tomtom had the same talents.

"Tinker?"

Windwolf still had his great sword sheathed, and he moved down the bridge in a stylistic stalk, like dancing in slow motion. She could feel the power he had gathered around him, the wind thrumming in his hold. He wore black leather pants, and a white silk shirt that blazed in the moonlight like a target. His long black hair was unbound, and it flowed out on the wind.

Of the *sekasha*, there was no sign. He was all alone.

"Is Pony alive?" His voice was quiet but loud, like a whisper over a microphone.

Pony was breathing, so Tinker said, "He's unconscious."

"Get him up," Windwolf commanded. "Get him to the other end of the bridge. The others are coming."

Tinker glanced down at the still unmoving Pony, a foot taller and easily fifty pounds heavier than her. How the hell did she move him? And where was Tomtom? What could the oni lord do—especially if he could throw illusions into Windwolf's mind?

Pony had dropped his sword, but he had other weapons on him. The guns were useless; the bullets would only feed energy into Tomtom's shield—assuming that wasn't an illusion. The knives placed her too near the much larger and better-trained oni. That left Sparrow's light bow and spell arrows. The arrows were all fletched white, which meant the same spell was marked onto the shaft and activated by the sound of the arrows' flight.

As Tomtom surely planned, Windwolf moved to the end of the bridge to cover her and Pony. He spoke a word, shifting his right hand with fingers cocked in stiff positions, and his shield extended out to cover the full end of the bridge.

"Go! Leave Pony if you have to." Windwolf commanded as the oni opened fire from the cover of the trees. The bullets deflected off his shield, but Tomtom could walk through it.

She didn't spend the last three weeks protecting Pony to leave him now, not even to save Windwolf. Tinker nocked an arrow—and looked for the factors of 73931. She could keep Chiyo from reading her mind by doing math, but that hadn't kept Chiyo from deluding her. She'd foiled Chiyo by noticing something that the kitsune had forgotten to disguise. Surely if Tomtom had two people to affect, there would be something he'd overlook, but what? The darkness itself would erase most of his errors. She lifted the bow, drew back the arrow, and tried to find a target.

"Tinker, what are you doing?" Windwolf growled.

"Trust me."

I can outthink him. I know I can.

Tomtom could fool her eyes. The gunfire covered his footsteps. What would he miss? His shadow? His smell?

Then it came to her—Tomtom would never think of hiding magic from a *domana*, since he couldn't feel magic himself—and she focused on the active magic in the area. There, passing through Windwolf's shields and nearly on him, was Tomtom's own shield spell.

She guessed the location of Tomtom's heart and loosed the arrow. As the arrow leapt from her bow, its whistling passage through the wind activated the spell written down its shaft; the kinetic energy of its physical form was transmuted into coherent light—a bolt of pure energy. There was a faint ripple as it passed through Tomtom's shield spell—apparently designed only for solid projectiles. Then it lanced its way through the oni lord, and he appeared with a gurgling scream. He was only six feet from Windwolf, sword upraised and ready to strike—with a neat hole burned through the right side of his chest.

Windwolf shouted, lifted his arm straight out, fingers splayed. The wind slammed Tomtom backwards thirty feet. Windwolf growled a spell to summon another bolt of lightning, moving his hands in interweaving circles, his fingers flicking through complex patterns. The brilliance struck Tomtom as the oni lord started to rise.

He didn't get up again.

There was a sweep of headlights on the far side of the bridge, and the *sekasha* spilled out of two of the Rolls and charged across the bridge.

Windwolf flinging lightning bolts, the arrival of the *sekasha,* and their own lord dead made the oni flee into the forest. The *sekasha* met no resistance as they passed beyond Windwolf's protection. Only when the *sekasha* had set up a line of defense did Windwolf loose his hold on the magic, letting it drain away.

He triggered a light orb as he walked to her, bathing them in light. People surrounded them, but he seemed to be the only one in focus.

"You're alive! My most wonderful, clever, little savage!" He lightly traced her face. She'd never seen him smile so widely. He blinked away a threat of tears, and glanced toward the waiting *sekasha.* "I must go and fight, but I will be back."

"Kiss me at least once," she complained.

"If I start, I will not be able to stop."

"Bullshit." She grabbed hold of his collar and pulled him down to her level.

He hadn't been exaggerating. Someone had to catch the light orb—he let it fall in order to crush her to him—and she had to finally push him breathlessly away after the third "*dame zae,* the oni" from the *sekasha.*

"Go," she said. "Deal with oni. Come back to me."

He kissed her fingertips and reluctantly left to chase after oni.

Tinker slumped down beside Pony, quite willing to let them fight
without her.

"*Domi?*" Pony croaked.

"Oh good." She took his hand. "You're awake."

"Yes." He frowned as she checked his attempt to get up. "Is it over?
Did we win?"

"Yes, we've won."

Hospice elves arrived, first-aid kits in hand. "*Domi*, are you hurt?"

"No, no, see to him first," Tinker lied, motioning to Pony.

There were, however, more than enough healers to treat them
both. One inked a healing spell onto her side and triggered it while
the rest dealt with Pony. In the desperate fight, he'd been hit more
times than she realized. As the healers stabilized him, enclave elves
moved into the forest to deal with the oni dead.

Sparrow's body was found and carried to the enclaves, along with
news of her betrayal. Apparently in an effort to keep searchers from
the Turtle Creek area, the female had planted evidence in the South
Hills: articles of Tinker's clothing, items from Tinker's pockets, Pony's
beads, scraps of paper with Tinker's handwriting. Windwolf and his
forces had been at the farthest point in Pittsburgh from Tinker when
she escaped, but the reports of gunfire at the construction site had
brought Windwolf literally flying back, out ahead of his bodyguard, to
save her.

The fighting had now moved far off, heading back toward Turtle
Creek; Tinker could track it from the sound of gunfire and the
occasional bright strokes of lightning.

That is so cool. "I'm really going to have to learn how to do that."

Or did she? Now that she was once again still, she could feel the
feedback, definitely stronger. According to the models she ran, the
orbital gate would soon shake itself to pieces, permanently returning
Pittsburgh to Earth.

Which world did she want to be in?

Earth? With Oilcan, Lain, all the neat gadgets, the Internet, colleges
full of like-minded people, and the possibility of returning to Elfhome
anytime she decided to build a gate back?

Or Elfhome? With Windwolf and Pony, but no humans or techno
toys, and the grim possibility that even if she could find the supplies,
she might be denied the permission to build a gate back to Earth?

On the surface, all logic seemed to say that she should get up and walk into Pittsburgh proper before Shutdown. Go back to Earth.

But it wasn't that simple. In truth, she'd never been to Earth. Every Shutdown, she'd clung to her scrap yard and waited for Startup. She disliked the dirty air, the noise, the confusion, and the crush of people that Shutdown brought to Pittsburgh. Oilcan—who knew her best—predicted she'd hate Earth for those very reasons. It was a foreign other place she always resisted visiting.

Becoming an elf didn't make Elfhome her home—it only strengthened her tie to it. She grew up praying to elfin gods, practicing elfin morals, and celebrating elfin holidays. What did she know about being human besides beer, bowling, junked cars, and advanced science? On Earth, she wouldn't be a human with fancy ears; she'd be a displaced elf—just like Tooloo had been.

What's more, Pittsburgh was filled with oni disguised as humans, and by now, all of them knew she could build a gate. She'd never be able to trust anyone again; every new friendship would have to be endlessly questioned. Oilcan and Lain would be in danger of being used as leverage against her.

"Oh this sucks." Much to the healer's dismay, Tinker started to pace.

The feedback was becoming a hard pulse, as if the ground and the sky beat out the word "decide, decide, decide."

There was another crack of lightning, and she looked in that direction, but it was already gone and all there was to see was the dark primal forest of Elfhome. Trees. Magic. *Sekasha*. Windwolf. That kind of summed it up. The world she considered home, the people she trusted, and the male she loved.

But Oilcan, Lain, her datapad, the hoverbikes, people that understood physics, clever little gadgets, pizza, and pierogies . . .

She found herself at the far end of the bridge, a city block from the Rim.

Was she so shallow that she'd give up everything she loved for stuff?

Without the stuff, though, she'd been bored to tears at Aum Renau.

But she could have spent her time learning the complex magic of the spell stones. Windwolf had said that he'd teach it to her. She'd ignored it—in what now seemed like childish spite. In hindsight, she certainly could have used the power in the last twenty days. And the oni magic opened up a new realm of possibilities—creating solid temporary matter.

She paced back to Pony, the feedback beating on her even harder. Any minute now, she'd lose the chance to decide. She wanted to stay on Elfhome, right? It felt more like her home than Earth, with or without Pittsburgh.

Except there was still the problem of Oilcan—if she stayed, she'd lose him forever.

The hospice elves had moved Pony onto a stretcher. They piled all the various guns and knives on beside him, and then checked at the light bow, obviously not a *sekasha* weapon.

"*Domi*, your bow and arrows."

It was simpler just to take the bow and quiver than to explain they were Sparrow's.

She trailed slowly behind Pony's stretcher as they started for the enclaves, trying to decide. Go or stay. She got as far as mid-bridge before coming to a complete stop.

She didn't know what to do, and she was running out of time.

"You're still thinking like a human."

She hated to admit it, but Sparrow had been right. She was thinking of tomorrow, next month, or next year. If she stayed, she wasn't going to lose Oilcan forever. Humans knew Elfhome was here. They had all the technology needed to build a gate. They had the oni desperately cluing them in. Sooner, more probably than later, another land-based gate would be built.

She'd stay.

Only after she decided did she realize Sun Lance had been trailing back and forth after her.

"*Domi*," the female *sekasha* said, "I don't think it's safe to stay on the bridge with the air shaking so."

There had been no sign of fighting for the last few minutes, so she went back to the new palace construction site. From there, she had a panoramic view of Pittsburgh. She should have only minutes left. The feedback had become a low roar, and everything shook with its vibration. She found a couch-sized stack of canvas tarps to sit on and drink in her last sight of her hometown.

"Tinker? What's happening?" Windwolf called to her as he and the *sekasha* came out of the forest. "The oni tried to retreat to Turtle Creek, but there was something very wrong with the valley."

"What do you mean 'wrong'?"

"It was—fluid."

She considered a moment. "The veil effect must be extending the area of the gate, so there's several layers of overlapping realities all being disturbed by the feedback."

"What do you mean?"

"The gate I built for the oni is creating a resonance effect with the orbital gate. The veil effect of the orbital gate is pulsing the local gate." She made a fist and flared her other hand out over it to show the radius effect. She pulsed her top hand in time with the feedback. "It's doing Elfhome, Earth, Onihida, Elfhome, Earth, Onihida."

"The area affected wouldn't grow?"

"No. The local gate doesn't have the power to affect more than a few"—she considered the possible range—"hundred feet. I think a mile from the gate would be the maximum range."

"You planned it this way?"

"Actually, I planned for it to tear the orbital gate apart—which it should do any second now—with Pittsburgh going back to Earth permanently."

He glanced to the city below and then to her. "Then you're staying with me?"

"Yes, this is my home."

Silence fell while he was kissing her. Being in his arms, knowing that they had forever together, made the pain bearable. Still, she didn't want to turn and see the city gone, so she kept her eyes closed tight, and thought of only how much she loved him. The kissing led to other things, and he eased her back onto the tarps, and careful of her cuts and bruises, made gentle love to her.

Sometime later, he grew still and silent. "Love, I do not think it worked."

"Hmmm?" She rolled over to follow his gaze. Pittsburgh was still there. "*Shit!*" She rolled on her back to look at the stars instead. "Oh damn. What could have gone wrong?"

"Perhaps your gate failed first."

"Oh, I was so sure it wouldn't. It didn't on any of the model programs I ran."

"It is no matter. We will settle it with politics."

Tinker made a rude noise. "The governments of Earth are not going to want to destroy it—it represents too much money."

"We can compromise. If they destroy the orbital gate, we'll fund land-based gates to replace it."

It sounded like a long, drawn-out mess with the oni interfering at every step.

A streak of light caught Tinker's eye. "A falling star," she pointed out. "Humans think they grant wishes."

Windwolf shook his head. "I will never understand why a race without magic can believe that so many random things are magical."

"Wishful thinking."

"What do you wish for?"

"That we can get rid of the orbital gate without triggering a war between dimensions."

"A wise wish. There is another falling star."

Tinker blinked at the night sky. "Is it my imagination, or is that one much larger than the first?"

"Look!" Windwolf said and pointed to a fireball. "And there too."

"For us to see anything falling, though, there must have been an explosion that kicked large parts of the orbital gate into the atmosphere. I'm surprised they didn't just bounce off."

"Bounce off what?"

"It's, um, all orbital mechanics and velocities." Tinker waved it aside. "Oh, oh, that's not good. We shouldn't be able to see the gate— if that is the gate. It's in orbit around Earth—oh shit, I think I might have yanked it into Elfhome space by accident."

"If it is broken, then it is off," Windwolf said. "Shutdown. Right?"

Tinker eyed the city lights spread out down over the hills to the rivers. "Oh, this is really not good. I-I-I think, I think Pittsburgh is permanently on Elfhome. I'll have to run some models, but I think I changed a constant by shoving too hard, or maybe it was the resonance between the two gates. . . ."

"Without the gate in orbit, we will not be able to return Pittsburgh to Earth," Windwolf pointed out.

"Oh, this is so bad."

"I thought you wanted to stay."

"Yes, me, but the city? Without the supplies from Earth, Pittsburgh will be starving within weeks."

"Ah, yes. Not to worry, love. We will work it out."

"<evil> Eh heh heh! </evil>
Finish the gate in 21.54 days or the
HEDGEHOG GETS IT!!!